A WELSH WITCH

A WELSH WITCH

A Romance of Rough Places

by

ALLEN RAINE

With an introduction by
Jane Aaron

HONNO CLASSICS

Published by Honno
'Ailsa Craig', Heol y Cawl, Dinas Powys,
South Glamorgan, Wales, CF64 4AH

1 2 3 4 5 6 7 8 9 10

First published in Great Britain in 1902 by Hutchinson & Company
First published by Honno in 2013

British Library Cataloguing in Publication Data
A catalogue record for this book is available from the British Library.

ISBN 978-1-906784-65-2

Published with the financial support of the Welsh Books Council.

Cover image: 'Ceridwen' by Christopher Williams,
City and County of Swansea: Glynn Vivian Art Gallery
Cover design: Graham Preston
Text design: Elaine Sharples
Printed & bound by Gomer Press, Llandysul, Ceredigion, Wales

CONTENTS

Introduction – Jane Aaron   ix

I	The *Lark* and the Glaswen	1
II	The Witch	13
III	Under the Apple Blossoms	31
IV	The Chase	47
V	Catrin's Questions	63
VI	Yshbel	80
VII	The Queen of the Village	94
VIII	The Dark Shore	103
IX	Awakenings	117
X	Catrin's Prayer	137
XI	Yshbel and Catrin	151
XII	Catrin's Letter	162
XIII	The Fate of Parcglâs	178
XIV	Granny's Angel	195
XV	Seeing the World	208
XVI	Glaish-y-Dail	221
XVII	Away to the 'Works'!	232
XVIII	An Uninvited Guest	247
XIX	The Colliers' Friend	262
XX	Tangled Threads	278
XXI	The Explosion	291
XXII	Under the Hawthorn Tree	309
XXIII	John Lovell	327
XXIV	On Tramp with the Gipsies	345
XXV	Sylvia's Wedding	362
XXVI	The Cribor	379
XXVII	The Two Aunts	390
XXVIII	Mountain Echoes	415

Glossary – Jane Aaron   437

Introduction

JANE AARON

Along the sheltered sands of a small Cardiganshire fishing village in the late nineteenth century four children grow up, their lives 'bounded by the seaward horizon on the one hand, and the fuzzy, heather-clad slopes leading up to the blue hills, which hemmed them in on the other.' As they mature towards adulthood, the trajectory of their lives takes them into very different environments. Three of them undergo their most formative and testing experiences in the coalfields of Glamorganshire, at this date attracting unprecedented numbers of incomers from the rural west, while the fourth goes north to find work tending sheep on the Snowdonia range. Whether deep underground or high in the thin air of the mountains, all four dream of a return to the happy middle ground of their sea-level birth-place, and all finally achieve this aspiration.

The life of the author of *A Welsh Witch: A Romance of Rough Places* followed a path similar to that of her four main characters in this novel. Anne Adaliza Puddicombe, whose pen name 'Allen Raine' had apparently come to her in a dream, was born inland, in Newcastle Emlyn, Carmarthenshire, in 1836, the eldest child of local solicitor Benjamin Evans and his wife Letitia. But every summer of her childhood was spent in the neighbouring seaside village of Tresaith in Cardiganshire, and it was to that spot she returned whenever possible throughout her later years, settling there permanently in 1900, after her husband, Beynon Puddicombe, had retired from his post as foreign correspondent to a London bank due to mental illness. By this time his wife had become a novelist of some renown, with four novels in print, each title selling hundreds of thousands of copies in Britain, America and across the Empire. *A Welsh Singer* (1897), *Torn Sails: A Tale of a Welsh Village* (1898), *By Berwen Banks* (1899) and *Garthowen: A Story of a Welsh Homestead* (1900), along with her first Eisteddfod-winning fiction, *Ynysoer*, serialised in 1894 and later published as *Where Billows Roll: A Tale of the Welsh Coast* (1909), were all set in a Cardigan Bay village, recognisably Tresaith in each case, though known as Abersethin, Mwntseison or Treswnd in the novels.

In the late 1890s, fiction set in Wales was no more popular with London publishers than it is today. *A Welsh Singer* was rejected by six publishers before Allen Raine presented the manuscript to Hutchinson, where she was discouragingly informed, as she paid £20 for the privilege of having it considered, 'that the firm had received no stories about this part of the country before.'[1] But once in print her success was rapid; she soon became one of the best-sellers of the day with her popular blend of social realism and romance. For some of her later male critics, her 'sandcastle dynasty' was too saturated with sentiment to withstand the test of time;[2] for others she succeeded not only in establishing a place for Wales on the international literary map but in representing with authenticity and precise detail the material and psychological world of her characters. According to her biographer Sally Roberts Jones, who hailed *A Welsh Witch* as the 'most ambitious' of her works, the romance element is only one strand within an oeuvre which also included 'a careful and lovingly absorbed study of Welsh society in nineteenth-century Cardiganshire'.[3]

As its sub-title suggests the 'rough' element in the novel's various settings is in tension with its more idyllic scenes throughout. Even Treswnd, to which its villagers look back with such yearning once exiled from its shores, is not without its harsher aspects. Of the four central characters whose tales we follow, only three – Goronwy Hughes, Yshbel Lloyd and Walto Gwyn – played together as children on its sands. The fourth child, Catrin Rees, watched the others from hiding, from the first an outsider; though she and Goronwy lived on neighbouring farms, they were not personally acquainted until, at sixteen, he witnessed local boys 'baiting' her as a witch and tried to prevent it. A belief in witchcraft apparently lingered long in some of the rural communities of west Wales. As late as 1926, when a dairy instructress from the Agricultural Department of the then University College of Wales, Aberystwyth, was called to a local farm where difficulty had been experienced in making butter, 'the farmer's wife explained matters by saying that someone had laid a spell upon her churn, but that the witch from the College, being the more powerful sorceress of the two, had been able to take it away.'[4] When Goronwy asks his grandmother whether she believes in witches he is regaled with a litany of witch tales, with historical equivalents. Susan Dwt, 'no bigger than a child', who spoiled the grandmother's buttermilk with her curses, bears close resemblance to Siân Bwt, reputedly referred to in Beaumaris as the 'little witch of Llanddona', who survived into the twentieth century.[5] The grandmother closes her account by warning Goronwy of Catrin: '"They say she's a real witch. Take care of her, my boy. Don't speak to her or let her eyes fall upon thee."'

The fifteen-year-old Catrin is imagined here as a wicked witch with an evil eye, but another concept of supernatural female agency, related to the old pagan traditions, was also available in the Welsh language, in which the word 'witch' translates as either *gwiddon*, a wise woman, or *gwrach*, a hag. Both types, but particularly the *gwiddon*, had frequently featured in the pages of Welsh local history, folklore and fiction before the appearance of Raine's novel. They owe their origin to the witch-figures of Welsh myth, particularly Ceridwen

from the *History of Taliesin*, first transcribed in its entirety in
the sixteenth century but with its origins in a much earlier oral
tradition; her well-known portrayal by Charles Williams was
painted in the same decade as that in which *A Welsh Witch*
appeared (see cover illustration). Ceridwen spent her days
brewing in her cauldron a potion 'of all charm-bearing herbs'
gathered in auspicious 'planetary hours', which would give its
imbiber 'knowledge of the mysteries of the future state of the
world'.[6] Her herbalist and astrological expertise would
categorize her as a *gwiddon*, but when her servant Gwion Bach
inadvertently swallows the potion, she hounds him with evil
intent through earth, sky and water, shape-shifting in his
pursuit like a veritable *gwrach*. A *gwiddon*, however, could be
very helpful to her local community as herbalist, soothsayer
and counsellor, and her usefulness probably accounts for the
fact that Welsh women were rarely persecuted in the law courts
as witches, though it would appear from the annals of local
history and folklore that virtually every village in Wales had its
gwiddon for most of the seventeenth, eighteenth and
nineteenth centuries.

Catrin, however, is in fact no *gwiddon*, or *gwrach* either; the
Treswnd community have associated such superstitions with
her image largely because she is a wild child, living like a feral
cat for the most part outside the domestic zone. Her gipsy
mother died giving birth to her, her alcoholic father is prone
to violence and, to avoid his abuse, she approaches her home
warily, but to snatch up her daily bread, and spends her days
and nights in hiding on the rough coastal cliffs. Though the
Treswnd doctor refuses to give credence to the notion of
witchcraft, declaring himself 'ashamed of my country' that
such 'tomfoolery' should still persist within it, his patients
point to Catrin's apparently supernatural ability to 'disappear
off the face of the earth' as a validation of their superstition.
When pursued, Catrin can throw herself over a local cliff edge
only to reappear elsewhere, unharmed, soon afterwards. All she

does in fact is to swing herself into a hidden cave just under the cliff top and climb out via underground water channels. Nevertheless, though she knows of course that there's nothing supernatural about this trick, Catrin has internalised the idea of herself as a witch. Because she is universally spurned and 'nobody is caring for me', she has accepted that 'Of course I am a witch.' The local vicar, however, after learning that she is in the habit of listening to his sermons in secret, standing outside the church walls at the 'old leper window', is moved to help her, but such is her position in the community that the safest future he can imagine for her is incarceration in the local mental asylum.

Like the leper, Catrin is the outcast scapegoat of her community. But in her isolation she relates to the natural world with a greater intensity than her neighbours and becomes familiar with its secrets, as Goronwy begins to learn. After she has shown him how she manages her cliff-jumping illusion, he realises that she must have a good working knowledge of the 'Deep Stream', the underground waterways which have always lain beneath his home village. He journeys with her down to this underworld, and is fascinated and terrified by the debris which the treacherous current of the Deep Stream has carried to its underground shores: 'Here were broken spars and oars and splinters which told of many a wreck; here a torn and sodden sail…and there, on the dry sand, lay a human skeleton, the two arms outstretched together, as if imploring help that never came.' But Catrin tells him, 'We need not be afraid, for they are God's rocks down there, and 'tis God's sea.' Underground is a place of wrecks and endings, but it constitutes a natural darkness which Catrin is brave enough to face and to become familiar with; it has no terrors for her compared with the unnaturalness of the social darkness in which she lives on the surface world. The psychology of the outcast is probed with some subtlety throughout this text. Made monstrous, even in her own eyes, by her community's construction of her, Catrin, like the monster of Frankenstein's creation, asks 'Why had God made her at all, if she was to be thus separated from the rest of the world?' The process by means of which 'this waif of existence' finally finds anchorage at home in the world constitutes a key element of the novel's plot.

But the social construction of the witch as outsider is only one of the shadows darkening the lives of the children on the sea shore, and arguably not the most damaging. Though Goronwy, Yshbel and Walto play together as equals, Walto in fact belongs securely to the gentry class. His mother Eleanor Gwyn, the 'meestress', is the main landowner in the area; Goronwy, a farmer's son, and Yshbel, an orphaned fisher girl, are Walto's social inferiors. As a reciprocated but as yet unexpressed attachment develops between the maturing Yshbel and Walto, Mrs Gwyn feels compelled to intervene; she warns Yshbel off 'raising thine eyes to Mr. Walter Gwyn', under threat of losing her home should she persist. Yshbel, from affronted pride more than fear, turns from Walto to Goronwy, who responds to her apparent interest while all the time denying even to himself his secret growing attachment to the 'witch' with whom he is by now spending his happiest hours, roaming the cliffs.

Goronwy's refusal to examine and give weight to his own emotions is indicative of another element of social critique in the novel, that is the questioning of socially constructed gender roles. Though Allen Raine was by no means a committed feminist, the conventional patterns of heavily polarised masculinity versus femininity prescribed during her Victorian era are often criticised in her work, and nowhere more clearly than in this novel. During the first half of the novel Goronwy is the very model of an embryonic Victorian patriarch; accustomed to lead and dominate over others, he believes that a necessary manliness resides in having a strong will and enforcing it upon one's environment. His repeated insistence that 'I always do what I say I will' very nearly proves as destructive to his own happiness and that of his three friends as Mrs Gwyn's class-motivated prejudices. Before the close, however, he is brought to admit that a man's will is not the be all and end all of his existence, and only after that submission does he find fulfilment.

As for conventional womanly models, the semi-feral Catrin stands of course from the outset as a polar opposite to the prescribed domestic role for the women of her day. Though her atypical lifestyle was forced upon her rather than chosen, the freedom she enjoys on the open cliffs is presented throughout as in itself life-enhancing, particularly when she has Goronwy to share it with. At one point, in an attempt to persuade her to conform, her father's maidservant Madlen tells her, '"See how different it might be – a tidy maiden in the house, making the beds and preparing the meals for her father, would be a comfort to us all; and going to church on Sunday with her prayer-book and her pocket handkerchief in her hand."' But this representation of the allotted narrow role of 'tidy' domesticated females only increases the allure of the wild zone as the only alternative space for women. And Yshbel too on one occasion acts with most unconventional courage and enterprise when through her quick-thinking and bravery she saves Walto, Goronwy and his father from drowning. The men must all stand passively by, helpless to save themselves on a stricken vessel, while their female knight in shining armour labours manfully with tempest-tossed elements, travelling through extreme peril to their rescue.

When Yshbel, after securing the men's safety, is herself caught in the treacherous currents of the 'Deep Stream' and nearly drowned, it is Catrin who saves her through her knowledge of the underground waterways carved out of the cliff by the currents. Alone she carries the unconscious Yshbel on her back up to light and life from the hidden shore where the 'Deep Stream' had deposited her, in a key scene in terms of their relationship as two rivals for Goronwy's love. As a number of critics have pointed out, two 'duplicate heroines', contrasting doubles of one another in rivalry for a shared love object, constitute a frequent motif in Allen Raine's plots.[7] The pattern had been set in earlier Romantic fictions, with contrasting figures such as the Highland Jacobite Flora MacIvor and the gentler Lowlander Rosa Bradwardine in Walter Scott's *Waverley*, for example, or Charlotte Bronte's Jane Eyre versus the mad Mrs Rochester. But in *A Welsh Witch*, the relation is subtler: it is not at first evident which of the two young women is the mad, bad or dangerous rival and which the true heroine. Particularly given that the saving of Yshbel is in part an act of penance on Catrin's part, as she had earlier momentarily succumbed to the temptation of attempting to call upon her non-existent witch's powers to curse her rival, it would appear that Catrin must be the 'bad' anti-heroine. Yet, unlike Yshbel, she is steadfast in her affections and their demonstration, ungoverned by pride or wilfulness and entirely impervious to vanity or the allure of materiality. Throughout the text she has a more profound understanding of her own feelings and those of others than any of the other characters, including Yshbel. At its close, she emerges as the truest heroine, though that resolution is achieved without casting Yshbel into the anti-heroine's role: it is as if the very concept of a necessary rivalry between women, thrusting each of them into polarised opposing types, is being deconstructed here.

But at this point in the text, after the shipwreck incident, the dispersal of the four main characters from their seaside home begins, with Walto in his chagrin after losing Yshbel's love leaving to take up a post as assistant manager at his uncle's colliery in Pontargele, Glamorganshire. Five years later Yshbel arrives at the same locality, having just been discovered and adopted by her dead father's nouveau-riche and childless relatives, who also (a little too coincidentally) own a colliery in the Pontargele area. Goronwy comes to claim her as his affianced bride because 'a man must do what he says he will do', though he is now conscious of his stronger tie with Catrin. As he awaits an opportunity to make his claim, he takes up work as a collier in Walto's pit. In Pontargele, class difference is thus starkly exposed, not so much, interestingly, as a barrier between the central characters but as a factor alien to them which drives them into one another's arms in defiance of its hierarchies, notwithstanding their mutual emotional reluctance. Yshbel, taking tea on the lawn with her new-found relations, is so troubled by the thought 'that deep down under the surface of the very hill upon which the gay party around her were enjoying themselves' her old intimate Goronwy is labouring at the coalface, that when he unexpectedly appears at the party, still in his collier's grime, she promises to marry him forthwith, to the great consternation of her aunt. They are only saved from this well-meant but potentially disastrous coupling by an intuitive clergyman who, recognising that the deepest affections of both lie elsewhere, forbids the banns.

Goronwy's and Yshbel's horror at the artifice of class difference, particularly the distinction drawn between the working and middle classes, is consistently presented throughout the book as part and parcel of their rural Welsh identity. In Treswnd none but the anglicised gentry, like Mrs Gwyn, speak English; that Welsh is the common language is indicated throughout by the characters' occasional use of Welsh-language terms, for which Raine rarely provides a translation (but a glossary has been included in the back pages of this edition). Social relations between the farmers and their servants are presented as those of near equals, with Madlen, for example, scolding Catrin as if her master's daughter was virtually her inferior. In Pontargele, the workers are also Welsh-speaking, most of them having newly arrived from the rural west, but those amongst them who are moving up the social ladder as officers, managers and owners of the mines change their language to English. Not only is English the language of business and social prestige, it is also the language by means of which origins are annulled and poor relations betrayed. Before she leaves Treswnd for her new home Yshbel is told by her uncle Jones that she 'must drop the Welsh'; in Pontargele she undergoes a name change to the more refined – and English – Isbel, and witnesses her aunt's abject fear that her own servants might guess at the nature of her origins. Many of Mary Ann Jones's collier relatives still live in the area but when her sister visits she has to do so secretly, 'sitting with her in her bedroom talking Welsh – soft so the servants won't hear.' Wales was slow to develop a middle class; when it came, as this text suggests, it was but a copy of an English original, not indigenous to the area and ill-suited to traditional Welsh lifestyles.

   Given that Allen Raine was herself born into the professional class, this focus may seem unexpected, but lawyers, doctors, teachers and the clergy are usually presented sympathetically in her fictions as working alongside the farmers, serving their needs and speaking their language. It is the nouveau-riche capitalists who are portrayed critically, with their wealth, for the most part in Wales, dug out of the earth through other men's hard and dangerous labour. Both Goronwy and Walto undergo a close encounter with those dangers when they are trapped underground for four days as a result of a pit explosion. This underground disaster scene, based probably on accounts of a disaster at Tynewydd Colliery, Porth, in 1877, when four men and a boy survived entrapment underground for nine days, is one of the first of its kind in Welsh fiction. Ann Beale had depicted a similar south Wales pit explosion in her novel *The Queen o' the May* (1883), but there events are described only from the point of view of the anxious watchers at the pit's mouth; Raine's account, however, focuses in detail on the thoughts and fears of the entrapped. Goronwy acts with great courage, at one point carrying on his back through the low passages the unconscious Walto, struck by a falling rock, in a scene which interestingly parallels Catrin's rescuing of Yshbel. The outcast witch saves the popular village beauty, the collier saves the manager, in accord with the bonds of attachment that have developed between them, notwithstanding the social constructions that would divide them.

It is also during his four days underground that Goronwy grows fully to recognise the hubris of his former macho stance, realising that 'I was a fool – so proud, so wilful. "A man can always do what he makes up his mind to do," says I and here's the end of it! – to die in a deadly hole, to be eaten by rats – and Catrin, oh, Catrin!' As the boy who was entrapped with them dies, Walto drifts in and out of consciousness and a fourth collier loses his mental balance, 'Alone! with the dead, the dying, and the frenzied around him, Goronwy was brought face to face with the deep mysteries of life.' But Catrin had from childhood known those deep mysteries of the underground, that darkness at the core of life; the tunnels of the coal mines and the 'Deep Stream' of Treswnd both appear to function in this text as tropes of the unconscious with its characteristic preoccupation with death and mutability, and its capacity to surface as madness. If that darkness can courageously be faced, however, it strengthens the human character rather than destroys it. The superficial reaction, however, is always to avoid such recognition and thrust the dark zone into a communal unconsciousness. In Catrin's case, 'it was considered the proper thing in Treswnd to ignore the girl's existence as much as possible': her wild existence and reputation for witchcraft were 'a slur upon the respectability of the neighbourhood, which it was better to thrust out of sight and forget so far as might be.' Similarly in Pontargele the dangers in which the colliers labour are thrust below the surface consciousness of the 'boss class' partying above.

This symbolic use of different locations as representing levels of consciousness is extended further in the final part of the novel in which Catrin too, after the death of her father and the apparent loss of Goronwy, leaves Treswnd. Motivated by the desire to live as independently as possible of a human society which cannot care for her, with the help of another group of self-appointed outsiders, the gypsies, she finds employment as a shepherd, guarding her flock alone along the highest peaks of Snowdonia. Like a hermit or anchorite of old, she opts for a high rarefied isolation, as close to the heavens as possible. Sally Roberts Jones finds these Snowdon scenes 'too little integrated with the earlier settings and themes to be successful,'[8] but in terms of the book's symbolism this final locality provides a necessary counter-balance to the Treswnd 'Deep Stream' and Pontargele underground chapters. Once established in her shepherd's hut, after her long solitary trek up and out from society, Catrin starts ailing, as if to fade into the ether from her high altitude was all along her goal. The symbolism suggests that, just as a life trapped in underground darkness is dangerous to human health and mental balance, so a life without shadow lived in isolation at heady altitudes is also iniquitous to humanity.

In the nick of time, Goronwy, himself saved at the last possible moment from the pit, comes searching for Catrin on a long penitential progress up from the deep mines of Glamorganshire to the topmost heights of Gwynedd. From afar on Cribin mountain Catrin hears him calling out her name as he encircles the summit, climbing steadily towards her. So convinced is she that human love will never find her out that 'the strangely familiar voice…seemed to come from some mysterious spirit world to mock her.' The scene evokes Rochester's supernatural call to Jane Eyre in Bronte's novel, but in this case, as well as providing the high point of romance in the text, it also brings closure to its more realist themes. Catrin considered herself a witch because 'no one cares for me'; her chosen isolation was a consequence of her socially constructed monstrousness. But now the searching eye of love has found her out and reclaimed her for the human race, to which she and Goronwy return, to the middle ground of Treswnd, where Yshbel and Walto, now also united, await them.

Of course the 'Deep Stream' still hollows its way under Treswnd's sunlit shores, but the suggestion at the close of the text is that this new young generation have acquired between them enough understanding to bring to the surface and heal some of their society's more corrosive underground tensions. Yshbel and Walto with their joint experience of the iniquities of social hierarchy are hardly going to take Mrs Gwyn's place as the autocratic English-speaking elite of the village. And the way in which Goronwy has already started responding with ferociousness to any reminder of Catrin's former witch status suggests that such scapegoating too is likely to become a thing of the dark past in modern Treswnd. In the novel's last scene Goronwy protectively draws Catrin's cloak about as they stand on the long beach with the moon rising above Penmwntan, the cliff overlooking the shore. Years ago on a similar evening the vicar had puzzled over the girl who listened to his sermons at the old leper window:

> The darkness had fallen deeper and deeper, the light had faded from the western sky, the stars were glittering above them, the moon was rising high above Penmwntan. The solemn stillness, the soft throbbing of the sea, the gentle breeze, which swept over his forehead almost like the touch of human hand, the companionship of this strange girl, whom he had always thought of as an outcast and a pariah – all combined to arouse in the vicar's heart the unsatisfied yearnings which lie deep in every human soul, though buried, perhaps, under a surface of conventionality or carelessness.

What is the vicar yearning for here? The chance to re-inhabit that darkness, perhaps, to take it back from the scapegoat or pariah and own it as part of the complex richness at the core of each and every human life. At the time in which she wrote *A Welsh Witch* Allen Raine had herself been forced to plunge beneath surface conventionalities as she faced the difficulty of coming to terms with the full reality of her husband's mental illness. But in this novel, for all that, or perhaps because of that struggle, she has succeeded in writing an everyday romance in praise of the middle ground and its humane balance, as achieved long ago in a rough Cardiganshire fishing village.

Notes:

[1] John Harris, 'Queen of the Rushes: Allen Raine and her public', *Planet*, 97 (1993), p. 66.

[2] Gwyn Jones, 'The First Forty Years: Some Notes on Anglo-Welsh Literature' in *Triskel One: Essays on Welsh and Anglo-Welsh Literature*, eds Sam Adams and Gwilym Rees Hughes (Swansea and Llandybie: Christopher Davies, 1971), p. 78.

[3] Sally Jones, *Allen Raine*, Writers of Wales (Cardiff: University of Wales Press, 1979), pp. 41 and 80.

[4] Russell Davies, *Secret Sins: Sex, Violence & Society in Carmarthenshire 1870-1920*, (Cardiff: University of Wales Press, 1996), p. 216.

[5] See Eirlys Gruffydd, *Gwrachod Cymru* (Caernarfon: Gwasg Gwynedd, 1980), p. 58.

[6] Lady Charlotte Guest, trans., 'Taliesin', in *The Mabinogion* (1838; London: T. Fisher Unwin, 1902), iii, 118.

[7] See Sally Roberts, *Allen Raine*, p. 28; Jane Aaron, 'The Hoydens of Wild Wales: representations of Welsh women in Edwardian and Victorian fiction', *Welsh Writing in English*, i (1995), 30-37; Katie Gramich, *Twentieth-Century Women's Writing in Wales: Land, Gender, Belonging* (Cardiff: University of Wales Press, 2007), p. 39.

[8] Sally Jones, *Allen Raine*, p. 47.

CHAPTER I

THE *LARK* AND THE GLASWEN

The lights and shadows of an April day, and the solemn silence that sometimes falls on a calm sea, were brooding over a sheltered bay on the Welsh coast, as the *Lark* ploughed her way through the green pellucid waters. She was only a small smack of eighty tons burden, very creaky as to masts, very patchy as to sails, and requiring much overhauling and caulking in hulk; but in the opinion of the master and owner, Morgan Hughes (Captain Hughes as he was always called), there was not a ship that crossed the bay that rode so gracefully, that weathered the storm so bravely, or carried more important cargoes, than she did. 'Slwbs', smacks, brigs, and 'schoonares' often flitted across the horizon, but the *Lark* steered straight into the little haven of Treswnd; for she only traded between that place and one or two of the seaport towns, situated somewhere on the edge of the unknown world lying beyond the left horn of the bay. The inhabitants of Treswnd knew these ports existed, for they saw tangible signs of them, in the cargoes of culm and limestone which the *Lark* discharged periodically on their beach; indeed, the sailoring folk had seen these strange places, and spun long yarns about them by the cottage fires in the evening, but to two-thirds of the people, the world beyond Cerrigduon Head was a subject of mysterious wonder. They spoke of distant shores sometimes indeed, in a tone of familiar intimacy, as, ''Twas over by there in Bermuda,' or 'Up yonder in Monte Video'; but the suggestion of familiarity really covered a complete ignorance of the comparative distance of these places from their sheltered, secluded corner. Their hopes and fears, their ambitions, their sorrows, were bounded by the seaward horizon on the one hand, and the furzy, heather-clad slopes leading up to the blue hills, which hemmed them in on the other.

No sound of shrieking engine, no rattle of high road, broke the soft stillness in which their lives were wrapped, only the lowing of cattle, the calls of the sea birds, and sometimes the horn of the farm servants announcing that supper was over – an old custom long discarded in the more civilised and thickly populated country behind those blue hills.

It was long before suppertime, however, on this breezy April day, when the *Lark* made her way towards Treswnd. The sky was flecked with fleecy clouds, with here and there one of heavy grey, its edges glistening with a silver radiance, never yet caught by mortal brush. The creaking of the mast and the lapping of the waters alone broke the stillness, except the hoarse voice of the captain, as he walked about the deck, and prepared to lower his sails, and to flit into the little haven under the cliff, as a bird folds its wings and drops into its nest at sunset.

Will Preece, the mate, also prepared for action; not so a lad who sat at the prow, idly gazing at the undulating green waters in deep thought, until roused by his father's rough tones of reproof.

'Wake up, Goronwy, you lazy lubber,' said the captain in Welsh; but he added his nautical instructions in English, as all Welsh sailors do— 'Leggo the jib sheet'.

His son started to his work, and as he hauled at the ropes and lowered the sails, there was no sign of laziness or want of energy in his actions. When all was neat and taut, and he had returned to the prow of the little vessel, the old man joined him there, and, fixing his eyes on a rugged cliff which they were approaching, asked eagerly: 'Is she there? Dost see her?'

'No – no, of course not,' said the boy, in a tone not untinged with impatient contempt.

The anxious look of expectancy died out of the captain's face, giving place to one of sullen anger, as the ship's course disclosed more and more of the shore which they were approaching.

'There she is now, in the same place of course,' said the lad. 'Why will you waste your thoughts and hopes upon such folly?'

There was a sigh and a muttered oath from his father, as he turned away, and applied himself to steering his ship safely into the narrow little haven.

He was a stout, well-built man, about fifty years of age, weather-beaten and tanned to the last degree; his strong, round jaws showed a week's growth of a grizzled, stubby beard, grey, like his hair, which had once been red. With his slouching gait, sou'-wester, and blue jersey, his much tarred fustian trousers and bare feet, he differed nothing from the other seamen who sailed about the coast; but in his eyes there was a look of discontent, which seemed strangely at variance with the tender and lovely aspect of nature around him. His son Goronwy resembled him in outward appearance, being of strong build and large boned, and though he was still but a boy of sixteen, he had the decided and somewhat masterful ways of a man. His brown hair covered his head with short, crisp curls; his blue eyes had a sparkle of wilful imperiousness perhaps, but were quite free from the look of anger which lurked in his father's eyes; while the firm, square jaw gave character to his face.

'Father,' he said, suddenly rousing himself, and standing before him, his hands sunk deep in his pockets, his cap pushed back, and that dogged look on his lips, which his father, and the others who lived with him knew it was useless to oppose – 'Father, l have something to say to you before we land. I have been thinking of it all the afternoon, and l have made up my mind.'

'What about?' said the captain, gruffly.

'Well, look you here – this is the last voyage I will take with you on the *Lark*.'

'Why, thee'st only been twice. Spending all thy time over those infernal books has turned thy mind away from the seafaring. And what'll I do with the *Lark*? Must I pay for a boy when my own son could fill his place and save my pocket?'

'Yes. If you must have a boy, take one of the Bullets with you. You say, "What will become of the *Lark*?" I say, "What will become of the farm if we both go to sea, and leave it to Will and Marged?" For poor old granny, you know, is quite unfit to manage things. No, father, I must stop at home; for I love the farm, and they must have a man at Sarnissa to look after them.'

'A man, indeed!' said his father, and he laughed loud and boisterously. 'A fine man of sixteen. You crow too early, my young cockerel; you want to idle your time at home, while your poor old father is out in the storm and the wind.'

'That is all nonsense,' said the boy, standing square and defiant before him. 'You know I like work, and I'm wanted at home. I'm only a lad, but I can manage the farm, and I will, or my name is not Goronwy. You may laugh as long and as loud as you like. I am talking sense, father, and you are talking nonsense. You know the *Lark* has been a loss to you for the last two years. Where's the sense of keeping her on, just because you have steered her so long, and because she's your own? Sell her, and come and live at home, at Sarnissa, and attend to your farm, and drop that nonsense about the stream. Wait till I'm twenty-one, father.'

'Twenty-one,' said the captain, in a sneering tone, 'and what grand thing wilt do when thee'st twenty-one?'

'Well, listen,' said the boy. 'We'll go to law about it – we'll go to Oliver Hughes, the lawyer – and we'll win. Leave it to me, father, and I'll get that field from Simon Rees!'

'Thou, indeed,' said his father, contemptuously; nevertheless, his son's words soothed him, for there is an innate love of litigation in a Welshman's soul, ever ready to be roused by the slightest cause.

Even while he spoke, his eye had glanced furtively towards the side of the cliff, down which fell from a height of seventy feet the little streamlet which formed the boundary line between the farms of Sarnissa and Pengraig. With a bound, it leapt from the narrow channel which came to so abrupt an ending at the edge of the cliff, and as it fell on the rocks and sands below it spread into a foaming, frothing sheet of spray and snowy lace work, which looked not unlike the flowing garments of some ghostly female figure, who stood against the black rocks, every movement of the sea breeze swaying the lacy folds of her skirts.

'There you are now!' said the boy. 'I see you looking at her. 'Tis time, indeed, I should take the management of things into my own hands.'

The old man turned to his work with a shamefaced embarrassment, unable to deny the soft impeachment.

'Well, have thy way, as thee always dost,' he said. 'Say no more about it, and go down tomorrow and see if Ben Bullet will come.'

'Of course he will,' said the boy, and together they applied themselves to their work, until, with a good deal of shouting, much jingling of chains and hauling of ropes, the little *Lark* was safely stranded on the beach and fastened to her moorings.

Sitting on the sands, Morgan Hughes and his son put on their shoes and stockings, and leaving Will Preece on board, took their way homewards, up the winding road, round the spur of the hill, to the uplands, where Sarnissa spread its straggling, sunny fields, and Pengraig, across the valley, reached in unkempt pastures down to the edge of the cliff. As they neared home, Morgan Hughes, before entering the house, roamed away round the farm, taking a survey of his crops and of the work done during his absence, but more particularly of the stream, which ran between his fields and those of Pengraig. The little Glaswen after meandering down a rocky ravine, when it had reached within an acre of the cliff edge, took a sudden turn to the right, thus leaving a small field of green and luxuriant pasturage attached to the Pengraig farm, although there were very evident signs that at some earlier period it had flowed on the left of this much coveted acre, whose rich, verdant crops were the outcome of its depth of subsoil, its curious formation showing plainly that it had been formed by the silting of the soil from the watershed above. It rose in a swelling knoll, between the two cliffs which formed the sides of the little haven, the sea ever washing its rocky base, and sometimes, in stormy weather, reaching dangerously high up its sides of soft loam. And it was this small plot of land which was the interest and bane of Morgan Hughes' life.

A hundred years earlier, Pengraig farm had belonged to Sarnissa, but Morgan Hughes' grandfather had sold it to the grandfather of the present proprietor, Simon Rees, farmer and carrier.

It had been sold according to the will of an earlier ancestor, the ambiguous wording of the document being the cause of all the unrest and anxiety which had destroyed Morgan Hughes' peace of mind. 'And whereas,' it set forth, 'the said stream of Glaswen shall always form the boundary line between the lands of Sarnissa and those of Pengraig, and whereas it hath latterly flowed on the left side of Parcglas, contrary to its former habits, that field must go with the lands to which it is attached, and therefore must remain a part of Sarnissa.'

This was all plain enough, in Morgan Hughes' opinion; but whereas, from his earliest youth and that of Simon Rees, the streamlet had run on the *right* of Parcglas, it had been decided in a court of law, after much litigation and the impoverishment of both litigants, 'that the said Parcglas must now be considered to belong to the lands of Pengraig.'

Simon Rees was well satisfied with the legal decision, but Morgan Hughes considered there was a conspiracy to rob him, and to defraud him of his rightful property, and he nursed in his heart a bitter hatred of the man in whose favour the case had been settled. He had a firm belief that some day the stream would revert to its original bed, which was still very plainly discernible, on the left side of Parcglas; and whenever he returned from his short voyages of a few days or a week, he was buoyed up with the hope that this event would have occurred, and that the waterfall would greet his eyes at a point fifty yards south of its present position.

As he stood this evening, with his arms folded, looking down at the brown waters of the Glaswen, he muttered to himself, as he had done a hundred times before, "Tis a cruel shame, that the best field on the whole hillside should be given up to that drunken devil.'

At last he turned his steps homewards, where Goronwy had already greeted his old grandmother, Gwen Hughes, and had taken his seat at a little round tea table under the open chimney.

'Well, and how's mother?' said the captain, as he unceremoniously passed Marged, the servant and friend of the household, in the passage.

'Oh, quite well; she's been having Madam Lloyd and the Queen and Garibaldi to tea with her since you been away.'

'Well done,' said the captain, laying his hand on the old woman's shoulder.

She looked up into his face with the pathetic simplicity of a second childhood, and with a smile of welcome. No false teeth spoilt that sweet, sunken mouth, no curled fringe or beribboned cap crowned that white forehead, but the full frill of muslin, which Marged ironed so carefully, tied down with the usual handkerchief of black silk; the complexion was still fair and white, the cheeks still of a delicate pink, but the grey eyes had a faraway look, which gave the face a touch of sadness.

'I am glad the wars are over, my boy, and that you and Goronwy are safe home again. And see what he has brought me,' she said, delightedly spreading on her knee a handkerchief of brilliant scarlet and yellow cotton; 'he says 'twas Bony's flag.'

'Why, of course,' said Goronwy; I took it from his own hand on the field of battle.'

'Was he killed?' she asked, timidly.

'Oh, dead as a red herring. *He'll* never trouble us again.'

And the old woman, reassured, presided at her tea table with happy content, often joining in the laugh which her quaint remarks occasioned.

Morgan Hughes was more cheerful than usual, frequently laughing boisterously at his mother's fancies, and entering thoroughly into the accounts of the farming operations, and the plans for future work.

'I think I will go to the singing class tonight,' said Goronwy, as he finished his third cup of tea. 'Are you coming, father?'

'Not tonight,' he said. 'I am tired, but go thou; the altos are weak, but the basses won't miss me.'

'Will you come back, my boy?'

'B't shwr, granny, and we'll sing the anthem together before we go to bed,' and he went out whistling merrily, Morgan Hughes looking after him with a little anxiety, lest he might change his mind, and stay at home after all; for it had suddenly struck him that his son's absence would be a good opportunity for asking his mother a few questions concerning the Glaswen; and Goronwy had scarcely disappeared round the thorn bush by the gap in the farmyard, when his father drew his chair up to the fire, and gently insinuated 'that it would be a fine day for a bathe tomorrow. Not in the sea, you know, but in the Glaswen.'

'Yes,' said the old woman, gazing vaguely through the deep-set windows at the gorgeous tints of the April sunset. 'We'll bathe in the minnow pool tomorrow.'

'Why not under the nut trees?'

'Yes, where mother used to bathe.'

'Did she now?' said the captain, rubbing his hands.

'Yes; before little Peggi and Betty died, she bathed with them there under the nut trees, and she said the cows came to the water's edge and looked at them.'

'What cows – Pengraig?'

'No, her own cows – Sarnissa cows.'

'Of course,' said Morgan; 'and now, mother, we could not bathe there. The grass grows green under those nut trees, and Simon Rees' horses and his two cows graze there, and the Glaswen runs down this side of Parcglas, and leaves the field on the Pengraig side. When did it change its course? Mother, try and remember.'

'Yes, yes,' said the old woman, with a troubled look, as she tried to call her memory to her aid. ''Twas a storm, I think, heavy rain and dark sky for days and days, and the river was very full, rushing down from the hills; and one morning when we went out it had made a new passage for itself; and now it is a broad, swift river passing by, and the ships sail down it to the sea, and some day I shall go in one of those ships, and sail on it out to sea.'

'Twt, twt,' said the captain, ''tis but a streamlet yet, but it flows the wrong side of the field. We are here by the fire now, and we are waiting for Goronwy to come back from the singing school.'

'Yes – yes, of course,' said the old woman, with a pleased smile.

'Don't talk of broad rivers here then, there are none at Treswnd.'

He spoke gruffly, but not unkindly, for Morgan Hughes had a strong affection for his old mother.

And while they chatted by the fire, Will, the farm servant, weaving willow baskets in the background, and Marged, scraping potatoes for the supper of 'cawl', Goronwy stood up in his place in the singing class, and joined his clear, powerful alto in the singing – in fact, leading the altos, for wherever he went, somehow or other he took a prominent part, and was deferred to by all his companions.

A Welsh Witch

'Look here,' he said, turning to a redheaded, freckled youth who stood near, 'thee'st singing wrong, Ben. Highsht then, man, till I teach thee the tune tomorrow' – and the offender was silent at once.

When the meeting was over, the whole party poured out to the 'cwrt'. It was a cloudy night, and the boys ran pell mell down the road, their heavy wooden shoes clattering noisily over the stones.

Suddenly, in the bend of the hollow, some dark object crossed their path, and sprang through the thorn hedge which bordered it.

''Tis the wild cat!' said the boys, ''tis the witch of Pengraig! There she goes across the field. Let's run after her and drive her over the cliffs. 'Twon't hurt her; she won't drown.'

And with a loud whoop they scrambled over the hedge, and ran in full pursuit after the dark figure, which dashed at full speed over bush and brier, making straight for the edge of the cliff. Goronwy was running too in the thick of the rush, but crying at the top of his voice: 'Stop! For shame, Dyc Powell, Ben Ty Brwyn! Stop all of you, I tell you.'

But the passion of sport was too strong to be checked at once. They did not heed him, but ran with more eagerness than ever, as the brown figure, suddenly turning aside, made for the grey, gaunt farmhouse on the hill.

'Catch her, boys, or she'll get to Pengraig!' said one, and, stooping, he picked up a stone and flung it after her.

Some of the others did the same, and suddenly the night air was rent with shrieks, only too familiar to the boys, whose favourite pastime it was 'to bait the witch', until she screamed in rage or pain.

'Stop, you diawled!' ('devils'), said Goronwy. 'Do you hear me?'

But, heated by their chase, they paid no attention to him, and, increasing their speed, caught the fluttering, flying figure which had so far escaped them. Goronwy, the foremost of the runners, though with a different intention, caught hold of the struggling girl, who, finding herself captured, set up a continued screaming, which filled the night air, and woke the echoes from cliff and mountain. The boys, satisfied with their success, stopped breathless, slouching back a little, their fears aroused by the eerie screams. Goronwy, however, annoyed by the shrieks of the girl, still kept hold of her.

'Highsht!' he said, in a tone of command. 'Silence, lodes; I am not going to hurt thee.' And he would have loosened his hold of her at once, had not her repeated screams aroused the masterful spirit within him.'Be quiet, and I'll let thee go,' he said.

'Loose her, loose her,' said the boys; 'she'll work thee mischief, Goronwy. 'Tis time for Simon to be home.'

'I don't care for her or Simon,' said Goronwy, and the girl struggled in vain in his strong grip. 'I'll master her, if she has never been mastered before. Be silent, lass, and I'll let thee go.'

But again she shrieked loudly, and the same moment stooping down, fixed her sharp teeth in the boy's hand.

Now, indeed, the lion within him was roused. Gripping both her hands in one of his own, he twisted his free arm round her neck, and holding her as if in a vice, let her scream herself hoarse, while the other boys, alarmed and frightened, slunk away one by one, leaving Goronwy and the girl to their struggle alone under the darkening sky. Neither spoke, but her cries and the lad's angry panting continued for some time, until at last the shrieks changed into sobs and moans, Goronwy still holding the quivering form in his firm grasp.

'Be silent then,' he muttered at last, when a fresh wrench betokened a renewal of the struggle. 'Be silent, girl, for I tell thee, if I stand here all night, thou shalt never go, till thee'st silent as that sheep which thee'st frightened with thine unearthly noise.'

For some time longer the gasping struggle went on, until at last even the moaning ceased, and the thin figure of the girl seemed to shrink and grow limp in his hands.

'Now,' he said, loosening his hold, ''thee canst go.' But instead of taking to her heels and fleeing for her life, as he had expected, she stood still, and continued to moan.

'Now then, why doesn't go?' said the boy, beginning to wipe the blood which trickled from an ugly blue wound on his hand.

The girl did not answer, but turning silently away, walked slowly towards Pengraig, crying softly, with both hands covering her face, Goronwy looking angrily after her before he turned homewards. When he reached the Glaswen, he held his hand in the cooling stream, and binding it round with his red pocket handkerchief, said nothing, and felt little more of his wound.

CHAPTER II

THE WITCH

Along the high road, Simon Rees, the carrier, was making his way to Treswnd. Twice every week he took the same monotonous journey, his waggon sometimes filled with rosy-cheeked women, each carrying her basket to the market. Sometimes the heavy lumbering vehicle carried only a deal box or two, a basket of eggs, a pig tied up in a sack, or a hat packed up in a bandbox, and many other incongruous and surprising articles. But Simon drove on with the stolidity of Fate, taking but little account of the quantity or quality of his load, so long as he started betimes in the morning, and returned some time in the evening. Punctuality was a virtue unknown at Treswnd, so the single passenger who sat in the waggon was not much surprised when, passing a cottage, she heard a clock strike nine.

'We are two hours late, Simon,' she said, standing up and endeavouring to attract his attention, by pommelling his shoulders with her knuckles. 'Nanti Betto will be frightened. Let me out, and I will run the rest of the way home.'

Simon drew up with a grunt. He had slept through the last mile, and the two horses, Captain and Bess, had slackened their pace so much that the girl was doubtful whether they were making any progress at all, for they put their noses together, and drooped their heads, apparently consulting as to how much time they could spend on the road.

'What's thy hurry, Yshbel?' grumbled the carrier, who resented being awakened by a slip of a girl. 'Didst sell all thy fish today?'

'Yes,' answered the girl. 'I am not in a hurry, but I thought Nanti would be waiting,' and, paying the small fare, she jumped out of the waggon and shook off the straws which clung to her.

'Good-neit,' she said, an English word often used by the peasantry.

'Good-neit,' mumbled Simon in return.

Turning to the dim and misty moor, she began to run down one of the sheep paths which led to the village below. Suddenly the air was rent with screams, and Yshbel stopped a moment to listen.

'Ach-y-fi! 'tis Catrin,' she said with a shudder; 'the boys are plaguing her,' and apparently thinking no more of the matter, she continued to run down the side of the hill.

Left alone, Simon resumed his nap, and 'Captain' and 'Bess' jogged on in their former somnolent condition, until they reached the point at which the road turned away from the stream whose course it had hitherto followed. Here the driver woke up a little, and shook the jingling reins to show he was alive to the difficulty of the abrupt turning.

Across green fields, where the grass-grown road was scarcely distinguishable, through rickety gateways and stony lanes, the jolting vehicle made its way across the valley towards Pengraig. Simon had just forded the little stream, when his ears were assailed by a succession of piercing screams. A quiver passed over his stolid face, and a gleam of anger sparkled in his bloodshot eyes. He shook the reins again, and the horses pricked up their ears as the uncanny sounds rent the soft evening air, but Simon shewed no further signs of disturbance. It was only Wednesday, and not until Friday did he begin to cast off the influence of the strong drink to which he was a slave, and which blunted his feelings and dulled his brain. In the early part of the week he was always in a sodden, semi-drunken condition, but on Friday evenings he arrived at home in a tolerably sober state, and generally devoted the whole of

Saturday to sleeping off the effects of the week's potations, thus enabling himself to appear, with the regularity of clockwork, in the corner of his pew at Penmwntan church on Sunday. This custom he clung to with the tenacity of a drowning man, feeling it was the last shred of respectability left to him.

His two servants, Bensha and Madlen, had entered his service in the early days of his married life, and had stuck to him and the farm ever since, with the old-fashioned dislike of change which was so marked a characteristic of the Welsh servant in the past. What qualities had recommended them to his choice, it is difficult to say; certainly, not their outward appearance, for Bensha had lost one eye, a circumstance which seemed to compel him to keep the other one very wide open, and Madlen had but one tooth, whose size and length proclaimed it the survival of the fittest. There were continual bickerings between them and their master, but the idea of parting never entered their heads or his.

On this particular evening, when he climbed off his seat on the lumbering waggon on arriving in his own farmyard, Bensha led the horses away, while Madlen greeted her master in sarcastic tones.

'Well done,' she said. 'Here's a nice pickle you are in tonight again. Ach-y-fi! Come to supper, if you've got any room in you for supper.'

'No, no,' said the old man, sitting down in the chimney corner, 'I don't want supper. What's the matter with her tonight?'

'Matter with her? She wants a good thrashing, that's the matter,' said Madlen. 'Go to bed, you drunken sot,' and, with a mumbled oath, the old man lurched up the rickety stairs.

In spite of this, on the following Sunday he might be seen sitting bolt upright at church, his bleared eyes fixed dutifully on the vicar, who was perfectly aware of his delinquencies during the rest of the week, but shook hands with him kindly in the churchyard after the service. He made inquiries concerning his crops, his waggon, his horses; never mentioning his daughter, however, for it was considered the proper thing at Treswnd to ignore the girl's existence as much as possible. Her eccentric mode of life, her screams, her reputation for witchcraft were all a slur upon the respectability of the neighbourhood, which it was better to thrust out of sight and forget as far as might be; so the vicar, who had only heard stray rumours of her uncanny ways, followed the fashion, and, in consideration of Simon's feelings, never mentioned her. Every Sunday the old pews were filled and emptied, and no one thought of the girl who lay among the furze bushes on the Pengraig cliffs, or basked on the rocks below. Had they roamed into the churchyard when the days were shorter, and the curtain of darkness fell early over the silent sleepers lying there under the night sky, they would often have seen a slender brown figure glide softly between the graves to the east end of the church, and there, mounting a tombstone, sit crouched upon it, peering into the dimly lit church.

On the same Sunday, Morgan Hughes was also at church, and decidedly in a happier frame of mind than that of his neighbour, Simon Rees. He had felt the fervour of the old hymns, he had joined in the service in his rough, broad tongue, and had shown the world how well conducted he was, how sober, how much better dressed than Simon! When the service was over, and they followed the diverging paths to their homes, each man cast frequent glances at the little field which spread its verdant pasture beside the stream under the spring sunshine, studded with cowslips and orchids, and edged with sea pinks, all turning their innocent faces to the blue sky, as if there was no such thing as envy and bitterness in the world.

When Simon reached his ramshackle old house, there was but little comfort awaiting him. Madlen had boiled a couple of fowls and a large piece of ham, which would do duty for every night's supper during the coming week. She had spread the knives and forks on the bare deal table, and had placed the barley loaf and the jug of buttermilk in readiness. When Simon appeared, she was standing at the gap in the farmyard that opened out to the fields sloping down to the cliffs. With a curious gurgling sound in her throat, not unlike the jodling of a Swiss cowherd, she called the two cows and her master's daughter at the same time. She would not call 'Catrin! Catrin!' lest, in the clear air, the echoes should carry the name from hill to hill and to the village below; for Bensha, and Madlen his wife, were much scandalised by the girl's wild ways, so she stood there making believe to call the cows only. Corwen and Beauty heard the call, but went on grazing peacefully amongst the cowslips, for they had become accustomed to the trick by which they were lured up to the farm, only to be 'shooed' back again with a flap of Madlen's flannel apron.

'Dinner's ready,' she said, as Simon passed her in the yard, and when he had sat down to the plentiful, though roughly served, meal, she filled the wooden bowls with the 'cawl' in which the ham and fowls had boiled together, not to speak of the barley dumplings which also tumbled about in the crock. Simon sat at one end of the table, Bensha at the other, and between the long-drawn sups of their cawl they interpolated their scant remarks.

'Wasn't at church?' asked Simon.

'Oh yes,' answered Bensha, 'but I was hungry, and came straight home; don't know where you spent the time.'

'Morris ffeirad was asking how I was, and I was telling him how bad my knee was yesterday,' said Simon, with pride.

'Hm!' said Bensha. 'Did you tell him how you was on Thursday and Wednesday, and the rest of the week?'

The head of the family made no answer, but, with a shamefaced sullenness, looked down at his plate, upon which Madlen was piling the boiled fowl and bacon.

At this moment the sunshine was darkened by a shadow, and slowly a footstep came sliding along the earthen floor of the passage, as a girl came in, flattening herself against the wall, her hands drawn over its rough surface, as if ready to clutch at it. Reaching the end of the passage where it opened out into the living room, she peered round timidly before she ventured to leave the protecting wall; then, seeing no stranger, she slipped noiselessly to the bench which stood beside the table, and looked eagerly at the viands. Simon Rees glanced at her for a moment, and Madlen flung upon her platter a portion of the boiled fowl. Bensha was too much engaged with his own share to make any remark. For some time the girl ate hungrily, in the sullen silence which had fallen upon the company; and while she eats, we may endeavour to describe her outward appearance. Though only fifteen years of age, she had the thoughtful look of an older woman, and was thin and worn, as though the want of home comforts had told upon her, in spite of the counterbalancing advantages which her life of freedom in the open air brought her. Altogether she gave one the impression of a *brown* girl; her long unkempt hair was brown, her eyes the same colour, her skin, naturally dark, was burnt and tanned by summer suns and winter winds, her tattered frock of rough homespun was of the same sombre hue, the neck cut low and the sleeves above the elbows; over it a blue cotton apron, changed once a week, when the Sunday luxury of a hot midday meal, and a pudding, or Madlen's idea of one, tempted her to spend a few hours within the walls of her home.

Bensha and Madlen, in consideration of being allowed to make their own small profits from the fowls and garden, took upon them the farm work, and the rough household menage; but they had long ago ceased their efforts to extend their management to the girl's behaviour. The window of the room in which stood her bed of chaff, with its rough coverlet of red and blue cloth, was always left open – in fact, for the want of a little carpentering, it refused to close. Through the aperture Catrin crawled in at night, if the weather was too severely cold or stormy for her hardy frame. Where she slept at other times was a matter of conjecture only to the inmates of Pengraig.

'Her window is open; she can reach it from the top of the garden wall, and can sleep in her bed every night of her life like any other decent girl,' Madlen would say sometimes, when Bensha, who was of a rather more kindly nature than her own, had compunctions of conscience.

As for Simon himself, if, over his sodden mind, there sometimes dawned a perception of his daughter's irregular and strange mode of life, the feeling was immediately stifled, and drowned in a stronger potation than usual, and Catrin was allowed to continue in her erratic ways.

But today being Sunday, and having shaken hands with the vicar, Simon's thoughts were a little clearer than usual. Suddenly looking up from his plate, he began to make inquiries which were not unnatural in a parent, but which seemed to frighten the girl, and to surprise Bensha and Madlen.

'Where hast been till today?' he said, looking with bleared, unhappy eyes at the girl, who stooped over her platter.

In a moment she was roused and on the defensive. She slipped from the bench, and keeping her brown eyes fixed upon her father in a defiant manner, answered:

'Out l have been – out in the fields and on the mountains. What harm's in that?'

The fierceness of Simon's anger seemed to quail under the girl's eyes, but, with an effort, he continued: ''Tis harm to make the whole neighbourhood talk about thee, and afraid of thee. Thee'rt fifteen today.'

'Fourteen,' interpolated Bensha.

'No; I read it on her mother's tombstone today, and Sunday it was too when she was born.'

'Yes. You were a different man then,' said Bensha, who seldom spared his master's feelings.'I remember you the day the little girl was born. Yes, you were a different man then.'

The words, or the memories awakened by them, seemed to exasperate the miserable man, for he started to his feet, and tried to recall the girl, who had disappeared into the passage.

'Come back,' he shouted, 'or by the Lord I'll give thee the cart whip. Dost hear, Catrin?'

'What?' said the girl, reappearing at the doorway, and fixing her eyes upon him once more.

'What wert screaming about a few nights ago, thou she-devil born to be a curse to me?'

'The boys were throwing stones after me, and one of them caught me and held me fast till I stopped screaming. 'Twas the son of Sarnissa, Goronwy Hughes. I hate him, and I bit his hand.'

'Goronwy Sarnissa,' said Simon. 'That's it, that's it. Be bound he went home and told his father how the boys ran after thee and called thee witch, and threw stones after thee. In my deed, I'm ashamed to think thou art my daughter; and listen, I've had enough of this, and as sure as my name is Simon Rees, I'll send thee to the "Sayloom", that I will.'

'Yes,' chimed in Madlen, 'Tan i marw, I'm ashamed to own I live with thee. To hear what the people say about thee; and to think thou art idling thy time about the rocks while I am working my fingers to the bone! See how different it might be – a tidy maiden in the house, making the beds and preparing the meals for her father, would be a comfort to us all; and going to church on Sunday with her prayer-book and her pocket handkerchief in her hand, and going to the singing class with all the other boys and girls, and indeed the tune they are learning there now is enough to draw any one to the class!'

Madlen's rambling reproaches seemed at last to have touched the girl's heart, for raising her blue apron to her eyes, she began to cry.

'Thee may'st well cry,' said her father, 'seeing thou art bringing shame and sorrow upon thy old father. 'Tis a good thing thy mother is dead; thou would'st break her heart.'

'Perhaps,' said Bensha, 'if she had lived, the "croten", would not be what she is.' This set Madlen off again in self-defence:

'Haven't I done all a mother could do for her? Nursed her and fed her and kept her tidy and scolded her when she wanted it.'

'Oh yes,' said Bensha, 'I'll allow thou'st done all that, especially the last; but there's one thing has never been done, that a mother, her mother whatever, would be sure to have done for her.'

'And what's that, I should like to know?' asked Madlen again.

'Pray for her,' said Bensha, looking confused and embarrassed at the mere mention of such a thing at Pengraig.

Simon said nothing, but Madlen deeply resented the implied reproof, and launched out into a flood of self-justification.

The object of their reproaches stood looking from one to another with apparent indifference, and as though the conversation in no way concerned her; but appearances are deceitful, for not a word was lost upon her. She had taken them all in, to be thought over, perhaps to be wept over, in some long vigil under the stars, when only the roll of the breakers broke the stillness. The singing class – that hour of charm that was for ever tempting her to leave her safe retreat on the cliffs, and to venture within the haunts of men – was it possible that she could ever have been allowed to enter with the other lads and girls, to stand up with them and join her voice with theirs in the harmonies to which she had so often listened, standing in the shadow of the schoolhouse? The very thought was overpowering, and the tears suddenly welled up into her eyes, and burst forth in deep sobs, which shook her slender form, and brought the blue apron into requisition again.

'I'll have no more of it,' said Simon. 'Thee can't be wise, or thee wouldn't go on like this. With a comfortable home and a dry bed ready for thee, to prefer the wind and rain and the bare hillsides; 'tis real madness, and I'll thrash it out of thee, or I'll send thee to the "Sayloom", by God I will!'

He had worked himself up into a fury, and starting towards

the girl, would certainly have wreaked his anger upon her in some form of bodily chastisement, had she not eluded his grasp by darting through the open doorway into the sunny farmyard. When her father reached the door, she was flying through the gap into the sloping fields beyond, and Simon returned to the table, his anger giving way to a maudlin self-pity and some bitter tears of humiliation.

'Let her go,' said Bensha, soothingly.

For once, he was sorry for the old man, so enslaved by drink that all his manliness had departed, and in whom the effects of the Saturday's and Sunday's partial sobriety only served to waken the dim consciousness of a ruined life and lost self-respect.

Meanwhile, having gained the open air, Catrin had forgotten the annoyances of the last hour. She ran through the gap into the fields, her brown hair flying behind her, the sea wind in her face and the blue sky above her.

All this took place on the uplands; the breezy 'bryns' and slopes rising in grassy solitudes or rocky escarpments from the strands and beaches below.

On the edge of one of these sandy shores stood the village of Treswnd, its houses grouped together at the opening of a ravine between the cliffs that towered behind it. Its inhabitants were for the most part fishermen, the owners of two or three boats, which luffed out lazily when the weather was quite satisfactory, and sheltered snugly behind the rocks when the wind showed the slightest sign of blowing more than a gentle breeze; for what was the use of toiling, when two or three nights' fishing in the autumn would fill up the nets, and provide herrings in abundance for the whole village, and for the neighbouring farmers over and above? Then there would be excitement and life, laughter and talk in the air, lights flitting about on the beach, and the eager waiting for the boats with their uncouth scaly owners; then the merry gatherings in shed or boathouse, where the herrings were salted and dried, to be hung up afterwards in rows inside the wattled chimneys, in readiness for the grim winters which would bring but a bare, unvaried diet of cawl and tea, until the springtime came again, and the cabbages and leeks grew up to vary the monotony of the winter's fare.

But the winter is far off at present, for it is April, and under the light of a crimson sunset, the long, fair reaches of sand lie wreathed with shells and seaweed, and bearing on their tawny bosoms the suggestions of pearls and precious stones, which add so much to the fascinations of a lonely seashore.

A long, peaked headland stretched out on one side of the harbour, broken up at its furthest point into jagged rocks that rose out of the deep green waters at low tide, their surface covered with tufts of golden brown bladder-weed, under the clammy branches of which the crabs lived and throve. These rocks, with their myriad pools, were the favourite daily resort of the village children, who roamed there at low tide, springing from rock to rock, and hunting with never-failing interest in the fissures and crannies, sitting on their edges, with bare feet dangling in the sunny water, shouting to each other, and singing with boisterous, but musical, voices.

The black rocks, or 'cerrig duon', as they were called, had great attractions also for the lads of the uplands. They came down daily, with a little restraint and aloofness in their manner towards the boys of the village, who, perhaps, gave themselves slightly a town-bred air, for there were twenty houses at Treswnd, which, for about two hundred yards, were ranged pretty evenly on both sides of the road, and were here called the 'stryt'.

Amongst the others, Goronwy was wont to come down, with his hands in his pockets, his sailor cap pushed back, and his lips generally drawn into a small circle, from which issued the merriest whistle imaginable. On the evening after his adventure with Catrin Rees, he was sauntering down as usual, springing from rock to rock, and peering, with the shrewd observant eyes of a coast-boy, into every hole and corner.

'No crabs today?' he called to a knot of boys and girls who stood looking at him.

'No,' they answered. 'Walto Gwyn has been here; there he is round there in his boat.'

Goronwy made no answer, but stood shading his eyes from the sunset, and looking towards its brilliant glare with a slight shade of annoyance on his open countenance.

'Well, he's got as much right as you have here, or I, or any one else; but, of course, with his boat he can reach some places better than we can.'

'I could bring father's boat,' said little Tim Powell.

'Tush! your father's boat; that lumbering old thing wouldn't go in between the rocks like that little cockleshell.'

There was no denying this, so the boys scattered towards the village, leaving Goronwy still looking at the tiny white boat, in which no oarsman was visible.

'He's asleep, I expect, lazy dog,' he muttered, and then he took to shouting – 'Walto! Walto Gwyn!' And from the bottom of the boat a figure began to rise, and a lad stood up against the sunset.

About Goronwy's age, perhaps, though looking considerably older; supple, and brown as a gypsy, he turned his dark eyes towards the rocks, and his handsome clear-cut lips curled a little defiantly as he shouted in return: 'Hoi! what's the matter?'

'Crabs?' called Goronwy.

'Yes, and two lobsters,' was the answer, and then Walto lay down again, and applied himself once more to the study of a dog-eared book without a cover, leaning on his elbows and taking no further heed of Goronwy, who still stood on the rock, around which the tide was beginning to lift the seaweed at his feet. Turning to retrace his footsteps, he saw coming towards him the girl who had ridden home the night before in Simon's waggon.

Ysbel Lloyd (Yshbel, as the country people called her) lived on the further side of the beach, where two or three thatched cottages were perched amongst the rushes, and coarse grass growing between the cliffs and the shore. There had always been hanging over the girl the halo of a traditional claim to 'gentility', very undefined and unsubstantial but still sufficient to surround her with an interest not pertaining to the other girls of the village.

Nanti Betto had received her into her keeping as a baby, and the large sum of £20 had been paid by the man who delivered the child into the old woman's charge. He and his wife had drifted to Treswnd in a honeymoon journey, and being, it may be presumed, people of refined natures, had felt the charm of the old-world simplicity of the place, and had stayed on there longer than they had intended. Here their first child was born. When she was a month old, her mother had died, and her father, known only in the village as 'Mishter Lloyd' had hurried away from the place that had been the scene of his short-lived happiness and his so sudden bereavement.

Time had thrown his usual mantle of romance over a very simple incident, and Yshbel's parentage was often the theme of a fireside gossip. 'At all events they were rich,' the villagers decided, 'for did they not have meat for dinner every day, and silver spoons with their tea?' and when the little one was handed over to Betto with a deposit of £20 and a promise that some day her father would send for the child, and pay her well for her trouble, she was considered a lucky woman. 'I don't say when it will be,' he had said, 'but *some* day I will come or send for her. Bring her up like one of yourselves, and I shall be satisfied.' Betto had received the child with many curtsies and promises of care – promises which she had well fulfilled, for she had grown to love the beautiful girl, and little Yshbel had found a happy home under the brown thatched roof that looked so perilously close to the great sea waves; though when she grew older, her thoughts often turned to the mother whose resting-place in Penmwntan churchyard was marked by a little grey headstone, and to the father who roamed in distant lands.

As she approached Goronwy on the cerrig duon, he looked at her with the careless indifference of a lad upon whose heart the enticements of beauty have as yet made no impression. She was Yshbel, whom he had played and sung with from babyhood; she was Yshbel, whom he despised somewhat for her want of skill in rough games, in crab-hunting, in reaping; also for the slight halo of romance which hung over her, and prevented his speaking to her with quite the same familiarity that he used to the other village girls.

He was glad she had come, for he wanted a companion, as that lazy Walto had not chosen to join him, but he took no note of the willowy grace of form, the crown of yellow hair, the dark-blue eyes, the slender, creamy neck which rose from the rough blue serge frock, fitting so close to her slight girlish form, the red parted lips, and the rosy hue which was gradually suffusing her face as she approached. He saw none of it. All this was to dawn upon him later on perhaps, but today he thought of nothing but the tide and the crabs.

'Yshbel, thou art late, lass, thou'st lost the tide. No crabs for thy tea tonight; that sly Walto has been before us.'

'Where is he?' asked the girl, shading her eyes as Goronwy had done. 'Oh yes, there he is,' and placing her two hands to her mouth, she called through them, 'Walto!'

The lad had heard her, and was sculling vigorously towards the rocks.

'He's awake at last,' said Goronwy. 'What d'ye want with him?'

'The mestress sent down for a lobster last night, but I had sold them all in town, and I was wondering had Walto found one for her tonight.'

Here the little white boat reached them, and Walto jumped out.

'Have you found a lobster for your mother?' said the girl. 'That's what I was coming for, because Nanti was vexing that she hadn't got one for her last night.'

'I was too late for the lobster pots yesterday, but I have two beauties today,' and he jerked his thumb towards the blue monsters clawing about at the bottom of his boat. He spoke with a slow, deliberate manner, unlike the short, brusque tones of the other villagers, but in quite as broad Welsh as they. 'If Ben will be fishing tomorrow,' he continued, 'mother asks will he bring some fish to Tredhû, Yshbel?'

'Yes; I'll go home and tell him.'

'Won't you come for a row in the boat?'

'Yes, come,' interpolated Goronwy, 'I'll take one oar.'

'There's no need for that,' said Walto, and Yshbel looked undecidedly from one to the other, Goronwy being too interested in the white boat and the lobsters to notice her hesitation, while Walto looked earnestly at her, as if hanging upon her decision; and if eyes speak the truth, not one of the charms which were lost upon Goronwy were unnoticed by him.

'Not tonight; I must go,' she said, turning away without a word of goodbye.

Greetings were unusual amongst the villagers, who met and parted so many times in the day. Goronwy followed Walto into the boat, and the two lads took naturally an oar apiece.

'Where dost want to go?' asked Walto.

'Only across to the Crugyn. I promised granny a crab for her tea.'

'Thee'lt go thyself then,' said Walto, rising and springing back to the rock.' No granny in the world would tempt me into the "Deep Stream"; the Crugyn is much too near it; the tide has turned and thou'lt be in the whirlpool before thee know'st it.'

'Nonsense,' said the daring lad. 'Stand you there and watch me then. I'll be back in five minutes;' and pushing the boat away from the rocks, he sculled towards one which rose like a tower straight from the green water.

As he neared it, he began to feel that he was doing a

foolhardy thing; for though he used his best endeavours to reach
the right side of the Crugyn, the subtle tide opposed him, and
drew him, against his will, to the other side, and he knew that
more than the tide drew him aside, for he felt the force of a
strong current which flowed at this point in the direction of the
high, black headland. It was a deadly and mysterious suction,
known to, and dreaded by, every man, woman, and child in the
neighbourhood. A crust of bread, an apple, a dead dog – or a
live one for the matter of that – thrown within its insidious
influence was gradually but surely drawn towards some invisible
point under the cliffs, somewhere down below the smooth
surface which looked so calm and harmless. Tradition told of a
sea cave beneath those rocky hillsides into which this strong
current drew its victims, washing them on to the sands of a dim,
dark shore, beneath those beetling crags. No one had ever
returned from that mysterious shore, so how the tradition had
grown and gained credence it is difficult to say. The Crugyn
rock was considered to be too near it to be safe, and the village
boys left it severely alone, so Walto watched with keen interest,
not unmixed with fear, as Goronwy neared the rock, and
shouted to him, 'Keep to the right, fool, or you'll get into the
Deep Stream.' Goronwy shouted something in return. He had
succeeded in reaching the rock, though not on the safest side,
and was already searching under the damp seaweed, and soon
drew out a crab of good proportions. Laying it on its back at
the bottom of the boat, he turned again to his oar, and not for
worlds would he have confessed to Walto the qualm of fear that
shot through him as he felt the hard straining of the boat to
resist his sculling. But it was over in a moment, and he was
beyond the magic circle of danger, and springing with outward
composure to the rocks beside Walto.

'What didst do such a mad thing for?' said the latter, with a
curl of his handsome lips. 'To brave danger for a good cause is
something to be proud of, but to dare the Deep Stream for the
sake of a crab to eat is silly and childish!'

'I said I would bring her a crab for her tea, and I always do what I say I will. There is no danger yonder. If you had come with me it would have been easy.'

Drawing the boat up to a place of safety, they turned together towards the village, where Goronwy dangled his crab for the boys' admiration.

'Fancy venturing to the Crugyn just for a crab to eat!'

'Don't I always do what I say I'll do?' said Goronwy, with a toss of his head.

'Oh! b't shwr!' said one of the older lads, 'thou'rt a wonderful man in thine own opinion. Thee'll have hard work to keep all thy promises though.'

'Which?' said Goronwy, defiantly.

'Didn't thee say thou wert going to get Parcglas back for thy father?'

'Did I? And I will do it I'll never rest till Parcglas belongs to Sarnissa again.'

'And didn't thee say thou would'st rid the place of the witch? And she was screaming as loud as ever last night.'

'I'll do that too, if I said I would. Any more? Come on, all of you. Have I made any other promise?'

'Yes,' said a pale-faced boy, with his finger in his mouth. 'You said you'd marry Yshbel Lloyd when you were grown up.'

'And so I will,' said Goronwy. 'You wait a few years, and I'll marry Yshbel Lloyd. Anything more?'

But there seemed to be no further arraignment, so the boys separated, leaving Goronwy and Walto to follow their course towards the village.

'I'll go to the Crugyn again some day,' said Goronwy, 'there would be no danger before the tide turned.'

'Thee'st better make no more plans,' said Walto, or thee'lt find thine hands too full, I'm thinking!'

Goronwy laughed, and tossed his head again.

'Oh, 'tis only to plague the boys I said all that but still it's true, Walto – whatever I say I'll do I'll do.'

'How art going to get the field from Simon Rees?'

'I don't know; but I'll get it. A man can always do what he makes up his mind to do.'

'And how art going to rid the place of Catrin Rees?'

'I don't know; but I'll do that too.'

'And Yshbel Lloyd?' said Walto. 'I'll tell her what thee'st said, and see how she'll like it.'

'Tell her if you like,' said Goronwy, 'I won't care a cockleshell for you, nor for her, nor for any one else.'

'Marry Yshbel Lloyd, indeed! Thee a common farmer's son and she a lady born! Dost remember?'

'Phruit! What's that matter?'

'And what if she won't have thee for a sweetheart?' asked Walto.

'Then I'll make her say she will,' said Goronwy; adding his favourite maxim, 'A man can always do what he makes up his mind to do.'

'Thee'st a fool, Goronwy. Thee'lt never get rid of the witch from Pengraig, and thee'lt never get Parcglas, and Yshbel Lloyd will never take thee for a sweetheart.'

'Wait a few years and see,' said Goronwy, laughing, as he came to the parting of the ways, where the path turned off from the stony road towards Sarnissa and the uplands. Walto did not answer, but turned in another direction, with a flush of anger on his face.

CHAPTER III

UNDER THE APPLE BLOSSOMS

On the following morning, Morgan Hughes stood in the cwrt at Sarnissa for full five minutes, with his telescope to his eye, old Gwen sitting in the morning sunshine, and watching him anxiously, as usual, when he contemplated sailing.

'There's the *Speedwell* and the *Jane*,' he muttered, 'and a good nor'-nor'-wester. I'll be in Milfwrt before night.'

'Art going then, machgeni? And going to take Goronwy with thee?'

'No, no, mother fach,' said the captain, 'I am going to take Ben Bullet's boy. Goronwy says he must stop at home to look after you and the farm.'

'To take care of me?' said Gwen, with a smile of sweet and shy surprise. 'He is my dear boy whatever!'

'That's me, I expect,' said Goronwy, appearing on the scene; 'now, you behave, old woman,' he said, holding his fist threateningly before her; 'look at my fist, as big as father's – so mind!'

Gwen laughed as she pushed his hand aside.

'Or else wilt beat me, lad, as Billo beat his old mother in the mill long ago?'

'Bh-r-r-r!' roared the boy, in mock fury, and Gwen laughed again till her shoulders shook.

The captain looked at his watch.

'The tide will turn at twelve,' he said; 'till then, I'll take a look round the farm,' and he took his way over the stubble, and towards Parcglas.

'He'll never be happy till he gets Parcglas, and 'twill be his before many years, or my name is not Goronwy Hughes,' said his son, picking up the spying glass; and resting it upon the wall of the cwrt, he gazed through it long and steadily. Old Gwen carried her knitting indoors, and sat crooning over the kitchen fire.

Meanwhile, the lad still gazed through the spying glass. Over there, across the valley, rose the breezy slopes of Penmwntan, its rugged head marked clearly against the azure blue sky of morning; and on its rock-strewn side, not far from where the cliffs broke off suddenly into the sea, stood the grey walls of Pengraig, showing sharp and distinct against its background of ill-tilled fields. Even in the bright morning sunshine it bore a grim, forbidding aspect, its grey walls unsoftened by ivy, its broken windows and thick oak doors bringing to mind all the old traditions of the countryside, which credited it with having been, in times not very long gone by, the resort of smugglers, and of having mysterious underground passages leading down to the shore. Catrin's eccentric ways, too, had not lessened the superstitious dislike with which the old house was regarded.

'Where is that witch today, I wonder?' said Goronwy. 'I'll manage her, in spite of her teeth and her screams,' and he scanned the house, the fields, the garden, in search of the girl. He could distinctly see the yard, where Simon Rees was already harnessing the horses into his lumbering waggon. Now it is done, and, whip in hand, he approaches the orchard, from the corner of which comes at his call the slender brown figure for which Goronwy had searched with his glass.

There she stood under the shade of the apple tree, while Simon evidently held an angry colloquy with her. He drew his long whip through his fingers, he stamped his foot, and in another moment the lash had descended on the girl's shoulders. Goronwy saw her distinctly as she flew round the apple trees, while again and again the lash descended upon her.

The lad's colour rose, but he continued to stare unflinchingly through his glass. Again another lash – the girl stands at bay, and in another moment springs like a cat at the uplifted arm, while scream after scream come clearly on the morning air. Goronwy flung his glass away, and breathing hard, began to race across the yard and down the valley, following the first impulse of his tender, though headstrong, nature. 'To strike a girl like that,' he muttered, as he climbed up the side of Penmwntan, 'brute, cythrael!'

The hill was steep, and as he toiled up, there had been time for a sharp struggle between Simon and his daughter. She had nothing but her teeth and her nails to defend herself with, so she bit and scratched like a frightened cat. The angry man, feeling that he was getting the worst of the struggle, suddenly wrenched himself away from her, and with great force flung her from him, as if she were a rat or a wild cat; then he climbed up to the seat of his waggon, and, gathering up the reins, shook them, and with a crack of his whip, drove out into the stony road without looking back. When the sounds of the wheels had quite died away, Goronwy reached the orchard wall, and peering over its loose moss-grown stones, looked round for the girl whose screams had a moment before awakened the echoes from every hill and crag in the neighbourhood. Now a solemn stillness reigned over the orchard.

Bensha and Madlen were accustomed to the frequent storms between the old man and his daughter, and were but little disturbed by them. He only dug his spade more fiercely through the clods, while she, with a click of her tongue and a toss of her head, went on with her cheese-making.

'Ach-y-fi!' she said, 'there's ashamed I am to belong to such people.'

So the girl lay quietly under the trees where she had fallen, and the apple blossoms fell over her, and strewed the ground around her. So white, so still, she was! Goronwy wished she would move, or even scream again, and at last, climbing carefully over the wall, he approached her on the soft spring grass. Was she dead? Or sleeping?

No; the brown eyes were wide open, and as he drew near, they turned upon him with the look of a hunted animal.

'Why don't you rise?' he asked.

'I don't want,' said the girl, sullenly.

'I don't believe you can. What's the matter with you?'

'I fell from the apple tree, and hurt myself.'

'You are telling a lie, you know you are,' said Goronwy; 'your father thrashed you shocking.'

'He didn't, he didn't,' cried the girl; 'I fell from the apple tree' – she moaned a little, and for the first time, the tears began to course each other down her cheeks – 'and – and I think my arm is broken.'

'Perhaps your arm is broken, but your father thrashed you – I saw him do it – and he deserves to be put in jail for it. I've a great mind to tell the vicar about it.'

'He didn't, he didn't!' cried the girl again. 'He didn't hurt me, I fell from the tree,' and once more she fell to screaming.

'Highsht!' said Goronwy, kneeling beside her. 'You know I made you highsht before – what night was it? – and if you make any more noise, I'll go straight to the vicar, and he'll pretty soon send your father to jail.'

Again the summer air was silent, except for the trickle of the streamlet in the thicket, and the birds that sang in the apple tree, whose blossoms dropped around them.

'Stop you there now till I fetch Madlen,' said the lad; but there was no occasion for this injunction, for Catrin had broken her arm, and every moment increased the pain that tortured her.

'Well, Bendigedig!' exclaimed Madlen, when Goronwy had told his tale, and she dried her hands from the cheese curds, with snorts of indignation.

'Don't scold her now,' said the boy; 'she's lying in the orchard with a broken arm. You and Bensha had better carry her in, and put her in bed, while I run for the doctor; I am sure to find him in the village today,' and down at the inn he found the doctor, who visited Treswnd every week.

'What's the matter with her?' he said, stepping into his gig, and taking Goronwy with him.

'She's broke her arm, sir, I'm thinking, or twisted it very bad. She can't move whatever.'

'How did she do it?'

'She said she fell from the apple tree.'

'But that oughtn't to hurt a witch – ought it? Poor old Simon! 'Tis pity he has such a daughter. Witch, indeed! A good whipping with a birch rod would soon take the witch out of her; and I'll tell Simon so.'

'No, don't, sir, please,' said Goronwy. 'He's not over kind to her, I'm thinking.'

'Well, we'll wait till she's well, anyway.'

Arrived at the farmhouse door, he flung the reins to Bensha, and passed into the ramshackle room where Catrin's bed stood. She was lying white and still under the quilt of blue and red, whose grandeur Madlen considered made up for any lack of sheets and blankets. Suffering acutely from the pain caused by her removal from the orchard, her cheeks were still wet with tears, though she had ceased to cry, and the long lashes lay on them placidly.

The doctor's cheerful 'Well?' aroused her, and opening her eyes, she looked into his face with the same hunted expression which she had fixed upon Goronwy.

'Well? Goronwy Hughes tells me you have had a fall – let's see the arm,' and he gently uncovered the injured limb, Goronwy standing by, with a strong feeling of pity for the girl who lay helpless before them.

'Now,' said the doctor, 'courage, 'merch i! I won't hurt you more than I can help. Goronwy, you stay here and help me, but you, Madlen, take yourself off, and take your snuffles with you.'

The former felt much disposed to follow Madlen, but stood his ground as manfully as he could, and helped with the splints and bandages.

When all was over, the doctor took a long look at the girl.

'Now listen,' he said, 'you are to eat everything Madlen brings you; I will tell her what to bring. You are not to scream, or scratch, or bite, or your arm will not get well. If you are quiet, it will soon be well. I will come and see you again on Tuesday.'

'Pretty little girl too,' he said, as he got into his gig. 'Pity she's "not wise". I wonder if she *is*, or whether it's all wickedness. I'll find out before she's well.'

Catrin had not spoken a word during the doctor's visit, and when Goronwy returned to the room, she was still silent and pale.

'Madlen is making bwdran for thee,' he said, 'and thee must drink it, remember.' Still not a word of reply. 'Why arn't thee speaking to me? I've done thee no harm.'

'I want to go out from here.'

'Out!' said the boy, 'out, indeed. Thou'lt have to be here many a long day, I'm thinking.'

'That will I not,' said Catrin.

'Oh yes, thou wilt; and I will come with the doctor on Tuesday to see how thou art. Fforwel now,' and Goronwy nodded as he went out at the door, still getting no answer from the uncouth, untutored girl.

When he was gone, however, she looked wistfully after him. Presently Madlen appeared, bringing a bowl of steaming bwdran, or 'sowens' as it is called in Scotland. Mindful of the doctor's injunctions to keep her patient quiet, she preserved an awful silence, indicative of her righteous indignation. Her bunch of yellow hair and her one yellow tooth looked more uncomely than usual, and when Bensha put his head in at the doorway, his one eye cocked with inquiring sympathy, he was instantly banished by a wave of his wife's forbidding arm.

'There's no need for me to scold thee now,' she said, slowly withdrawing from the room,' thy mad pranks have brought their punishment, as I often warned thee, and thee'd better give them up, or worse will befall thee – so there! Go to sleep now, and be quiet;' and she closed the door with a bang.

Catrin heard little of this tirade, her thoughts being fully occupied with anxiety lest the strange boy should bring trouble upon her father. This waif of existence had never before held familiar intercourse or friendly converse with any human being beyond those of her own household, but, from her childhood upwards, had consorted only with the animals around her, loving them with all the strength of a passionate heart, which must perforce find some outlet for the tenderness with which it had been endowed.

Now, as she lay there, sick and sore, her thoughts revolved round one point. The strange boy Goronwy (she knew his name) had not divulged to the doctor his doubts as to the way in which she had been hurt. The lie by which she had endeavoured to shield her father troubled her not at all. 'Oh, I hope they won't put father in jail,' was the thought uppermost in her mind, as her eyes closed in fatigue, the long lashes resting on her cheeks in the silence of profound sleep.

Goronwy went down to the shore, where he watched his father sail away in the *Lark*. On the strip of sand edging the full tide, the children gathered round him, listening, with breathless interest, to the history of Catrin's accident.

'Diwss anwl! I am glad,' said Tim Powell. 'Our cow died last night, and mother says she'll swear Catrin Rees had been in the field with her, because she saw the flowers she dropped there; old "bysse cwn" and snake flowers they were too – ach, smelling shocking!'

'Perhaps that's why she threw them away,' suggested Goronwy.

'Well,' said Dyc Pendrwm, with a shrewd nod, '"bysse cwn" are poisonous whatever, and she is a witch. Thee'lt get rid of her for us without much trouble after all, perhaps.'

'She's safe enough now,' said Goronwy, 'lying in that old bed, with such a grand quilt over her.'

'Art sure she can't move?' asked little Tim Powell. 'Let's go up and look at her tonight; the window is open at the top – let's go!'

'Indeed I won't,' said Dyc. 'I'm afraid of Madlen's tooth and Bensha's cock eye.'

'No, just you leave her alone,' said Goronwy, with the authority generally conceded to the strongest will in a knot of boys. 'She's quiet enough now, so you let her be.'

'I'll go home and tell mother,' said Tim Powell. 'Indeed, 'tis an odd thing that the anthem tonight at the singing school is "Praise be to God!"' And the little company walked up the village singing their anthem with gusto, paraphrasing the words to suit the event which they were celebrating, 'Praise be to God! the witch is conquered. He giveth us the victory over all our enemies.'

The words were English, so they did not entirely appreciate their sanctity. At all events, each knew his part, and the voices blended harmoniously. In the still country air, the music floated up the side of Penmwntan, and reached the old grey house where Catrin lay sleeping wearily.

The window being open, the sounds came in on the sea breeze and awoke her. She opened her eyes and listened, a smile of happiness lighting up the brown face, and making it almost beautiful, her senses soothed and charmed. The tears gathered in her eyes, although she smiled, and coursed each other down her cheeks.

When Simon arrived in the evening, he had but a dim remembrance of what had occurred in the morning, and came blustering into the house as usual.

'Highsht!' said Madlen, running to meet him with uplifted arm. 'Highsht! The girl is in bed with a broken arm, and the doctor has been here, and he says if she's not kept quiet she'll die; and I don't know what did you do to her this morning? She is saying it was a fall, but I know better than that.'

'Broke her arm,' said the old man, his jaw falling in horror. 'What did I do to her? O Lord, what did I do? Some day I'll kill her! I'm a miserable man,' and sitting down with his elbows on the table, he leant his muddled head upon his hands and sobbed in sheer depression of spirits, for it was Friday, and he had not drunk his usual quantity at The Hunter's Arms as he passed.

'Come, eat your supper,' said Madlen. 'Indeed, to goodness, between everything, I'm moidered to death. Catrin's wild ways and you drinking so hard; and now there's Bensha beginning to be religious, if you please! He's bothering me about Morris ffeirad, wanting to ask him to come and pray for the girl. 'Now's the time,' he says, 'when she's shut in, and she'll be obliged to listen. 'Tis a most ungodly house,' he says. Tan i marw! I don't know what's coming to Bensha, but I'm thinking good strong bwdran, and eggs and milk, will be better for her than all the ffeirads in the world.'

Here Bensha himself entered, and joined Simon at the supper which Madlen placed for them.

'Bad business,' he said, shaking his head solemnly. 'I don't know what you did to the girl, but there she is, lying like a wisp of straw, and I'm afraid there's no hope for her! How can she get well in such an ungodly house as this?' and he turned his one eye inquiringly upon the bewildered old man. 'D'ye think Morris ffeirad could do anything for her?' he added.

'What's the man bothering about?' said Madlen. 'If thee'st so keen after prayers, why dost not pray thyself?'

'Me?' said Bensha, and he laughed, as if his wife had perpetrated a huge joke; 'me pray? No, no; 'tis the prayer of a righteous man is wanted for the girl, and I'm going to get it for her if I can. She shan't go to hell if I can help it; and if Morris ffeirad won't come – well, I'll ask Jeremy Schoolin; I believe *he's* got the root of the matter in him too, as much as those devils of boys will let him have,' and he nodded shrewdly over his cawl.

'Will I go and see her?' said the old man, humbly, as he rose from his supper.

'Yes, go,' said Madlen, giving him a slight push.

Simon opened the door, and stealthily looked in. The red light of the setting sun shone full upon the bed where Catrin lay, still and white. She had heard the rumble of the waggon, and the sound of the voices from the kitchen, and knew that her father had come home – that it was Friday too, she remembered, and had gleaned a little comfort from the thought. She felt no anger against the father who had struck her; neither did any compunction for her fierce attack upon him trouble her. Her teeth and her nails were her only means of defence, and she had always used them in her frequent struggles with her human persecutors.

There was nothing in her room to withdraw her attention from her pain. The boarded walls, the dark coffer in the corner, the old broken grate – there was nothing in these to interest her, so she kept her eyes fixed on the square of sky visible through the upper half of the window which would not close, and her untaught soul was filled with longing for the sea breeze, the smell of the cowslips, the call of the sea gull, and the cawing of the little sea crows.

The door creaked, and Simon's round red face appeared, he peering anxiously at her out of his bloodshot eyes.

'Catrin,' he said, still standing outside the half-open door, his face only visible – 'Catrin, how art, 'merch i? Wast hurt this morning? Thee must forgive thy miserable old father.'

'Forgive' – what was that? She knew not the meaning of the word, knew only that her heart was filled with conflicting feelings.

'Yes, I was hurt; my arm is broken. You whipped me shocking, but I stopped you.'

'Yes, yes, 'merch i, I'm glad you did. I might have killed you! I'm a miserable man, Catrin. Can't somebody do something for me? Dost think, lass, thee could'st pray for me? Lying there now, thee has nothing better to do. Try it, 'merch fach i – just a word or two – perhaps God would hear thee;' and he shuffled uneasily from one foot to another. He did not wait for an answer, but closed the door gently.

'Pray,' what was that? She knew the meaning of it no more than 'forgive', but a little smile flickered over her face as the old man disappeared. 'Pray! He means, I suppose, will I ask God to make him leave off drinking. Of course I will – You know, dear God, I've asked You many, many times – I am asking You continually. "Pray – Gweddio." 'Tis a funny word whatever. I've heard it many times, on Jenkin Gower's tombstone, when I've been listening through the church window.'

The red sun set in the west, the twilight darkened, and Catrin endured in silence; for to be cooped up within the walls of a house was a bitter experience to the girl who had lived her life in the open air. Oh, how she longed to escape – to fly down the grey fields through the twilight, with Merlin the sheepdog bounding after her, to rush headlong to the cliffs, and there to disappear in the mysterious manner which delighted her, and excited the wonder and suspicions of the villagers!

She heard Madlen's step approaching.

'A basin of milk porridge thy father hath sent thee – wilt drink it?'

'Yes – I am hungry.'

'Caton Pawb!' said Madlen, as she brought out the empty bowl; 'she'll eat us out of house and home in this way.'

'That's the way she'll get well,' said her father.

'Here's what l want to know,' said Bensha, 'now we've got her here, can't we keep her? Perhaps, if we mended the door – but then there's the window, that'll never close without breaking the framework. I'll go to Morris ffeirad tomorrow.'

'Well – do as thee pleasest,' said Madlen. 'The girl is getting well, there's no mistake, so I don't see what thee want'st to bother anybody to pray with her.'

'She'll be the same as ever once she gets well, and I want to give her a chance, d'ye see?' and he turned up his eye inquiringly.

'Let her be, I say,' mumbled Simon; 'there's no harm in the girl when she's quiet.'

The next few days were weary ones for Catrin, but she endured them with tolerable patience, her loneliness being much solaced by the visits of Merlin, who frequently darkened the upper half of the window, as he lumbered in and took his place at the foot of her bed, invariably disappearing at the sound of approaching footsteps.

Goronwy frequently directed his telescope towards the grey walls of Pengraig. On Sunday he saw Simon, dressed in his best brown frieze, come down the mountain side, and pass up the rocky road to the church, Madlen and Bensha following him, books in hand.

'Catrin's alone then,' he thought; 'I'll go and see her,' and off he went, climbing up the hillside with vigorous strides.

Reaching the dust-begrimed window, he tapped, and heard the girl answer from within.

''Tis me, lass, Goronwy Hughes, only come to see how thee'st getting on,' and drawing the wheelbarrow up to the wall, he stood upon it and looked in, leaning his arms on the open window.

'Oh, I'm very well, if they would only let me out. I would be quite well then, but I can't go, Madlen has locked up my clothes. 'Tis very dull lying here; I wish I could hear some more music like I heard the other day. Oh, 'twas nice! The boys were singing together.'

'Oh yes, they were singing the anthem; 'twas singing class that night' – he grew very red as he spoke – 'did'st hear the words?'

'No, 'twas too far; but there's beautiful the music was!'

'Hast heard that Malen Powell's cow is dead?'

'Yes, I know,' said Catrin, 'they were giving her medicine the other night, but 'twas no use. She sent her dog after me one day, and he bit my leg shocking. I didn't want her cow to get well.'

Goronwy looked puzzled. 'Thee'rt a wicked girl to say that, and I half believe what they say about thee.'

No answer from Catrin.

'Well, I'm going,' said the boy. 'Would'st like a drink of water or anything?'

'No,' said the girl; 'I don't want anything but the key of the coffer.'

'Has it a pink tape on it?'

'Yes,' she answered eagerly.

'There it is then, on the window of the penisha, but I won't give it thee. Jari! No, not I. Thee'st got to lie there, and Dr Jones will come to see thee tomorrow or next day.'

He turned away and as he strolled down the hill he sang at the top of his voice, a hymn whose minor, melancholy tones rolled across the valley and reached Sarnissa, where old Gwen heard them, and smiled as she sat by the fire, her open Bible before her. ''Tis Gronw,' she said,' singing *O fryniau Caersalem*,' and closing her book she joined, with her quavering treble, in the well-known hymn.

On Tuesday morning Goronwy was early at the Anchor Tavern, where Dr Jones was accustomed to meet his patients.

'Hello, lad!' he said. 'Art coming with me to see that witch today? Well, let me kill or cure these others first, and I'll be ready for thee. Thee canst sit in the gig and flip the flies off Dragon's ears till I come.'

And Goronwy gladly did as he was bid, and sat in the gig, surrounded by a knot of envious village boys. They were all at home in a boat with the oars, but a horse and carriage were not common at Treswnd.

'Now,' said the doctor at last, tossing off his morning's glass of whisky, 'I am ready for the witch,' and he laughed jovially as he mounted to his seat and took the reins from Goronwy.

On reaching the farmyard, they found Madlen busily scouring the milking pails.

'Well,' said the cheery doctor,' and how is the lo's fach getting on today?'

'First-rate, sir, l should think. I took her her breakfast at seven o'clock, and she cleared out two bowls of milk porridge. There's eating she is!'

'That's right,' said the doctor, passing into the house and entering the room in which stood Catrin's bed, Goronwy following closely at his heels.

The red and blue quilt was spread smooth and flat on the bed; Dr Jones turned it down, but – the bed was empty. Catrin was nowhere to be seen!

'Bendigedig!' said Madlen at the doorway, raising both hands, with fingers outspread, in astonishment. 'The hussey's gone!'

'Where's she gone to?' said the doctor, looking round the room.

'Jar-i! There's a girl!' exclaimed Goronwy, not without some admiration of her pluck.

'Gone,' said the doctor, 'with a broken arm!'

'Yes; and with her clothes locked up,' said Madlen, 'for I thought we'd keep her now we got her.'

Goronwy peeped round the door into the untidy kitchen, where, on the windowsill, he saw the key still lying with its bit of pink tape.

'See if she has taken her clothes,' said the doctor; and Madlen unlocked the lid of the old coffer.

'Every rag of them,' she said; 'the clean ones, and left the dirty ones folded here. She's as odd as her mother was about clean clothes, and if it wasn't for them, and the pudding on Sundays, I don't believe we should ever see her in the house.'

'But what the diwss d'ye mean?' said the doctor, waxing wroth. 'D'ye mean to tell me a girl can disappear like that, with a broken arm too, and no one be able to find her? Nonsense!

She's hiding under hedge or bush or haystack. Go you out, Goronwy, and look for her – be bound she's not far off.'

Here Bensha joined them. 'Yes, sir, you may say behind some bush or wall or haystack; but what bush? what haystack? That's what I want to know – eh?'

'Well, have you fastened the horse up?' said the doctor. 'Then let us all go and look for her. Where's her father? Gone to Caermadoc, eh? Well, I'll have to give him a bit of my mind about this girl. Never heard such a thing in my life – the impudent baggage! Come on – you take that field, and I'll take this – we'll find her somewhere.'

But neither behind hedge, or rock, bush or haystack, was there any sign of Catrin.

''Tis no use, sir,' said Bensha. 'I have searched for her many and many's the time. Sometimes, indeed, she would come flying towards me – *she* would find me, but that wasn't *me* finding her! No, no. I have seen her run down that field which falls straight into the sea, and l have run to the very edge, and looked down for her, but she was nowhere to be seen! Here's Merlin lying behind the pigstye – he knows where she is, but he won't tell. Jar-i! I think sometimes he's in league with the "old boy" himself, he's so fond of that girl. Glad he is when she comes in, as if it was the Queen, and downhearted when she's gone.'

Goronwy was beginning to be deeply interested. There was a spice of daring and bravado about the whole matter that appealed to his own bold spirit. 'And yet she must be somewhere,' he said, 'for she'll turn up again and scream. I wonder are the boys right in saying that she is a witch after all?'

'A witch?' said the doctor, irritably. 'Such tomfoolery has died out of the world. I am ashamed of my county. I don't think such a word would be heard, except in this out-of-the-way corner of the world.'

'Oh, we are no worse than other places,' said Bensha; 'nor more ignorant. No one believes in witches now, of course; but

when a girl disappears off the face of the earth as this girl does
– how does she do it? That's what l want to know – eh?

And he cocked his eye as usual.

'Well, I'm not going to waste my time talking to a parcel of
idiots,' said the doctor, now fast losing his temper. 'My belief
is, you know where she is. Anyway, don't bother me any more
about her,' and he turned to his gig indignantly. 'You,
Goronwy Hughes,' he called back as he was driving away, 'you
search for her. Don't leave a stone unturned nor a bush
unbeaten until you find her – d'ye hear?'

'Very well, sir, I'll try,' answered the boy.

But somehow or other he had very little hopes of success.
Had not he and the boys of the village had many a hunt for
her, but in vain? Indeed, it was a favourite pastime, when the
country dullness waxed too heavy for the boys. Then they
would gather together, and with whoop and halloa, sometimes
with sticks and stones, would scour the country, more for the
fun of the sport, than with a real desire to capture the girl, who,
everyone knew, was harmless enough if let alone.

'I'll have a good hunt whatever,' said Goronwy, leaving
Madlen and Bensha in the farmyard.

'Hunt away,' called out Bensha, 'but you'll never find her,
unless, indeed, she chooses to come – then she'll come.'

CHAPTER IV

THE CHASE

Before beginning to explore, Goronwy found the temptation to run down to the village and inform the 'boys' of his intentions irresistible. A little pity stirred within him when he remembered how Catrin looked, as she lay on her bed, and pleaded for the key with the pink tape. 'She got that key,' he thought, hurrying down the hillside. 'She got the key and dressed herself, and went out at the door, like anyone else would do, no doubt; but the boys will swear she flew out through the chimney or something. Jeremy Schoolin will never knock that out of them – indeed, I used to believe it too, although I knew better.' When he reached the sands, he was surrounded by a knot of boys, who listened, with gaping mouths, to the story of Catrin's disappearance. 'Not a sign of her,' said Goronwy, emphasising his words with outspread hands. 'The old red and blue quilt spread out there, as flat as an empty sack, and when Dr Jones turned it back – nothing. We all went out to look for her, but nothing – not a sign of her. Dei anwl! Didn't he swear! And, "Don't bother me any more about her, but you, Goronwy, find her out," says he; and so now, boys, you can come and help me if you like. We'll scour the country, and well find her out before night, or else my name is not Goronwy Hughes.'

'Oh, yes,' said Dai Pendrwm, with a sneer. 'Thee always dost what thee say'st thee'll do.'

'Well, I say I'll knock thee into a pleat if thee doesn't hold thy tongue, and then thou'lt see whether I keep my word or not. Now listen! Whoever comes with me to hunt the witch, must not carry a stick or a stone, and whoever catches her, must treat her kindly till l come; and then I'll settle what we'll do with her. The best thing, I think, would be to take her back to bed, and lock the door and nail her window. Now mind – do you all promise?'

'We promise.'

'Then off we go,' and without further ado, they tore up the hillside, shouting, whistling, whooping. Once in the bare Pengraig fields, the chase was in full hue and cry, under the broom bushes, round the rocks, behind the hedges, by cornstack, haystack, and barn, up over the rushy moor, where the sheep fled distractedly from their path, and at last, when noontide came, and suggested bowls of cawl and slices of bacon, down to the edge of the cliffs, at the bottom of which the sea tossed and foamed against the rocks.

'There,' said Dai, 'we've searched every inch of ground. Who can say now that Catrin Pengraig is not a witch? Now, Goronwy, what shall we do with her? Put her in bed? Lock her up? Ha, ha! machgeni!'

'Well,' said Goronwy, 'I give it up; but I'm not such a fool as to believe in witches. Granny believes in them, but the world is wiser now.'

'Where is Catrin then?' asked the boys, derisively.

'Well, since she's not on Pengraig land, she's most likely hiding somewhere in the Tygwyn fields, or up in Penmwnta churchyard perhaps – I don't know. I'm sick of her and her ways, and I'm going home to dinner.'

And off he went with his hands in the pockets of his frayed fustian trousers. He had been frustrated in his object, so he went to his work in the field, in the afternoon, much ruffled in temper; and for the next day or two, nothing quite satisfied him. The speckled trout in the Glaswen were more confiding than usual. He had found the kingfisher's nest which had hitherto eluded his keen eyes; he had found, too, the hole in the old belfry, where the white owl was rearing her young. But nothing withdrew his mind from those grey walls, which stood up against the sky on the opposite hillside. He was constantly peering through that wonderful telescope which his father had left after one of his voyages, and which was the envy of all his companions, or climbing up the stony path to the farm, roaming over the bare fields, or sitting on the edge of the cliff, gazing over the broad bay, and wondering – wondering what had become of Catrin!

When Simon Rees had returned from Caermadoc, on the day of his daughter's disappearance, he had accepted the fact with stolid indifference, his usual state of mind.

'Oh well, let her be,' he said, 'let her be. She'll be all right if you let her alone.'

And so the event was allowed to sink into forgetfulness, Bensha alone being exercised in mind as to the girl's whereabouts.

'She's alive and well, and that's all I care about,' said Madlen.'Go and look at the crock of 'bwdran' that I left nearly full in the pantry last night, and the bread and cheese on the shelf – they'll show signs of her, I can tell thee!'

But the mystery of it got hold of Goronwy. He could not withstand the desire to turn his footsteps towards Pengraig. He haunted the place morning, noon, and night. On the third evening after the girl's disappearance, he was sauntering along the edge of the cliffs, looking keenly at every bush large enough for a girl to hide behind, when suddenly, through a gap in the hedge, Catrin came towards him, her brown hair blown about her shoulders by the fresh sea wind. The sun was near its setting, and the girl's face and figure were bathed in a flood of crimson light.

'What are you wanting with me, Goronwy? I am not doing any harm,' she said, her brown eyes half merry, half defiant. 'What art hunting me for?'

Goronwy stood confounded before her. 'I didn't say thou

wast doing any harm, and I don't want to do thee any,' he said.
'But what art thou running away for? Why dost not stop in
thy bed till thine arm is well, like any other girl?'

'Because I hate it,' said the girl stamping her foot. 'Because
my arm would never get well in there, with the cobwebs and
the dust. I will get well sooner out here under the sky, with the
wind blowing round me. Thee wouldn't give me the key, but
thee told me where it was. And dost think I was going to lie
there after that?'

'Why dost not stop at home, like other girls?' said he,
'instead of sleeping out anywhere, and spending thy time on
other people's lands; for I'll swear thou wasn't on Pengraig land
the other day when we hunted for thee.'

The girl burst into an uncontrollable fit of laughter, so fresh,
so blithe, so heartsome, that Goronwy was obliged to join. Her
face dimpled, her eyes swam, and her whole expression was so
transformed by her gaiety that the lad was astonished.

'Oh dear, oh dear. I will never forget it. Oh, it was funny
indeed – Dai Pendrwm and little Tim Powell and Dyc Penlan
and Goronwy Sarnissa, all shouting and calling and running,
with their breaths in their throats, as if 'twas a hare they were
hunting, and me watching them all the time! Indeed, I was
laughing, and I must laugh when I think of it.'

Goronwy pushed his fingers through his hair in
bewilderment. Suddenly the girl's expression changed into one
of sad and serious reproof.

'But, Goronwy Hughes, thou art a cruel boy after all,' she
said, 'to call thy friends together to hunt a poor girl who never
did thee any harm.'

'Why art so different to other girls then?' said Goronwy,
beginning to be ashamed of the part he had taken in the witch
hunt.

'In what am I different? Because I like to be out with the
stars and the sea and the birds and the sheep, better than to be
shut in with Bensha and Madlen, and – and my father?'

'No; but thy screams, thy biting, thy scratching Ach-y-fi, thou art altogether different from every other girl.'

The eyes drooped, and a glow of crimson overspread her face, even deeper than that of the sunset light.

''Tis when I'm angry I do that – when people are cruel to me. I hate them; I don't want to be with them.'

'If thee art not different from other girls, then why do the boys hunt thee, and throw stones after thee, and call thee "witch"?'

'Because I am a witch, I suppose,' said the girl.

'A witch!' said Goronwy, scornfully. 'Dost think I believe such nonsense? Dost believe it thyself?'

'Of course I am a witch,' said the girl seriously, with large open eyes fixed upon him.

'Nonsense! A witch indeed! Why dost think thyself a witch?'

'Because I am one,' said the girl. 'Nobody is caring for me, and I am living out here by myself, and I am hearing many things in the wind and in the sea that people can't hear in those dark houses; and I am watching the stars, and they are teaching me many things.'

Goronwy flung himself down on the sea pinks, and Catrin sat down beside him, leaning against a broombush, her bandaged arm resting on her lap.

'Come then, let's hear what canst do more than I can?'

'I can hide where thou canst not find me,' she said, the dimples reappearing in the cheeks and chin. 'Canst do that, Goronwy Hughes?'

'No, that beats me.'

'Dost know where the Deep Stream flows?'

'Oh, under Penmwntan somewhere, deep in the bowels of the earth. They say there's a sandy shore there, where the seals breed, though how they know that I don't know, for nobody has ever seen it.'

'I have seen it,' said Catrin. 'I have walked often on that sandy shore, where the waves break in the dark, as they do here

in the sunshine. There are strange things there, Goronwy
Hughes, and I have seen them, and nobody else has ever seen
them.'

'Dir anwl!' said the boy, rising to his feet, and making a deep
salaam before her. 'No wonder Catrin Rees thinks herself a
witch, and doesn't care to consort with such simple people as
the rest of us at Treswnd! Indeed, 'tis a wonder thou car'st to
speak to me at all, after hiding from us all these years, and
frightening everybody off the lands of Pengraig. Mind thee,' he
added, with a sudden qualm of suspicion, 'I have no mind to
consort with the devil nor any witchcraft though I am so simple.'

'The devil?' said the girl, looking up at him with wondering
eyes. 'I don't know him, perhaps he is in the houses, with the
cobwebs and the darkness. He is not out here, with the stars
and the rain and the sunshine. Ach-y-fi! No, 'tis only God out
here,' and she waved her hand towards the sea, the sky, the
darkening landscape.

'Well, why dost make friends with me all at once?' said the
boy, sitting down again.

'Because you are kind to me,' said Catrin, 'and nobody else
has ever been kind to me. Oh dear, oh dear, oh dear,' and
burying her face in her hands, the girl, who was still a child,
burst into an uncontrollable fit of crying – crying that seemed
to shed the tears of a long pent-up sorrow, sobs that shook the
slender form with the strength of long-endured, but suddenly
freed, bitterness.

The tide of sorrow and the rain of tears that overcame her,
surprised and agitated as much as they shook her, for she was
perfectly unused to any such storms of emotion. Hitherto, the
want of companionship and of home tenderness had never
been realised by her. She had fed her life from the fountains of
Nature's never-ending supplies, and had been satisfied; her only
deviation from the paths of peace and content being the fits
of fierce anger roused in her by the antagonism of her fellow-
creatures. On such occasions, tears and screams had been her

first resource, her teeth and nails her weapons of defence. But tonight the magic charm of human companionship, the tone of friendliness in Goronwy's voice, scant though it was, had touched the warm heart beating beneath that frayed serge bodice, and the unusual feelings could find no expression except in that shower of tears, which were still trickling through the brown fingers. But if she herself was surprised at the suddenness of her storm of feeling, Goronwy's state of mind was indescribable.

A lad of sixteen, who had no sisters, and whose mother had died in his childhood – what did he know of floods of tears? He had never heard of such a thing as 'a good cry,' and to him, the sight of Catrin's heaving shoulders and fast-dropping tears, spoke only of trouble and distress beyond his power to relieve. He had never seen such a thing, and his first feeling was one of contempt, that even a girl should be so weak. Gradually, however, his contempt gave way to a strong desire to stop those tears, and to see once more the dimpled smiles and the dewy eyes, which gave such a charm to the brown face.

'Catrin lodes!' he said, trying to pull away the blue apron which hid her face. 'Don't cry. What art crying for?'

'I don't know indeed,' said the girl, whose sobs began to grow less frequent. 'There's foolish I am. Art angry with me, Goronwy Hughes? 'Twas something sudden came over me. I am never crying, and I like for you to come and talk to me sometimes, because you've been very kind to me.'

'Well, I'll come,' said Goronwy, beginning to soften, 'if thee'lt promise not to cry.'

'Oh, I won't, I won't – never again indeed. What'll I cry for?' Suddenly her expression changed, and with her eyes fixed upon the boy's hand, she asked in a low voice, a deep blush spreading over her face,'What is that?'

'Why, the mark of thy teeth,' said Goronwy, presenting his wrist for inspection. 'See! A regular half-moon. I'll bear that mark to my dying day, I'm thinking.'

Again she covered her face with her hands. 'Oh dear, oh dear,' she moaned, and Goronwy, fearing lest this should be the prelude to another burst of tears, hastened to console her.

'Twt, twt, 'tis nothing, lass. Dost think I mind a scratch like that?'

To this Catrin made no answer, but, keeping her face still hidden, swayed backwards and forwards, as if too ashamed of herself to make any excuse.

'Goronwy,' she whispered at last, 'I will show thee where I hide from everybody.'

'Wilt show me that dark shore too? And wilt promise not to scream any more?'

'Yes indeed,' said the girl, surrendering without capitulation. 'Wilt have courage to come with me?'

'Courage?' said Goronwy. 'Tchwt! When I say I'll do a thing, I'll do it. But, jar-i! I must go now.'

The sun had set, the red pathway had died out of the sea, the rocks and cliffs stretched away to the right with their bordering of white foam. Behind them Penmwntan reared its craggy head against the clear blue evening sky; the crescent moon was rising behind it, attended by one brilliant star.

'Art going into a dark house, when 'tis so nice out here?' said the girl.

'But there's no supper, and I'm hungry,' said Goronwy. 'Where art *thou* going, Catrin?'

'Where thou canst not follow,' she answered, the dimples and smiles of laughter playing over her features.

'I'm not afraid to follow thee anywhere.'

'Wilt turn thy back till thou hast counted twenty, then?'

'Yes,' said Goronwy, and he stood square and broad, looking up at the moon. 'Now can I look?' but there was no answer, and turning hastily round, he saw the girl was gone. There was no sign of her along the bare cliff, and she could not have escaped up the hillside without his seeing her. Bewildered, startled, and angry, he walked to the edge of the cliff. 'She must have jumped over,' he said, looking down the perpendicular rocks, where there was no foothold for any creature, except the birds, who built their nests there. 'Catrin,' he called, but there was no answer; no sound, but that of the waves breaking down below, and the tinkle of a sheep-bell on the mountain side. He heard the bark of his own dog across the valley – at Sarnissa, and turned homewards in a disturbed and bewildered state of mind. 'She's gone,' he said, 'but where she's, gone I don't know and I don't care. Gone to the devil, perhaps!' But no, the innocent face, the bewitching play of changeful expression forbade that thought, and as he entered the farmyard, his mind was still full of doubt and bewilderment 'Diwss anwl!' he said, 'perhaps she's a witch after all.'

It was a merciful and accommodating dispensation of Providence which made Marged the constant companion of old Gwen Hughes, for this arrangement enabled her to give full play to her powers of imagination and to use them in what she considered a perfectly legitimate manner. Generally speaking, Gwen Hughes was what is politely called in Wales, 'not wise', and in Marged's opinion, there could be no moral obligation to speak the truth to a person in such a state of mind. Sometimes, indeed, Gwen's memory returned, the mists which obscured her mental vision cleared away, and reason resumed her sway. Then was Marged sore perplexed, but the ingenuity with which she managed to emerge from the entangled meshes of her past exaggerations was astonishing.

When Goronwy returned home after his talk with Catrin, he had but half crossed the farmyard when he heard the sounds of laughter issuing from the low, thatched doorway. The red culm fire lighted up the window, and as he entered the house his heart was filled with the warm glow of home love and life, for, in spite of her wandering mind and erratic memory, his grandmother was very dear to him, and her happy laugh as he entered awoke an echo of cheeriness in his own heart, though tempered a little with the underlying sadness connected with her simplicity and aberration of mind.

'Hello!' he said, as he reached the glowing kitchen and seated himself on the settle opposite to her. 'What's all the fun about? Come on, let's have supper; I'm as hungry as a hound.'

Marged was on her knees washing the red brick floor, and as she reached into the corners under the benches and tables, her conversation seemed to follow the cloth in sweeps of imagination.

'Telling your granny about the *Lark* I was,' she said.

'She was asking where was your father.'

'Yes,' said old Gwen, with a happy smile, 'I was wondering why didn't he come home to tea. Of course, I didn't know the Prince of Wales had sent for him.'

'No, no,' said Marged, making a long sweep with her cloth under the table,' she didn't know the Prince of Wales was going to buy the *Lark*!

'Oh, I see,' said Goronwy. 'That'll be a fine thing, granny!'

'Yes, indeed,' said the old woman.

'Yes,' added Marged, with a wink at Goronwy, 'your father had a letter by the post this morning from the Prince of Wales, telling him to come down to Milfwrt at once, "for I am determined," said he, "to buy the *Lark*. I am going for a trip to America, and I have heard the *Lark* is the neatest, purtiest ship in the bay," says he, "let alone the fastest sailing in the world; and I have heard," says he, "there's a patch on her sail put on so beautiful that 'tis quite an ornament; so come down at once," says he "– here she reached behind the door – "and name your own price!" So there,' she added gathering up her cloth and pail, and emptying the dirty water down the sloping farmyard. 'Supper now then,' she said, as she blustered in again, and spread the little round table by the hearth.

'Well, granny,' said Goronwy, 'that's fine news. We shall make our fortune at last.'

'Perhaps, indeed, 'machgen i,' said the old woman, already

forgetting the glorious destiny of the *Lark*, in the present pleasure of filling her dear boy's cup, and piling his plate with the buttered toast of brown bread. 'Where'st been all day, my boy?' And Goronwy entertained her with the history of the day's adventures.

'Do you believe in witches, granny?'

'Why, of course,' said the old woman. 'Haven't I known them and seen them? There was Susan Dwt. She lived in a bit of a turf hut on the moor. Ah, many's the churn of buttermilk I've seen spoilt by her! There, in that very spot,' and she pointed to the doorway, 'she stood one day, when we were churning here, and begged for buttermilk. "Avaunt, witch!" said my mother, in a flash of temper. She was sorry directly afterwards, and tried to speak fair to Susan, but 'twas too late. She only stood there and looked at us, with her bright black eyes under the hood of her red cloak. A little thing she was, no bigger than a child. "You'll churn long before that butter comes," she said; and she turned away from the door, and true enough we churned all day. The men had to come in from the fields to help us, but thinner and thinner got the cream, and at last we had to throw it away.'

'What became of her?' said Goronwy.

'One morning,' said Gwen, 'when the men went out to work in the fields, there was nothing to be seen of Susan's cottage, except a few smouldering sticks and thatch, and under them a few charred bones. Then there was old Mali Ben. My mother often told me about her. She said people would turn back, and walk miles out of their way to avoid meeting her. So she never got a word from any human being, and they say, before she died she had forgotten how to speak. Well, then there's Simon's daughter. They say she's a real witch. Take care of her, my boy. Don't speak to her or let her eyes fall upon thee.'

Goronwy laughed, the merry lightsome laugh of youth, and flipped his fingers.

'I don't believe a word about her being a witch. I'm not afraid of her. She'll never do me any harm.'

After supper old Gwen went to bed, happy and content, and Goronwy, looking at the pattern of the window bars which the moon made on the brick floor, said: 'I am going down to the shore to see what luck they have had with the fishing tonight.'

'Look then,' said Marged, 'what an apple I found today.' Twas hiding in the straw in the loft. Didst ever see such an apple? As big as a baby's head!'

'Yes, and its cheeks as rosy,' said the boy, going out into the moonlight, carrying his apple, which refused to be stowed away in any pocket. Down on the shore there were merry voices, and clattering of wooden shoes on the rocks – lights bobbing about, and much shouting from the fishermen who were landing their spoil. Amongst the crowd of boys and girls looking on, Yshbel Lloyd stood, light and supple as a willow-wand; near her, hovered Walto, silent and awkward.

'Art going to the fair tomorrow?' he asked at last, in a careless, offhand manner, which he was far from feeling. How delightful it would have been to push his way through the crowded fair, his arm necessarily curved round Yshbel's shoulders to protect her from the crush, though not daring to touch her, and then to stop at the gingerbread stall, and fill her pocket with cakes and nuts and apples!

'I don't know,' answered Yshbel, her heart fluttering under the woollen bodice. 'I have not heard Nanti speak about it,' and into her mind, too, flashed a vision of the gingerbread stall, she choosing her cakes modestly, Walto's black eyes looking at her with pleased interest; but she would show none of this in the calmness of her answer.

Walto was Mrs Gwyn's son, and although there was no outward difference between him and the other boys of the countryside, yet she knew what the 'gentriss' felt on the subject. Walto would look upon her as a fisher girl only, and would think he might talk and laugh with her as much as he liked, and then turn away to a 'ladi' and leave her to her life on the lonely rocks.

'No, no,' she thought, with a toss of her head, 'he should see she was no silly peasant girl, glad to receive a smile and a kind word from a gentleman.' But there was no time for reflection now. The boats were in, and the silvery flapping haul was turned out on the sands, and divided amongst the whole gathering, Yshbel receiving her basket full like the rest.

'There,' said n'wncwl Ben, as he handed her her basket, 'there'll be a fine smell of frying by-and-by.'

Yshbel smiled, well pleased at the prospect of the only little delicacy which varied the monotony of the cawl, or tea, of every meal at Treswnd.

'Art going to the fair tomorrow?' said Goronwy, dangling his 'quantum' of fish on a willow-withy stuck through their gills.

'Well, indeed I don't know,' said Yshbel. 'I haven't heard whatever, but I have three pairs of stockings and some thyme and chives to sell.'

'Who can tell me then?' said Goronwy, 'for I want to know; because, if thou art going, I'll go too, but Dei anwl! I'm not going there by myself, to hang about after the ballad singers. Tis dull work.'

'Oh! most like Nanti and I'll be there,' said Yshbel 'but I must take my fish home. Ach-y-fi! I'm tired, standing about the rocks tonight.'

'Wilt have this apple?' said Goronwy, holding up the monster in the moonlight. Fruit was scarce in that salt sea air, so Yshbel took it with a pleased smile.

'Well, well,' she said, 'I never saw such a big one. Nanti will make a large dumpling of it tomorrow.'

Walto would have said, or at least would have felt, 'No, 'tis for thee, for thyself,' but there was not much romance in Goronwy's character. She had accepted the apple, that was enough, and he turned homewards well content.

When he was gone, Walto once more approached.

'Here's a sewin for thy supper,' he said, holding out his sling of fish. 'Wilt have it?'

'No,' she said. 'Caton pawb! what will I do with more? Look! see, my basket is full. The mestress will like that for her breakfast;' and Walto, easily repulsed, withdrew his fish.

'What is that?' he asked.

'An apple Goronwy gave me.'

''Tis the largest I ever saw. Goodnight;' and he turned moodily away.

At another time he would have waited for the girl, but tonight he was feeling offended and sore. She had accepted Goronwy's apple, and refused his sewin, and as he turned towards the sloping fields which led to Tredu, and left the sand and rushes behind him, he was full of bitter feelings towards Goronwy. How was it that he always got what he wished? – always carried his plans through with a head so high? While he, Walto, felt the whole good of life was denied him if Yshbel turned away her pretty head. 'One has not to wait till one is old,' he thought, 'to bear a heavy heart.' And as he reached his own home, for the first time in his life he looked at it with discontent. It had all seemed fair and beautiful to him when he left it two hours earlier – its yellow walls warmly lighted by the evening sun, his mother nodding to him as she tended her flowers in the square, box-edged, front garden; but now all was changed, and when Mrs Gwyn opened the front door to receive him, he held his fish out without a smile.

'A sewin for supper, mother,' he said, throwing himself moodily into a rush chair beside the fire in the hall, or living room, which he and his mother used in preference to the 'Parlours' which were considered too sacred for everyday use.

'You are very late, Cadwalader,' said Mrs Gwyn in English. 'Where have you been?' and Walto knew, by the use of his full name, that she was not well pleased.

'The moon is so bright, mother. The fishers were in, and it's not very late after all.'

'The fishers were in? H'm – Ben Lloyd, I suppose – was Yshbel there?'

'Yes,' said the boy, sulkily.

'Cadwalader Gwyn,' said his mother, solemnly holding up her finger, 'you'll make a fool of yourself with that girl. And I would rather see you dead and buried.'

Walto was silent: in some measure annoyed at his mother's displeasure, but more surprised and pleased at her evident admission of the fact that he was grown up at last.

He coloured like a girl and only laughed, as he stretched out his long legs and crossed his arms behind his head.

'Twt, twt, mother, fach,' he said; 'don't be foolish.'

Mrs Gwyn made no further remark, but sniffed a good deal as she bustled about until the smell of the broiled sewin restored her good humour. She was a tall woman with a florid complexion and a hard look on her face, which completely hid the real kindness of her disposition. Her gown of grey homespun differed in no wise from that of the ordinary peasant women of the village, except only in the band of black velvet which bordered its skirt. A narrow band of the same material crossed her forehead, keeping in place two flat curls, or loops, of her jet-black hair. A cap of black lace covered her head, full bordered at the sides and flat on the forehead, and much trimmed with black satin ribbon. She wore a pair of black lace mittens, which left her hard-tipped fingers free for the household work. She was proud of her old furniture, her old spoons, and her old silver teapot, and grudged neither time nor trouble for their preservation. The broad low windows were always clear as crystal, the blue stone threshold always clean and speckless, and above all the brass knocker shone in resplendent brilliancy, for, with the exception of Mari's daily rubbing, no human fingers ever touched it. The villagers knew that, and if they found the back door closed, would stand half an hour at the front door, endeavouring by any means to make their presence known rather than touch that sacred sign of gentility. Indeed, Peggi Jones, the carpenter's wife, having dared to announce herself by that means was severely rated by her neighbours.

'Certainly, thee hastn't been living here long,' they said, 'so hastn't learnt manners yet; but remember thee, never touch the knocker again! Ach-y-fi! When Mari takes such pains to clean it every morning too.'

'Oh, anwl! I will never again. I tried everything to make them hear, but nobody came. I shook the handle of the door, and pulled it and knocked it with my knuckles, and I called through the keyhole, because I never saw a knocker before as I know, but at last I just touched it, and it knocked; and there's frightened I was when Mrs Gwyn opened the door and I could ask her did she want my chicken!

'"No, I don't," she said, quite short; "and next time you come, don't you touch my knocker." But she bought my chicken after all.'

''Tis a very good sewin whatever,' said that good lady, when she and her son were halfway through their supper. 'I had a letter from John my brother, today, and there's something about you in it, Walto; and I hope, indeed, you will try to please him, because he can be a great help to you in time to come. Here, read it; 'tis very small writing.' But Walto's young, clear eyes found no difficulty in deciphering the letter.

'He's a very kind man, I'm sure, but 'tisn't likely I will ever see him, unless he comes here, or I go there.'

'Well, no, of course,' said Mrs Gwyn; 'but I daresay he will come some day.'

'Or perhaps I will go there,' said Walto.

'Go there! Don't talk nonsense, Walto;' and she hastened to change the subject, and wished she had never shown her boy the letter, for all his life the possibility of his leaving home had hung like a cloud over her, and henceforth there was a fresh anxiety in her mother heart, before which that concerning Yshbel somewhat paled.

CHAPTER V

CATRIN'S QUESTIONS

In spite of his grandmother's advice and his own misgivings, Goronwy's visit to the Pengraig fields were very frequent during the next fortnight. After all, what wonder was it that he should feel attracted by Catrin's wild Crusoe life? No boy worthy of the name but would have felt its fascination. The long hours spent on the lonely hillsides, the happy roaming over the untrodden sands, the treasures of shells or seaweed, coming fresh with every tide, the search for sand eels before the sun had risen – all, all was full of that nameless charm which hangs like a golden cloud over our early years. Especially delightful to Goronwy were the impromptu meals which Catrin devised and prepared under some sheltered hedge side, or in some shell-strewn cove.

'Let's have supper,' the girl would say sometimes, flinging away the shells with which they had played at 'Dandiss' together.

'Supper!' Goronwy would answer with scorn, not unmixed with confidence in his hostess' resources. 'Supper of what? Sand or seaweed?'

'No, no. Come up to the heath field and thou shalt see;' and, arrived on its short, crisp turf, he would watch with interest while Catrin lighted a fire of dry sticks; and would help, with the clumsy willingness of a lad.

'Two big stones? Here they are then. What for?'

'To make the grate,' said Catrin. 'Now some dry sods to make the fire solid. Now, here's the bread and butter I brought with me this morning – plenty, see, in my cupboard,'— and she drew from a hole in the rocky hillside her store of barley bread and butter. Then, with deft fingers, she placed an old gridiron, which she drew out of the same cranny in the rock, over the glowing embers.

'Bread and butter's not much of a supper after all,' Goronwy would say, tentatively.

'Oh, stop you there now, and I will find the supper,' and in another moment she was flying over the field, returning quickly with her blue apron filled with smooth, white mushrooms.

'Salt and pepper I have in my cupboard too. Come and help to peel them, Goronwy.'

'Jar-i! they smell nice too,' he exclaimed, as, laid on their backs on the gridiron, the tender, pink-lined mushrooms turned to brown, and the evening air was full of an unwonted scent, not at all unwelcome to the hungry lad. Sitting on the soft turf beside their crackling fire, they ate their long slices of barley bread and butter, and snatched the frizzling mushrooms from the glowing heat. Oh, what meals those were! What laughter! What hungry enjoyment, never to be forgotten in the long years to come! The evening sky turning to pale violet above them, the sea murmuring and whispering below, the shy birds passing to their nests for the night, Merlin, attracted by the savoury smell, bounding down from the farmyard as guest.

Having once partaken of Catrin's providings, the meals were constantly repeated, Goronwy bringing his own share of bread and butter, and trusting to Catrin's resources for the comestibles which should give zest to the feast; for when mushrooms were not in season, there were sand eels, blackberries, shrimps, crabs, or, as a last resource, there were eggs from the hayloft at Pengraig.

'Well, thou art a "cute girl"!' said Goronwy, as he watched his deft companion not only draw from her 'cupboard' an old tin pot to boil the crab in, but also break her eggs on a slate which had been blown off the roof in a gale.

'It is washed clean in the stream,' she said, 'and now it is hot, the eggs will fry splendid.'

'Well, indeed' he would answer, 'it is nice out here under the sky by ourselves. I will get as fond of it as thou art, I think. Dei anwl! I never ate such a supper in my life,' and Catrin would watch with delight while the viands disappeared with wonderful quickness, forgetting her own hungry appetite in the pleasure of seeing Goronwy's enjoyment. As for her broken arm it had healed in a marvellously short time, and was, she declared, when Goronwy sometimes asked after it, stronger than the other.

May had come once more; and the monthly fair at Caermadoc, the largest and most important of the year, was drawing near. There were few of the inhabitants of Treswnd and its neighbourhood who felt no interest in its approach. Old Shân Gweydd had a piece of cloth of her own weaving to dispose of, mulberry coloured, with crimson stripes. John Davies Pantgywn had a snow-white heifer to sell, for which he expected pounds and pounds. Yshbel Lloyd had knitted several pairs of stockings. Even Mrs Gwyn had four fat ducks which she was going to send surreptitiously in Shân Gweydd's basket with strict injunctions that no one was to know that she was the sender, and Shân blushingly declared to intending purchasers, that they were her own feeding, on the best of meal and 'the clearest duck pond on the road'. Even Betty Powell intended to sell some thyme and marjoram, and had ironed the lace frill of her cap with extra care, in anticipation of her visit to the fair. Catrin alone was unconcerned. On the hilltops, no sordid care, no yearning for a bargain, troubled her. Although her acquaintance with Goronwy had introduced some fresh interests into her life, and she was beginning to feel the unrest which is ever the result of increasing knowledge and broadening sympathies, the long days came and went in peaceful monotony, every morning bringing the same buoyant exultant delight in life, every evening the same happy fulness of satisfied desires and healthy fatigue, bringing with it its own cure, in the heavy, dreamless sleep that always came at her call. Leaning on the turf at the edge of the cliff one day, she idly plucked a pale blue flower which nodded in the breeze.

'There's pretty it is,' she said, holding it out for her companion's inspection. ''Tis as blue as the sky. You can smell the honey in it. I wonder what is its name?'

'I don't know,' said Goronwy, looking thoughtfully at it. ''Tis exactly the same colour as Yshbel Lloyd's scarf I was telling her it was like some flower, and here it is.'

The light died out of Catrin's face, her dark eyebrows fell, and her mouth took a sullen curve.

'I don't care about Yshbel's scarf,' she said. 'I hate her and her scarf.'

'Why?'

'Because I do, and because she is afraid of me. She is shaking like this when they are talking about me,' and she shrugged her shoulders and shuddered.

'Afraid of thee?' said Goronwy, scornfully. 'Yshbel afraid of thee? What is she afraid about, I'd like to know? Thee canst not harm her.'

'*Can't* I?' said Catrin, a fierce look in her eyes that Goronwy had never seen there before.

'Thee canst do wonders, if we believe thee. Where is that wonderful shore thee wert going to show me? And how dost disappear from sight so sudden sometimes? Show me these things, or I will know thou art a boaster.'

The hot blood surged through the girl's veins, reaching even her brown face and neck.

'A boaster?' she said. 'Then thou hatest me; but I am not. I will show thee now where I go when I want to get away, but the shore I cannot show thee till evening, for 'tis then the tide will be down. There is no shore now, nor cave; 'tis all full of green swelling water, but tonight, when the sun is going down, I will show thee. Come now to that point,' she added, her voice trembling with some inward emotion, which Goronwy neither saw, nor would have understood; but he was pacified, and they turned their steps towards the point together, and standing at the edge looked down at the heaving, green waters, which lurched up the sides of the cliffs, and receding, left them wet and shining.

'Well,' said Goronwy, looking at his companion with something of a taunting expression, 'what next?'

'I am going,' said Catrin, 'but thee must not follow me.'

'I will follow – if I like,' he added with a little hesitation, as he saw the girl prepare apparently to leap over the cliff, for stooping, she laid her hand on the stump of an old furze bush, which projected from the ground at the extreme edge of the cliff, and with a slipping motion, let herself fall over the side.

A few yards below, a hawthorn berry had long ago taken root in a chink of the rocks, and, in spite of the strong sea wind, had grown into a bush of goodly size, though flattened against the rock in a matted mass little distinguishable from the short scrub covering the rest of the hillside.

Goronwy was horrified at the girl's disappearance, but, looking over the edge, was relieved to see her alight on the fringe of the thorn bush, her weight separating it entirely from the rocky surface over which it spread. With a dexterous movement of her agile limbs, she slipped between the matted thorn and the cliffs, disappearing with apparent ease into some aperture which the flattened tree hid from view. Left alone, Goronwy looked round him helplessly.

What should he do? Follow? Diwss anwl! No! 'I would never catch that bush; and a fall from there... ach-y-fi!' and he shuddered.

He wandered about the cliffs aimlessly for an hour or two, often peering down over the edge, where the girl had disappeared. But in vain; only the heaving sea was to be seen, rising and falling below, flecked with the snowy seagulls, which hovered over its surface. At last he turned slowly homewards, his eyebrows knitted in puzzled thought. By this time it was broad noon, no time for superstitious fears, but it must be confessed that his face paled a little, as, coming down the mountainside, he saw Catrin's brown figure, her face dimpling with a mischievous smile. Pretending not to see her, he ran hurriedly down the steep fields; nor in the evening, when the red sun was sinking down behind the sea, did he return to afford her the opportunity of redeeming the rest of her promise concerning that underground shore, which from childhood had been a shadowy horror to him. There were rumours of it always floating about, and the indefinite nature of these accounts augmented the mystery which surrounded it. He believed now that Catrin was familiar with this dim, uncanny shore, and, as he hurried homewards, he felt no inclination to make a closer acquaintance with it.

She waited long for him on the cliffs, but the sun went down, the evening breeze lifted her hair, and still he did not appear. Accustomed to long waiting and lonely vigils, she lay patiently looking over the darkening sea, and, later, into the deep blue sky of night, until at last, rising and roaming down to the shore, she turned her steps towards Yshbel's home, following an uncontrollable impulse which often led her to the further side of the beach.

Making her way through the darkness amongst the sandy hillocks, overgrown with rushes and sea holly, she reached the low, thatched cottage in which Yshbel lived. The fishers were all a-bed, the soft night air throbbed with the monotonous breaking of the waves on the shore; the curious heaving sound of the Deep Stream's undercurrent adding a muffled murmur to the ordinary sound of the sea. The glittering stars hung like lamps in the silent night sky, which brooded over the undulating waves, the mellow moon sinking down behind the sea.

It was a curious mixture of repulsion and attraction which

drew Catrin there, a feeling she could not have explained or understood but that was a thing this simple child of nature never attempted. As her lonely figure crossed the darkening beach, she walked with bent head and dragging footsteps, scarcely knowing whither she went. Goronwy was often speaking to Yshbel. She was pretty, and Catrin was moved by his remarks in connection with the blue flower on the cliffs. She had not expected to see Yshbel tonight, for it was late, and the cottagers went early to bed. Perhaps in the glow of the firelight a glimpse of her little shoes lying side by side on the hearth; perhaps a sound of her sleeping breath through the open window. But, to her surprise, a light was burning in the cottage, and approaching on tiptoe, she watched with intense interest the girl who sat within.

She was bending over a little piece of feminine adornment, which, to Catrin's unsophisticated mind, was the acme of grandeur. Yshbel's fair face was full of varying expressions, as she pinned into a little black felt hat the white wing of a sea bird which she had picked up upon the beach. At one moment a pleased smile lit up her countenance, as she held the hat at a little distance to judge the effect, then a look of dissatisfaction, and the feather was pulled out again – another attempt and another examination of the effect; then placing the hat on her head, she gazed at herself in a little cracked looking-glass, which hung on the whitewashed wall.

Above the neck of her faded blue dress hung a necklace of coral, which she had worn from babyhood, and which was looked upon by the villagers as a badge of the gentility from which she had sprung, and to which she would certainly be some day recalled. A smile of perfect content spread over her features as she took off her hat at last, and hung it on a nail on the wall. Next, the best frock of dark crimson was shaken out, and also hung up; then, from a little square box covered with wallpaper, the greatest treasure of all was extracted, namely, the pale blue tie, just the colour of her eyes, which was to put the finishing touch to her attire. A wave of bitter envy swept through the heart of the dark-faced girl who stood outside under the night sky, and looked in at the little delicate refinements, which give charm even to the life of a peasant girl, who may have only a blue tie to treasure, and a papered box in which to keep it.

'Where is she going?' thought Catrin, and she suddenly remembered that tomorrow was the fair at Caermadoc, and doubtless Yshbel was going there. She had but a vague idea of the glories of a fair, for she had never been to one, but she knew that the girls enjoyed it, and returned laden with apples and sweets and gilded gingerbread. At fifteen these delights awaken strange yearnings in country girls, and as she turned away from that cottage window, it would be hard to describe the bitterness of spirit which overwhelmed her. She walked slowly back through the loose sand. Hitherto, she had lived happily in the solitude of the hillside, but tonight she realised that something was wanting in her life.

'How beautiful Yshbel would look in her crimson dress and white feather! And oh, the beauty of that pale blue tie!' and her eyes were full of tears as she took the steep path up the hill and in the darkness drew her fingers over the ragged roughness of her brown bodice.

Next morning, when the sun rose red and round above the ridge of Penmwntan, she let herself out quietly through the loosely latched door at Pengraig, having first breakfasted and taken with her the remaining half of a barley loaf, with butter and cheese sufficient for the rest of the day. She took her way over the dew-spangled grass to the edge of the cliff where, hidden behind a furze bush, she could watch, without being seen, the world below her. Away to the right lay the rushy strand on which Nanti Betto's cottage was perched, and to this point Catrin's eyes were continually directed. It was long waiting for the inhabitants of Treswnd to open their doors and windows, for in the coast villages, as a rule, they are not early risers, unless they have some strong reason for bestirring themselves. At the springtide, for instance, they were out at two o'clock in the morning, with buckets and spades, digging at the furthest edge of the tide for the silvery sand eels, which, fried or baked, made a much-enjoyed addition to the homely breakfast. At last, the blue smoke began to curl up in the morning air, doors were opened, white-capped women emerged from them and flapped their tablecloths, exchanging pleasant greetings, or snappish, as the case might be.

Catrin took no heed of any of them until she saw the whole herd of the Sarnissa cows trotting down the stony road to the beach, playfully butting at each other, whisking their tails over their backs, and never stopping till they reached the snowy fringe of the blue tide. Here they would stand for hours, just up to their fetlocks in the cool surf, sometimes retiring further up the beach to lie on the warm dry sand and ruminate, until 'Sezzar' came barking and bounding down to the shore and drove them back to their neglected pasturage. This morning Goronwy ran down the hill behind them, 'how-howing' in his throat some mysterious directions, evidently understood by the cattle – Goronwy, who had been so kind to her, who had promised to come again to see her, and to see the underground shore, which she alone could show him. Would he come today? she wondered. He was dressed in his everyday suit, so perhaps he would not go to the fair. But hark! in the clear air she hears him whistle shrilly to another lad who sculls a tiny boat across the bay.

'Are you going to the fair, Walto?' he shouts, getting for answer only a loud 'No.'

'There will be "shows" there, and, they say, two swinging-boats. Come on, bach'en.'

But the lad in the boat sculls on without answering, and soon disappears beyond the rushy end of the shore. Goronwy wastes no time in persuasion but turns homewards, with hasty steps.

'He's going,' and Catrin's heart sinks a little. 'He's hurrying home to put on his best clothes.'

And then she watches, with unflagging interest, the blue smoke that curls from Nanti Betto's one chimney. At last she starts, for out of the cottage door comes Nanti herself, arrayed in scarlet petticoat and 'gwn bach' of mulberry colour, a yellow handkerchief tied over her head, surmounted by a broad-brimmed, tall-crowned hat. She is carrying over her arm a basket containing the stockings and herbs which Yshbel had knitted and grown. The latter follows from the cottage door, and Catrin watches her with the deepest interest, taking in every detail of the dress whose preparation had filled her with envy the night before. Yes, Yshbel too would be at the fair – shows, swinging-boats, gingerbread, nuts and apples! Yshbel and Goronwy would be in the midst of it all while she – why should she be so different? Why had God made her at all if she was to be thus separated from the rest of the world?

Why should Yshbel enjoy all these pleasures – the blue tie, the coral necklace, the dainty white wing? And a look of sullen bitterness fell upon her face, the dark eyebrows were drawn down, the brown eyes flashed, and the red lips were pressed together. 'I hate her,' she said; 'she has everything, and I have nothing.' And as long as Nanti Betto and her slim companion were to be seen toiling up the hill, Catrin lay, face downwards, under the furze bush, her chin resting on her hand, her eyes following the lessening figures. At last they were gone, and she fell into a deep reverie, which resolved itself, as her musings generally did, into a heavy trance – like sleep, lasting two or three hours. At last starting to her feet, she looked up the dusty, white road, where Yshbel and her companion had disappeared, her mobile features wearing a very different expression to that which had darkened them before she had fallen asleep. She waved her hand towards the top of the hill.

'Thee canst go,' she said, 'if thee likes, to thy fairs and thy gingerbread. I have all these,' and she looked round at the brown hillsides, shading off into the vivid greens of spring, the golden tints of cowslips on the meadows, the breadth of blue sea, which sparkled under the noonday sun; and stooping down she kissed the tufts of sea pinks which cushioned the bank on which she had lain. All day she roamed over the cliffs and sat under her bushes contentedly, until the long summer day had melted into the soft grey tints of evening.

Twilight was deepening fast, the stars were coming out one by one, the air, redolent of flowers, softly rose and fell, too light to be called a breeze. It had been a glorious day, the May sun reigning undimmed in the clear blue sky. The fair at Caermadoc had been brisk and crowded, and those who had attended it came home in the evening in a little group together, chattering so volubly that Catrin could distinctly hear and distinguish the different voices. That was Nanti Betto's, sharp and metallic; that was Yshbel's, soft and cooing; that was Ben's bass. Yes, she knew them all, for she was always watching them from her eyrie on the cliff.

She sighed a little sadly as the merry voices passed down the road, but the bitterness of the morning had entirely disappeared, and when the little company dispersed on reaching the village, she turned away to the more solitary and secluded side of the hill. The twilight still lingered in the west, but behind her the night was falling fast. Suddenly a voice broke the stillness, a man's voice, calling her name. She turned, startled, and saw coming towards her a figure, clear cut against the evening sky, a man whose form and features were familiar to her, though she was quite unknown to him. It was Morris ffeirad. Had she not often listened to his sonorous voice, and watched his clean-shaven, pleasant face by the dim light of the two mould candles, which illumined the gloom round the pulpit at Penmwntan Church?

She knew him well; had heard him say strange things, and

had longed to ask his meaning; but what could he want here? Was he going to reprove her? To compel her, perhaps, to live within the walls of a grimy house? She stood still, her attitude not altogether friendly, while the dark figure advanced steadily. He carried a book, and as he drew nearer, he spoke again.

'Is it Catrin Rees?'

'Yes, 'tis me,' said a musical voice in reply.

Catrin had a peculiar softness in her voice, attributable perhaps to the pure sea breezes in which she spent her life.

'How art, merch-i?' said the vicar, holding out his hand.

He was not altogether at his ease in the presence of this uncanny creature, of whom he had heard no good; and he thought it wise to conciliate her at once, by holding out his hand in a friendly manner. This was a mode of greeting with which she was but little acquainted. She scarcely knew what it meant, but some strange, new yearnings for human sympathy impelled her to place her hand in his.

'What do you want?' was her first question, and the vicar did not find it easy to answer.

'Well,' he said 'I wanted to see you, and Bensha said I would find you perhaps on the cliffs – h'm, h'm. 'Tis a fine night, but – h'm – but l expected to find you at home in bed, with a broken arm. 'Tis not fitting that a young girl, who has a comfortable home, should sleep under the stars,' and he laughed good-naturedly, as he generally did at the end of a sentence.

Catrin did not quite understand him, but there was no censure in the tone, so she waited, somewhat reassured.

''Tis very nice out here,' she said; adding suddenly, 'but what do you want?'

'Well,' said the vicar, fumbling rather awkwardly with his books, 'I am Morris ffeirad. Hast heard of me?'

The girl nodded.

'Well, Bensha came to fetch me to thee. I have been away from home till yesterday, but he left word that thou wast very ill, and asked me to come and see thee. So I came, thinking thou wert dying; but here I find thee, alive and well, so my ministrations are not wanted.'

'Why not?' said Catrin, fixing her lustrous brown eyes upon him. ''Tis easier to die than to live!'

'H'm, h'm,' said the vicar, 'that depends. You must come to church like other girls. There you would learn how to prepare to die.'

'Oh, I am quite willing, if God wants me.'

Catrin had seated herself on one of the rocks scattered about. The vicar sat opposite to her, studying the dark silhouette of her figure against the pale glow of the west.

'Caton pawb!' he exclaimed, 'how dare you say that, child? 'Tis shocking! A girl who has never been to church, or school, or singing class, who cannot read or write – I suppose?'

The girl shook her head sorrowfully.

'And then to say she's ready to meet her God! Art not afraid, girl?'

'Afraid,' said the girl, in blank astonishment. 'No; I am speaking to Him so often, and He's so close to me here on the hillside. Can you feel Him so near in the house, and in the dark church, where I hear you speaking about Him?'

'Hast been in the church then,' said the vicar, mollified, 'and I have never seen thee?'

Perhaps, after all, this waif had drifted into his church and been touched by his ministrations.

'Oh no, no,' said Catrin. 'I would not venture in there. It is so gloomy and so dark, and so many people are there. They would drive me out. No, no. I stand outside, on John Gower's tombstone. 'Tis very high, and 'tis close to that little window near you, when you are speaking.'

'The old leper window,' said the vicar in an undertone; and he thought with pity of this isolated being, who had listened, where so many sad hearts had yearned in ages gone by.

'I don't know what is that,' said Catrin, 'but 'tis a very good little window for me whatever, only the boys are driving me from there sometimes; and Dyc Pendrwm kicked me shocking, when he caught me there one night. He would not catch me, only my foot was lame, where Malen's dog bit it.'

'H'm, h'm,' said the vicar, and his round, good-humoured face took an expression of perplexed annoyance.

'You are speaking in church about many things I don't know,' said Catrin. 'Will you tell me?'

'What do you want to know? Ask, and I will explain anything to you.'

Catrin stood before him, clasping and unclasping her hands.

'Well, first, where is heaven?' she said, still keeping her eyes fixed on her visitor.

'Well, to be sure!' he answered. 'No one can tell you that, for no one has returned to tell us, but we know it is where the good people go.'

'Yes, yes, but where do they go? Up there?' and she pointed up to the night sky. The vicar's eyes followed the direction of the brown finger, and in his heart, too, awoke the question that troubled this simple child of nature; but the moon rode on in silence, and the golden stars gave no response. 'Or everywhere?' said the girl, a little impatiently. 'They must be somewhere, they who are dead, and I thought you would know. You are speaking as if you knew in Penmwntan Church.'

'You ask a foolish question, child,' said the vicar. He was annoyed and disturbed in mind. Never, since his ordination, had he been subjected to such a cross-examination. 'No one can answer that question.'

'Perhaps it is here then,' continued the girl, with anxious, inquiring eyes.

'H'm,' said the vicar. 'We don't know. We must be content to wait. Perhaps you are right, and it is wherever noble souls are gathered together.'

Catrin nodded emphatically.

'That's it,' she said. 'I thought so. They are here, they are there,' and she spread her hands out to the sky.

The vicar was becoming interested, but felt rather nervous, fearing lest he might be enticed beyond the safe lines of orthodoxy.

'Yes, indeed. I know it. My mother, my little brother, and Gelert – they are here sometimes,' and she crossed her hands over her bosom.

'Who is Gelert?'

'My dog that I was loving so much, and that was so faithful to me, but the boys caught him, and tied a stone round his neck and drowned him.'

This was indeed venturing beyond his depth, and the vicar recoiled in affright.

'You are a very ignorant girl,' he said. 'When a dog dies, he dies, and there is an end of him – an end to his pleasures and his pains.'

'I don't believe you,' said Catrin. 'You have not asked God about that, I'm sure; I have, and I know.'

'I tell you again you are a very ignorant girl, and the best advice I can give you is to come to church regularly. I will give you a Prayer Book, and in it you will learn all that is necessary for you to know.'

Catrin looked at him despairingly.

'But you are not knowing much more than me, after all,' she said. '*Who* will teach me, I wonder?'

The darkness had fallen deeper and deeper, the light had faded from the western sky, the stars were glittering above them, the moon was riding high above Penmwntan. The solemn stillness, the soft throbbing of the sea, the gentle breeze, which swept over his forehead almost like the touch of a human hand, the companionship of this strange girl, whom he had always thought of as an outcast and a pariah – all combined to arouse in the vicar's heart the unsatisfied yearnings which lie deep in every human soul, though buried, perhaps, under a surface of conventionality or carelessness.

'I want to know,' asked Catrin again, 'where do the wicked

go? John Jones Pensarn, and Betti, the miller's wife – where have they gone to? Surely you know where the wicked go to? And I want to know, where is hell?'

This plain speaking flurried and distressed the vicar. John Jones of Pensarn had been his churchwarden, and had died in the odour of sanctity; 'Betti the Mill' had also been a member of his flock, in spite of some rumours of scandal to which he had closed his ears! He pushed his fingers through his hair in perplexity. The questions which press most heavily upon the human mind he was unable to elucidate.

'We know, at all events,' he said, 'that the good are safe with God, and that the wicked are cast out from His presence.'

'Perhaps they are very close to Him, and He burns their sins out of them,' said Catrin.

'Good heavens!' thought the vicar, 'where was this witch leading him to?' No doubt discretion was the better part of valour, and he rose from his rocky seat.

'Goronwy is going to teach me to read, and God will teach me the rest perhaps,' said the girl.

'Come to church, child. Get your father to give you a new bonnet, and come to church and Sunday school, like any other girl.'

Here the vicar felt he was on safe ground once more.

'Will I come to church, where all the people are? And the dogs in the churchyard? No, indeed will I. But the night is coming on, and you have far to go, and you didn't tell me yet what was it you want me to ask God for you?' And standing up, Catrin stretched her hands towards the deep blue sky, with its glittering company of stars.

The vicar dropped his Prayer Book in shocked bewilderment, but as the girl continued to point towards the sky, he felt unable to cast off the influence of the solemn silence around them.

'Highsht a minute! while I speak to Him,' and, spellbound, he was silent, while on the clear night air Catrin's voice fell soft and distinct.

'Dear God! I ask You to bless this poor man, and to teach him as You teach me. He doesn't know much, and he wants to feel You near him in the close house and the dark church. Near as You are here on the hillside.'

For the life of him, the vicar could not restrain an 'Amen,' which fell as softly on the night air. He stooped to pick up his book, and turned away without a word, Catrin looking after him. At last, she, too, turned slowly away. The day had been fraught with excitement, and she turned towards the dark grey cliffs with a feeling of awakening interest. After all, human beings were not all cruel, Goronwy – Morris ffeirad, Yshbel? Ach! The moon rode serene and pale above her; the night wind sighed; a dog barked on a distant farm; a labourer sang a weird Welsh hymn, as he trudged homewards over the heather. All the sweet sounds of night fell on her ears, the grey slopes shimmered in the faint moonlight, a snow-white farmhouse stood out clear on the ridge of the hill. The scene, the sounds, were all familiar to her, but unconsciously they awoke in her that satisfying delight, for which she had no words, and which only those who have lived alone with nature can understand.

CHAPTER VI

YSHBEL

The stars that glittered in the sky above Penmwntan, the moon that shed so soft a light over the landscape, looked down also upon the solitary figure of a girl, who had sat long in the same position, leaning against the rough-shelled rock which she had chosen for her seat; her feet hanging down so near the water's edge that sometimes the swelling wave reached them, and wetted the soles of her little wooden shoes. It was Yshbel, whose footsteps often turned to the broken rocks lying under the cliffs. She looked at her cottage home, where the fire lit up the tiny window and the open doorway, but she took no step towards it. The moonlight was so enticing, the waves lisped so softly at her feet, the breeze blew so gently around her, and all the mysterious sounds of night which came to her over the sea, awoke within her such dreams of beauty and happiness that she could not leave her rocky seat. She was often musing thus, dreaming of the wonderful world beyond the horn of the bay, the towns, the cities, which she heard the sailors speak of sometimes.

Fate, or rather Providence, had ordained that her lot should be cast in scenes where the rough exigencies of life brought out the stronger traits of her character, and checked the tendency to romance which was strong within her. They could not, however, entirely quench the poetic temperament with which she had been endowed, and as she drew her fingers over her coral necklace, it not only reminded her of the scenes of grandeur and beauty with which it might link her in the future, but also led her back in thought through the past years of her life, the happy wanderings on the shore, the joyous hours spent idling on the shimmering sea, the cosy hearth where her childhood had glided so peacefully away, and the constant companionship with Goronwy and Walto, which used to be so easy, so simple, so free, but had latterly been more constrained.

Why was it? What had come between her and Walto? Goronwy was unchanged, but Walto? And then she drifted into a maze of fancies, offspring of the mingled sounds which came to her on the sea breeze. Surely, with the murmur and whish of the sea there was a sound of singing – perhaps the voice of a mermaid, sitting, like herself, on one of the rocks, and thinking sadly of some one who had changed and drifted away from her. And she pictured – oh, how falsely – the tide of human beings away in the busy world, all happy, all beautiful, all noble, marching to the strains of some mysterious music, through scenes of splendour and beauty to a glorious destiny. She felt her coral necklace, and wondered when all this would be for her. When should she be called to take her place in that happy world? 'Some day,' her father had written, 'I will come or send to fetch her.' He had never done so; and if he did, could she leave the humble home that was so dear to her? The shore? The sea? Goronwy? And Walto?

Suddenly she was startled by a boat coming round the point – a tiny white boat which she knew well – in it, a figure which was too often present in her dreams. Quite unconscious of her proximity Walto stood up and sculled, his figure showing clear in the moonlight. He was tall and strong beyond his years, broad shouldered and firm of limb as a man of twenty, and as he worked at his oar, his athletic figure showed to advantage. Drawing nearer, he came in sight of Yshbel, sitting there, where he had often seen her before, where he had often sat beside her.

'And why not now?' he asked himself, as he flung down his oar, but he could not land with his former ease and confidence. A spell seemed over him, which he could not shake off.

'Yshbel, is it you?' he called at last.

'Yes, I suppose it is me, indeed,' said Yshbel, 'though I was beginning to think I was somebody else – a mermaid, perhaps, or a water spirit – what do I know? 'Tis a good thing you called, perhaps I would fly away with my dreams.'

'Indeed, I am glad I came then,' he said sitting down beside her, and glancing around him.

'What are you seeing?' said Yshbel beginning to rise from her seat, and she looked towards the light in her mother's cottage, with intention in her glance.

'Oh, don't go in yet. I was looking round and thinking, how this place would be without you, Yshbel. Tan i marw! 'Twould be dull.'

''Twould be dull for a little while, perhaps.'

'A little while!' said Walto, and he looked at the receding tide, and mused, while the girl stood undecided. Should she go home? Should she stay? There was a time when her companion would not have scrupled to clutch at her skirt and pull her down again, but now, he looked at the tall, graceful girl and dared not touch that rough blue serge.

'You're in a great hurry tonight, Yshbel,' he said.

He was never addressed as 'thee' or 'thou' himself by his village companions, and he observed the same slight formality in his mode of speaking to Yshbel. For her part, she was pleased at this rather than otherwise. It distinguished her somewhat from the other girls of the village, and perhaps showed that Walto, as well as others, felt the suggestions of that coral necklace.

'Oh, I'm not in a hurry,' she said, 'only I've been here such a long time. 'Tis thinking I am, when the moon is shining and the sea is lap-lapping like that round the rocks.'

'Yes, and 'tis singing you used to be, Yshbel, but I never hear you now. What is the reason? The sound of the sea always makes me think of your voice.'

The girl seemed nervously anxious to confine the conversation to generalities this evening.

'There's beautiful the sky is, tonight,' she said, 'such dark blue.'

'Yes; 'tis the colour of your gown exactly.'

'Well, indeed,' she laughed ''Tis prettier than my shabby old frock whatever.'

Walto laughed too.

'Well, yes. 'Twould be hard to make even velvet so soft as that sky. What were you thinking about before I came, Yshbel?'

'I was thinking what if I was a mermaid, and my home was down in the sea, and I was coming up sometimes, to see the moonlight and the stars, and my friends down below would be calling me, and I would refuse to go, and I would be pointing to our cottage and saying, "'Tis better here.'Tis warm and cosy and my friends are wanting me."'

'Stop, stop,' said Walto.

A peal of laughter from Yshbel showed that she too had noticed her mistake.

'Oh, yes; of course, they wouldn't be my friends then.'

'No, no,' said Walto, flinging the shells into the sea. 'Couldn't you alter it to "lover?"'

'Lover?' she said, with a toss of her head, and a fine pretence of sarcasm in her voice, 'a chit of a girl like me? No, I wouldn't be talking nonsense even if I was a mermaid,' and she rose abruptly to her feet, shaking the shells off her blue gown.

'Are you going?' said Walto, frightened lest he should have offended her. 'Nay, stop and tell me how did the fair go off?'

''Twas beautiful indeed,' she said. There was a "show", where the horses were dancing and pretty ladies were jumping through hoops. 'Twas wonderful! And Goronwy said—'

'Was he there?'

'Yes. He treated me and Ellen Bowen and Mari Jones. There's kind he was indeed. Apples and nuts and gingerbread, as much as we could carry.'

'Well, you didn't tell me you were going; but I couldn't go, because my mother was expecting my cousins, and she wanted me to stop with them. But they didn't come after all, so I wish I had gone.'

'The Miss Joneses of Caermadoc?'

'Yes.'

There was a long pause after this, Yshbel dipping the point of her wooden shoe in the water, Walto looking out seawards. When they had both mused for some time, he turned to her, asking suddenly: 'I wonder what you are thinking of, Yshbel?'

The girl blushed a deep crimson, which was invisible in the moonlight.

'Oh, I don't know. Many things – mostly, that I ought to be going home.'

'Not yet,' said Walto. 'What is the reason you are always wanting to go now – whenever I am with you at least? I see you often sitting on the rocks with Goronwy. Are you constantly saying to him, "I must go; Nanti is wanting me"?'

'Well, of course,' said the girl, with an attempt at a laugh. 'Why would I be different? I am the same to both of you.'

Walto pulled at the mussels on the rock, flinging them one by one into the sea.

'Why is it,' he said, 'that we can't be such friends now as we were long ago?'

'Aren't we then? 'Tisn't my fault if we aren't,' and suddenly, with more seriousness in her tones, she added, ''Tisn't your fault too, Walto, because now we are grown up.'

'Grown up?' he said, with a laugh. 'Not one of us three is eighteen.'

'Well, you have many friends besides me now. There's the squire's son and your cousins. Nanti says they are very nice young ladies, and that you are often going to see them.'

'My cousins they are,' said Walto, 'but they are not you, Yshbel.'

'No, no. I know I am very different. They are ladies, and you are a gentleman. I am only a poor fisher girl. We will be friends always, Walto, but you mustn't be angry because I remember the difference between us.'

'You remember it continually, Yshbel – too often – and you are always reminding me of it.'

'Perhaps 'tis well,' she said, rising and looking towards the cottage door, where, against the glow of the firelight, she saw Betto standing and waving her arms like a windmill.

'What is she doing?' asked Walto.

'I don't know; I must go and see. Good-neit.'

'Yshbel,' he said, snatching at her hand, 'wait a moment.'

'I can't, Walto.'

'Goodnight then,' he said, still clasping her hand, as if reluctant to let her go. 'Yshbel!'

'Walto!' and she laughed so merrily that Betto heard her from the door, and sent a call through the evening air, waving her arms more rapidly than before.

'Nanti fach, what is the matter?' said the girl, as she reached the house.

'Enough the matter, I should think,' said Betto, limping about the room, holding on to the chairs and tables. 'Here's a botheration. 'Twas pouring water on the tea I was, and that 'andras' of a kettle slipped and scalded my foot; and mestress sending Nell down to say she must have a sewin tomorrow morning, and a lobster or a crab for tea; and Ben, thee know'st, is gone to Caermadoc and won't be home till tomorrow night. And more than that, she wants the boat for the afternoon, to take the young ladies for a row, because the Miss Joneses, of Caermadoc, are coming to see her and Walto.'

'Oh, stop, Nanti! let me understand. She wants a sewin and a lobster. I had better go over to Shacki Owens' at once. He will be out fishing early, and the lobster I daresay I will find in the pots; but the boat, Nanti – who's to row it?'

'Walto, she says, will take one oar, Ben ought to take the other, but thee must find some one to take his place, or thou must go thyself.'

'Oh, Nanti, I can't! I won't!'

'l can't! I won't!' said Betto, indignantly, bringing her fist down on the table. 'What's the girl meaning? Dost remember that this house belongs to the mestress and our boat belongs to her, for we haven't paid all for it yet. She could turn us out on those rushes at any moment. Art not ashamed of thyself? Can't! Won't! Indeed! And me with a scalded foot. Thee must take the fish up tomorrow morning too, and thee must take Ben's place in the boat if thee can't get any one else. So there!'

Yshbel made no answer, but sat long, pondering.

'Well, go to bed, Nanti, while I run over to Shacki Owens. Perhaps his John will go for me. Oh, I hope he will,' she added, as she ran out into the moonlight. Glancing towards the rock where she had lately sat, she saw, against the night sky, the figure of Walto, still reclining, still musing, and she sighed as she made her way through the rushes.

'A sewin?' said Shacki Owens; 'no doubt – no doubt! Two if she likes, but to row for thee in the afternoon! No. John is going to Aberynnis with a load of lime.'

'Oh, anw'll!' said Yshbel, clasping her hands in real distress. 'What will I do? Will Meilor go for me, d'you think?'

'No,' said Shacki Owens; 'I'm sure he can't, but perhaps Will can go.'

'Perhaps, indeed,' and she flew away under the shadow of the cliff. But, alas! Will had promised to help in unloading the *Lark*.

'Will Goronwy go, l wonder?' thought the girl, as she turned homewards, and in the early dawn of next morning she climbed up the path to Sarnissa, where Goronwy was already out in the farmyard, passing in and out of the old barn, his sleeves turned up, his strong arms bearing the weight of the golden straw, with which he was loading the waggon, his rough, tangled hair blown about by the morning wind.

'Diwss anw'l, Yshbel! What brings thee here so early?' he said.

'Oh, Goronwy, wilt do me a kindness?'

'Well, of course, if I can.'

'The mistress wants our boat this afternoon, to row the Miss Joneses, Caermadoc, on the bay. They are coming to see her, and she wants them to enjoy themselves.'

'The Miss Joneses, Caermadoc? Why doesn't Walto row them himself?'

'Well, he'll take one oar, but 'n'wncwl Ben is gone to Caermadoc, and there is no one to take the other.'

'Can't thee take it thyself?'

'Well, I can, of course, but I don't want to.'

'I have no more fancy than thee for rowing Walto's fine cousins, but I can't refuse thee, Yshbel – nobody can,' he added gallantly, 'so I'll come for certain if Jones Pantgwyn does not come to buy the heifer.'

'Of course,' she said, 'I will not expect thee then.'

'Well if he doesn't – thee can depend on me.'

'Can diolch! A hundred thanks!' and she turned homewards, much relieved.

At noon, carrying her fish to Tredu, she earnestly hoped she might reach the door, and return through the farmyard unobserved. Mrs Gwyn was sitting stiff and uncomfortable in the parlour, her mind distracted between anxiety lest Nell should burn her pastry, and a desire to appear at her ease. Ellen and Majory needed no entertainment so long as Walto laid himself out to be agreeable, but his mind, too, was not at ease. Where was Yshbel this morning? Betto, no doubt, would be bringing up the fish, and Ben would bring the boat round. Over the box hedge of the 'cwrt' he could see a corner of the farmyard, just where the white gate led out to the road. As he looked up from the album through which he was wading with his cousins, he caught sight of a pair of shapely blue shoulders and a white sun bonnet, under which, as the owner turned to close the gate, he saw Yshbel's blue eyes and golden hair, and a hot blush suffused his face. Ellen and Marjory saw nothing of it, but it did not escape Mrs Gwyn's keen eye.

'What was that?' she said, alluding to the click of the gate.

'The fish you ordered,' said Walto.

'H'm,' said his mother, and she made a note of the blush and determined to ask Nell who had brought the fish.

'You would like a row on the bay, my dears, after dinner. Walto will go with you.'

'But won't you come, Aunt Jenny?'

'No, my dear. I haven't been on the water this twenty years. It isn't agreeing with me.'

The young ladies glanced at each other with a sly smile. Their aunt's English afforded them much amusement, their own being quite correct, though seasoned with a broad Welsh accent. They were willing, however, to condone all Mrs Gwyn's shortcomings, in consideration of their cousin's good looks.

In the afternoon all was propitious for a row, but in the little thatched cottage by the sea there was disquiet in more hearts than one. Looking out through the doorway, her foot supported by a chair, Betto limped and chafed and grumbled.

'Was there ever such a thing? The mestress to want the boat, and Ben to be from home, and he never stirring away except twice in the year; and Yshbel so slow and unwilling, she that was always ready enough to go on the water when nobody wanted her to! 'Wirione fach anw'll!' there never was such a thing.'

True, Yshbel was dilatory and unwilling today. She went out a dozen times, and stood amongst the rushes looking up the Sarnissa fields for a sign of Goronwy's coming, but the brilliant May day changed into afternoon, still he had not arrived; and there, coming down the Tredu lane was Walto, accompanied by two white-clad figures. She could delay no longer. She must at least take the boat round the point to the landing rock. Walto would be expecting Ben. How would he take her coming instead? Of course, she would explain at once; but at the first sight of her, what would he feel? Would he think she was glad of the opportunity to accompany him? Oh, that Goronwy would come!

'Thou'rt not going in that old "hooden",' said Betto. 'Put on thy straw hat and thy best shoes, child.'

'Not I indeed, Nanti' answered Yshbel with a disdainful toss of her head. 'What are they to me, any one of them – the Miss Joneses or Walto Gwyn? I don't care what they think of me,' and reluctantly she crossed the beach to the cove where Ben's boat was moored, Betto looking after her, with a smile full of meaning.

'"I don't care, indeed!" but I know better than that, 'merch-i! Nanti Betto is not too dull yet to see where sweethearting is going on – but that old white "hooden"! the girl must be daft. Yes, yes. For all the mistress' pride, Walto is doting on Yshbel, but I'm afraid that "hooden" will do for her today;' and thus musing and mumbling she watched the boat, as it glided under the girl's easy sculling, across to the landing rock, where Walto and his cousins had already arrived, and where the former was much disconcerted at its approach.

Yshbel sculling? What was the meaning of it? And how should he greet her in the presence of these town girls? And into the calm atmosphere of Treswnd life, there entered, perhaps for the first time, the disturbing element of social distinctions; but Walto's feelings for his old playmate were too strong and deeply rooted to be much influenced by these trifling difficulties. He was not left long in doubt, too, as to the cause of her presence, for before the boat had reached the rock she called out to him:

''N'wncwl Ben is at Caermadoc, but Goronwy is coming instead of him. Nanti has scalded her foot, so could not bring the boat,' she added, as she reached the rock.

'Well, indeed,' said Walto, every shade of embarrassment flying before the sight of the beautiful face that looked out from under the white 'hooden'. 'I was thinking 'twould be too hard for thee to pull all the afternoon, Yshbel; but if Goronwy is coming, wilt stop and have a row with us?'

The two Miss Joneses stood silently waiting. They were

pretty brunettes, and, at the sight of the rower's fair complexion, were at once filled with envy.

'There's a pretty girl,' whispered Marjory, nudging her sister.

'Hm, pretty well. Look at her necklace.'

Yshbel was too flurried by the situation to notice the whisper, but she did not fail to observe that Walto helped his cousins into the boat with careful politeness, and she saw, too, Marjory's smiles and evident appreciation of his attentions.

'Where was Goronwy? Why did he not come? Could Jones Pantgwyn have come to buy the heifer?'

Suddenly a whoop reached them from the hillside, and Goronwy came running down.

'Here he is,' said Yshbel with much relief in her voice, which Walto at once misinterpreted with all a first love's power of self-torture, as he stepped into the rocking boat. Yshbel turned to Goronwy a face suffused with a rosy flush, so rejoiced was she at being relieved from the prospect of two hours of the 'ladiss" company.

'Well din, lad. There's glad I am,' she whispered, and once more Walto took note of the blush and the smile of welcome.

'Well, didn't I say I would come? And don't I always do what I say I'll do?'

The tone of voice, the favourite maxim, recalled to Walto's mind the evening when Goronwy had formulated his plans for the future, in which Yshbel Lloyd was to bear an important part. The memory of these words threw a shadow over the bright sunshine, and spoiled his row on the bay.

As Yshbel having given up her oar, stood on the rock and watched their departure, Marjory Jones, unable to restrain her curiosity, asked: 'Where didst get that necklace, girl?'

Walto's dark face lowered, but Yshbel took no notice of the question, letting Marjory imagine that she had not heard it. Walto knew better, however, by her heightened colour, so quick to come and go. Goronwy alone was unconscious of any awkwardness.

'Well, indeed, now,' he said, 'where did Yshbel get that necklace? 'Twould be a pretty story to tell the young ladies when we are on the water, but I won't tell them, Walto, I'll leave it to you. My English is not good enough.'

'Oh, hold your tongue, do, lad!' said Walto, in an undertone. 'I don't want to prate about Yshbel. Tell it thyself.'

'Not I,' said Goronwy 'I don't want them to laugh at my English.'

'Well,' said Marjory, 'I'm sure I don't care where she got it, only it looked such a good one for a common girl like that.'

'A common girl like that!' The words fell like fire on Walto's ear; even Goronwy winced a little and dug his oar so deep in the water that he narrowly escaped a 'crab'. Marjory felt she had made a false step, and hastened to retrieve her position.

''Tis a pretty boat whatever, and a beautiful day on the water, Walto. 'Twas very kind of Aunt Jenny to think of it.'

Walto mumbled something as he bent to his oar, but his temper had been ruffled. He was restless and unhappy, and the afternoon row was by no means a pleasure to him.

Yshbel, meanwhile, left standing on the rock, looked after the boat pensively, and even when it had receded so far, that it seemed but a speck on the water, she still stood lost in thought, and at last sitting down, continued her musing for some time, fingering her necklace, a frequent habit of hers. At length she rose, and stamped her little wooden shoe on the rock.

'Get up, foolish girl,' she said. 'Awake from thy dreams; indeed 'tis full time,' and stepping on to the sand she turned her face towards the village, walking steadily and deliberately, her hands clasped behind her, her eyes cast down. Reaching the roadway she followed its uneven course, until, having passed the straggling houses at the further end, she came to the smithy, from which, on the still afternoon air, the sound of Deio's anvil rang out its rhythmic beat. At the doorway she stood a moment, watching the bright sparks that flew from his hammer. At last, looking up and seeing whose figure it was that had darkened the light, Deio, who was a gallant man in his way, and an indiscriminate admirer of all the pretty lasses in the village, showed a row of white teeth and a sparkle of black eyes in the gloom of the smithy.

'Jari! Yshbel, is it thee, indeed? Who'd think of seeing thee here? Dost want to be shod, lass? Come, I'm making a shoe, but 'tis for Simon Rees' big Captain, and wouldn't fit thy foot, I'm thinking.'

'No, 'tis nothing wrong with my foot, Deio. 'Tis something on my neck. I want thee to loosen my necklace. It has never been off since I can remember, but 'tis getting too tight for me now. Hast any tools small enough to use on such a thing?' and taking off her bonnet she stooped her neck for Deio's inspection. The golden curls, the slender white neck, were bewildering.

'Tools!' said Deio, laughing. 'Will I get my sledgehammer, lass, or those big pincers perhaps? Phruit nonsense! I could do it with my finger and thumb, but this little file will be safer,' and in a few seconds, the coral necklace fell apart, and Yshbel gathered it into the palm of her hand.

''Tis a purty thing,' said Deio, 'but, tan i marw, lass, 'tis not so purty as the neck it was clasped on.'

'Oh, stop thy flattery, Deio. My neck is very well, and my necklace was very pretty on it, only 'twas getting too tight.'

'Will I make it bigger for thee, Yshbel?'

'Well, not today,' she said; 'some day perhaps I will bring it to be altered. What will I pay thee, Deio?'

'Pay,' he said, 'for such a trifle as that? Nothing, of course, only fling me a pleasant word sometimes, Yshbel, and a smile as thou passest.'

''Tisn't often I pass, but I promise thee the smile when I do,' and she turned away with a nod.

'There!' she said to herself, as she crossed the warm sands towards home. 'There! I will finish with it all. No more thoughts of the towns, the music, the silks, and satins. I have been a fool long enough. There are none of them for me. How do I know my father was a gentleman? I am Yshbel Lloyd, the fisher girl of Treswnd, and I put them all away from me – my dreams, my songs, my fancies, and – and Walto,' and as she reached her home, she brushed from her eyelashes a few tears which had gathered there.

CHAPTER VII

THE QUEEN OF THE VILLAGE

Mrs Gwyn of Tredu had a very high opinion of her own good sense, and considered that the present occasion demanded its exercise more emphatically than any event in her life had hitherto done. It was very evident that her only son Walto was, in her own words, 'making a fool of himself,' and it behoved her, therefore, to come to his rescue, and extricate him from the meshes which threatened to entangle him. Other women would temporise, she thought, would dally with circumstances, would trust to Time to dispel the difficulty – but then it was wonderful how little sense women in general had! She was not blaming them, poor things – they couldn't help that – but it was astonishing the small amount of sense with which Providence had endowed some people! Now there was Walto, with eyes closed, rushing madly to his own destruction, and there was that wily fisher girl, laying herself out in every way to entrap him. Rowing with him, sauntering about the shore with him in the moonlight, and, in fact, seizing every opportunity of attracting his attention. What was plainer? The remedy lay with her. It was her duty to lay the matter at once before this 'impident girl', not before Walto – for, indeed to goodness, she was afraid to rouse his temper. Not that he ever lost it in the ordinary way, but he had a dark and silent manner with him when angered which was very aggravating to her. All things considered, it was better to act at once; so in the gloaming of the next evening she donned her scarlet cloak and tall black hat, her lace mittens, and her creaking shoes with the black bows on the instep, and firmly turned her face towards the village. Her progress was marked by a series of bob curtseys and tugged forelocks. She was the queen of the village and knew it, and, in spite of her affable and friendly manner, she kept her dignity, and resented the slightest sign of its being forgotten.

'Well, Mali, fach,' she asked of a woman who stood at her door, 'and how is the rheumatism tonight?'

'Bad enough, mem, indeed.'

'Well, Sara, child, thee'rt rather stiff in the knees, I think. Hast got the rheumatism too?'

Mali hurriedly pressed her daughter's shoulder, reprovingly.

'A deep cwtchi, this moment, for mestress, lo's.'

The child bobbed, and Mrs Gwyn passed on, Mali administering a thump in the girl's back as a reminder.

'Well, Ben,' she said, meeting that worthy, who was lazily inclined, 'thee'rt as busy as usual, I suppose?'

'Yes, mem – what with the lapsters, and the boat to caulk, and the potatoes to earth up.'

'Yes, indeed,' said Mrs Gwyn, interrupting. 'Is Betto at home?'

'Yes, mem, and Yshbel,' and the queen of the village stepped firmly over the threshold.

Her creaky shoes roused Yshbel, who was sitting on a low stool by the hearth, idly throwing branch after branch of dried bracken on the fire. She started to her feet, and her cheeks paled a little. Instinct told her that the visit boded no good to her, for Mrs Gwyn was in her war paint and feathers. The scarlet cloak and hat were never worn, except on Sundays and other special occasions. But the good dame was on the war path this evening, and thought it wise to open fire at once. Betto was 'cwtching' and smiling for dear life, for she too felt that the mestress' best attire must mean something. She apologised for the rickety chair she offered, for the remnants of the meal on the table, for the fire being so low, almost for her very existence, while Yshbel felt for her coral necklace, forgetting its absence.

'I'm glad to see thou'rt not alone tonight, Betto. 'Tis dull work for us elderly people to be left alone, while the young ones go gadding about. Well, Yshbel, there is something the matter with thy knees too, as there was with Mali's croten, but I'd have thee to know who thee art – a thing thee'st been forgetting lately, I'm thinking. 'Tisn't often I come to the village, but don't thee think I'm asleep. No, no! I've heard of all thy flighty ways – idling about on the rocks and on the water. Thy blue scarves and coral necklaces have turned thy head, I'm thinking, and if thou art raising thine eyes to Mr Walter Gwyn, thoust better stop thy foolish ways. Dost remember that this house and all thou hast belong to me?'

Betto could only gasp and look from one to the other, while before Yshbel's mental vision passed a picture of herself and Betto turned out on the rushes, and standing there with the brass pan and spinning wheel for company. At last, Betto found her breath.

'Mestress, fach,' she said, 'that such a thought should have crossed your mind! The croten to raise her eyes to Mr Walto! D'you think, mem, Ben and I would allow such a thing? No; I would teach her better manners, and as for Ben, he'd break his thickest bastwn on her shoulders.'

Yshbel could only ejaculate her poor little excuses at intervals.

'Oh, I never, never! What have I done? Oh dir, oh dir!' She had grown white – in fact, her courage had all deserted her at the first sight of the mestress' red cloak.

'Well, well,' said the latter, relenting a little at sight of the girl's fright, and Betto's abject humility. 'I daresay it has been the want of some one to remind her of her place that has caused the croten to forget herself, Betto, and I don't want to threaten thee, but I would bid thee remember.'

Once more Betto burst forth into protestations of innocence

and good intentions. She had never dreamt of such a thing, and the mestress might depend upon her putting a stop to anything of that sort, ach-y-fi!, if she had to shut the girl up in the loft and feed her on bread and water.

'Nanti,' said Yshbel at last, with hot indignation, 'how can you, how dare you say such things?'

She looked desperately from one to the other, and was in no wise appeased by the furtive wink which Betto gave her.

It was terrible to the girl, this dragging of her precious secret into the garish light. The tender flower of her love for Walto to be thus exposed and laid bare – the love that she had scarcely confessed to herself, had scarcely realised the existence of! She was so chilled and shocked by the charge, that the nature of that love was almost changed, and as the tender lily withers before the east wind, so her love seemed to shrivel under the mestress' sharp tongue, and for a moment there sprang up within her the fierce vindictive feelings of her Celtic nature. She would have nothing to do with these people. Catrin Rees was wise indeed, to live up there on the hilltops, with only the sea and the sky around her, and only Goronwy for company. Would she could do the same! Walto, as well as his mother, should suffer for this insult, and turning her white face to her mestress she said: 'You are wronging me, mestress. I have never done you any harm, and never will. I will not come between you and your son. B't shwr, we were all brought up together – Goronwy, Walto, and me – and you cannot wonder that we have grown up friends. We are none of us more than lads and lasses yet, so if there has been anything displeasing to you in our conduct, there is plenty of time to set it right,' and, covering her face with her apron, she ran out of the house.

'Dyr Caton Pawb!' said Mrs Gwyn, sarcastically. 'Grand words for a fisher girl indeed! She learnt all that in her English copybooks, I expect, for I hear she has stuck hard to her English at school, and what use she meant to make of it I don't know.'

'Oh, mem, there's an odd girl she is,' said Betto. 'I have often heard her say that everything she could learn was a gain to her, if 'twas only how the shells grow. So I suppose that's why she has pained so much with her English.'

'H'm,' said the mestress, 'let her stick to her shells and her fish then. That will do for. her, I expect. English indeed! Ach-y-fi! what's the world coming to? I have only one word more to say to thee, Betto, and thou canst pass it on to her, Cofia – remember,' and, drawing her red cloak around her, she creaked out of the cottage, stooping her tall hat to clear the low doorway.

She crossed the sands in the twilight, and disappeared up the path to Tredu, well satisfied with her prompt action in this matter, and sundry jerks of her tall hat marked her approval of the course she had taken.

'Yes,' she said to herself, as she entered the cwrt, 'I think I have quashed that business in time,' and she sat down to supper with a happy confidence, in which lurked no suspicion that love laughs at locks and bars and all human restrictions.

Betto watched the mestress till she disappeared up the grey hillside, before she called softly at the doorway, 'Yshbel!' and slowly, out of the moonlight, the girl made her appearance. She was very pale still, her eyes red and swollen with the tears she had shed abundantly. How she hated this woman who had thus torn her beautiful fancies to shreds! Oh, how she hated her, and yet how she had once thought she could love her – Walto's mother!

But now all was changed. Her whole life was upset, and the girl who answered Betto's call was not the same light-hearted lass who had hitherto crossed the threshold.

'What do you want with me, Nanti?' she asked, quietly.

'What do I want with thee indeed! Want to tell thee what a little fool thee art to stand there gaping at the mestress without a word of excuse, instead of swearing thee hadst never spoken to Walto, but about fish. But there! thee'lt have to be wiser in future. The shore is wide enough without coming here, where there may be curious eyes 'kiwking'at thee, and ready to tell anything they may see. There's the sands beyond the cerrig duon and Traethyberil up here on the right. Thee and Walto must keep to these, and the mestress will know nothing about it,' she said, with another shrewd wink.

'Nanti,' said Yshbel, calmly but firmly, 'I have never done anything that I would be ashamed for the mestress to see, and I will never; and neither the sands beyond the cerrig duon, nor those on Traethyberil will ever be marked by Walto's footsteps and mine – not together – whatever!'

'Little fool!' was all Betto's answer.

Tonight Yshbel could not argue the matter. She felt sick and sad, weary of the cruelty of mankind, and sick of their falseness, more especially of her foster-mother's perfidy. 'All those promises to the mestress, and meaning me and Walto to deceive her!' She raised her fingers to her neck. The coral necklace was not there, but more than ever she wished her father would come, and take her away to that happy life where all the men and women would be good and beautiful. She had determined upon the course of her future conduct, while she had sat in the darkness and cried her heart out to the plashing waves. She would never pain Walto by an unkind word, but it would be easy so to divest her manner of all tenderness that he would think she did not love him. And what nonsense! Of course she loved him as she did Goronwy, and as all lads and lasses who have been brought up together love each other. Oh, the weariness of it all; so much talk about it. It would be so easy for her to set it all right. 'Easy!' she said under her breath, when she heard Betto calling her, 'Easy! I wonder will it be easy?'

It was not long before she had the opportunity of putting her resolutions into practice. It was not difficult to avoid meeting Walto, but in the following week, market day at Caermadoc compelled her to pass Tredu on her way thither.

As she approached the low, rambling house, the blue smoke curling above its yellow chimneys, she endeavoured to escape observation by walking close under the shadow of the tall thorn hedge which divided the 'clos' from the high road. And she succeeded so far as to reach the little market town without any sign of Walto, but once there, she met him at every turn, and his sad eyes tried her firmness to the utmost. At the seed stall she came upon him, as he examined a handful of the tiny heart-shaped clover seed.

'Yshbel,' he exclaimed, dropping them carelessly on the ground, instead of returning them to the sample bag, 'where have ye been these three days and nights? Not well?'

'Oh, well, can you think of me not well?' and she laughed a light ringing laugh, as false, in its way, as Betto's protestations had been. ''Tis busy I've been, weeding the garden and mending the net. 'Tis getting very rotten, and I don't believe 'twill bear a heavy haul of herrings in the autumn. Clover seed you are buying. I am wanting leeks.'

'So light-hearted – so easy – so pleasant!' thought Walto, 'and yet so indifferent; while he – should he ever be able to make her understand his feelings towards her?'

Again she met him at the broom girl's stall, at the cheese-table, and where old Peggi Pant sold her oatcakes in the corner. She had known before she left home that today would bring her a severe ordeal, but she had not expected to find it so trying. How hard it was to keep up an appearance of easy familiarity, without a shred of the consciousness which had underlain their former intercourse, but she succeeded so far as to check Walto's ardour without giving him any definite cause for complaint.

'What time are you going home?' he said, when the shadows were beginning to lengthen.

'As soon as I've sold this pair of wings.'

So he hovered about in sight of the road which led to Treswnd, while Yshbel made friendly advances to a farmer and his wife who, she knew, would be walking her way.

'Thee'rt going home soon, I suppose,' said the woman, as she saw the girl dispose of her last wings. 'Wilt come with us?'

'Yes, indeed. I will be glad of company,' and they set out together, Walto, who had waited and watched so long, joining them, and feeling much annoyed at the presence of the farmer and his wife. It was useless trying to get a quiet talk on the way home, for Yshbel, though as friendly as ever, seemed perfectly content with the state of affairs.

'Come in and see the new calf,' said the woman, and the girl made no demur. She stayed so long at the farm that Walto's patience at last gave way. There were tantalising glimpses of her, indeed, as she followed the good woman from kitchen to barn, then over the golden straw in search of the new calf. She waved her hand once or twice towards him, with the merry ease of their old friendship, but a cloud had fallen on his spirit, and there was a depth of sorrow in his dark eyes, which Yshbel pictured to herself, as she sat chatting over her tea in the cosy farm kitchen.

'Well, if that's how she feels,' he muttered to himself, 'I will not force my company upon her;' and as he tramped gloomily down the road, he was full of bitter feelings and upbraidings.

What had changed Yshbel? Why had fate ordained such a cruel experience for him? Was it possible that after all he had been mistaken, and that the happy friendship of their childhood had, in Yshbel's case, changed into indifference?

'Well if it is so,' he thought, 'I must bear it; but, in my deed, 'twill be hard.' And, looking round at the familiar landscape, where the soft greys of twilight were falling upon mountain and sea, he felt that every place looked changed; and giving way, in the solitude and darkness, he flung himself down on the grass beside the pathway, and, leaning his face on his folded arms, shed some silent tears, which he would have been ashamed for any one to see. After all, in spite of his tall figure and manly form, he was but a lad of seventeen, and the feelings which were so strong upon him had grown with his growth, and were rooted in the memories of his childhood. An hour afterwards he rose to his feet and, with a stretch and a yawn, took upon him to make light of his sorrow. He had his mother to face, he had the world to fight, his life to live, and he would neither be a fool nor a coward. Suddenly a light footstep approached, and in a moment his good resolutions were held in abeyance. It was Yshbel. What would she say? And in the darkness he waited in a fever of impatience.

Pit-pat, pit-pat, nearer came the footsteps. 'Was it she?' and he listened intently, while Yshbel, quite unconscious of his presence, hurried by. It had been a day of trial to her too, and as she passed, a deep sigh escaped her, a sigh which fell like balm on Walto's wounded feelings.

'Yshbel,' he said, 'have you come at last? I have waited so long.'

If he had hoped that the girl was in a more tender mood than when he had last seen her, he was doomed to disappointment, for with a light and careless laugh she answered: 'All this time, Walto? Well, indeed, what for then? The mestress will be wondering what has become of you.'

How easy it would have been at one time – yes, even a week ago – to say, 'I waited for you, Yshbel; I hungered for a word from you, a glance from your eyes, a smile on your lips.' But tonight it was impossible. The cloud that hung between them was cold and damp. It choked back his words and depressed his spirits.

'Oh, well,' he said, in a tone as light and careless as her own, 'I only wanted to be sure you were safe. Now I see you are safe and hearty, so I will go in and relieve mother's fears. Be bound she's been out a dozen times to look up the road. Unless you would like me to come as far as the shore with you, as 'tis getting dark.'

'Walto,' said the girl, 'fancy Yshbel Lloyd afraid of darkness, or sea, or storm! Can you think it?' and her laugh rang out in such a merry peal that all the echoes woke, and sent it back from hill and crag. Yes, 'twas a merry lightsome peal, but never did laughter so belie the feelings which prompted it.

CHAPTER VIII

THE DARK SHORE

Thus it will be seen that down on the shore these two at sixteen and seventeen had already passed that turning in the road of life, where it changes so completely. Already they had stepped into that path so thickly strewn with roses – and thorns – that gleams so golden in the sunshine, but has such deep shadows – that path, overarched by God's blue sky, yet imprinted with the footsteps of those who have trodden through bitter waters; and Yshbel had already seized upon the heritage of joy and sorrow, the possession of which is woman's education, and which fulfils her destiny. Above them, on the cliffs of Penmwntan, Catrin and Goronwy, at fifteen and sixteen, still trod the ways of youth's unconscious simplicity. Their sunshine had no shadows, their roses had no thorns, and their hours of play, or serious talk, left no bitterness behind them. True, Goronwy began sometimes to feel ashamed of his participation in Catrin's wild life. The freedom, the slight mystery of it, had still their magic for him, but at home he ceased to speak of it, and never expatiated upon their daring pranks.

He always shrank, too, from disclosing to the lads of the village how many hours he spent on the crags of Penmwntan; not that he ever neglected the work at the farm; that was punctually and carefully attended to, so much so that Marged and Will had been heard to declare, that everything had prospered at Sarnissa since Goronwy had taken his place as master. Every spare hour, however, when he could throw his farm implements away, and close the old barn door with an easy conscience, he might be seen climbing the stony fields of Pengraig. Sometimes the round moon rose high in the sky before he was able to run up the slopes to Catrin. Granny grumbled sometimes, and Marged said she believed the lad was bewitched.

One night, when the moon was shining as bright as day and the sea was touched with golden ripples, Catrin and her companion sat on the cliffs together, their feet dangling over its very edge.

'Thee'st never shown me that dark shore,' said Goronwy.

'But I will tomorrow, if thee'rt not afraid to come.'

'Afraid!' he scoffed.

'Well, 'tis low tides now, and tomorrow at sunset, I will show thee; but thee must not drop down there as I do; thee might not catch the bush.'

'Oh, as for that, I could do it if I liked, as well as thee.'

'No indeed,' said Catrin; 'I could not look at thee; it would frighten me too much.'

'Oh, well then, I'll bring a rope. I'm not afraid of any crag on this coast with a rope to hang by. We'll fasten it to this stump, and I'll manage all right.'

'Mind then, that it is a strong cord, lad, for thee'st grown so big and heavy.'

'Oh, I'll mind that,' said Goronwy, and all next day he waited impatiently for the evening hour, until, when the sun was setting red and round, equipped with a knotted cord, he made his way up the hillside. He was still a little incredulous about this underground shore. That Catrin disappeared somewhere in the side of the cliff, there was no doubt of, but perhaps it was only a cleft in the rocks, behind the thorn bush, in which she hid herself. How she returned to the upper world again was, however, a mystery which he longed to solve.

'What next?' he said, as he looped the cord on the jutting thorn stump.

'I will stay here, till thou art safe behind the thorn bush.'

'What for?'

'To loose the cord, and throw it into the sea, for fear any one will try to follow us.'

'Oh Dei!' said Goronwy, 'not for the world, lodes! Dost think I'm going to cut myself off in that way? Not Goronwy Hughes, I can tell thee!'

Seeing his look of horror, she burst into laughter, leaning back in an abandonment of mirth.

'Well, indeed,' she said. 'Art a coward after all? Canst not trust me then, Goronwy? I will follow thee at once, and will bring thee safe up here again. Wilt trust me?'

'I am not a coward,' he said, 'and looking in thy face, lass, I will trust thee, so here I go,' and in a moment he had seized the rope and carefully lowered himself over the edge of the cliff. Reaching the thorn bush, he found, as Catrin had predicted, that his weight easily separated it from the cliff, and disclosed an opening, into which he dropped, and which seemed to lead into a dark cave.

It must be confessed that a qualm of fright came over him, as he remembered that the rope which had just swung from his grasp was his only means of communication with the upper world. But before he had time for much thought, there was a movement at the opening, and the thorn bush bent outwards again, admitting Catrin's slender figure. With the ease of long practice, she slipped on to the firm floor of the cave, and Goronwy grasped her hand, with something very much akin to fear.

'Where are we, lass?' he said, trying to look round in the darkness. In every direction he heard the sound of dripping water, while the scant light that pierced the bush at the entrance only served to make the gloom more oppressive.

'We are quite safe,' said the girl. 'I will go before, and mind thee follow close behind me.'

'I will,' said Goronwy, 'though, in my deed, I think we must both be tired of our lives, before we would come to such a place as this.' Catrin seemed familiar with the way, for she walked bravely onward, until, the path suddenly taking a turn to the left, she stopped, to bid her companion beware of stepping over its edge.

'It gets worse and worse,' said Goronwy, who was beginning to lose his fear, and enjoy the adventure.

A strong wind met them, blowing Catrin's long hair in a fluttering cloud behind her, its roar mingling with the sound of rushing water.

'Listen!' she said, pointing downwards over the ledge upon which they were walking, and below them they heard the sound of waves, which broke in regular succession upon some invisible shore. Goronwy was by this time full of interest, and Catrin had some difficulty in preventing him from taking the lead.

'No, indeed,' she said; 'for once thou must be willing to be second. What if thou mad'st a false step?'

Here, descending some rough-hewn steps, evidently of human workmanship, they reached the bottom, and stood on a bank of soft dry sand, finding themselves in a high-roofed cavern, on whose sandy floor the sea was breaking in foaming waves. A faint green light shone through the lurching water, which rose and fell at the low opening, whose highest span was now a foot under the surface. For a moment Goronwy stood spellbound.

''Tis an awful place,' he said, almost in a whisper. 'Is there no opening to the sea?'

'Yes,' said Catrin, in the same low voice. The ghastly light, the frowning overarching rocks, seemed to oppress her, for all her dimples were gone, and her large brown eyes looked almost luminous in the gloom. 'Yes, there's an opening twice a year – in September and March, when the tides are at their lowest. There's room for a boat to come in, but the rowers must lie flat down, I'm thinking. 'Twas so the smugglers used to come, and they who made the steps in the rock most like.'

Becoming more accustomed to the darkness, they began to look around them.

'Why did'st never show me this before?' asked Goronwy. 'No wonder thine eyes are so deep and so serious sometimes, for thou knowest this place is under us, when we are laughing up there in the sunshine.'

'Oh, I'm used to it now, and I am not afraid,' said the girl, 'but, indeed, we couldn't laugh on this shore whatever.'

'What's that?' he cried, starting, as a plaintive moan broke the silence. What is that? Catrin, lodes, what is it?'

''Tis only the seals,' she said. 'This is their breeding place, and the little ones are calling 'Ma Mam! Ma Mam!' It is just like little children. See, there it is!' and in the darkness, Goronwy saw two solemn eyes, that looked at him through the gloom.

''Tis the mother,' said Catrin. 'We won't frighten her, poor thing! See, all along the shore, these 'gwrecs' that the waves have left here.'

'Oh yes, I was forgetting,' said Goronwy. ''Tis here the 'Deep Stream' carries everything,' and with intense interest he ran from one dark object to another. Here were broken spars and oars and splinters which told of many a wreck; here a torn and sodden sail, there a heap of bleached bones, that rattled about on the shingle.

'The tide is beginning to turn now,' said Catrin, 'but it never reaches this dry sand. Oh, don't go there! I have only been once, but I cannot forget it.'

'Who's the coward now?' said Goronwy. 'I will go,' and, stooping low, he advanced towards the further end of the cave, Catrin holding his jacket and following reluctantly.

'It is there,' she whispered, pointing to a heap of debris and there, on the dry sand, lay a human skeleton, the two arms outstretched together, as if imploring the help that never came. Goronwy started backwards.

'Come, come!' he said. 'Come back, Catrin. Come back to the sunshine and the blue sky. There's a fearsome place it is!'

and retracing their footsteps, they drew near the flight of steps by which they had entered the cave, but here Catrin turned sharply to the left.

'This is the way out. I never walk upon that shore now, though l did when I was a little girl. Somehow I was not afraid then, but now, when I come down here I always run round this corner of the sand.'

'Run?' said Goronwy. 'I would run now, if the path were not so steep.'

It led up the side of a fissure in the rocks, at the further and uppermost end of which the light of day struggled dimly in. Faint as it was, it disclosed the rugged sides of the fissure, ere long beginning to show tufts of fern and grass in the interstices. Sometimes a bat would flit across their path, and once a large owl swept by them. A strong current of air blew downwards from the opening, fanning their faces with a refreshing coolness. Goronwy hurried onwards, as they neared the opening, until, having reached the outer air, he took a long breath, and looked round him in astonishment.

'l don't know more than the dead where I am,' he said; and Catrin, amused, looked on, laughing.

'Dost not know the rocks at the top of our garden at Pengraig?'

'Of course!' he said, 'where it reaches up the side of Penmwntan! Well, indeed, I didn't believe there was such a place as that shore, and even now 'tis hard to believe it. Ach-y-fi,' and, shrugging his shoulders, he shuddered.

'So that's where the Deep Stream sucks its food in? Indeed, I was always afraid of it. I'll never go to the Crugyn again.'

'There is an opening at the other end,' said Catrin, 'where the tide runs out again. We need not be afraid, for they are God's rocks down there, and 'tis God's sea.'

'Yes,' said Goronwy, with a shake of his head, 'but 'twas God's sea, and His rocks, when the poor man walked about that shore in the dark, and died there.'

'Yes,' said Catrin in a low voice; 'I can't think how is that,' and, returning together over the springy grass of the slopes, they talked their simple, serious thoughts in the twilight.

'Look at old Ben's boat rocking down there on the tide,' said Goronwy. 'Dei anwl! wouldn't Yshbel scream if she knew where the Deep Stream leads to? She wouldn't row so often by herself, I know; and look at the light at Sarnissa. Granny will be waiting for me.'

'Wilt tell her about the cave?'

'No; she wouldn't sleep a wink tonight. I won't tell any one about it, and I'll never go there again. Wilt promise me, Catrin, never to go there again?'

'I cannot,' said the girl; 'but one thing I will promise, Goronwy, I will never go there – I don't want to go there – unless some one drives me there. 'Tis a dark, awful place, but 'tis better sometimes than cruel people.'

Returning down the mountain side, Goronwy met little Tim Powell, stooping under the weight of a basket of fish, which he was carrying to Tredu for the mestress' supper.

'Where'st been, Goronwy?' he said, a sly twinkle in his eye. 'With the witch again? Dost remember thy promise to get rid of her from here?'

Goronwy did not deign to answer, but pushing his hands deeper into his pockets, and whistling more loudly than ever, tramped on towards the light in Sarnissa kitchen. As he went, he thought rather ruefully upon his inability to keep his promise.

''Tis true, I said I would,' he thought, 'and I always do what I say I will, and now they'll laugh at me. But I have stopped her screams whatever, and that's the same thing.'

Still, he was not altogether happy concerning the opinion of the village boys. Yes; they would certainly laugh at him. What should he do? And Catrin's dimpled face and liquid eyes rose vividly before him.

'Let them laugh,' he said. 'She does them no harm.'

In the farm old Gwen was waiting for him, sitting in the chimney corner, where the greater part of her peaceful life was spent. Before her, over a glowing peat fire, the big crock hung on a long chain which reached up the heights of the brown-smoked chimney.

In her rush chair, whose rounded back curved like a cosy hood over her head, the old dame sat, and wove the happy fancies which were mingled so closely with the events of her everyday life. Goronwy's cheerful 'Well, granny, fach!' roused her from a reverie, which had evidently been a pleasant one, judging by her happy smile.

'Thinking I was, my boy,' she said, 'how grand it will be when thou art a man, and canst take thy father and me down the Glaswen in the *Lark*, out to sea, and over to the land where little Betti and John are waiting for us. There's nice 'twill be, Goronwy!'

'Well 'tis supper now,' said Goronwy, and the rattling of the bowls and platters soon told that the meal was in full swing.

'Morris ffeirad has been here,' said Marged, as they drew near the end of the meal.' Something about Catrin Rees, he said, wanting thy help to catch her he was. They are going to take her to the sayloom; and quite time too, tan i marw! Madlen tells me she's worse than ever, never darkening the door, except on Sunday, and there's fat she is, and smooth as a new laid egg! Where she feeds, and what she gets, Madlen doesn't know, unless the devil helps her.'

'Devil!' said Goronwy, startled by the suddenness of the news. 'Thee'rt a devil thyself, and more fit for the sayloom twenty times than Catrin is.'

'Perhaps, indeed,' laughed Marged. 'I am fool enough sometimes, when I put up with thy tongue. Bensha been asking him to come and pray for her, if you please; and when he went there, books and all, she was pranking about on the cliffs, and wouldn't listen to him. There's a wonder that the devil doesn't come and fetch her away.'

'Hold thy tongue, thou prating ass!' said Goronwy. 'Tomorrow, first thing, I'll go and see Morris ffeirad.'

But next day he was less alarmed. It was only some of Marged's foolish talk, he thought she was drawing one of her long bows, as usual, and Catrin was as safe as ever she was.

Still, when the day was over and the soft twilight brought its hour of rest and relaxation at the farm, he took his way up the left side of the mountain, away from the sea, and walked towards the grey vicarage, but little different from the farmhouses around it. He would explain to Morris ffeirad how cruelly the girl was misjudged by the villagers – nay, more, he would persuade him to see her; and again a vision of Catrin's slender form and sensitive face rose before his mind's eye. No 'ffeirad' in the world could judge her harshly, or doom that pleasant sight to the oblivion of a lunatic asylum. He shuddered as he thought of it.

'Jari!' he soliloquised, 'there's a dull world this would be then. In my deed, they'd soon have to put me in too. I could not live without Catrin.'

He had reached the breezy moorland which stretched away into the undulating inland country. On the still air, away from the rush of the sea, the trickling of some hidden streamlet fell musically on the ear, the cry of the plover came down the long brown furrows, a wood pigeon cooed in the coppice, and the rooks cawed as they flapped lazily homewards. There was no conscious romance in Goronwy's nature, but the sounds which reached his ear awoke within him some pleasant associations, which flushed his cheek and brightened his eye with the vigorous joy of youth.

As he opened the gate which led to the coppice, where the doves were cooing peacefully, a sound broke the silence, startling him, and bringing him to a sudden standstill. He listened breathlessly, and again came a cry which, he knew too well, was Catrin's scream of terror. In a moment he had turned his back on the scene of quiet inland beauty, and, facing the sea wind and the rugged side of the hill, he ran as if for dear life. His cap blew off, but he stopped not for that. On he ran, eager and panting, hearing no more screams, but picturing to himself the terror of the girl who had promised him never to scream again, unless driven to it by cruelty.

What were they doing to her? Would he be in time? These bare cliffs which he was already reaching, what would they be without that brown-clad figure so closely interwoven with his boyish pleasures? He almost sobbed as he heard on the evening air the sounds of voices in altercation. Yes, there they were, in one of the bare Pengraig fields, sprawling against the skyline, four men with a cart and horse, and before them, with her back to a hayrick, Catrin alone and undefended! They had ranged themselves in a semi-circle around the girl, and were closing in upon her when Goronwy arrived.

'Come on, Goronwy,' called Dr Jones, who, with the vicar and Deio the blacksmith, made three of the company. Bensha was the fourth and most excited of the group.

'Thee, Bensha!' said Goronwy; 'art not ashamed of thyself, man?'

Catrin stood at bay before them, her dark eyes flashing, her lips parted in hard breathing, her teeth gleaming white between them, her hands clenched, and every limb quivering with the eager desire to escape.

'Tis for her good,' cried Bensha, 'Mishter Morris has shown me 'tis for her good. There's a parson in the sayloom ready to preach or pray at any moment, day or night, and 'tis her only chance, poor thing!'

'That's for *thy* good then, thou cock-eyed fool!' said Goronwy, administering a blow which sent Bensha sprawling on the ground.

'Run, lass,' he cried to Catrin, but the injunction was needless. Already she had seized her opportunity, and rushed through the broken ranks of her enemies, even springing over Bensha, as he clumsily rose to his feet.

'She's off,' cried the doctor, and in a moment he and the blacksmith were in hot pursuit, Goronwy and the vicar being left to watch the chase. Catrin was making straight for the cliffs, and Goronwy felt quite at his ease as to her safety. The vicar, on the contrary, was much distressed. His round, good-natured face had changed into an oval shape, every feature depicting horror and fright.

'Stop! for God's sake!' he shouted after the pursuers. 'Don't drive the girl over the cliffs.'

But it was too late. Already she had reached the cliff, and disappeared over the edge. Meanwhile, Goronwy had administered an impromptu drubbing to poor Bensha, whose anxiety for Catrin's spiritual good he did not appreciate.

'There, go home, thou coward,' he said. 'Ask Madlen for a bowl of bwdran, and go to bed. Art not ashamed of thyself, to hunt down a poor, friendless girl like that?'

'Friendless,' said Bensha, rubbing his shoulder. 'Dei anwl! l wish I had such a friend. But 'twas for her good I did it whatever,' and he went off grumbling, though, if the truth were known, not ill pleased at Goronwy's rescue of the girl.

'Merciful heavens!' said the vicar.' Have I been the cause of driving that poor creature to an untimely end? On my honour, Goronwy Hughes, I meant her no harm. I thought it was terrible that a young girl like that should be out in the rain and wind and darkness, while we are in our comfortable beds; and it would be better for her to be housed and fed, and kept warm in the asylum, and safer for the people here. And now, where is she? Oh, God, I can never forgive myself!'

'Twt, twt, sir,' said Goronwy, now perfectly restored to his equanimity; 'she's all right. I've seen her do that a dozen times.'

'Nonsense,' said the vicar. 'I'm not such a fool as to believe all that stuff about her supernatural powers. She has gone over that cliff, and nothing but a miracle can save her.'

'She's safe, indeed, sir,' said Goronwy. 'Would I be standing here, cheerful and happy, if I didn't know she was safe?'

At this moment Dr Jones and the blacksmith returned, breathless and crestfallen, the former much exhausted and out of temper.

'Well, sir,' laughed Goronwy, 'you see 'tis no use trying races with us boys and girls of the mountains.'

''Tis no use running races with witches,' said Dr Jones, while the vicar looked on in frightened perplexity.

'What's become of her, Goronwy Hughes?' he said. 'I wish I'd let her alone.'

'She's all right,' said the doctor. 'She's been known to jump over those cliffs before. How she does it I don't know, but 'tis certain she appears again next day as fresh as a lark. Confound the hussy! She may go to the devil for me. I'll never interfere with her again. If you want to send her to the asylum, Morris, you must manage it yourself, for l swear I'll never come near her again.'

'What you didn't hold her tight for, sir,' said Deio, 'when you ketch her first?'

'She screamed so shocking, and slipped through my fingers like a trout from the Glaswen.'

'Well, Goronwy Hughes,' said the vicar, 'I will leave the girl to your care, under God's guidance, since you declare she's safe. Will you undertake the responsibility?'

'Yes, yes, sir; I promise you Catrin shall come to no harm. But why did you want to send her away? What harm has she done?'

'Well, look here,' said the vicar, in a low, confidential voice, while Dr Jones and the blacksmith prepared to get into the cart, 'between you and me, my lad, now there is something very uncanny about the girl – isn't there? Why, what do you think she did one night when I came here to see her? At Bensha's request, mind you. She p-p-prayed for me. She did, indeed!'

'Well, sir,' said Goronwy, 'I can't see what harm was in that.'

'Ach-y-fi,' said the vicar, 'You're as mad as she is, and I bid you beware of her, Goronwy. Try and convert her, my lad, and bring her to church.'

'Oh, that,' said Goronwy, 'I'm afraid I'll never do – not while the boys are about, and the dogs ready to bite her. But, indeed, to goodness, I must say the truth, sir – I don't think Catrin Rees' prayers would hurt a saint, there now! And I'll promise you she sha'n't do it again, nor be any trouble to you or any one else.'

'Very well,' said the vicar, delighted so easily to retire from the affair. 'Well, remember you are responsible for her good behaviour.'

'Yes, yes, sir,' said Goronwy again, with a smile playing about his mouth, and a twinkle in his eye.

'Jar-i!' he said, as the three men drove away over the soft grass, one can never tell in the morning what fun there will be before night. Where's Catrin, I wonder?' and looking up towards the rocky ridge to which Pengraig garden reached, he saw a girlish form, and a blue apron waved aloft. 'She's all right,' he thought, as he turned homewards, 'and neither doctor nor parson will trouble us again, I'm thinking. As for Deio the blacksmith, I'll call in and have a few genteel words with him as I'm passing.'

'What did they want with me?' asked Catrin next morning, when Goronwy stole an hour from the turnip field to see how she fared, and explain yesterday's adventure.

'Well,' he said awkwardly, 'Morris ffeirad, after seeing thee on Penmwntan that night, was sorry for thee and sorry to think that a young girl should be out under the skies, while every one else was warm in bed.'

'There's kind he was, indeed,' said Catrin. 'I thought he was a very nice man, and there's unhappy he was, poor man. He couldn't tell me any of the things I'm wanting to know so much. I thought, being a ffeirad, perhaps he would know. But to where was he going to take me then?'

'Oh, I don't know. Somewhere where they would take care of thee.'

'Take care of me! To the sayloom?' asked Catrin, horror depicted in every feature. 'Oh, Goronwy, thee'lt not let them!' and her face blanched, her brown eyes growing tearful.

'Let them? No, don't thee fear, lodes, they'll never trouble us again, and if they did, thou canst laugh at them, while thou hast that cave to fly to. Tan i marw! They'll have more courage than I think they have if they follow thee there. But thou canst take my word for it, thou wilt never see their heads nor tails again, not in search of thee whatever!'

CHAPTER IX

AWAKENINGS

'Come on to Traethyberil,' said Goronwy one morning. 'The sand is as hard as a board today.'

But it was not without many a start and many a glance towards the heights that Catrin ventured to follow him.

'I can't think,' she said, as their wooden shoes clattered down the rocks together, 'what did I do, that they wanted to take me away from here. Goronwy,' she said, stopping and looking seriously into his face, 'I am not a child now. I am fifteen.'

'No,' said her companion, 'thee'rt growing everyday; thou art nearly as tall as Madlen, but not a bit like her,' he added, with a smile.

'Well, but listen, lad, if they sent me away from here, I would die – yes, I would die!'

'Twt, twt, thee'lt never go away from here,' said Goronwy, thinking with some compunction of the promise he had once made to the village boys. 'Trust me, lass, they shall never trouble thee more. I trusted thee, and followed thee into that nasty hole.'

'Yes, indeed, and I'll trust thee, if I can.'

'Well, come to thy A B C then.'

Goronwy was right, and they were no further molested, but seemed to be forgotten by everybody – in truth, no one had time to think of a useless waif like Catrin, for the summer days had brought on the hay harvest, and all the countryside was alive with the sound of the whetting of scythes, and the rumble of heavily laden waggons, and in the evening, the call of the landrail.

In the hay fields the hedges were gay with wild roses and elder flowers, under them the children sat eating their barley bread and butter, and searching for the tiny frogs which lurked under the green swathes of newly mown hay.

Goronwy worked hard day after day, not only in the Sarnissa fields, but with equal zest in those of his neighbours, Catrin watching him from the cliffs with eager interest, and wishing sometimes that she too could take her rake on her shoulders, and join the string of maidens, who stretched like garlands of flowers across the hay fields. The days wore on rather wearily, when there was no hope of the evenings bringing Goronwy up the hillside, for during the harvest he worked so energetically that evening found him thoroughly fatigued, and fit only, after tea with granny, to throw himself down on the settle opposite her, and sleep till roused for supper.

Before the hay had ripened, he had devoted many an hour to Catrin's education, the hard, dry sand being her book – her pen, a feather dropped from some sea bird's wing – and Goronwy was a tolerably patient instructor.

'Thou'rt much more slow at thy figures than thou wert at thy letters,' he had said one day.

'Yes, indeed,' she had answered, 'I like better the letters; they make words and names – thy name and father's – but figures – ach-y-fi! What for are they?' and after much endeavour in that line Goronwy was fain to abandon the task, and the mysteries of arithmetic remained a sealed book to Catrin.

'Thee'lt never be able to count thy money,' the teacher had argued.

'My money!' exclaimed the pupil, with one of those dimpling laughs which would have been the distraction of a more susceptible youth, and which often, in later years, returned to his memory, as if to avenge his former indifference. 'My money! Oh, there's nonsense! I will never have money – I don't want it. It cannot buy sky nor sea nor air nor moonlight – nor anything—'

'But food and clothes,' said Goronwy.

'Oh, God will give us those. Look at the birds and the flowers – they haven't any money.'

'Thou hast learned to read suddenly, I'm thinking, lass, for that's in the Bible.'

'In the Bible? Is it indeed? How is it? Tell me the words.'

'I'm not sure,' said Goronwy, 'but here 'tis, I think: "Behold the birds of the air, they have neither storehouses nor barn, yet God feedeth them" – "and see the lilies how they grow, and Solomon in all his glory was not arrayed like one of these."'

'There's for you,' said the girl, in a tone betwixt awe and delight. 'Didn't I tell you then, I will have food and clothing as long as I live, so there's no need of money for me, nor figures' – and after this arithmetic was much neglected in the curriculum of Catrin's education; but she continued to apply herself with great diligence to her sandy tablet, and when, one day, Goronwy brought home from the market a copybook, a pen, and a bottle of ink, her happiness was too deep for words, and brought a moisture into her eyes. But literature had to be cast to the winds when the corn harvest came, when the air was luscious with the smell of the apples in the orchard, and the blackberries in the brake, when the corn stooks bowed to each other in the hazy fields, and the land was alive with the shout of the reapers and the song of the 'harvest home'.

With all its golden beauty, however, that autumn brought to Catrin the first pang of the unrest with which she was to become familiar hereafter.

On the opposite side of the valley, at Sarnissa, she watched a field of barley as it fell before the sickle of the reapers, among them Yshbel, and next to her Goronwy. Sitting there alone under the broom bushes, she fell into a state of deep abstraction, induced by the heat of the day, and the blank caused by Goronwy's absence. Her reverie, however, was gradually dispelled by a multitude of thoughts and feelings

which swept over her with a strength and vividness new to
her.

Morning glided into noon, and noon to evening, yet she sat
on, motionless, her eyes fixed on the reapers, her mind passing
through a conflict of feelings to which she had hitherto been
a stranger, but which found in her emotional nature a soil in
which they took deep root for good or ill. Up to the time of
her first acquaintance with Goronwy, her inner life had flowed
on peacefully, although in a narrow groove. She was now
beginning to feel the influence of human intercourse, for she
had stepped from her solitary path into the road of life, which
sooner or later must lead to bitter and sweet experiences, and
today there were born within her the germs of many thoughts
and sentiments which went to the formation of her character.
New desires and strange longings swept over her, as she lay
there, half reclining on the bushes, and watched the reapers
through the hot quivering air, her fingers twitching, her bosom
heaving with long-drawn breaths. Within her soul awoke the
dreams and longings natural to youth. 'Why should she not
too be one of that merry company, and take her part in the
labour and life of the harvest field?' She saw them all, but
chiefly her eyes followed one figure, whose blue dress and white
sun bonnet she recognised as Yshbel's. She saw how Goronwy
ceased his work to chat with her sometimes, and when the
noontide meal was spread in the shade of the hedge, she saw
him sit beside her, while they ate their uwd and milk, and a
feeling much akin to jealousy took possession of her, as she
thought with bitterness how different was Yshbel's life from
hers. True, she had always been very happy, and had never
hankered after the pleasures which went to make up the life of
the village girls, but the future – what did it hold for them and
what for her?

The warmth and comfort of home began to have a charm
for her – pretty gowns, blue scarves, white wings; and these
girls would have each her lover – oh, wonderful thought –

would marry – would perhaps have little children to call them 'Mother!' The brown eyes became humid, and presently a large tear rolled down her cheek, and fell on her hand. She did not move to dry it, but continued to gaze at the reapers, heedless of hunger and thirst, heedless of Merlin, who had found her out, and was sitting beside her, much puzzled at not receiving his usual caress. As the afternoon wore on, she began to move; she sighed, clasped her hands together, and a smile, though a wistful one, passed over her mouth. After all had she not Goronwy, her friend and companion forever and ever – and what was anything else worth, in comparison with this?

Goronwy, whose very presence was as a fresh sea breeze to her! She did not connect his name with the idea of the possible lover, with whom, in imagination, she had endowed the other girls. Her mind was as fresh and unsullied as the stretch of sand upon which she and Goronwy engraved their alphabet She rose to her feet with outward composure, although the long vigil of that day marked a turning point in her life. It seemed even to have wrought a change in her appearance, and to have left a more pensive curve on the lips.

'Hello, Merlin, bachgen, hast been waiting for thy kiss,' she said at last, and, dropping on her knees beside the dog, she clasped her arms around his neck, and pressed his head to her bosom for a moment before turning away.

In the Sarnissa fields Goronwy worked with a will: he was aware of Catrin's watchful figure on the cliffs, and felt, with a sort of resentment at his own weakness, an occasional longing to be up there too.

'It was shameful,' he thought, 'that a youth of his age and strength should enjoy the boyish pleasures which had hitherto filled up so much of his life and Catrin's. He was thankful that none of the men and maidens around him were aware of the manner in which he spent his time at Pengraig. How they would laugh at him, these sturdy labourers! A man must be a man to take his place amongst them – must not dabble with

childish pleasures – must do a little drinking, a little
sweethearting, a little swearing, and a little church or chapel-
going!' And Goronwy began to think it time that he should at
least make a show of these things, and approve himself in the
eyes of the world as a proper inhabitant of Penmwntan parish.
He even fell into a serious reverie during the noontide meal,
upon which Yshbel rallied him, with considerable mirth.

'Well, indeed, lad,' she said, 'there's a wonderful thing I have
never seen before – Goronwy Sarnissa quite silent and serious,
thinking about something! What is it then?'

'No, I wasn't,' said Goronwy, using the first excuse that
presents itself to the rustic mind.

'Yes, thee wast. I called thee twice, but no answer, only
staring at thy bowl thou wast, as if there was a frog in it.'

'Oh, thinking of his sweetheart he was,' said one of the
labourers; 'and his thoughts hadn't far to go, I'm thinking.'

An awkward blush suffused the faces of both the accused,
while Walto's dark face turned a shade paler. Rising suddenly,
he said: 'Well we chose the hottest corner of the field for our
dinner whatever. Pouff! There's not a breath of air today,' and
he sauntered back to his work, the others slowly following his
example.

'Thee'st always a dullard, Simon,' said Yshbel as she passed
him, 'but thee need not be impident too.'

'Haw, haw!' laughed the dullard, looking at her blushing face.

Goronwy was annoyed and partly pleased.

'B't shwr,' he thought, 'he ought to be looking out for a
sweetheart, and where could he find a prettier than Yshbel?'

And during the day he thought the matter over with due
seriousness, and concluded to begin his wooing when the
harvest was over. Not today – for Simon's rallying had brought
dire confusion upon him, and evidently frightened Yshbel too,
for she was careful to chat no more with him; and when the
day's work was done, she disappeared in some mysterious
manner, giving him no chance of 'Good day' or 'Good e'en.'

This gave Goronwy no pain whatever; he was matter of fact and unsentimental in the extreme, and considered that Yshbel had acted like a sensible girl. There would be plenty more opportunities for sweethearting – there was no hurry, and Yshbel's pretty face would not pale by keeping.

Yshbel's fair face had paled a little, though, lately, and she had laid the blame on the hot weather, or the hard work in the corn fields; but her little bed under the rush-covered roof could have told a different tale – of wakeful nights and tear-stained pillows.

She had succeeded in repressing Walto's ardour, and in crushing his love, she thought, without giving him any tangible cause of offence – succeeded so well that she ought to be satisfied – but the pale cheeks which that sun bonnet shaded, the forced gaiety, the long musings in solitary rambles on the beach, were scarcely signs of content. The slight awkwardness between her and Goronwy soon wore off, with the continual companionship of the harvest field and the latter's blunt good nature.

He had lengthened out wonderfully lately, had grown from a rather square and squat figure into that of a youth of fine proportions, and his face – well, that had always been the cheerfulest and pleasantest in Treswnd. 'Not the handsomest,' Yshbel thought, with a little sigh, which she cleverly followed up so closely with a smile, that none would have detected it.

It was late one evening when she sat by the hearth on the little three-legged stool, not for warmth, for it had been a sunny day, and she had come home heated and tired from the field where Nanti Betto still lingered for a final gossip. It was autumn, and the sun had set, so the little room was in partial gloom, only the smouldering turf fire throwing a faint glow round the hearth and the moon looking in at the window. Yshbel sat silent, leaning her head against the whitewashed wall of the big chimney, her hands lying listless on her lap, her bonnet thrown on the earthen floor beside her.

Suddenly a sound of voices came in through the open doorway – voices as familiar to her as those of her own home, and yet one of them caused a flutter and a bound of the heart. But that slight girlish figure was tenanted by a spirit capable of firm determination and strong endurance, and there was no outward sign of the pain which she felt.

Goronwy's voice was loud and buoyant, Walto's softer and more musical. In the clear evening air every word fell distinctly on her ear.

'When art going then?' asked Goronwy.

'Very soon, if I go at all,' answered his companion. 'Mother is not willing, of course, but when a man gets an offer like that, he is foolish to refuse.'

'When a man,' said Goronwy, laughing. 'Hear him then; he has grown ten years older already.'

He was always rather sensitive on the subject of age, feeling that he had not made such rapid strides towards manhood as Walto had.

'Jari! We shall soon he hearing you're married to a ladi, and you'll be bringing her down here to see our country ways.'

'Well, I would never marry anyone but a lady,' said Walto, thinking how fully Yshbel answered to his idea of one.

'You're a lucky chap,' said Goronwy. 'But, indeed, Walto, I'm thinking you'll long for the smell of the sea breeze sometimes in that smoky place.'

There was no answer, as the speakers had reached the threshold.

Yshbel rose to meet them, and through the doorway the moonlight fell full upon her and hid the paleness of her cheek.

'Nanti Betto,' shouted Goronwy. 'Hello, Yshbel, lass, art alone in the house?'

'Yes – Nanti has not come home. Well indeed, Walto! I haven't seen you two together this long time.'

'No,' said Goronwy; 'no more we have been,' and he looked at his companion, suddenly realising the fact.

'True enough,' said Walto. 'I suppose we are both too tired with the harvest work to go out again.'

'I was so tired tonight,' said Goronwy, 'I didn't know whether my arms and legs belonged to me or not, but I borrowed them to come down here whatever, to see if Betto had one little fish for granny's supper; she is not well, and she is not eating more than a bird this hot weather.'

'Dear anw'l! Yes,' said Yshbel; 'plenty of beautiful herrings fresh from the sea today.' And she brought out a dozen strung on a willow twig. 'Here's for thy supper, too, Goronwy; and, Walto, will you take this other dozen home for your mother? There's more than plenty left for us.'

'Well,' said Walto, awkwardly, not liking to refuse, ''twas just what she was wanting,' and he dived in his pocket for a sixpence.

'Pay for herrings?' said Yshbel with a light laugh, which covered a feeling of bitterness. 'There's nonsense. Indeed no.'

'Diwss anwl! no,' said Goronwy. 'Has it come to money between us three? We are grown up indeed then. Hast heard the news, Yshbel? This man has had a letter from his uncle, offering him a good place in his "Works," and he is going, los.'

'Going? Walto?' said Yshbel. 'No, no! What will we do without him, Goronwy?' And, clasping her hands, she put on a melancholy look, whose extravagance was intentionally evident.

'Yes,' said Walto, with assumed indifference, 'you'll break your hearts without me, I know. P'raps I'll come back some day, and see how you are all getting on here.'

'Oh yes, you'll come back sometimes to see your mother,' said Yshbel.

'And bring a wife with him,' said Goronwy. 'A lady with thin shoes, and a little umbrella to keep the sun off.'

'Perhaps, indeed,' said Yshbel, laughing, her face wreathed with smiles, her cheeks flushed, and her eyes full of mirth.

She looked more beautiful than ever, Walto thought, as he

turned away rather brusquely, leaving his fish on the table –
forgotten.

This was not the view Yshbel took of his action, however,
and she quietly covered the herrings, lest Goronwy seeing them
might offer to take them to Tredû.

'Granny will enjoy her supper, Yshbel, and that's better than
thanks to thee, I know, and better than money between friends.
What's the matter with Walto lately? I didn't notice it much
till thou wert speaking about it today, but now I do remember,
he has been very strange lately – fforwel, lass, and can diolch!'

When he was gone and his footsteps had died away, Yshbel
seated herself once more on the little round stool and waited,
her lips pressed together, a line of thought on her forehead,
and tried to quell the aching at her heart. A sob rose in her
throat, but she gulped it down.

'Oh, there's a foolish girl I am, to waste my thoughts upon
a lad who doesn't care a cockle shell for me! Why can't I feel
the same to him as I do to Goronwy? But I can't, I can't. I
thought my life was going to be so happy, but I've heard Nanti
Betto say that 'Man is born to sorrow, as the sparks fly
upwards.' 'Tis in the Bible, I know, and I suppose I must bear
my share – but why, I wonder?'

When Nanti Betto returned, she found the girl listlessly
spreading the table with the simple preparations for supper,
the wooden bowls, the spoons, the jug of milk, while over the
fire the crock of porridge bubbled.

The days passed wearily on, the sun still gilded the sands
and rocks at Treswnd, the sea gulls still stood preening their
wings at the edge of the tide, the little waves still ran caressingly
up to her feet, but Yshbel walked with more sober mien, with
eyes that looked sadly over the sea, though a footstep had but
to catch her ear, a voice but to call her name from rock, or
shore, or cottage, and at once she was blithe and merry – a
joke, a repartee, ready for every one, a little more bitter than
of old, perhaps; but still, as ever, Yshbel was the pride of

Treswnd. She felt a little more drawn to Goronwy than hitherto. 'He was not the rose, but he had been near the rose!' and as week followed week their companionship became closer, although, perhaps for that very reason, there was not a grain of romance in their friendship.

Sometimes Walto met them on the shore, or the stryt, or on the hillside, and at such times, neither he nor Yshbel showed any signs of the strained feelings which had taken the place of their old intimacy.

From the Pengraig fields Catrin watched them with intense and increasing pain. Goronwy's visits to the cliffs were becoming less frequent. 'Was it possible he was getting tired of their happy intercourse? Was that cruel Yshbel going to steal from her the one bright gleam in her existence?' So thought Catrin, in dumb pain, unable to express the bitterness which had come into her life, since that silent day when she had watched the reapers at Sarnissa.

Goronwy was as cheerful, as kind, as full of gaiety as ever, when sometimes in the twilight after the day's work he found his way through the broom bushes up the side of Penmwntan.

One day she asked him, 'Why dost not come up here as often as thee used, Goronwy? I see thee often with Yshbel – art tired of being out here with me? There's shoals of mackerel coming in with the tide; we could dip our baskets from the rocks, and fill them tonight, and have our supper up here as we used to do, but I'm afraid to ask thee, Goronwy – indeed to goodness, feel my heart now; it is thumping here 'cos I'm afraid!'

A burst of laughter from Goronwy, as he felt the beating under the brown dress, laughter that echoed from Traethyberil to Penmwntan and died away over the sea.

'Dei anw'l! thou art a girl for speaking plain. Wilt believe me now, Catrin, I've been as dull as a wet day the last three weeks – but Catrin, lodes, 'tis time for me to be thinking of something better than loitering here on the cliffs with thee, playing 'dandiss', paddling on the shore, and hunting for eggs. Tan i marw! I'm ashamed of myself sometimes and I'm trying to be wiser; but supper, lodes – fish fresh from the sea, and broiled up here on the slopes? If I was a hundred I wouldn't say "No" to it.'

When their baskets were full of shining mackerel they hurried up from the shore to cook their spoil but were astonished to see, on the side of the hill a blaze already rising from the spot on which they were accustomed to light their fire. The flames leaped up against the dark blue sky, while round the fire passed and repassed the forms of many people.

Catrin and Goronwy stared at each other.

'What does it mean?' he asked, and the girl looked equally puzzled.

Creeping behind the furze bushes, they approached nearer, unobserved, and soon discovered a gipsy encampment located on their own particular haunts.

'Tis the gipsies!' said Goronwy, indignantly. 'What business have they here in your father's fields?'

'Oh, I know,' said Catrin, 'they were here once before, and my father told them to come when they liked, because my mother was related to them.'

'Well, I have heard indeed thou wert related to the gipsies. Will we go nearer?' And, stealing nearer, they took a closer view of the strangers.

There were carts and vans scattered about, donkeys and children also, while near the glow of the fire reclined an old woman, whose face, wrinkled and worn with nearly a century of hard life, still showed signs of the acuteness and energy which had been the chief traits of her character. Her keen, black eyes gleamed fiercely under the red shawl which she wore as a hood, and she watched with interest while the younger members of the company prepared the crock and the viands for supper. Near her a man stood leaning against the tent with folded arms, his dark, handsome face lit up by the blazing fire.

''Twas a good bargain, and no mistake,' he said. 'Barlow called him "Alexander", so well keep to that.'

The old woman croaked something in return, and they both gazed at a big, strong horse, which, tethered to a cart, munched his hay near by.

'I like a good 'oss,' said the man, smoothing down his fetlock. 'If I only drove a barrow I'd like a good 'oss in it.'

'Well, you can afford it, John Lovell,' said his aged companion; 'but I wish ye'd had time to ask Simon Rees' leave before we camped. I always like perliteness – it pays.'

'Well, they can't see the fire from the farm, nor the village, and I'll see him first thing tomorrow. Oh, he'll be all right when he knows ye're with us, mother, but who the dewss are these?' he added, as Goronwy and Catrin, irresistibly attracted by the scene before them, emerged from the darkness.

'What d'ye want, young man, and who are you?'

'I am Goronwy Hughes, Sarnissa, and this is Catrin Rees, Pengraig, and we are bringing you some fish for your supper. Will you take them?'

'Well, what's the price?' said John Lovell, diving into his pocket. 'We can catch plenty for ourselves, so I'm not going to pay much for them.'

'No, no – 'tis a present, I meant,' said Goronwy, while Catrin gazed shyly from one to the other of the dark-skinned company. 'We got them down there by the rocks – they're thick in the sea tonight – and going to light a fire here we were, to broil them.'

'Well, come on,' said Lovell, 'there's enough for us all. Here, Sylvia, child, wilt fry them – nicely now? Well, we saw the marks of your fire.'

'Bring them here,' screamed the old woman, 'the lad and lass, I mean.'

'Yes, go and speak to her,' said the dark man and remember you, she's Nancy Wood, so mind your manners.'

Goronwy's manners were never of the gentlest, and this

injunction made him throw his head back and approach the old woman with rather a defiant stride. Catrin's manner, however, must have been all that Lovell desired, for she hung her head and trembled in her shoes. From childhood she had had her relationship to the gipsies flung in her teeth, and Nancy Wood, in her childish imagination, had been literally a name to conjure by, so it was not without dire misgivings that she now found her hand clasped in the claw-like fingers of the old woman.

'Catrin Rees?' said the latter. 'What, daughter of Simon Rees, the carrier? Yes – I'll swear it without waiting for an answer; there's Dolly's eyes, and her small hands and feet!'

'Jinny was my mother's name,' said the girl, timidly.

'Yes – but Dolly Wood was your great grandmother's name, and Catrin was your father's mother's name, and you're fifteen years of age since last April! There, I know all about you, d'ye see? Come, speak up, child,' she continued raising Catrin's chin in her hand. 'I'm not goin' to hurt ye. My, ye're my own blood relation! Ay, ay! Many's the prank we've had, Dolly and I, in these very fields. And now, who's he?' she added, looking at Goronwy.

'Goronwy Sarnissa,' said Catrin.

''Twas fishing on Traethyberil we were,' he explained.

'But how are you out so late then?'

'Often I'm out all night,' said Catrin, 'and sleeping in that shepherd's hut. I can't bear to be shut in with Madlen and Bensha.'

'Ha, ha!' laughed Nancy Wood, ''tis the gipsy blood in you, child; and he,' she added, pointing to Goronwy, 'is "keeping company" with you, I suppose.'

'Yes,' said Catrin, unembarrassed, for the expression had only its literal meaning for her, and fortunately it had struck Goronwy in that light also.

'Well, I must go soon, or they will shut the door at home,' he said.

Meanwhile, the fish had been broiled, and John Lovell who seemed the ruling spirit of the company, called all to supper, and made room for the guests beside him on the ground, where Goronwy seated himself, well pleased to escape from Nancy Wood's glittering eyes and claw-like hands. Catrin, however, she insisted upon keeping beside her, questioning her closely, and easily extracting a fund of information from the guileless girl, and forming her own shrewd opinion as to the state of domestic affairs at Pengraig, as well as of the friendship existing between the lad and lass who had so suddenly made her acquaintance.

''Tis good fish,' she said, 'and I'm glad thee'st brought it. Tell thy father that Nancy Wood bids him look after his daughter better. Let me look at thy hand, lass, before thou go'st,' and, holding the brown palm to the firelight, she examined it closely.

'H'm,' was her only remark, followed, however, by a long look at Goronwy, whose honest, good-natured face was at that moment full of interest, as he leaned back from his platter to look at 'Alexander's' good points, upon which John Lovell was dilating.

When the mackerel had been disposed of, the contents of the crock, which steamed and bubbled on the fire, was handed round. The merry talk, the laughter, the toddling children who pattered bare-footed round the fire, were all so new and interesting to Goronwy and Catrin, that the time sped on unobserved, until, suddenly starting to his feet, he called, 'Catrin, lass, 'tis time to go!' and Catrin, unable quite to throw off the fears of her childhood, was not sorry to bid her new-found relative 'goodnight.'

'Come on, lodes,' said Goronwy.' In my deed, I won't be sorry to see that John Lovell again, but the old woman's talons – ach-y-fi!'

'Yes; I was afraid of her at first,' said Catrin, 'but she was very kind.'

'They are off tomorrow, so we won't see them again.'

After a little silent musing, Catrin returned to the subject uppermost in her mind. ''Tis a pity we must grow up,' she said.

'Yes,' said Goronwy, taking a long breath; 'I don't believe we'll ever have such suppers then.'

'When we are quite grown up, Goronwy – how will it be then? Wilt never come up here?'

'I don't know,' said the latter, with a shake of his head. 'I suppose not. T'will be very odd seeing a man and woman playing dandiss in the moonlight. Ach-y-fi! Don't let us think of it. That time hasn't come yet, though, in my deed, lass, thou hast grown so tall!'

'And so hast thou,' she answered.

'Yes, there's no doubt about it,' said Goronwy, 'we'll have to grow into two stupid old owls, instead of two happy seagulls. Seagulls or owls, I must fly home now. Granny will want to go to bed, and she'll never go till I come in. Goodnight,' and he left her on the cliffs.

Long she sat there and pondered, not altogether unsatisfied with Goronwy's explanations, for there was no doubt of the matter, they had both clung too long to the ways of childhood, and Goronwy was wise and firm, and it behoved her to be the same – but oh, how could she? Give up the happy scrambles, the long rests in the shade of the furze bushes, or some sunburnt knoll, the quiet rambles round the shore, under the stars, the impromptu meals, and all the joyous ways of their youth – how could they?

In spite of her wayward and impulsive nature, she had her full share of common sense, and more than her share of self-abnegation, and now that the cause of Goronwy's less frequent visits had been made plain to her, her one desire was to share his feelings, and act as he would wish her to do.

These were her musings for the first hour after his departure, but as the twilight faded and the darkness came on, a cold wind arose, and compelled her to quit her seat, and seek for exercise to restore warmth to her limbs, and folding around her an old cloak of her mother's, which she fetched from the shepherd's hut on the hillside, she began to roam the cliffs, as she had often done before, drinking in the soothing influences of her solitary communion with Nature.

A glimmering light in Yshbel's window attracted her notice. She could see the glow of the firelight through the open doorway, until a dark figure obscured it and passed into the cottage. It was not Ben Lloyd, for there was his boat out at sea, where he was evidently at his late fishing; it was too broad and tall for Betto or Yshbel. Who then? Was it Goronwy? And the dark brows were drawn together, the eyes flashed, and disturbance was depicted in every feature of her face, and every movement of her body.

Up and down on the dewy grass, backwards and forwards, with her hands clasped under the old cloak, her breath drawn hard and fast, while a host of bitter feelings assailed her, and took the place of the sweet reasonableness that she had gained a while ago. All around her, too, there were signs of change, the long spell of fine weather was evidently coming to an end, and everything spoke of an impending storm.

Two hours earlier all nature seemed sleeping in a soft swoon of calm and rest; but already the sky was overcast, and Catrin shivered as she drew her cloak closer around her. The night wore on, the stars glanced between the driving clouds, and yet the girl paced up and down.

The lights in cottage windows went out one by one, a low murmuring seemed to float over the sea, which, as the night advanced, increased in depth of sound. The wind sighed ominously round the broom bushes, the reeds and grasses shivered, and the sleeping cattle lifted their heads as if scenting a storm.

In the darkness Catrin still paced restlessly, feeling neither cold nor hunger, so absorbed was she in her own thoughts. 'Yshbel' was the bitter drop in her cup, the thorn in her flesh, and the cloud that threw its shadow over all her happiness. Alas! for all her good intentions, her strong desire to identify herself with Goronwy in his wise actions! The old headlong passions were upon her, the fierce, vindictive anger of an untrained nature took the reins and swept her before them. 'Yshbel!' She could not live in the same world with her. 'I know it! I feel it!' she said to herself, as she paced faster and faster along the cliffs. 'She is going to be happy in this life, and she's going to make me miserable. I know it, I know it! Before she began to be friends with Goronwy, we were blithe and happy; now she is drawing him away from me – she, who has Betto and Ben and Walto to love her, while I have no one but Goronwy. Is that right? 'Tis not, 'tis not!' and falling on her knees, she lifted her hands to the night sky, over which the clouds were racing, as if to some appointed place.

'Oh, dear God,' she cried aloud in her vehemence, ''tis not right, and You who know everything, know it; and I ask You – oh, I beg of You – to take her from this world. Make me Your tool – I will do it. Only send her to me, O God! For I know she is angering You, so help me to get rid of her. 'Twill be very easy – a push over the cliff when she is passing will do it; and I will, I will! Oh, dear God, hear me. I am begging it here by myself, and You are strong. I do not ask for wings, for scarves, or necklaces – but only to get rid of Yshbel. Only send her in my way, O God and I will do it – I will, I will!' and, letting her hands drop on her bended knees, she remained some time lost in a maze of tumultuous passions.

At last rising, chilled to the bone, she sought shelter in the shepherd's hut, where she had often spent the night in worse storms than the present one, but no sleep came to soothe her. Lying wide awake, on a bed of bracken, she watched the flying clouds, and the brilliant stars that glinted between them.

She had ever gathered peace and happiness from the sight of them hitherto, but tonight there was no rest in her soul. She was alone in the universe – no home, no friend, no God!

For, in spite of her confident prayer, she felt within her that the God whom she had addressed would not respond to her appeal. And, as the night wore on, and hour after hour passed wearily over her, her misery and despondency increased, until, when the first faint streak of dawn appeared, it surely fell upon no sadder, lonelier being than Catrin.

Hitherto she had always found her solace in the close, pressing presence of the Unseen, the God Whom she loved with the simple faith of a child, the spirits of the departed, whom she still felt near her; but tonight she could not stand, with outstretched arms, looking up to the sky in silent happiness. All was gone – the world was empty – and when that first faint streak of dawn broadened, and the sun approached the edge of the hills, it only served to show her how cold and grey and dead was the world around her. At last he rose, that bright effulgent orb, which she was wont to greet with the adoring welcome of a simple reverent soul, and as his golden beams reached rock and hills and ocean, a strange reaction began to set in upon the girl's worn-out spirit.

There was Sarnissa gleaming white in the sunshine, its inmates and the cattle in the fields not yet stirring. There was the village down below her still asleep, all safe in the care of the God to Whom she had prayed, while she alone in her misery was shut out from His loving care. There was Goronwy now crossing the stubble, and opening the big barn door – what would he say, if he knew what she had asked for? Should she ever again be able to look into his clear, honest eyes without this heavy weight in her heart? Should she tell him? No; she would be ashamed for him to know how wicked she had been. What then of God, Who heard her prayer, and knew the evil feelings which had been in her heart? And a flood of bitter regret and penitence swept through that passionate, impulsive spirit, until the sensitive slender body seemed to writhe with the weight of its burden.

Rising from her bed of bracken, she ran out into the

sunshine. Behind the hut the broad sea stretched out to the dark horizon, the clouds still hanging overhead. The world was awaking, and Catrin's heart was awaking too.

Once more she flung herself on her knees, and with her hands uplifted as before, she prayed while the tears rolled down her cheeks, imploring that her former prayer might not be heard or answered.

'O God! Have pity on me, and forget my wicked prayer – blot it out. Forgive me, and take me back to Your loving care, where I have been so safe and happy.'

She remained long on her knees, her head bent in silent devotion, and when at last she rose, her face had regained its look of happy confidence, although her body flagged under the strain of long abstinence and the uncurbed passions of the previous night.

She would go home to Pengraig, and breakfast with Bensha and Madlen; but ere she went she looked across the sea, with the shrewd, observant eyes of one accustomed to, and intimate with, the changing face of nature.

''Tis from there 'twill come,' she said, pointing towards the north-west, where from one point the clouds spread outwards like the ribs of a fan. The sea too showed the same broad pathway narrowing to the same point, its troubled waters roughened as with the footsteps of an invisible host. 'Yes, and 'twill be a bad one,' she said; and passing up the rough fields, reached Pengraig, where the usual objurgations of Bensha and Madlen awaited her.

CHAPTER X

CATRIN'S PRAYER

It had come to the last day of Walto's home lingering. He was filled with a restless longing to get away from Treswnd, which battled with a leaning as strong towards his old home and the scenes of his happy childhood. But the ambitions of youth were upon him, the desire for a new field of work, a longing to see the world, and, above all, a feeling of deep disappointment with the turn which his life had taken lately. Mrs Gwyn, who had at first been much averse to his leaving home, had lately become more reconciled to the idea, as she saw it would be the surest way of separating him from 'that impident hussy'. There were a few last purchases to be made, all important in her eyes, such things as were not to be procured nearer than Caermadoc, so, in spite of the scudding clouds and the rising wind, Walto accompanied Goronwy thither. On reaching the town, they separated, Walto to make his purchases, Goronwy in search of his father, who he knew would be sailing down the river that day and up the bay to Treswnd. After searching in many inns, he met him coming out of Mr Robert Oliver's office, with all the signs of flurry and excitement which a visit to that gentleman invariably left upon him.

''Tis all right, Goronwy,' he said, excitedly. 'Mr Oliver says we can take proceedings, and we needn't wait until you are twenty-one; so we'll go at old Simon at once, and Parcglas will come back to its rightful owners, my boy. You go and ask him if I'm not telling the truth;' and Goronwy, who was also much interested, entered the little office known as 'Oliver's den'.

When he rejoined his father in the street, it was with a heightened colour and an exultant air, for litigation is as the breath of life to a Welshman. Let him but see the slightest prospect of being engaged in a lawsuit, and his mien and bearing are at once altered. He scents the battle from afar, and metaphorically snorts and paws the ground in his impatience to enter the lists.

'We'll do it, father, all right,' he said; 'a man can always do what he makes up his mind to do. When are you sailing?'

'At four o'clock.'

'Well, I'll come home with you, and bring the new hen coop for Marged. Now I'm going to buy a handkerchief for granny.'

On leaving the shop, having bought a brilliant cotton handkerchief, he met Walto.

'I am going home with father in the *Lark*,' he said. 'Will you come, Walto? There's a storm brewing.'

'Yes, indeed, I'll come,' said Walto.' If there's wind in it whatever, I'd like a last blow before I go.'

At four o'clock they reached the *Lark*, which was riding at anchor on the broad river. The captain had not arrived.

'No, no,' said Goronwy; ''tis another glass at the Mermaid, or a 'blue' at the Mariner's, is keeping him.'

Little Will Bullet was leaning over the side of the vessel, and crooning a song to himself. The bright red pennon fluttered at the mast head, and the wind was in the rigging.

'Hoi, hoi!' shouted the captain as he stepped on board, 'here you are, my lads. We won't be long getting to Treswnd, if we can cross the bar.'

'We'll have a tossing, I think,' said Goronwy; 'and if you take my advice you won't sail today. Stop here at Peggi Bowen's; she'll give you a clean bed, and a good breakfast.'

'Hold thy jabber,' said his father, whose last few glasses had not improved his temper, 'we'll be at Treswnd before the storm comes. You two land lubbers can stop at Peggi Bowen's, if you like.'

'Oh no,' said Goronwy 'if you go, I will go too.'

'And I,' said Walto; 'but I think we'll have a bit of a blow when we get out to sea.' And they sailed down the river, somewhat sheltered from the force of the wind by its high bare banks.

At Treswnd, it was evident that every moment increased the strength of the gale, and before the sun set, the storm was upon them in all its fury; straight from the north-west, it blew with unremitting violence, not a break nor a pause in its relentless force. The sea, which had been restless and turbid for many hours, now tossed and frothed in huge breakers, rolling in from the horizon, tossing their angry crests into the crimson sunset light.

Catrin, sheltering under a thorn bush, peered round the horn of the bay, anxiously watching the flying foam and the furious sea, for Goronwy had told her of his intention to return with his father; while Yshbel stood in the cottage window, her eyes fixed in the same direction. Shacki Owens, who had returned early from the fair, had dropped a word or two which had frightened her.

'I met Walto Gwyn and Goronwy in the town,' he had said. 'Going down to the shipping they were, coming home in the *Lark*, they said. There's a tossing they'll have – dei anw'l! No ship could live on that sea!'

She had answered nothing, but had gone home with the roar and the dash of the waves in her ears and a strange sinking at her heart. She had never seen such a storm in her sixteen years of life. The very air trembled with the strength of the blast.

Just as the sun was sinking into the troubled waters, a little ship, grey and indistinct, was visible in the murky haze. 'Surely not the *Lark*,' said Yshbel. But it was – it was! Her eye, familiar with every boat that crossed the bay, could not be mistaken. The sails were furled, and she was evidently riding before the gale straight into land, to which the strong nor'-wester drove her mercilessly.

Catrin saw it too, and waited with cheeks that blanched and eyes that swam in tears. 'What did it mean? How could Morgan Hughes have dared to leave his port in such a storm?'

Louder and more fierce grew the wind, and higher tossed the angry waves in the red light. Down sank the sun upon the scene of wild confusion. The elements were at war, and the only object upon which they could wreak their fury seemed that frail vessel which rocked and tossed as it rapidly neared the land.

'Three men on board – who can they be?' said Catrin – 'and little Will Bullet!'

But Yshbel knew, and tying Ben's red fishing cap firmly on her head, she went out into the storm: Betto tried in vain to wrap a shawl round the girl, but the wind tore it from her grasp, and Yshbel ran on without it.

Betto had a hard fight to close the door. 'Is the girl mad,' she said, 'to venture out in such a storm, and what for, I wonder?' But she too ventured out before long, for all the inhabitants of Treswnd were gathered on the beach. The news had spread that the *Lark* was dragging her anchor, and being driven on towards the cerrig duon, those cruel rocks which had proved the destruction of so many good ships.

'Oh, isn't there something to be done?' said Yshbel, running towards the little crowd. 'Won't some one go to their help, and take the life-belts with them?'

Shacki Owens shook his head sorrowfully. 'No, nothing to be done. No boat could have a chance in such a sea as this. Druen bach! Pwr things! So near land too!'

'There's three of them and the boy,' said Ben. 'Who can they be?'

''Tis Goronwy and the captain, and Walto Gwyn with them,' shouted Shacki.

Yshbel moaned in her distress, for no one could hear her. So near land, so near home, and no one to help them. 'Oh! will not one of you venture?' but no one volunteered for such a hopeless mission, but watched despairingly for the destruction of the *Lark*, and the loss of those on board of her.

Yshbel alone continued to urge, to implore, and finally to upbraid. 'Cowards, cowards!' she cried, wringing her hands. 'If I were a man, would I let my friends be drowned without trying to save them?'

''Twould be madness, lodes, to throw away our lives. We would only be dashed on the cerrig duon ourselves, and we can't love our neighbours more than ourselves.'

'I can,' said the girl, turning from them, and running as fast as the wind would allow her towards the other end of the shore, and as she ran she kept repeating under her breath, '*more* than ourselves, more, much more!' Once she turned back to beseech for help, 'Come, one of you then, and help me to lift the rope into the boat.'

'What use, thou little fool?' said Ben, clutching at her arm. 'Thou shalt not go to thine own certain death.'

'I will,' cried the girl, dragging herself away from his grasp, and Deio, the blacksmith, followed her, saying: 'I'll put the hawser in the boat for thee, but for God's sake, Yshbel, don't venture out with it!'

The rope of which they spoke was knotted to a strong ring of iron, fastened to a rock deep buried in the bank beyond the rushes. Could she but carry this rope to the *Lark* they would be saved, for hauling it in would counteract the force of the nor-wester, and bring them safely away from the cerrig duon and towards the further end of the shore.

'Yes, yes, she would try it; God would help her,' and springing into the boat, she waited while Deio brought coil after coil of the rope, and flung them into the boat at her feet.

'All in!' he shouted, and she pushed the boat out into the foaming surf.

'On my soul, I won't let her go alone,' he cried, leaping in after her.

The little crowd of watchers on the beach were as much

astonished at Yshbel's rapid action as at her courage, and the utter hopelessness of the task she had undertaken.

'Deio of all men too,' they said, 'who knows nothing about steering.'

'Well, he has nothing to do but keep her head to the north, and he'll be driven back to the cerrig duon safe enough.'

Breathlessly they watched while the little boat toiled through the foam, sometimes quite lost to sight, sometimes riding high on the crest of a foaming wave, making so little way, too, against the furious gale. Sometimes a groan from the watchers showed the tension of their nerves, when some huge breaker, more angry than usual, tossed the little cockle shell, and hid it in its seething fall.

'Oh, Yshbel, fach! We shall never see her again – nor Deio! Why did she do such a mad thing? We ought not to have let her go – poor thing, fach! Oh dear, oh dear!' and the women hid their faces in their aprons.

Catrin saw it all from her high watchtower. Powerless to help, for no boat or rope was hers to use, she could do nothing but strain her eyes to watch the labouring vessel. She did not weep, no sound escaped her lips, but in her heart there was an agonising prayer for help. At last, from the far end of the beach, she saw Yshbel and Deio push out their boat to dare the stormy waters, and for a moment a wild feeling of envy rushed into her heart. Yshbel was risking her life for her friends, while she could do nothing. They would all be drowned but not separated, while she must be left to bear it all.

Drowned! And like a flash of lightning came the realisation of what this would mean for her; and with such vivid force did the knowledge strike her, that for a moment she nearly swooned. 'Yes, she saw it all – the God whom she had offended was going to punish her by granting her wicked prayer, and fulfilling her revengeful desire to rid the world of her enemy.' And as the little boat tossed and rocked in the foam, her terror grew more and more intense. 'It is my doing,' she thought, 'I have wished her evil and it has come. Oh, if I had wings that I might fly to her, and be drowned instead of her!' But stay – was Yshbel to fail in her mission? No; for gradually the boat had drawn nearer and nearer to the toiling vessel, and in an agony of excitement Catrin saw Deio fling one end of the rope on board, while the three men seized it and fastened it to the vessel. She knew they were practically saved, and Yshbel had done it. But stay – again a fresh terror lay hold of her, for surely something had happened. Deio was safe on board, but Yshbel, alone in the boat, was drifting swiftly away from the *Lark*. She saw her fling herself down as if in despair – no oars, no sails, no rudder! 'Twas certain death – for already, not only to Catrin, but to a crowd of anxious spectators on the shore, as well as those on board the *Lark*, it was evident that Yshbel was rushing towards her destruction; for tide and wind setting in the same direction added to the strong suction of the Deep Stream, and every moment her frail boat was drawn swiftly and more swiftly towards the frowning cliffs.

That she realised her danger was very evident, from the imploring attitude in which she knelt, and raised her clasped hands towards the stormy sky.

On board the *Lark* the excitement was intense. They had watched the girl, who had risked her life for them, with nerves strained to the utmost, had greeted her near approach as that of an angel of mercy. They had caught the rope end which Deio had flung up to them, and hope, which had all but died within them, had sprung up, giving them new life.

'She has risked her life for us,' said Goronwy. 'God bless her!'

'She has risked her life for thee,' said Walto, 'and we all share in thy blessing,' and they strained both eyes and hands of greeting towards their brave rescuers.

Deio was quickly on board, and eager hands were stretched towards Yshbel, but, by some unlucky chance, her oar slipped overboard, and even while she tried to secure it, a ponderous wave lifted up one end of the boat. At the same moment the furious wind caught the other oar and sent it flying into the foaming water.

Walto sprang towards the side of the *Lark* in his first impulse to reach her, but Goronwy and Deio gripping him ere he had cleared the side, dragged him back with all their force. He struggled furiously, panting and writhing, until he fell inert and unconscious between them.

'Mawredd anwl! she's gone,' said Deio. 'See her racing in the Deep Stream.'

'Yes.' said the captain, 'in another minute we should have been in it too – we were within five yards of its grip. Better we had all gone with it than that brave girl!'

But there was no time for many words, for the north wind drove as hard as ever, and the rope strained as they hauled it round the capstan. God grant it may not break!

In a few moments Walto revived, and again began to struggle for freedom.

'Let me go, let me go, you coward. She is losing her life for you, and you will do nothing to save her.'

'Highsht, man,' said Gorowny, holding him forcibly down, 'till you've listened to reason. I tell you, you shall not throw yourself to useless destruction. If mortal man can help her, she is already saved.'

'What dost mean?' said Walto. 'Who could save her from the Deep Stream? No one.'

'I say – if mortal man can save her, Catrin Rees will do so.'

'Catrin Rees!' said Walto in bewilderment, standing up and looking over the scene of wild confusion.

There was no sign of Yshbel or her boat, nothing but the angry, foaming billows, and the grim cliffs rising behind them.

'Listen, lad,' said Goronwy, as well as the storm would let him. 'I saw Catrin spring over the cliff. She knows where the Deep Stream casts up its victims. 'Tis not more than three minutes since Yshbel – God save her! – was drawn under water, and something tells me Catrin will save her. Pluck up heart, man; help with the rope. Come on; it will be as much as we can do to fight this cursed wind.'

And Walto followed him to where Morgan Hughes and Deio were steadily, though very slowly, hauling in the hawser, and nearing the further end of the shore. Slowly, but surely, they left the cerrig duon behind them, and followed the good strong rope, at last reaching the little cove under the lee of the north horn of the shore, where they were able to cast their anchor in comparatively calm water. The boat was lowered, and there were not wanting willing hands to help them to land, where the greetings were mingled with deep dejection and sorrow for the fate of Yshbel.

Betto was inconsolable, for she loved her foster child with all the depth of affection which no child of her own had lived to call forth.

Mrs Gwyn of Tredu, was one of the knot of anxious watchers, and as she clasped her son to her heart, she whispered in his ear:

'I am conquered, my boy. God bless Yshbel!'

'Go home, father,' said Goronwy, 'and tell granny I'm all right, I will be home soon.'

There was no talk of searching for Yshbel or her little boat, for every one knew that once within the clutch of the Deep Stream there was no chance of rescue.

'Too late, mother,' said Walto.

And the poor woman could only sob and cry:

'Not too late to be forgiven, I hope, whatever.'

But Walto and Goronwy, hurrying across the shore, and up the hillside, were not without a faint hope, the former relying on Goronwy's assurances, and the latter auguring well from Catrin's sudden disappearance.

They were both very silent as they rapidly covered the ground, helped on by the force of the wind, which almost lifted them off their feet.

When they reached the high ground around Pengraig:

'What dost expect, Goronwy?' said Walto. 'If thee hadst left me alone I should be out of this miserable world by this time. It was cowardly to let her drown before our eyes. We might at least have died with her.'

'Died with her?' said Goronwy. 'I daresay I am a stupid farmer, and thou art a gentleman's son, but dei anw'l, man! It will be better to live with her than to die with her, and that's what I'm expecting whatever. If not, then God help us, for we can never forget today, Walto; but some strong feeling is in me that Catrin has saved her.'

'How?' said Walto, impatiently.

'There she is!' cried Goronwy excitedly; and, looking up, they saw a blue apron waved in the wind. 'It means good news, I believe. Come on.'

Panting with fatigue, for they were well-nigh worn out with their exertions in the *Lark*, they hurried through the farmyard, to meet Catrin, who was running towards them. She was very pale, and there were traces of tears in her eyes, but there was a reassuring smile on her lips.

'She is here,' she said; 'and Madlen is putting her in bed now. I must go back and help her, only I knew you would be wanting to know.'

'Oh, God bless thee, lodes, for thy good news!' said Goronwy. And Walto, seizing her hand, wrung it without a word.

There was not much in the action, but to Catrin it meant much. It was a link of friendship with the world from which she was estranged, a message of kindness – nay, more, of gratitude – from one of her fellow human beings, whom she had always shunned, and from whom she had experienced little but harshness. The hot blood kindled through her whole frame, and mounted to the cheeks and forehead which, a moment ago, had been so white. To hide her feelings she turned quickly away, and the two youths began their way down the hill bearing the good tidings.

'Yshbel saved! Catrin saved her! Where? How?

They were assailed by a hundred questions. The villagers crowded round them, some incredulous, but all rejoicing; Goronwy secretly exulting in the fact that, for once, all must acknowledge their indebtedness to the girl, whom they were accustomed to despise, if not to execrate.

'Well, it is all very well,' said Ben, 'to say Catrin saved her, and it behoves us to thank God for His mercy. Indeed, I don't know what would the hearth look like at home with only me and Betto, and the big crochon on the fire. But 'tis plainer than ever that Catrin Rees has friends where we have enemies. If she can save from the Deep Stream, she must have help from some one, and we can all guess who that is.'

'Yes, yes,' said another of the crowd; 'there's no need to doubt it any longer, and no use in people laughing at us. Witchcraft is among us as strong as ever, and thou, Goronwy, hadst better keep away from Pengraig slopes; I often see thee going up there.'

'You are a lot of fools,' Goronwy said, indignantly, 'and I am sick and tired of your nonsense. Tan i marw! 'tis no wonder that Catrin Rees keeps away from you all! I tell you, you are wronging her shamefully. Here has she delivered us from a trouble that would have shadowed our lives for ever, and you then turn round and abuse her for it.'

'How did she do it, then?' asked Shacki Owens.

'She knows the way to the underground shore of which we have all heard. I have been there with her, and I tell you 'twould take stronger brains than yours to bear the gruesome sights there, but Catrin is so good, so much better than us all, that she can bear it without fear. No doubt she found Yshbel there, and carried her up to Pengraig.'

'Dei anwl! Perhaps indeed,' said Shacki Owens. 'I have heard my grandfather tell of a deep sea cave, where the smugglers who lived at Pengraig used to keep their spoil, and of a path leading up to Pengraig cellars, but 'tis news indeed that Catrin Rees is a good girl, and better than us all!'

'Well, never mind,' said Peggi Bullet, whose little son was cabin boy in the *Lark*. 'Never mind, since she has saved Yshbel.'

'Shall we venture up to see her? I have never been inside Pengraig,'

'No, no,' said Goronwy, in his masterful way. 'No one is to see her tonight – not till tomorrow – and then I daresay she'll be down amongst us once more.'

But here he was mistaken, for when the morrow's sun rose, it shone upon a flushed and fevered face lying upon Catrin's coarse pillow, and it was several days before Yshbel, who had struggled painfully back to life, felt sufficiently restored to rise from her bed, Madlen and Betto doing all in their power to bring back health and animation to the listless form.

Of the horrors of the Deep Stream, and her being cast up on the dark underground shore she knew nothing; happily unconsciousness had overtaken her, before she had been drawn through the opening to the cave.

Catrin had seen the racing swiftness with which the little boat had been carried onwards to its destruction, with feelings acutely self-condemning and with an agony of repentance. Nearer and nearer to the dark cliffs came the frail cockle shell, almost under where she knelt watching it; now it sinks in the swirling waters, and now she knows it is carried with the rushing tide into the dark forbidding cave. Suddenly she realises that it is possible yet to save Yshbel, and instantly without wasting a moment she fastens the rope which lies hidden under a furze bush to the thorn stump at the edge, for the wind is too strong to venture on her usual mode of reaching the cave. For a second or two she sways perilously backwards and forwards, but at last is safe behind the flattened bush, and beginning a rapid descent to the cave. She was consumed by an intense anxiety. 'Was it possible that after all she would be allowed to save the girl towards whom she had felt such bitter enmity?'

Down, down against the rushing wind into the darkness and at last on to the sands, where the waves were breaking with their usual monotonous regularity, for here the storm did not enter. With beating heart she crept along the edge of the tide, examining every dark object carefully, lifting the sodden sails, tearing away the accumulated heaps of seaweed, until at last she saw in the foam of an incoming breaker a swirling garment, which, at the risk of being herself caught by the receding wave, she rushed to grasp, and to draw to land.

It was Yshbel! Yshbel! And now it was well indeed that Catrin was strong and sinewy, for, with her dripping garments clinging to her, the rescued girl was no light weight. Catrin lifted her on her shoulders, and, with a strength and swiftness imparted by excitement, carried her up the flight of steps and through the rest of the steep ascent and, hurrying down the rocky slopes to Pengraig garden, entered the house, breathless and faint with her exertions.

'Well, Bendigedig!' said Madlen, as the girl deposited her dripping burden on the hearth, 'what in the Lord's name have you brought with you?'

'Oh, come,' said Catrin, 'it is Yshbel Lloyd. She has been drowned, but you know how to bring the drowned to life again, I have often heard you say so, Madlen, fach,' she cried, for the first time in her life using a term of endearment to that repellent woman. To do her justice, Madlen readily responded to her entreaty, and Yshbel was soon wrapped in warm, dry clothing, while Madlen proceeded to put into practice her often boasted power of restoring the apparently drowned, Catrin aiding her with a deftness which astonished her.

'Tan i marw!' she said afterwards to Bensha, 'you might think she was used to nursing all her life. More shame to her, the lazy hussy, to spend her time about the cliffs.'

When Yshbel showed satisfactory signs of recovery, Catrin watched the closed eyes intently for a first awakening glance, but Madlen pushed her aside.

'There, thee can'st go,' she said. 'Thee'st helped me very well, considering, but thee't better go before she opens her eyes, for 'twouldn't do to frighten her, and she mightn't like to see thee so close to her.'

Catrin turned to the window with a patient humility, accepting the repulse without resentment. She was used to it; it had been her portion since childhood!

Coming across the farmyard in haste, she saw Goronwy and Walto, and, as we have seen, hurrying out to meet them, was comforted by Walto's warm grasp.

Returning to the house, she timidly peeped into the sickroom. 'Can I do something else, Madlen?' she said, gently.

'If thee wast like any other girl, I would tell thee to go down to the village, and tell Betto she is safe. Where didst find her?'

'Down below, washed up by the waves on the shore,' and Madlen, supposing she alluded to one of the many coves which indented the cliffs, inquired no further.

'Betto knows by this time, for I have just told Goronwy and Walto.'

'Oh, I don't want thee any more then. Hisht! she is opening her eyes.'

Catrin longed for that first glance of recognition, but she was accustomed to be hated and despised, and she dare not thrust her presence upon the reviving girl, lest she might quench the frail spark of life, which had so nearly been extinguished, as she thought, by her impious prayers. With a warm glow of gratitude suffusing her whole frame, she returned to the cliffs; and Betto arriving at Pengraig, Yshbel was soon nursed back to life, though some days elapsed before strength returned to her.

CHAPTER XI

YSHBEL AND CATRIN

Mrs Gwyn, always active and energetic, had risen before the sun on the morning of her son's departure. She had had a sleepless night and her eyes were red with weeping, for she had pretty well gauged Walto's feelings, and realised that his leaving today would mean 'Goodbye' to his boyhood and to their close companionship. On the preceding day, when she thought that Yshbel was drowned, and that Providence had delivered her from her anxieties, she felt keenly regretful that she had nursed in her heart such bitter animosity towards the girl and would even have given much to recall the guileless life which, she shrewdly guessed, had been risked for Walto's more than Goronwy's sake. But when, before night, the astonishing news reached her of Yshbel's safety, she felt that her brave action would but confirm her son's infatuation, and that it would perhaps be well for her, if possible, to acquiesce in his choice, and crush down all her objections if she ever hoped for his return to his old home.

It was no wonder, therefore, that she had spent a wakeful night, and was subdued and silent when she entered the cosy 'hall' in the early dawn. Mari had already kindled a fire and laid the breakfast; the tins and coppers glistened in the firelight the fish frizzled appetisingly in the pan, but when Walto came down, looking scarcely less weary than herself, the mestress felt that the zest and pleasure of life were gone, and to both the sunshine seemed overshadowed by a heavy cloud. They were but half through their breakfast when a cheerful voice in the kitchen startled them.

'Maybe 'tis Goronwy, come to say goodbye,' said Walto.

'Not so fast, 'machgen-i!' said Goronwy, entering. 'I'm coming with you as far as Caermadoc, to see you safe in the coach.'

'Well, indeed! there's kind of you,' said the mestress, 'and I'm very much obliged to you, Goronwy Hughes.'

There was generally a little patronage in her manner towards Walto's village companions, but today she was too broken-spirited to remember that her son was better-born than his friend.

'Yes, 'tis very kind of thee,' said Walto. 'But, indeed, lad, I think I would rather go alone. 'Tis no use making a long goodbye, thee see'st and—'

'And 'tis to shake off Treswnd and all your old friends at once you're wanting, Walto; but I won't let you, not I. Why, we've been friends ever since we wore pinafores, and I'm not going to be shaken off as if we were strangers! 'Tisn't long, lad, since we were on the point of beginning a longer journey together.'

'No,' said Walto, gloomily. 'Hast heard how Yshbel is today?'

'Yes; I have been up to Pengraig to ask – I was thinking you would like to know before starting. Getting on splendid, Madlen says, and there's cross the old woman was because I called her so early. Her tooth grows longer every day. There's a brave girl, Yshbel Lloyd! Mestress, Treswnd ought to be proud of her, oughtn't it?'

'True enough,' said Mrs Gwyn, with a tremble of the lip which even Goronwy noticed.

He was not an acute observer, but when he saw his way, was prompt to act.

'I will go and bring the car out, and there's no need for Shoni today,' and mother and son were left to their final leave-taking.

She clasped him in a tender embrace.

'Perhaps, my boy,' she said,' I will never see you again! 'Tis a long way to Glamorgan, and I am getting an old woman. Don't be taken in by any of the foreigners you'll be meeting in the 'Works', Walto, bach! English, Scotch, and Irish girls, and all setting their caps at my handsome boy, but beware of them, Walto. Rather than that, my boy, l would prefer to see you take up with Yshbel Lloyd.'

'Mother,' said Walto, holding her at arm's length,' what nonsense you are talking. I am but a lad yet, and Yshbel Lloyd is nothing to me. What folly have you got in your mind? She is nothing to me – no more than the shepherdess on yonder mountain – so never waste another thought on Yshbel Lloyd except, indeed, in gratitude for saving our lives. Goodbye, mother, fach; I'll write often, and come and see you, perhaps in a year's time.'

Goronwy was already tapping his whip handle on the window.

'Come on, man,' he said, as Walto took his seat beside him in the car, and they jolted out of the yard together. 'Coaches and trains, they say, won't wait as our country cars will. Your mother is shocking heavy-hearted, Walto.'

'Yes,' said the latter, turning round to wave a last goodbye, 'she is full of all sorts of foolish fears. Women are odd creatures.'

'So they are,' said Goronwy, 'but, in my deed, you and I and father must always swear by them, since a woman saved our lives. Yshbel Lloyd and Catrin Rees are women, and there's old granny! Tan i marw, she's the best and sweetest of them all,' and thus chatting, they reached Caermadoc betimes, where Walto took his seat in the mail coach, which every alternate day met the train at a station twenty miles off.

On his return to Tredu, Goronwy gave Mrs Gwyn a cheery account of Walto's departure, considerably coloured by his desire to make the best of things, as well as to raise his own spirits.

''Twas a good thing the rain kept off, not to spoil Walto's new suit – indeed, he looked as much a gentleman as young Mr Rice Gwynne.'

'So I should think, indeed!' said the mestress, with a toss of her head, 'considering they are related. Why, Walto's aunt's mother was first cousin to Mr Rice Gwynne's grandmother, and because they have put two letters to the end of their name is no reason why Walto would not look as well as him. Did you mind his great coat, to put it in with him, Goronwy?'

'Yes, yes; and he went off as jolly as a cricket.'

'Well, indeed. Great thanks to thee; and come and see me sometimes – and – tell Yshbel Lloyd I am asking about her, and will never forget what she did for thee and Walto.'

'No, indeed,' said Goronwy, turning back at the gate of the clos, 'we can never forget that;' and away he went with an uncomfortable sense of loss, for Walto and he had been inseparable companions from their childhood.

At Pengraig, Yshbel was lying listlessly on Catrin's bed. The strain of the last few weeks, together with the excitement of the storm, had been a heavy drain upon her strength. The long tension of the nerves, which she had borne with great fortitude during the last few weeks, was suddenly relaxed, and she felt almost reluctant to take up again the battle of life. It was pleasant to lie there, in the old black bedstead, letting her thoughts roam at will back to the scenes of her happy childhood, and to know that her brave act had saved her friends and restored Walto to his mother's arms.

Madlen and Betto had been unable to withhold from her the account of her miraculous rescue by Catrin, and she had shrunk a little upon hearing it.

'Thee must get up tomorrow,' said Betto, who knew little of nerves and less of sensitiveness.

'Yes,' said Yshbel, 'I think I am lazy, for I feel quite well,' but she still lay quietly under the red and blue quilt, until one afternoon Goronwy came blustering into the kitchen.

'Look here!' he said,'we can't live any longer without Yshbel down there in the village. Tell her the people are all wanting to thank her, and I have a message from the mestress for her. Go, fetch her, Madlen, fach.'

'Well I'll try,' said Madlen; ''tis quite time she should get up. Come, lodes!' she said entering the 'penisha'. 'If thee doesn't get up, I think Goronwy Hughes will come in himself to fetch thee.'

'Tell him to wait and I'll come,' said Yshbel, and dressing herself hurriedly, she entered the kitchen. Goronwy waved his cap in the air.

'Yshbel, lodes! what'll I say to thee? Thou hast saved our lives, and if Walto were here now, he would have plenty of fine words to tell thee how grateful we all are to thee; but jar-i! l can't find anything better to say than "thanks from my heart, lass." 'Tis nice to be here today, to see thee looking so pretty after all, when we might be dragging about the bottom of the sea now if it wasn't for thee!'

'Oh, hisht!' said Yshbel, ''tis nothing to thank me for, because I couldn't help it; and, indeed to goodness, you owe as many thanks to Deio as to me, because it was he coming with me gave me courage to face the waves; but don't say more to me about it. I am not very strong yet, I suppose, and every word you say makes me feel like to cry.'

Goronwy, who had a masculine dread of a woman's tears, hastened to change the subject.

'Oh, as for Deio,' he said, 'the people nearly carried him home. I went to Caermadoc with Walto Gwyn on Tuesday. Didst know he was going so soon? There's sorry the mestress was to lose him; and she bid me tell thee, Yshbel, she will never forget what thou hast done for her and for us all. But there's a fool I am! See what I've done!' Yshbel had turned very pale, leaning her head against the whitewashed wall. 'Bring her a cup of tea, Madlen – that always cures women, I've noticed. 'Tis no wonder she's shaky. I'd better go, Yshbel, or I'll be making thee cry perhaps.'

'I'll come home tomorrow, if I shall sleep here one night more,' said Yshbel.

'Well, b't shwr,' said Madlen, 'as long as thee likes, for there's the bed empty. Catrin sleeps out as often as in.'

Yshbel drank her tea silently. She had known that Walto was on the eve of departure, but she had a faint hope that he might come to bid her goodbye, perhaps to thank her; and as she lay herself down once more to rest, she closed her eyes, and tried to disperse the tears which would well up in them. ''Tis better so,' she thought; 'Walto is gone, and I must forget him.'

Madlen, with a wonderful stretch of generosity never accorded to Catrin, had brought in a rushlight and left it on the windowsill.

Outside, in the twilight, a silent figure had drawn near the light like a brown moth. It was Catrin, who had been struggling with a strong desire to see and speak to Yshbel. Ever since she had carried her, with panting breath and trembling limbs, up the rugged path from the cave, a new-born interest had awakened within her towards the being, who, but for her, would have perished in solitude and darkness; the natural longing also for fellowship with one of her own sex possessed her. The old hatred was dying out, and giving place to a dawning and timid desire for sympathy and friendship. She hovered round the half-opened window, thinking how easily she could slip through the aperture and alight by the bedside, but she feared to startle its occupant. A dread that she might be repulsed, too, deterred her, and she decided to run the risk of being waylaid by Madlen, and enter in the ordinary fashion. The gloom of the kitchen favoured her, and Madlen's wooden shoes were clattering in the dairy. The door stood a little ajar, and, thus encouraged, she gently pushed it open and entered.

Yshbel, who had watched the slow opening of the door, was startled at the sight of Catrin. The perfect oval of the face, on which the dimples played like sunbeams on a lake; the dark, clear skin, like polished marble; the fine glow of health in cheek and lips; and, above all, the brown, velvety eyes, which so easily sparkled in mirth, or grew humid with feeling; the symmetrical moulding of the bare arms; the graceful contour of the bust and figure revealed by the thin brown frock – all made a picture of such uncommon beauty that Yshbel was struck with astonishment. She had been accustomed to think herself beautiful, accepting the fact without vanity; but here was a creature of far greater beauty than any she could boast of – this, at least, was her first impression as Catrin glided in through the slowly opening doorway. A connoisseur might have found it difficult to decide to which of these entirely contrasting styles of beauty belonged the palm, but Yshbel at once mentally surrendered her claims.

Timidity and anxiety to please vied with each other in Catrin's expressive face.

'Oh, Yshbel Lloyd,' she said, extending her hands, ''tis only me – Catrin Rees I am.'

'Well, indeed, I am glad thou hast come, Catrin, because I wanted to thank thee for bringing me safe to land. I would surely be drowned if it wasn't for thee.'

'Yes, I carried you up safe.'

'But where did you find me?'

'On the underground shore.'

'Ach-y-fi! 'tis a dreadful thought,' said Yshbel, with a shudder. 'I cannot bear the dark. I am keeping thy bed, I'm afraid. Where wilt sleep tonight?'

'Oh, in the shepherd's hut on Penmwntan, perhaps. Merlin is always finding me there and sleeping at my feet. 'Tis nice out there. I can see the stars through the roof, and I am happy when they are over me.'

'Art not afraid?'

'Afraid?' said Catrin, in genuine astonishment. 'Afraid of what? With God, and I don't know how many spirits, around me! No, indeed, I am not afraid.'

Yshbel looked long at Catrin before answering.

'Well, 'tis at home with Nanti Betto, and in the firelight and in the sunshine I like to be. Doesn't Madlen want thee to help her in her work?'

'No,' said Catrin, 'she does not want me, and father doesn't want me, nor Bensha; nobody in the world wants me, except, sometimes, Goronwy.'

'Art very fond of him, then?'

'Yes,' said Catrin, crossing her hands on her bosom.

'Yes, indeed, 'Twas for his sake I brought thee up from the cave.'

Here she suddenly became confused, and the colour mounting to her face, she bent her head a little as she added: 'But 'twas most for another reason.'

'What then?'

'Oh, because – Yshbel Lloyd, I want you to forgive me 'twas because I had wished you evil, and I would give my life to undo my wicked thoughts, and so I went over the cliff and found thee on the dark shore.'

'Over the cliff? Dear anw'l! then it is true what they are saying about thee, and what they are calling thee?'

'Oh, no, no!' said Catrin, dreading to hear the word which once she had been proud of. 'No, no; 'tis not true,' and shame scorched her heart and burnt her cheeks. 'I am only a poor simple girl.'

'Why did'st hate me then?' asked Yshbel.

Here was a question impossible to answer, so Catrin's head bent lower.

'Can'st not forgive me?' she said at length.

'Well, b't shwr,' said Yshbel, 'for thou hast saved my life,' but a little chill crept over her, which Catrin, watching her anxiously, detected at once, and a corresponding shiver swept over her.

'I will go now,' she said; 'the night is coming on. Will I put a shawl over you? 'Tis cold about two in the morning.'

'No,' said Yshbel, rather coldly; 'I am warm here, in thy bed.

But 'tis cold, I am sure, outside, or in the dark sea cave. Ach-y-fi, lodes! Stop at home and give up the stars and the spirits, and the sleeping out and things.' But Catrin had already half disappeared behind the door.

'Goodnight, Yshbel Lloyd,' she said, looking back with dark, earnest eyes, and a slight tremble in her voice. 'Indeed, I thank thee for forgiving me.'

'Goodbye,' answered Yshbel; and the brown moth flitted away as silently as she had entered.

In another moment a flood of regret rushed into Yshbel's heart, and she cried aloud, 'Catrin, Catrin! Come back!' But for answer only Madlen's face presented itself in the doorway.

'Wast calling?' she asked.

'Yes, I was calling Catrin. She has been here, and I didn't thank her half enough. Oh, I was cruel to her. Call her back, Madlen, I must thank her before I sleep.'

'Call her back?' said Madlen. 'Thou might'st call her back till midnight, and she wouldn't come. There's no telling where she may be by this time. Let her go, lass, and think no more of her,' and Yshbel was obliged to acquiesce, and slept one night more in the old black bedstead.

Catrin, lying awake in the shepherd's hut, looked thoughtfully out at the stars and pondered.

What was it? Was there some spell upon her? Was she a witch after all, so that she could never break through the line that seemed to divide her from her fellow creatures? For she had seen the tremor of suspicion that had crossed Yshbel's mind and quenched, as she thought, the friendliness which was beginning to grow up between them. What had she done to arouse that feeling of fear or distrust? Was it because she had spoken about God and the stars? Surely no! They must be the same to Yshbel, and she must love them too. What, then, could it be? Would she never see her again? Never have another chance of making friends with her? Yes, for it would please Goronwy, and she would try once more. Tomorrow she would take Yshbel a

present. What should it be? The chain of birds' eggs hanging on
the heather walls of the hut? The basket of shells which she had
decorated with seaweed? Or the hat of green rushes that she had
plaited for herself, and trimmed with a wreath of brown barley?
No; for Yshbel owned a hat with a white wing, a blue scarf also,
and would not care for a rough, rush hat. And she pondered
again, until suddenly a bright thought struck her, and pleasure
danced in her eyes and covered her face with smiles. The deep
red apples in the orchard, which had grown so delicious in the
sea breeze and the sunshine!

A basket of these would be welcome, she knew, for fruit was
scarce on that wind-blown coast; and with this happy fancy
gilding her thoughts, she fell asleep.

Next evening, in the twilight, she gathered her apples in the
orchard, where the old trees, gnarled and bent by the sea wind,
still bore fruit in abundance.

The ground was strewn with them, but none of these would
do, and climbing up into the branches, she filled her basket
with the crimson fruit. Sitting on the grass, she sorted them,
casting aside any that were marked with speck or flaw,
polishing them on her blue apron, and at last eating those
which she had cast aside, her small, white teeth biting into
them with ease, and disclosing the pink-tinged core and the
dark brown pips. She waited impatiently while the darkness
settled down upon rock and shore and whispering sea.

'She will like them, I know,' were her thoughts. 'They are
so pretty, and their sour is mixed with sweet.'

The storm was already a thing of the past, and there was no
trace of it in the gentle breeze that blew on Catrin's face as she
crossed the shore and neared the cottage, with the intention
of leaving her basket of apples on the sill of the little window,
through which she had watched Yshbel's preparations for the
fair. That window was dark tonight, but that on the other side
of the doorway was bright with the glow of the firelight; the
door was open as usual, revealing a scene of cosy home

comfort, which was strangely unfamiliar to the homeless girl without.

She heard the sound of voices as she approached – Yshbel's soft and musical, Goronwy's too – and with intense eagerness she watched them through the window, the former sitting on the little oak stool, Goronwy standing opposite to her and leaning against the chimney wall. He was looking unusually thoughtful.

''Tis no use trying to tell these things,' he was saying, 'because, lass, they are too deep to tell, but thee know'st how grateful we are to thee. We belong to thee, Yshbel; thou hast a right to order us anywhere – my father and Walto and I – for thou hast given us our lives.'

'Goronwy, don't thank me more; because, indeed, I am quite surprised myself that I was so fearless. God helped me no doubt, or I couldn't do it.'

'No, I suppose,' he answered, looking pensively into the fire.

'And then for Catrin to save me! Wasn't that wonderful? Oh dear, I didn't thank her half enough. There's pretty she is! Perhaps it is true what the people are saying, that she will bewitch thee, and some day thou wilt marry her.'

Catrin's cheeks burnt in the darkness; such a thought had never crossed her mind. She turned away, but a scornful laugh from Goronwy arrested her for a moment.

'Marry a witch,' he said, 'and fly to church on a broomstick!'

It was terrible. Catrin felt her heart shrivel within her, and hurriedly leaving her apples on the windowsill, she turned to the darkness, and fled across the sands, and up the mountain side to the shepherd's hut before she stopped. The words, 'Marry a witch, and fly to church on a broomstick!' rang in her ears as she flung herself down on her rough bed of heather, gathering her cloak around her. She shed no tears, and made no moan, but silently gazed through the broken roof at the stars that glittered above her, until in the early dawn she fell asleep.

CHAPTER XII

CATRIN'S LETTER

The *Lark* had not escaped without damage from the storm which had brought so much excitement to Treswnd, but her injuries not being of a serious nature, were only a boon to her owner, as they afforded him employment for the long months which must intervene, ere the stormy gales of winter should subside sufficiently to render it safe for such small crafts as 'slwbs and schoonaires' to venture once more out of port. Not only Morgan Hughes, but all the sailoring folk whose voyaging did not take them to too distant shores, spent their winters at home. It was, therefore, a time of pleasant home gatherings, which were impossible in the summer, or, at all events, lacked flavour while all the men were away.

At this season the herrings were salted, nets were dried and stowed away; the lasses dressed more carefully, and the lads more jauntily, as they dropped in of an evening to the hearths of their neighbours, where the women sat round knitting, while the men wove baskets, or read their newspapers, and argued hotly on points of politics or topics of religion. Ballads brought home from the fairs were read aloud in a sing-song voice, gossip was retailed, and songs and choruses made the rafters ring. At Sarnissa, old Gwen knitted in her chimney corner, Marged helping her through all intricacies, such as heel-turning, or 'increase' and 'decrease'. Goronwy read or made up his 'count book,' while his father sat smoking, his eyes fixed on the glowing embers.

'Oh, dang it! I can't get it right,' said Goronwy, pushing his fingers through his hair. 'You see if you can do it, father,' and he flung his pen aside.

'I was thinking,' said the captain, slowly rising, 'if we better leave Simon to mend the rails in Parcglas before we go to law?'

'Wait ten years then, or twenty,' said Goronwy. 'When did Simon Rees mend anything?'

'True,' said the captain summing up the 'count' with a dash under the total.

'There's a man for figures you are, father!'

'Yes, he was always doing his sums,' said old Gwen, smiling. 'He was a good boy, only too fond of the boats.'

'Well, we'll go to Caermadoc, and see how Mr Oliver is getting on with them papers,' said the captain; and a few days afterwards, when the fields were hard with the frosty east wind, and the sun shone like burnished gold on road and river, Goronwy and his father set off together, in the jingling car which had made so many journeys between Treswnd and Caermadoc, stopping at the blacksmith's, as Goronwy thought Flower's shoe required attention.

Deio seemed not a whit the worse for his adventure in the storm, and was standing at his anvil, in full talk with a young man of a pleasant countenance, whose town-made, well-fitting clothes, gave him the advantage over the country lads of the village. He passed out as Goronwy entered.

'Who was that?' asked Morgan Hughes, while Deio hammered at Flower's shoe.

''Tis the son of our new agent. They say Colonel Lloyd is not doing anything without his advice; he is looking after all the woods on the estate. 'Forrester,' I think they call him!'

'What does he want here?'

'Well, that's the thing, what *does* he want all the time, all the time? A new lock to the Garth gate he is wanting today; but 'tis wonderful what a lot of trouble people will take to get a lobster or a crab, and 'tis odd that Ben Powell's are so much better than others! There, that shoe will go to London with her!'

'What dost mean, man?' said Goronwy.

'Well, I mean that Yshbel is a very purty girl whatever, and it's my belief that 'tis her this youngster is looking after, and not lobsters nor locks. There's a lucky girl she'd be, but not more lucky than she deserves.'

'No, indeed,' said Goronwy, whipping up his horse to a trot, and passing Simon Rees as he drove his waggon into town.

'There's a face he's got,' said Goronwy, adding, 'Poor Catrin!' under his breath, for he had become very reticent about her lately; even the thought of her, which used to bring with it a buoyant sense of happiness, now brought a haunting disquiet.

'I wonder,' said his father, 'how that witch girl will like it when Parcglas comes back to us?'

'I don't think she'll care,' said Goronwy, 'only for her father. She is one that never thinks about herself, but all for other people.'

'She is a fool then, if she *is* a witch; and look ye here, Goronwy, 'Deio Go' was saying one day that she may bewitch thee into marrying her, for they say she's purty enough, but d— me if I'll ever consent to that. Remember Sarnissa's a good farm and large, and the *Lark* belongs to me nearly all, and thee'rt my only son, so I expect thee to pick out some tidy girl, with a good name, if she has no money, not a ragged croten like that, who sleeps no one knows where, and consorts with the devil, they say.'

'Oh, don't bother me,' said Goronwy, whose temper was none of the calmest, 'with your jumble of witches and money and courting. Who's thinking of such nonsense? Not me for many a long year. I think Parcglas must have muddled your brain, father, or you wouldn't be talking so foolish,' and Morgan Hughes, who was a little afraid of his son, said no more.

Arrived at Caermadoc, they made their way to Oliver's den, and were soon entangled in a labyrinth of legal terms, from which they emerged at length, very little wiser than when they entered. One thing was plain, however. Mr Oliver advised a short delay for his own accommodation as well as for further opportunity of looking into matters, a delay which Morgan Hughes had grudgingly assented to. His son had some difficulty in persuading him to leave the town before the sunset, as the streets were full of sea-faring men, whose ships were moored in the river for the winter, and at every corner they jostled up against an acquaintance, a 'blue' at the Mermaid being the inevitable result. At last they were safe in the car and rattling out of the town, their conversation never ranging far from Parcglas, or the probable course of the lawsuit which they were about to commence. As they drew near Treswnd, at a distant turn of the road they saw Simon Rees' waggon. "Tis a wonder he has got so far,' said Goronwy. 'There's drunk he was in the market today! But where is he?' he added, as, drawing nearer, they saw that Captain and Bess were grazing quietly on the bank at the side of the road.

'Be bound he's in the Hunter's Arms and the horses have gone on without him.'

'No doubt,' said Goronwy, but drawing still nearer, they saw a dark object lying on the road, and coming up to it found it was Simon, who had, in fact, lain there for nearly an hour, for it was a little-frequented road, except when market or fair drew people to Caermadoc.

'Dead drunk,' said Goronwy. 'What'll we do? We can't drive over him.'

'Lift him aside,' said Morgan Hughes, 'and leave him there till he sobers; Captain and Bess won't stray far.'

'Oh, jari! that will never do. I'll come back and drive them home,' said Goronwy, and alighting, he bent over Simon. He was sober enough now, and as Goronwy endeavoured to lift him, he groaned and opened his eyes.

'Leave me alone to die,' he said.

'What is it,' said Goronwy; 'has the waggon gone over you?'

'No; but I fell, and l broke something inside, I'm thinking.'

'Are you in pain?'

'Yes, but I don't feel my legs.'

'There's no doubt he's badly hurt,' said Goronwy, returning to his father, who sat in the car stolidly looking straight before him.

'What do I care,' he said, 'let him die.'

'I couldn't be such a brute,' said Goronwy, 'and if you won't help me, I must run back to the Hunter's Arms and get Jones to come and lift him into his wagon,' and running hurriedly back to the inn, he procured the assistance of the landlord and a friend who was smoking by the hearth.

When they reached the injured man, they found that Morgan Hughes' bark was worse than his bite, for he had alighted and was standing by his fallen enemy.

'Can't thee move, man?' he asked.

But Simon answered only with a groan.

'Well, here come Goronwy and Jones.'

They raised him carefully, and laid him at the bottom of the waggon, Jones, the Hunter's Arms, taking the reins and slowly driving homewards, his friend turning up a rough lane in search of Dr Jones, who lived somewhere in the vicinity. Goronwy also remounted.

'We better go on to Pengraig,' he said; and at the corner where the lane to Sarnissa branched off from the main road, he stopped, saying, 'There, father, take the reins; I'll run up to prepare Madlen;' and Morgan Hughes sullenly obeyed.

'What's the need?' he said; 'Jones will take him home safe enough. Come thou to thy supper.'

'No,' answered Goronwy.' I'll be home soon, but don't wait,' and his father jogged on, mumbling something about 'a headstrong mule as ever lived.'

Madlen received the news which Goronwy imparted with her usual exclamation.

'Well, bendigedig! I wonder it didn't happen long before. Is he alive?'

'Yes; and Dr Jones will be here soon, I expect. Put his bed ready.'

''Tis all ready,' said Madlen, turning down the bedclothes of a cupboard-bed which stood in a corner of the living-room. ''Tis upstairs he is sleeping when he is sober, but oftener than not he is tumbling into this one.'

'Well, he can't tumble in tonight, and how'll we raise him I don't know. Here's the waggon.'

The lumbering vehicle came slowly over the stubble in the yard, and as near the door as possible; Bensha, who had met it in the lane, following in a state of bewildered fright.

'What's the matter?' he gasped, realising that it was something more than drunkenness that kept that familiar figure so straight and still.

Goronwy explained, and Madlen, whose temper was invariably aroused by fright, added: 'Why, dost not see, thou dolt, that 'tis hurt the man is? Go and help to lift him out, thou old fool, instead of standing there like a hen with the gapes.'

And, with a push between the shoulders, she sent him stumbling towards the waggon, where Goronwy and Jones the Hunter's were already endeavouring to move the injured man. Instinctively the two elders took their instructions from the younger man, and gently they bore their heavy burden into the house, and placed him on the bed. They were surprised to find that Simon showed no signs of acute suffering, and augured well from the fact.

'Cheer up, man,' said Jones. 'Thee'lt soon be all right again, and we'll have a right hot glass of hollands ready for thee on thy first journey, from that square bottle, thee know'st!'

But Simon only gazed vacantly from one to another, though his eyes seemed to rest meaningly on Goronwy.

'Can I do something for thee?' said the latter. 'Dr Jones will be here soon.'

'The lo's fach,' was Simon's answer.

'I'll go and fetch her,' said Goronwy, and he left the house at once.

Jones the Hunter's, stayed on till the doctor arrived, who, after a careful examination, shook his head gravely.

'Is he badly hurt, sir?' he asked.

'Yes,' said the doctor, seriously; 'and that's all I can say at present.'

'Will he die?' asked Madlen.

'Yes, some day; and so wilt thou,' he said tartly, Madlen being no favourite of his.

Meanwhile, Goronwy had hastened over the fields to the cliffs in search of Catrin, but, failing to find her, had turned towards the shepherd's hut.

The wattled door was open, a fire of peat burnt on the ground, the blue smoke curling upwards and escaping through the 'star window,' as Catrin called the hole in the roof. The girl lay on the ground, leaning on her elbow beside the fire, while, with the other hand, she wrote carefully and slowly on a leaf of the copybook which Goronwy had given her. As he entered, she started to her feet.

'Goronwy!' she said, 'well, indeed. 'Twas writing to thee I was, lad. There's grand!'

'A letter?' said Goronwy. 'What for then, when I am here so often?'

'Thou hasn't been a long time, and I was afraid perhaps thee would never come again.'

'Catrin,' he said, seriously, 'thee'rt a good girl, and thou seem'st to have some strength that others have not got. Well, call it now to thy help, and be brave, for I have bad news for thee.'

All the colour had fled from the girl's face; her eyes were dilated and her voice trembled.

'Bad news? Of my father? What is it? Is he drunk?'

'No; he has had hurt. 'Twas a fall from the waggon. The doctor is with him, and he is in bed.'

But he spoke to the wind, for Catrin had already flown, on the wings of love, over the grey fields towards Pengraig, where, on entering the house, she was clutched by Madlen.

'Stop, lodes – don't frighten him! No screams, mind!'

'Away,' said Catrin, thrusting her aside, and, without ceremony, pushing between the doctor and the bed. Bensha tried to intercept her, but she shook off his hand.

'Away, all of you!' she said. 'This is my place. Father anwyl!' and stooping over the bloated face, now grey and pale with pain, she kissed his forehead and drew her fingers over his cheek. The old man fixed his eyes upon her, but could only whisper 'Catrin'. Still continuing her loving touches on his face and hair, she turned quietly to the doctor, saying: 'Isn't this my place, sir? I will never leave him again.'

'Right, my girl,' said Dr Jones; 'thou seem'st quiet enough, and wise enough. Drop thy mad pranks, and stay at home and nurse thy father. How's the arm?' he added.

'Oh, well, quite well! I am well and strong – tell me what to do for father.'

'Keep him quiet tonight,' said the doctor, 'and I will see him tomorrow.'

Later on, when he was gone, and the shades of night were closing in on the old grey farm, the girl sat on by the sick man's bed, murmuring soothing words of love and comfort, and making her requests known to Bensha and Madlen in such calm and womanly tones, that they obeyed in silent astonishment.

Goronwy meanwhile, when he had watched the last flutter of her brown skirt and the last wave of her hair, as it floated behind her in the wind, turned into the shepherd's hut. The fire still glowed brightly, Catrin's copybook lying beside it on the ground, where in the first shock of fright she had flung it. Picking it up Goronwy turned the leaves over with a smile, half of sadness and half of amusement. Here were the lines and pothooks which they had bent over one day on the cliffs. Here the first rude letters learnt on the sands at Traethyberil; here was the fast improving, though imperfect, writing; and here, at the end, the ink still wet upon it, the letter upon which she had been engaged when he found her. It began 'Anwyl frind – I am going to write you a letter. There's grand for me, Catrin Rees! You taught me, and I will never cease to thank you for that, but I am sorry that my first letter must be to say 'Goodbye' to you. I am thinking continually lately about our happy ways here on the cliffs and sands, and the more I am thinking, the plainer I am seeing that it is time for us both to give them up now, because I am not a child any more – I have nearly had my sixteen – and I see 'tis at home I ought to be now. Madlen will not be liking it, but I won't mind that. When we ask God to show us the way, we must walk in it when He makes it plain, mustn't we? So don't come up to the cliffs again to look for me, because I won't be there; not in the shepherd's hut too, nor on the sands when the moon is shining. And so goodbye, Goronwy. l am thinking I am helping you too, by this.'

'Catrin Rees wrote this letter!'

And this was the outcome of her silent communing with the starlit sky! When he had read the last word, he looked round with a weight at his heart that he had never felt before. Going out, he closed the wattled door, slipping the wooden bolt into its latch, and with something like a sigh he looked over the familiar landscape, now growing dim and dark. The sea still shone faintly with the last glow of the west; the puffins, too far out to be seen, alone disturbed the stillness with their hoarse cry of 'Arron! Arron!' Old Penmwntan reared his rugged crest behind him, the roar of the surf on the shore reached his ears, the lights glimmered in the cottages below as of old, but Catrin was nowhere to be seen, and the whole landscape seemed sad and lonely. He saw a light in Pengraig too, and wondered what scene had greeted her eyes when she entered. 'Perhaps,' he thought, 'Simon would be better tomorrow, and Catrin would again be out on the cliffs.' But no! He could not shake off the inward conviction that tonight was a turning point in his life, that tonight he would part with his boyhood, and take upon him the ways and feelings of youthful manhood, too long thrust aside for the charms of a Crusoe life.

On his way homewards, he stopped at Pengraig door. The light streamed out from the kitchen, and with it came the sound of low moaning, mingled with a murmur of soothing tones, which he recognised as Catrin's. Reluctant to disturb the sick man, he stood a moment listening, before he turned away to meet Madlen coming from the cowhouse.

'How is he now?' he asked in a whisper.

'Oh, the same; groaning sometimes, and talking about Catrin and Bess and the waggon. But think! Madam has come in, if you please, and 'tis "speak soft, Madlen," or "Open the window, Bensha," as if she was used to it all her life.'

'Well, 'tis a good thing, I should think. Hasn't thee always been grumbling because she wouldn't stop at home and help thee?'

'Oh, to help is all very well, but I'll have no one here to "mistress", I can tell thee!' and she raised her voice so that her words might be heard in the kitchen.

'Well, goodnight,' said Goronwy; 'and my advice is the same as Catrin's, "Speak soft, Madlen."'

It was a pity he could not see the toss of the head, and hear the snort with which she re-entered the house, it would perhaps have brought a smile to the lips which were unnaturally grave, and a lightness to the heart that was weighed down with a dull foreboding. Catrin had heard his question, although so subdued, and the voice with which she spoke in words of endearment to her father had trembled a little, but the shadow of her hand, on the old black dresser, continued to rise and fall regularly, as she fanned the damp face of the invalid.

The night fell, and the dark hours sped on; Madlen, in a half-hearted manner, offered to sit up, but was relieved to find the 'croten' would not abandon her post; so Bensha and she retired to the barn, and the old house was left to gloom, only lightened by the rushlight, which burnt on the shelf at the bedhead, and to silence, only broken by the moaning breath of the old man. Catrin sat on, watching the face grow paler and more collapsed, as the effects of the day's drink wore off, leaving in their place that terrible exhaustion which is often both cause and effect of excessive drinking. Towards the small hours the night grew bitterly cold, but she was inured to cold and hunger. She was not, however, indifferent to the unpleasant pests of indoor life, and watched with terror the black beetles that at midnight invaded the floor, and the spiders that wove their webs undisturbed in the corners of the room. Her thoughts wandered to the clean, dry heather in the shepherd's hut. She remembered the sweet smell of the furze blossom and the freshness of the sea breeze; and a deep throb of longing surged through her for the freedom of the life which she had relinquished. But a look at the helpless form on the bed banished the rebellious thoughts, and drew her, with the strong bands of love, towards the parent who had neglected her, and had often treated her with cruelty. That was all forgotten now; she remembered only that he was 'father', and that her love for him had never died out.

Contrary to every one's expectations, the doctor included, Simon recovered his strength considerably in the next few days, and continued to improve so much in appearance that Catrin was full of hope, as she sat patiently attending to his wants. He was soon well enough for her to rest many hours of the night on a small truckle bed, which she placed beside his, and carried to the 'loft' each morning when she rose. But the doctor continued to shake his head gravely, as she each day inquired eagerly:

'Isn't he better? Will he get well?'

In her anxiety for her father, she had forgotten the part which Dr Jones had taken in the attempt to immure her in the asylum. But as one day he gazed at her intently before answering her question, her first impulse was to fly, but 'love', the ruling motive of her life, conquered her fear, and she bore the doctor's scrutiny unflinchingly.

'What were you trying to catch me for?' she said, her voice trembling a little. 'I am only a poor girl, with plenty of troubles, who is not doing any one any harm. I am not mad,' she said, 'and I want to stop at home to nurse my father.'

'No, by Jove! you're not mad,' said the doctor. 'You're a very good nurse, and a very bonny lassie. I won't try to catch you again, 'merch i.'

'Will my father get well then?' she said, returning to the point of interest.

'I don't think so,' said the doctor. 'He may live for months, perhaps for years, but 'tis die he must at last, 'merch i. He will never be able to walk again.'

Catrin clasped and unclasped her fingers.

'Then he will never be able to drink again?'

'No, no, no!' said the doctor, 'only what I allow him. You hear? We must not cut it off at once.'

'No, sir; but gradually, I suppose – 'twill be less and less.'

'That's it; you're a sensible girl, and what the diwss we wanted to catch you for, I don't know! Goodbye now; give him plenty of bwdran. D'ye hear, Madlen?'

'No, I don't,' said Madlen. 'I don't hear people who talk to others; if they've got anything to say to me let them say it.'

'Well, then,' said the doctor, 'give Simon plenty of bwdran and plenty of fowls in the cawl.'

'Oh, b't shwr, I'll see to that,' and, to give her her due, Madlen catered well for the invalid, leaving the continual watching, the tender touches, and the soothing words, to Catrin as her share of the trouble, and the girl was well content with this arrangement.

Gradually she became more reconciled to her indoor life, although at first nothing but her strong love for her father would have enabled her to conquer her aversion to being pent up within the walls of a house. She was indefatigable in her attention to him, and before long began to feel that that dingy old living room held for her much of the interest and pleasure of life. Sometimes an intolerable yearning came over her for the freedom of her earlier life, and at such times, while her father slept, she would steal from the room, and race down the sloping fields, between the furze bushes, to the edge of the cliff, or up the side of the hill to its rocky summit – anywhere, anywhere for a breath of the fresh sea breeze, and the sense of communion with nature, which was the essence of Catrin's religion.

But the old kitchen was the scene of her daily life. There she conquered her discontent with her lot; there the most beautiful traits of her character were developed; and there, at length, she had the satisfaction of seeing her father's better nature awake, and shake off the depraved passions which had of late years enslaved him.

Occasionally, Goronwy came to inquire for Simon, marvelling much at the brave spirit which sustained the girl in her new mode of life; one which he knew must be entirely distasteful to her. Generally he saw only Madlen, whose wooden shoes were forever clattering around the house door. He had a strange reluctance to meet Catrin. It would but impress upon him more forcibly the loss of their happy days together, which, in spite of his unsentimental nature, he missed sorely.

One morning Madlen was absent and, entering the passage, he heard the voice which was so intimately interwoven with his life. Surely she was reading, and he listened in astonishment. She had made more rapid progress than he was aware of, for she had spent many hours of the long sunny days, poring over her books, a dog-eared *Robinson Crusoe* and an equally tattered Bible. Since she had been domiciled at home, a *Pilgrim's Progress*, which she had found on the 'llofft', had been added to her store of books, and out of these wells she drew both instruction and delight. Today it was the Bible from which she was reading. She was sitting on a low rush stool near the cupboard-bed, just where the sun, shining in through the deep square window, made a patch of light upon the red-brick floor: her brown hair was coiled into a knot at the back of her head. Leaning with one elbow on her knee, she held the big Bible spread out on her lap. Raising her eyes, she met Goronwy's. There was the old cheerful face, the keen bright eyes, that had danced with hers over many a joyous adventure.

'Goronwy,' she said, starting up, but instantly came the memory of those cruel words: 'witch!' 'broomstick!' Oh, shame, shame! and a hot blush overspread her face; but with the memory came the determination which had sustained her through the bitterness of the hour, when she had peered through Yshbel's cottage window, and overheard Goronwy's words. 'No, no; he shall see,' she thought, 'I can be quiet and peaceful, like other girls. I will make friends with the people, I will nurse them when they are ill, I will play with the little children.' All this, so rapid is thought, passed through her mind before she spoke again.

'He's asleep,' she said, pointing to her father.

Goronwy nodded.

'How art, lass?' he said, his face beaming with the pleasure of meeting his old companion, and into his mind, too, darted the memory of his conversation with Yshbel; and the words 'witch!' and 'broomstick!' which had made no conscious impression upon him at the time, now stood out in lurid clearness. Catrin, rising, stood before him, tall and slender, her face regaining its composure, and its peculiar look of peace and calm.

Spirituelle is the word that best describes the expression of her countenance. 'Witch, indeed!' he thought. 'Goronwy Hughes, thou wert a mean dog then!'

'Yes, I am well,' she said; 'I am glad to be with my father.'

'Dost not long to be out on the hills sometimes, lodes?'

'Yes,' she said, bending her head to hide the tears which suffused her eyes, 'but 'tis better like this, isn't it? Say yes, lad, for oh, indeed, 'twas for thy sake I was making up my mind to leave my old wandering life; because I thought, Goronwy, thou would'st be happier, with thy farm and thy work and Yshbel, if there was nothing up on the cliffs to draw thee away from them.'

'Hisht hisht!' said Goronwy. 'I have read thy letter in the shepherd's hut, and I see as plain as the daylight that thou art right, but tan-i-marw, lodes, I can't bring myself to say that I like it.'

Let us look at Goronwy as he returned from Pengraig to his farm work at Sarnissa. It was late autumn, and under the dull November sky, the landscape wore its mantle of sober browns and greys, the sea was still and of a leaden colour, the sands dry and white with the keen east wind. There was no outward brightness in the scene, and Goronwy's face reflected its want of life. An indescribable change had come over him – a change which had been chased away for a moment, by the sight of Catrin and a sound of the familiar voice, but it had resettled on his face as soon as he had left the 'clos'. He looked older, graver, more determined, and he walked with a more sober mien. Overtaking Dyc Pendrwm, who had grown into a lanky, knock-kneed bully, he would have passed him with a dry nod, but Dyc was never easily shaken off.

'How's the old man?' he said, walking abreast with Goronwy. 'I suppose thee'st been there?'

'Yes. He is better, the doctor says, but not likely ever to walk again.'

'Dei anw'l! there's a loss to the Hunter's,' said Dyc. 'They say that witch girl is nursing him like any Christian.'

Goronwy made no answer.

'I am going up one day on purpose to see her,' said Dyc. 'They say she's a very purty girl, and I daresay she is, indeed, or thou wouldn't have been so much in her company. Diwss anw'l! There's strange things happen, Goronwy! Dost remember how thou used to say "a man can do anything if he makes up his mind to?"'

'Well, what of that?' said Goronwy, stopping a moment at the corner of the Sarnissa lane, and looking at Dyc with a threatening air.

'Oh, nothing,' said Dyc; 'only there's Catrin settled down here for ever now, and there's Parcglas still belonging to Simon, and there's Yshbel Lloyd – well they say the agent's son is courting her; and if that's so, be bound she'll marry him. Don't thee look so fierce, man – I'm only saying what the other lads are saying.'

'Well, go home, and say the rest to the other lads then,' said Goronwy, as he turned abruptly up the lane.

CHAPTER XIII

THE FATE OF PARCGLAS

The subject which provided the gossips with the greatest interest was the evident courtship of Goronwy and Yshbel Lloyd. True, they were never seen together, but that was a strong proof of the truth of the rumour. Betto allowed herself to be approached upon the subject with evident satisfaction, though giving the usual mysterious denials.

Yshbel had altered much in appearance; she lost none of her beauty, but she did lose the spirit of animation which had given piquancy to her speech and bearing. The lips were not so ready to smile, nor the cheeks to blush. The small affairs of the household seemed to occupy her fully. She had put away from her entirely the memory of the coral necklace, with all the hopes and dreams connected with it, and had thrown in her lot completely with those around her. Goronwy was the brightest spot in her life; ever ready with his strong arm to help her and Ben with the boating or the fishing, prompt to suggest a remedy for every ill, always tender and kind, and withal so evidently bent on sweethearting, that she gradually came to look for his attentions, and to miss them if he were too long absent.

Betto was accommodatingly indulgent. On Friday nights – the night given up to courting in the country – she was sure to pile up the fire with peat and logs, to sweep up the hearth, pack Ben off to bed, and to find herself unaccountably weighed down with sleep about nine o'clock, when Goronwy generally arrived; and with her arms folded in her apron, she would sit in the background amongst the pots and pans, complacently dozing, but still keeping an eye upon the couple who sat in front of the glowing logs, chatting of old times, of wrecks, of the country gossip anent births, deaths, and marriages; and if sometimes Goronwy's arm slipped round Yshbel's slim waist, Betto gave a reassuring snore and was more awake than ever!

There was not much occasion for watching these two, for Goronwy, though warm enough in his attentions to satisfy Yshbel, was by no means an ardent lover, nor was he at all likely to be carried away by his feelings. He had grown sober beyond his years, and although Yshbel and he seemed perfectly content with each other's company, the other girls of the village would have considered him a 'laggard in love'.

The fire burnt up brightly, and the two shadows on the wall bobbed up and down with the flame, while the wind roared in the chimney.

'Hast seen Catrin lately?' asked Yshbel looking up from her knitting. 'There's a strange thing that her father's illness changed her so suddenly!'

'Yes,' said Goronwy, laconically; and he was silent so long, staring into the fire, that Yshbel asked again: 'Hast seen her lately?'

'No, indeed,' he answered, starting; ''tis nearly a month since I was there. I must go again on Monday. Poor Simon will never get well, they say. My father is shocking vexed about it, because he doesn't like to go to law while Simon is ill, but now he is determined, and 'tis coming on at once.'

'Well, indeed,' she said,' 'twill be hard to lose a large slice of their land like that.'

'It has been hard for us this many a long year then. Right is right, thou seest, and law is law!'

'Yes, yes – 'tis only right I know.'

''Tis a beautiful field,' said Goronwy.

'Yes; and 'tis such an odd shape, standing out by itself like that, the sea is nearly making its way round it.'

'It has been the same for hundreds of years, but even if 'twas an island 'twould belong to Sarnissa.'

'Yes, no doubt,' said the girl, and after a short silence she once more ventured a suggestion. ''Twas a long time ago it went to Pengraig, Goronwy, and 'tis a small field – canst not persuade thy father to let it alone?'

'Dei anw'l! No! He thinks of it night and day, and besides I have made up my mind, since I was a boy, to get it back to Sarnissa, and I always do what I say I will! Thee know'st how hard 'twas to plead with thee, but 'twasn't likely I was going to let that Forrester gather the prettiest flower that grows on the coast! Not Goronwy Hughes!' with a side jerk of his head.

Yshbel blushed and laughed, and Betto snored more loudly than ever. And so they chatted and wiled the hours away, while outside the waves plashed on the shore, and the rushes bent before the wind.

At last Ben thumped on the wooden partition, and Betto started up.

'Come, children!' she said. 'Caton pawb! what a time of night! Why did you let me sleep so long?'

Goronwy rose, and, holding Yshbel's hand, drew her with him through the doorway into the blustering night. In spite of the wind, she drew her shawl around her, and accompanied him a little way.

''Tis too cold to be out tonight,' she said, stopping at the turning of the path.

And he let her go without much ado, and hurried up the lane, breasting the high wind with a cheery song on his lips.

Yshbel, too, turned homewards contentedly.

The stars shone brightly, and the moon was rising. Once these charms would have tempted her to linger on the edge of the tide, to dream, to muse; but now there was little lingering or dreaming in her life. She knew the stars were bright, and that the waves broke musically as ever on the shore, but the wind blew keen, and the hearth at home was warm and cosy.

She had her work to think of, her small duties to attend to, and all the sweet dreams and fancies of girlhood must be thrust aside and buried with the memory of her coral necklace.

As for Walto, she never allowed herself to think of him, and quite believed that her love for him was dead, unconscious that in her bosom dwelt a warm and living bird, that was ready, at the first glint of freedom, to flutter its wings and start into life again.

On the following Sunday Goronwy made his appearance at Pengraig. It was ten o'clock, and on the still morning air came a little tinkling from the belfry of Penmwntan church.

Simon, shaved and washed, looked clean and comfortable in his bed, supported by pillows, in a sitting posture. There were signs of sickness and weakness in his face, but the expression was strangely altered from one of sullen discontent, to one of patience and almost of cheerfulness.

Goronwy's usual greeting of 'Hello!' roused him from a doze. 'How are you, Simon!' he asked, a little awkwardly, for Parcglas and the pending lawsuit came into his mind. 'There's comfortable you look, man! In my deed, I wouldn't mind being in your place.'

'Oh,' said Simon, ''tis easy to say that, but thee doesn't know what it is to lie here, and hear Captain and Bess neighing in the yard. But I'm not complaining. 'Twas time to stop me, before the devil had me.'

Goronwy was silent, not knowing what to say, while the old man fumbled for something, which he at length drew from under his pillow.

'This letter,' he said, his voice and his hands trembling, 'I had yesterday from Oliver, the lawyer.'

'About the lawsuit, I suppose?' said Goronwy, a hot feeling of discomfort flushing his face. 'Father waited as long as he could, but Oliver says it must come on now or never. "Right is right, and law is law," and—'

'Yes, yes,' said Simon. 'No one has more respect for the law than I have, and the law has given me Parcglas, so I will never give it up. 'Tis nothing to me now – Parcglas or Parcgwyn, nor any of the fields – but for the sake of the lo's fach I will fight for it, if I have to spend my last penny.'

'Well, b't shwr,' said Goronwy, soothingly, 'if you were well now, you would enjoy it.'

Simon again muttered something about 'the lo's fach'.

'Oh, leave her out,' said Goronwy. 'Diwss anw'l! Catrin wouldn't care a straw, only for your sake.'

'Morris ffeirad was here yesterday; he was asking me if I had made my will. Of course I have, long ago. A man won't die a bit sooner for making his will I don't remember it exactly, but I know Jones, the lawyer, said 'twas the best I could do for the lo's fach. He's got it safe.'

At this moment Madlen entered.

'There's grand doings here today, Goronwy,' she said.

'What'st think, bachgen? We're going to church if you please, and here's the lady!' and Catrin entered, blushing with shyness, while Bensha followed, his head bent almost on his shoulder, in his endeavour to take a whole length view of the girl.

'There's for you!' he said pushing her towards the bed, where Simon lifted his head to look at her. And Goronwy thought she was worth looking at.

'Art going to church, Catrin?' he said. 'Wel din!'

'Yes,' she answered, with her old nervous habit of clasping and unclasping her fingers. 'Yes, I think I want to go to church, like other girls; but, indeed, Goronwy, there's afraid I am! Will any one speak to me, dost think?'

'Yes – b't shwr,' said Goronwy, 'I will. Come on; we'll go together.'

'There's no need for that,' said Simon, hurriedly. 'Bensha is going, but look here, lad, thee'lt not let them laugh at her!'

'Laugh at her? What for? She looks better than any of them!'

'Was this possible?' thought Catrin. 'Was the world so beautiful, so golden, that she should walk to church with Goronwy, and feel herself no disgrace to him? Dressed in good clothes, the blue sky above her, the church bell calling her to prayers!'

Such a state of things would be like Paradise to her. But no! It must not be! What would Yshbel say? What would Goronwy feel, should any one point to her, and whisper 'witch'? And almost before the happy thought had suffused her mind with joy, she had put it away from her.

'No; I had better go with Bensha,' she said. 'He will be alone, because Madlen is stopping at home for me today.'

And so the matter was allowed to arrange itself, and Goronwy sauntered off alone, but accompanied by the image of a lovely face, blushing and dimpling with pleased shyness.

When, half an hour later, he entered the church, he saw Catrin seated at Bensha's side, and looking much perplexed at the intricacies of a prayer book, which he had thrust upon her. Her presence seemed to excite the congregation, for, in every direction, heads were turned round to look at her; the country girls tittered, and the lads nudged each other, while Catrin, trembling and confused, rose and sat down with her neighbours, and longed for the cliffs and the fresh sea breezes!

Even Mr Morris, as he read the 'Te Deum', fixed his eyes on the girl whose slender figure filled Madlen's usual place. Goronwy looked as heated and annoyed as he felt – he knew not why. Catrin's appearance was in his eyes absolutely pleasing, and although Yshbel Lloyd sat near, in all her pale pink beauty, no one could look at Catrin without feeling her superior charms.

Why, he would like to know, should that yahoo, Dyc Pendrwm, stare at Catrin, and then stoop in his pew to laugh? Why did the girls titter? Why did Yshbel even, after looking round, turn towards Betto with a smile of amusement?

It was altogether hateful; and Goronwy's face burned with indignation and resentment.

Catrin's toilet had been well considered; for days she had prepared for this, her first appearance at church, diving into the old coffer in the llofft, where her mother's clothes had lain stowed away for many a long year.

'This one,' she said to Madlen, 'dost think it will fit me?'

'Yes; fit it on, 'twas one of her gowns before she was married, and when she was as slim as thee, I'm thinking.'

'Was she very pretty?' asked the girl, as she buttoned up the front of the gown, and pulled out the loose sleeves which were reeved at shoulder and wrist.

'Oh, anw'l!' said Madlen, 'they say there wasn't such a pretty woman round the bay.'

'What will I wear round my neck with it?' asked Catrin, for the bodice was cut low.

'This red silk handkerchief,' suggested Madlen.

'Oh no; this muslin with the frills. I like this gown – the brown is like the ploughed fields, and the green splashes are like the young corn growing in them.'

Madlen tittered into her fist at this remark, but on the Sunday morning, when Catrin was dressed, she graciously allowed that 'she would do!'

The girl herself was perfectly satisfied with her toilet, until the important matter of headgear came to be considered. Her mother's tall hat lay in the coffer, swathed in paper bands, and she had fitted it on, but she could not make up her mind to wear it.

'No, not that,' she said. 'I can't, I can't! What will I do?' and she had resorted to her hat of rushes with a wreath of barley, which, in truth, was perfectly suitable to the rest of her attire. Under it, her face, with its ever-changing expression, its play of dimpling smiles, the liquid brown eyes, and the straying curls of brown-black hair, looked bewitchingly charming, and Goronwy had felt it so.

On Sundays, the village girls abjured their rustic costume entirely, vying with each other in their attempts to follow the

English fashions. Simplicity was a thing to be shunned on the first day of the week, and the girl, who on weekdays felt quite at home in a ragged skirt and wooden shoes, was complacently happy on Sundays in a hat as expensively trimmed as a lady of fashion's.

It was no wonder, therefore, that Catrin's rush hat excited the risibility of the congregation, which, as it streamed out into the churchyard, divided itself into little groups, all having for their centre of interest Catrin's hat of rushes, while the unconscious owner of it walked serenely home by Bensha's side, very happy in having accomplished the grand event, on which her thoughts had been centred for many a day. She had been to church! She was dressed in Sunday clothes! Goronwy Hughes had nodded and smiled at her as she passed him in the churchyard! She was going home to take off her best gown and kerchief, and lay them carefully away in the coffer. She was just like any other country girl.

In the evening, when the sun had set, when the tea things had been cleared away, and Madlen was sitting by the fireside singing hymns, while Bensha had departed for the evening service at church, she made her escape from the house, and, running down the fields, had reached the lonely cliffs, where, between the furze bushes, she could feel herself once more alone. Here, standing in her favourite attitude of prayer, with her hands outstretched, a smile parting her lips, her eyes fixed upon the brilliant stars, she held communion with her God. In the morning she had tried, in Penmwntan church, to realise that she was there to pray, and had found it very difficult to do so, but here on the hillside there was nothing to come between her soul and the Great Spirit Who had created her; and when, in the darkness, she returned to Pengraig – although Catrin was not free from the sorrow which must ever be the companion of love unrequited – there was no root of bitterness to trouble her heart.

'Come here, lass,' said her father, as she entered. 'Dost know

that that devil Morgan Hughes is trying to get Parcglas away
from us, as his great grandfather did before?'

'Yes,' she answered, her mind full of the soft impressions of
night, which had surrounded her outside on the cliffs, the
heaving sighing of the sea, the glorious galaxy of stars, the
soughing of the sea wind. 'Goronwy has told me; 'tis a pity,
but 'twill not make much difference to you, lying here, father
bach, we shall have enough without Parcglas, though the
flowers do grow finer there than anywhere, I think, and the
smell of the cowslips is stronger.'

'Smell of the cowslips!' said Simon, contemptuously.

'Thou'lt miss more than the smell of the cowslips, when that
thief gets Parcglas; but I'll spend my last penny to fight him.
The law was my grandfather's friend, and the law will be mine!
I swear it shall, if money can do it; and listen to me, lodes –
thee'lt never side against thy old father, and be friends with
those who rob him of his lands – eh?'

Catrin was standing by his bedside, her head bent, her
fingers picking at the coverlet. She had never realised that her
father felt so keenly the possibility of losing the little field,
which had been the object of interest and litigation to so many
of her own, as well as Goronwy's ancestors.

'Oh, father!' she said at last, 'I will never side with those who
are your enemies, but—'

'"But" won't do for me,' said Simon, raising himself on his
elbow. 'I must have it plain from thee tonight.'

His cheeks were flushed, and Catrin, observing this,
endeavoured to soothe and pacify him.

'Goronwy is not your enemy, father – indeed, indeed, he is
not, and I know—'

'Goronwy is the very one that I want to be sure of my
revenge upon. Thee must never speak to him.'

'Oh, father, father!' cried Catrin, 'I can't promise that. I can't,
indeed, indeed; and I won't. Goronwy and I have been friends
so long time!'

'That's it, that's it,' said Simon, 'and that's why I must have a promise from thee tonight, that if the case goes against us, thou wilt never marry Goronwy Hughes.'

'Oh, father – hush!' said the girl, and covering her face with both hands, she burst into tears, Simon falling back on his pillow and watching her impatiently.

Marry Goronwy! Why, oh why, was such a thought thrust continually upon her mind? Goronwy, who had never thought of such a thing? Goronwy, who loved Yshbel, and would marry her some day!

It shocked and pained her to have the idea thus forced upon her. It brought before her so plainly the truth which she was for ever schooling herself to forget; for, if such a thing as a perfectly pure, unselfish love is possible, it glowed in Catrin's heart for the companion of her youth, and it was the sudden realisation of this, occasioned by her father's words, the sudden development of the passion that had slumbered in the girl's heart so long, that burst into flame in a moment.

'What art crying about, child?' asked the old man, irritably. And Catrin dried her eyes.

''Tis nothing, father. I will promise you, indeed. I thought you wanted me to promise never to *speak* to Goronwy – that, I would never! But marry him? Such a thing never came into his head, nor mine. He is going to marry Yshbel Lloyd, and they are very fond of each other.'

'Is that true?' asked Simon, 'then it's all right.'

He slipped contentedly into his place, and Catrin sat patiently beside him, watching the drooping wick of the dip candle and listening to Madlen's low crooning, as she sat on the settle swaying backwards and forwards, and nursing her arms in her apron, while the old clock ticked, the owl hooted in the chimney, and the two stunted ash trees that grew at the pine end of the house stooped in the wind, and swept the roof as though the wing of some large night bird had brushed over it.

Night followed night and day followed day, and still Simon lay helpless in his bed, and Catrin watched and tended him with unflagging tenderness.

The winter had passed, the spring had come with bud and blossom, but it had been a season of unprecedented rains, and the world seemed sodden and damp, so that nothing less than the hot summer sun would dry it.

The *Lark* was away once more, and Goronwy had gone with his father to make some purchases at one of the seaports on the bay. There had been a thunderstorm in the evening, the sun sinking in a bed of lurid light. Lights glimmered late in the village, the cottagers being somewhat disturbed by the unusual violence of the storm, but at last all was darkness, and every one had fastened his door and retired to rest.

At Pengraig alone a light still burnt, and many times during the night, a slim white figure might have been seen stooping over the old man's bed.

About two o'clock in the morning, when the night was coldest, Catrin rose again, and was relieved to hear, by his regular breathing, that sleep had come to chase away the nervous excitement which the storm had caused. She was about to retire again on tip-toe, when a strange and weird sound startled her, and caused her to stand still in affright.

What was it? A hollow, rumbling sound, a tremble of the ground, and surely a surging of the waves which she had not noticed before.

Her father still slept on, but Bensha and Madlen had been roused from their slumbers, for the house door opened, and the former, only half dressed, appeared, pale with fright, his eye more askew than ever.

'What is it – eh?' he asked. 'The end of the world – eh? But I didn't hear the trump – eh?' and Madlen followed him, in great agitation and terrible *déshabille*.

'What is it, Catrin? Thee'st a good girl; canst not pray, lodes?

Bensha, thou old fool, thee'st always talking about prayer – canst not raise a bit of prayer now, man?'

'Hush, hush!' said the girl, endeavouring to calm their fears, though, in truth, she was much alarmed herself. 'There it is again! But, Bensha, if it is the end of the world, God is with us – wait till I dress a bit, and we'll go out and see. Something has happened, no doubt—'

'Out?' almost screamed Madlen. 'I, out on such a night? Never! Go you, Catrin fach, and see what's the matter.'

Catrin was soon cloaked and hooded, and leaving the house, made her way down to the cliffs. Once under the night sky, she felt safe, and all her fears vanished as she saw the stars which glittered between the clouds.

All was still as usual, only the dashing of the waves at the base of the cliffs, and the sighing of the wind in the broom and furze bushes.

Presently voices reached her on the wind, and lights moved about on the shore. She determined to make her way down to them, and although she shrank a little from encountering the villagers, curiosity impelled her to venture.

Passing down the slopes, she entered the field immediately above Parcglas, where Goronwy had struggled with her at their first meeting. Reaching the low hedge of sods which divided the two fields, she climbed over it, only to see, in the dim starlight, that something had strangely altered the conformation of the ground, and she stepped hastily back, deciding to wait for daylight to discover what had happened.

Making a detour, to return on the other side of the farm, she saw approaching her a knot of people, guided by the glimmering light of a lantern.

'Take care,' said somebody, 'keep to the right.'

''Tis plain enough,' said another, 'Parcglas has slipped into the sea! Come back! Ach-y-fi! We're on uncanny ground; p'r'aps it's some of that witch girl's tricks!'

'Oh, nonsense,' said Ben Bowen's bass voice. 'What for

would she ruin her own land? No, no; the girl seems quiet enough now; but, indeed to goodness, dear people, I think the Lord is dealing with Pengraig somehow!'

Catrin shrank back into the darkness, and reaching Pengraig, succeeded in allaying Bensha's and Madlen's fears, sufficiently to persuade them to return to the barn and wait for morning.

With the early dawn she was out again, but not before the villagers were astir. Parcglas was evidently the centre of interest to all, and as she made her way down towards that portion of the land that abutted upon it they trooped up to meet her. In the night there had been a strange falling away of the coast, one of those sudden subsidences which from time to time break up the rugged outlines of the bay. Parcglas had gone, and where it had once adjoined the cliff, there was now a deep fissure in the ground, beyond which the little field lay spread abroad on the sands below, a jumble of earth and sods and stones, the sea pinks and primroses still smiling up at the sky in some spots where they had slipped uninjured among the debris.

Catrin's eyes filled with tears, as she saw the cowslip clumps which would never bloom again, for every incoming tide would wash away all that remained of Parcglas, and leave but the stones and gravel to mark the place where it had stood.

'Here's a strange thing!' said one of the villagers, lifting his hands. 'Such a thing hasn't happened since the time of my great-great-grandfather, when I have heard my father say that a part of Tredu fell into the sea.'

Catrin ventured closer to the knot of people.

''Twas a dreadful noise in the middle of the night,' she said.

'Yes,' said Mali; 'thee wasn't out when it happened?'

'No; I was watching my father.'

'Dir anw'l! Thee wast in thy right place then;' and she drew away, rejoining her companions.

''Tis very plain,' she said, 'that the Almighty is angry with Pengraig!'

'Yes; and Sarnissa too! Not one of them shall have it for all their law.'

A little child, impelled by curiosity, approached the edge of the fissure, and Catrin, drawing him back, stooped to kiss him, but his mother hurried towards them, and dragging the child roughly away, said: 'There, let him alone!'

Catrin turned homewards silently, her heart saddened, not only by the loss of her favourite field, but still more so by the evident dislike of the villagers. 'No, they will never love me,' she thought. 'Their little children will never be allowed to put their arms round my neck – oh, gwae fi! That mother had lived, perhaps then they would never have called me a witch!'

She wondered how to break the news to her father. Would it hurt him? Would it excite him? Perhaps it would kill him! And, in fear and trembling, she entered the house door where Bensha and Madlen awaited her.

''Tis Parcglas,' she whispered, 'has fallen down!'

'Dei anw'l! There's a good thing,' said Ben' 'that the cows were not there last night! How will we tell the old man?'

'I will,' said Catrin, drawing near the bed where Simon was just stretching in his first yawn.

'Father, see this cup of tea that Madlen has just brought you,' and when it had been disposed of, she added, 'and now let me tell you my news. I have been out early, father, and what do you think – some of the cliff has slipped away!'

'What part?' asked Simon, eagerly. 'Near Parcglas?'

'Yes.'

'How much of it? Has any of the field gone?' and he lifted himself on his elbow in excitement.

'Yes, father.'

'How much, child? How much?'

'All, father! It is lying in a tumbled heap on the shore below.'

'Gone?' said the old man. 'Art sure, lodes?'

'Yes, indeed! gone, father. Don't vex about it.'

She was dreading the effects of her information, and when

she saw the old man fall back on his pillow, as if in a state of collapse, she feared lest she had caused him mortal injury. What then was her astonishment, to hear from the bed a low chuckle – there was no mistaking it – a chuckle of enjoyment.

'Well, tan i marw!' said Simon, 'I never heard such a thing in my life! I couldn't have managed it better myself! Morgan Hughes may whistle for it now. Catrin, lodes, art sure he can't plough it, or plant potatoes on it down there on the shore?'

'Never again, father! Two or three tides will wash it flat, and two or three months will cover it deep in sand.'

There was another chuckle from the bed; Simon rubbed his hands, his eyes gleamed with pleasure, and he called for his breakfast before Madlen was ready with it.

'Well bendigedig!' she said, 'losses seem to agree with some people"

As the morning advanced, the clouds broke up more and more, the sun rose bright and warm, and the sea sparkled and curled under the light breeze.

Round the right horn of the bay a little ship appeared, making its way with the foam at its prow and a smooth line in its wake. The sails were full, the red pennon fluttered in the wind, and Marged's patch on the sail showed out bravely in the sunlight, for it was the *Lark*, with Morgan Hughes and Goronwy on board, and little Tim Bullet asleep on a coil of ropes.

'Wake up, boy,' said the captain, 'or thee'll be a lazy land-lubber some day. Sailors don't sleep when port is in sight.'

The boy rubbed his eyes, and was wide awake at once.

''Tis a fine morning after the rain,' said the captain.

'Thee'lt have to fetch Ben Bowen to help us get this machine into the boat, Goronwy.'

'Yes; yes, 'tis an awkward passenger no doubt but 'twill be fine in the fields at Sarnissa, father.' The captain did not answer; he was standing at the prow looking through the telescope, and there was scarcely an exclamation or oath in the

Welsh language which did not fall from his lips, as he stood transfixed, with the glass to his eye.

'Well, mawredd anw'l! 'tis true,' he said at last, laying the glass down and walking excitedly up and down the deck.

'What, in the name of wonder, is the matter with you?' said Goronwy, and, taking the glass, he too stood transfixed with astonishment.

'She's not there!' said the captain hoarsely, grasping his son's arm. 'She's gone, bachgen! Not a sign of her waving hair, nor her skirts – nor anything! Good God! What's the meaning of it?'

''Tis true,' said Goronwy; 'the 'White Lady' is gone! The stream has altered its course, father, but where is the waterfall I don't know.'

'Put on full sail,' said the captain, and the little ship ploughed through the water bravely, her masts creaking, the wind whistling through the rigging, and the captain stumping up and down in great excitement, which increased as they drew nearer the land, and saw plainly what had happened.

'Parcglas has slipped down, father; 'tis a heap of rubble on the sands. The tide is reaching it now; 'twill be all swept away soon.'

Morgan Hughes was silent; the completeness of the catastrophe overpowered him, and in silence he cast anchor in the usual place.

Goronwy, though much disturbed himself, endeavoured to hide his excitement, for his father's sake, dreading lest this unexpected downfall of all his hopes might upset the mind which had long been too much occupied with the subject.

The mowing machine was safely landed, and the neighbours crowded round with expressions of admiration, mingled with descriptions of the collapse of Parcglas.

'Such a noise,' said one; 'we thought 'twas the day of judgment! What wilt do now, man? There'll be no need for a lawsuit now, for the Lord has taken the matter into His own hand.'

Morgan Hughes made no answer, but, returning to Sarnissa, sat long, lost in thought. At last he rose, and stretching himself with a yawn, said:

'Well, I don't care a cockle shell if Parcglas has gone to the devil. So long as Simon Rees doesn't get it, I'm satisfied!'

CHAPTER XIV

GRANNY'S ANGEL

Five peaceful, uneventful years have passed away since we last looked at Treswnd and its inhabitants. They had been years of that dull inaction which sometimes falls over a country neighbourhood with no apparent reason. No abnormal storms had visited the bay. Walto Gwyn's departure, which somewhat interested the community, had been forgotten. Simon Rees' accident, ending so tamely, had also sunk into oblivion; even Catrin Rees' eccentricities were things of the past. A few old people had died, and had been carried to Penmwntan churchyard. A few babies had arrived on the scene; but, upon the whole, a restful quiet had hung over the countryside, and the months had rolled on with unvarying monotony. The lads and lasses had grown into men and women, each taking his or her part in the business of life; while the children took their places on cliff and sea and shore. Over those whose simple history we have followed in the foregoing pages, time had flowed with outward tranquillity too, though their inner lives had not been exempt from man's usual share of joy and sorrow, of peaceful happiness as well as silent endurance, and strife with the strong passions and emotions that underlie the most uneventful life.

One evening, in early spring, Deio Go worked late at his forge. It had been a busy day for him, and now, at the last moment, Goronwy Hughes had brought two horses to be shod, saying, as excuse for the lateness of the hour, that he had been to Caermadoc fair.

'What today?' said Deio. Why didst not go yesterday? The second day's fair is only pigs and girls, they say.'

'That's just it,' said Goronwy; ''twas pigs I wanted.'

He had altered much since we last saw him. He was broader and more manly looking, with the same open countenance and same pleasant mouth, and withal the same rough-and-ready manner, with the same rather dictatorial tone of voice as of old too, which had made him more admired than loved in the village; but there was a something gone from his personality, an indefinable something that had lent a charm to the otherwise rather overbearing manner. Was it the sprightliness of youth only that was missing? Or was there a tinge of sadness and discontent in the face, which, when we saw him last, beamed with the keen enjoyment of youth and health. Perhaps it was only the inevitable impress that time leaves upon us, as he steals from us, one by one, the romantic visions of early youth!

Deio, who always hammered his thoughts well before he uttered them, sent the sparks flying, and asked, 'What size?'

'About fifteen score.'

'H'm, I might have saved thee the trouble of going to the fair; I have two pigs in the sty would have suited thee exactly, but thee'st so silent and to thyself lately, man! What's the matter with thee? Diwss an'wl! there's no one in all Treswnd ought to be happier than thee;' and again he made his anvil ring.

Goronwy, far from resenting Deio's remarks, sat down on an upturned cask, and burst into a laugh, which showed the strong white teeth were still there.

'Well, tan i- marw! Deio,' he said, 'there's never a shoe to one of the horses, but I can count a scolding with it. What's the matter with thee, man, lately? There's neither right side nor wrong to thee – not when I come near thee whatever. Ever since that day of the storm thou hast scolded me, whenever thou hadst an opportunity, and, indeed to goodness, thou hast a right. But have it all out, man. What's the matter with thee?'

'Well, then, why dost not get married? There's the matter with me! 'Tis five years ago, Goronwy, but I will never forget Yshbel Lloyd's face that day. I don't know much about angels, but I think they look like that, when they have a message to deliver. Her body was with me in the boat, but her spirit was with thee in the *Lark*. Before that time, I had a thought of trying for Yshbel myself, but, jari! after that day I would as soon go up to the squire's daughter, and ask her to marry me! And that's the girl thou art keeping waiting thy good pleasure all this time. Marry her off at once, man. Marriage is a smooth sea, when you have once dashed through the breakers, they say.'

'Well, that's thy opinion, but thee know'st no more than me about it. Some say marriage is a smooth sea at first, but there's breakers ahead. Make haste with that shoe, and I'll tell thee something that I wouldn't tell any one else, because they'd have no business to know. 'Tisn't me, 'tis Yshbel that is putting it off continually. Dang the women! They never know their own mind, I'm thinking. 'Tis always, 'Oh, wait for the spring,' or 'wait till the harvest's over,' or, 'I'm so young to be mistress over a large farm', or something of that kind. But at last whatever, I have made it plain to her, it must be before this year is out or never.'

'Right, 'machgen-i! Oh, there's no use giving way to the women – not too much whatever, or they'll walk over you when you're married.'

'Not Yshbel,' said Goronwy, who, like all men, liked to have the monopoly of finding fault with his women kind. 'She is different to every other woman, I think; so gentle she is, and so patient, and spirited with it all – no, I'm not afraid to say there's not a better temper in the world than Yshbel's!'

'Not a better girl nor a prettier, in the world, thee'st right,' said Deio; 'and I won't blame thee any more. I didn't know 'twas that way,' and he nudged Goronwy, gently as he thought, but with such violence that a box of nails which he held fell to the ground.

'Thy elbows are like sledge hammers, man,' said Goronwy, as they both fumbled about on the floor for the nails.

'The village people are all blaming thee shocking, Goronwy,' said Deio, rising. 'What'll I say to them?'

'Say what thee likes. I don't care that, what they say;' and he flipped his fingers, as he led his horses out of the forge. But although he treated the matter in such an off-hand manner in Deio's presence, his smile died away as he rode down the road on one horse, leading the other beside him, and he looked grave, not to say cross, as he turned them into the night field at Sarnissa. It was Friday night, and, by the light of a dip candle set in an old bottle, he made a hurried toilet in the barn. Any other night he would have gone boldly to the loft in which he and Will slept, to perform his ablutions, and brush his hair before the cracked looking-glass, but this was courting night, so it behoved him to act with the usual mysterious secrecy, and slip away from the premises unseen. To have walked straight down the road, and spoken to any one openly of the object of his walk, would have robbed the whole affair of its romance, and would have certainly offended Yshbel, who would have felt hurt at such publicity. No; Goronwy put himself to much inconvenience, in order to reach the shore without being seen, and when Dyc Pendrwm suddenly shambled out through a gate into the lane, he – well, he wished him away!

'Where'st going?' said Dyc, with a broad grin.

'They say there's mackerel in the bay,' said Goronwy.

'Aw! and thee'st put thy best waistcoat on to catch them.'

Goronwy made no reply, but strolled on towards the glowing west, with a decided scowl on his honest face. Everything had combined to annoy him this evening, and when, upon entering the cottage, he looked round the familiar fireside, he was irritated beyond the power of control.

'Yshbel,' he shouted, and Betto answered from the garden. 'She is gone to Tregelly to buy some yarn for me, and I expect Mari 'Gweydd' made her stop to have tea with the girls.'

'Tea!' said Goronwy, 'supper I should think. Well, I must go home; there's plenty to do at Sarnissa, so l can't waste my time loitering about here,' but going out hastily, he straightway took the road to Tregelly, a weaver's cottage some miles up the valley. The glow of the sunset still lingered in the west, while before him the new moon rose above the hills. It was spring time, and the earth was full of awakening life, every hedgerow newly decked in fresh green. In the fields the lambs bleated, lying warm beside their mothers for the night. All around him the daffodils bent their heads, and in the brake the streamlet trickled musically. The frown died away on Goronwy's face, and he forgot his discontent, as he saw Yshbel approach in the gloaming, her hands full of bluebells, her skeins of scarlet wool thrown over her shoulders, her fair hair plaited in long braids, and twisted round and round her head, her white hood dangling from her arm. She had lost not a whit of her beauty; on the contrary, every charm had developed and ripened, and as she came in sight, Goronwy realised it all, and forgave her all her wilful ways.

'Well, indeed, lodes,' he said, 'thee'st just like the pink lily Marged is tending so carefully on the parlour window.'

'Well done,' said Yshbel, clapping her hands, 'here's a wonderful thing! Goronwy Hughes, Sarnissa, has made a pretty speech! Indeed to goodness, that's not so common from thy lips but I must remember this one. I am going to Sarnissa tomorrow with some of this yarn for Marged, and I will ask to see the pink lily in the parlour window.'

'Yes, 'tis there,' said Goronwy, 'with shells all round it; but where'st been, Yshbel?'

'Oh, at Tregelly, having tea with Ann and Martha. Mari made me stay, and then we went to fetch the cow, and then—'

'Oh yes; and then – and then – and then thou forgottest all about me!'

'And then I came home, and met Goronwy Hughes on the road as cross as two sticks, and his smooth face full of puckers.'

'Oh, 'tis all very well to laugh, but listen thou, lass. Thee'st not been treating me well lately, and I've come tonight to have it all settled with thee – there now!'

'Caton pawb! and what about, I would like to know?'

'What about, indeed? Well, about being married. Art going to marry me or not?'

'Thee'st asked me a dozen times, if thee'st asked me once, and haven't I always answered "Yes?"'

'Yes, and hast not always put me off with some excuse when I wanted to fix the day?'

'The day? There's the year to be fixed first, then the month, before we settle the day! Dir anw'l! Goronwy, I never saw thee look so serious.'

'I am serious,' he said, sitting down among the daffodils. 'Come, sit down by me, lass, and talk some sense. I will not rise from here till I fix the year, the month, the day, of our wedding. The year is already fixed – 'tis this year or never. Sarnissa wants thee badly, Yshbel; there's granny failing shocking, and a woman like thee would know how to soften the downward path for her, God bless her, for Marged is very dull since she has grown deaf, and I have waited long enough, so make up thy mind tonight. Sometimes I think thou dost not care for me; if so, say so tonight. Dost want to have done with me, or art going to be true to me?'

Yshbel's colour came and went, there was a flutter in her breath, and her fingers played nervously with the bluebells she was carrying.

'I am going to be true to thee,' she said at last, fixing her blue eyes on his earnest face.

'When will we be married then? Next week?'

'Oh no, no; not so soon. Don't thee hurry me, Goronwy.'

'Hurry thee? Dei anw'l! Dost call waiting five years hurrying thee? If not next week, when, then?'

Yshbel put on her white hood, as if to prepare for the serious business of life.

'Goronwy,' she said, 'it shall be any time thou wishest.'

'Well,' said Goronwy, somewhat pacified, and charmed by the blushing face under the white hood, 'next week perhaps won't do, because the banns are not out, but next month!'

'Next month Nanti is setting the garden: how can I leave her when she is so busy?'

'That will be done in a fortnight.'

'Well, I am willing,' she said; 'but the hay harvest will be coming on then, and then will come the corn harvest, Goronwy, and thou wilt be busy and—'

'There, there – that will do, lass. Wilt be married in October or *never*?' and he started to his feet, with the old dogged look that they knew so well at Sarnissa.

'Well, yes, indeed, if thee art going to look like that. Ach-y-fi! Goronwy, I never thought before thy face could look ugly. Oh, October it shall be, lad, only smile again,' and Goronwy did smile again, and deliberately throwing her bluebells away, took both her hands in his, and looking into her blue eyes, made her repeat, word for word, after him: 'I, Yshbel Lloyd, sitting here on the Sarnddu, do promise to drop all my provoking ways, and to marry Goronwy Hughes ('with all *his* provoking ways' interpolated Yshbel) on the tenth day of October in this year, as witness, the daffodils all round me and the new moon above me;' and they both laughed together, and were friends again, and when they went home and sat by Betto's cheerful fire, she nodded complacently to herself over her knitting. Later on in the evening, returning homewards, Goronwy walked with a firm step, nodding his head occasionally, in answer to his own thoughts, and altogether bearing the look of a man who has settled a matter in accordance with his own wishes. When he had reached that part of the shore on which Penmwntan looked frowning down, a light on the side of the hill caught his eye.

''Tis those gipsy tinkers, no doubt,' he thought.

The new moon lay low in the sky, the stars glittered

overhead, the sea whispered through the darkness, and the
wind came laden with the smell of the brine and seaweed. The
pleased smile died out of his face, a sober, almost a sad, look
taking its place, and looking up to the side of the hill where
the gipsy fire glowed against the sky, he sighed – this man full
of life and energy, who had just plighted his troth to the
acknowledged beauty of the village, one too, who was as good
as she was beautiful, and one whom he had spared no pains to
win. Perhaps, if Yshbel had been more ready to acquiesce in
his wishes, he would not have been so persistent in his
endeavours to obtain her, but her evident reluctance to put on
the bonds of matrimony roused all the obstinacy in his nature,
and tonight, having gained his end, he ought surely to be
happy. He raised his eyes once more to the hillside.

'This is just the night,' he thought, 'that Catrin used to love,
and that fire is on the very spot where we often fried our fish
and our mushrooms. Dei anw'l! 'tis no use wishing to be a boy
again.' And then he looked at the grey, gaunt farmhouse, where
a glimmering light showed Catrin still kept her vigil by her
father. Reaching Sarnissa, he entered quietly, so as not to
disturb the inmates, who generally retired to rest on Friday
nights before his return. On this occasion, however, he found
his father still sitting by the kitchen fire. He was looking better
and less morose than of old. He had sold the *Lark*, and had
settled down kindly to the work of the farm, the bitterness had
gone out of his life with the fall of Parcglas, and the neighbours
declared Morgan Hughes was a different man and had taken a
new lease of his life.

'How are you so late?' said Goronwy.

''Tis mother – she has been so strange tonight, and looking
so frail – indeed, lad, I'm afraid we'll not keep her with us
much longer – but she's better now, and asleep. Marged has
just gone to bed. I will go now, too, and we'll send for the
doctor tomorrow.'

A shadow had fallen on Goronwy's face, a heavy weight on

his heart for he loved his old granny with all the depth of his tender nature.

Lose granny? It would be a blank in his life indeed!

And, as he approached her bed on tip-toe, a thrill of joy sprang up within him, as he saw the gentle eyes open and a welcoming smile on the lips.

'Goronwy bach,' said the old woman, stretching out her soft veined hand.

'Granny fach,' was his only answer, as he grasped it between his own strong palms.

'Where'st been so long, 'machgen-i?'

'Oh! to the forge with Flower and Bell, and after that down to the shore. Have you been ill today?'

'Ill? No, my boy – only tired a little bit because I have been up to Penmwntan to look for thee, and on to the shore and out on the sea, and now I have found my boy.'

'You were wonderful strong all at once; you who can't walk to the garden. How did you go? You had wings perhaps?'

'No, no; I haven't had my wings yet. I don't know how I went indeed,' and then she laughed, as if amused at her own embarrassment. 'Go now, my boy, and sleep all night,' and she smoothed his hands. 'We must part now. Goodnight, dear heart.'

'No, we won't say goodnight,' said Goronwy; 'I'm going to sit here till you fall asleep;' and he drew the curtain so as to shade the light from the frail face. 'We must have some one to sit with you always, granny fach. Very soon, Yshbel will be here to nurse you; you will like that – won't you?'

'Yes,' said the weak voice behind the curtain, 'Yshbel will be very kind; but better I like God's angel, who comes to me in the night. Go you now, my boy; perhaps she won't come if any one else is here.'

'God's angel?' said Goronwy, with an indulgent smile, 'What pretty fancy have you got in your head now?'

'No, no,' said the old woman; ''tis no fancy. She smiles at

me with her red lips, and draws her soft fingers over my cheek, like my mother used to do when I was a—'

The tired voice ceased, the eyes had closed in sleep. Goronwy sat on, lost in deep thought. His life, that used to be so plain, so straight and simple, had become somewhat of a tangled web, and yet he knew not why. The deepest shadow over it, to which he could have given a name, was the fear of losing his grandmother, and yet it was not that alone which weighed his spirits down. Yshbel loved him, he believed, with warmth and tenderness, and had promised to marry him in October; but there was a something wanting, which he felt dimly. The quiet content was his, but the rapturous joy of reciprocated love was not. The uncultured mind is slow to express, but the Celtic nature within him was sensitive to feel. He had never kept watch by a sick-bed before, had never known how wearily the hours could drag on. The clock struck twelve, and still he sat silently brooding, sometimes listening to the feeble breath behind the curtain. One o'clock, and still the household was quiet and granny slept. Two o'clock, and the night grew colder, the wind sighed round the house, the candle burnt low in the socket, and the old woman stirred a little. A touch on the window, and it was softly raised. Goronwy, hidden behind the curtain, watched curiously; while some one, stooping through the opening, came silently into the room. It was Catrin! and he watched more intently, while granny stirred again, and opening her eyes, recognised her nightly visitor. She stretched her hand towards the girl, who stood looking at her with that smile which Goronwy remembered so well.

'Gwen fach, 'tis me.'

'God's little angel?' asked the old woman.

'Yes, indeed; 'tis God sends me whatever. Now you must drink this milk.'

'Where is my boy?' said Gwen, her hand wandering over the coverlet. 'Goronwy was here when I went to sleep.'

'Here I am, granny,' said Goronwy, appearing round the curtain. She took his hand in hers, and unintentionally drawing it towards the other, clasped Catrin's and Goronwy's together. The situation had not been of his seeking, but feeling Catrin's hand within his own, after so long a separation, he could not resist the sudden impulse to grasp it, and hold it tight. It lay in his, trembling, burning, while Catrin, although embarrassed, was filled with an indescribable joy, which lasted but a moment, and for a moment only did Goronwy retain her hand.

'Goronwy,' she exclaimed, 'I wasn't thinking to see thee.'

'So this is granny's angel,' he said, his face aglow with pleasure. 'Indeed, I thought 'twas one of her fancies, but I will confess that when she said the angel smiled at her with her red lips, I thought 'twas thee.'

'Yes; 'tis the little angel,' said the old woman again. 'Goronwy told me Yshbel was coming, and asked me would I like her, and I say "Yes, but God's angel would be best,"' and again the eyes drooped, and she was asleep. Her last words left her hearers confused and awkward. Catrin was the first to regain her composure.

'People whose minds are astray say odd things sometimes,' she said.

'Yes,' answered Goronwy, 'but 'tis strange how wise they are sometimes.'

He had not intended the inference which might be drawn from the remark, and was once more in his turn covered with confusion; but Catrin, with a woman's tact, dissembled so successfully that he thought she had not noticed his mistake.

'Can' diolch, to thee, for thy kindness to granny,' he said; 'I will never forget it. To think that 'twas a stranger who first watched with her! 'Twill always trouble me.'

'But I'm not a stranger to her, indeed,' said Catrin; 'I am with her every night, the last fortnight.'

'Losing thy sleep like that, lodes, when thou hast enough to do to watch thy father!'

'No, no. Madlen takes my place at two o'clock always, and 'tis nothing for me to run down here, and give an hour to Gwen; I can always sleep in the day, too. I am used to watching now, and I know how the sick fail about two in the morning, and how a little milk, or a cup of tea, is welcome to them; then to shake their pillows, and lay them comfortable, and they sleep till morning.'

'God bless thee for it,' said Goronwy. 'How is thy father?'

'Oh, just the same, only weaker every day lately.'

'I have not been up to see him this long time.'

'No,' was Catrin's only answer.

'There's a fire on Penmwntan tonight.'

'Yes; 'tis the gipsies.'

"Tis on the same spot as when we went to see them.'

'Yes.'

'Dost remember it Catrin?'

'Oh yes.'

'And the suppers we used to make? The mushrooms and the blackberries? And catching the fish down in the moonlight?'

For a moment Catrin was almost overcome by the memories which she thought had been her own only.

'Yes,' she answered; 'and dost remember when the tide caught us at Traethyberil, so busy we were with our writing on the sands?'

'Yes, when I carried thee through the surf, Catrin! 'Twas a happy time. Dei anw'l! Did ever boy and girl have such a happy time as we did?'

'No, I think, indeed,' said Catrin. 'I must go now,' she added; "tis time.'

'I will come with thee across the stream.'

'No, no; I wish that thou wilt not. Nosweth dda;' and, before Goronwy had time to answer, she had slipped through the window and flitted away into the darkness.

After she was gone, sitting down again in silent thought, he began to recall her appearance as she had stood before him.

How fair she had grown! How delicate the creamy complexion! How soft the velvet brown eyes! A little graver, perhaps, and the dimples not so ready to play on cheek and chin. A little darker under the eyes, from watching probably; but there was a serene peacefulness on her brow, a gentle tenderness in the voice, whose tones were so familiar to him. The curve of her slender neck he saw too, the delicately moulded hands and arms which had grown white and smooth. Altogether, there was a charm about her, which, Goronwy was not far wrong in thinking, belonged to no other woman.

'Well, there she is gone,' he said, rising and peering into the darkness. 'I have not seen her for months, and I will not see her again for months, perhaps; perhaps not till after I am married. Will Yshbel be kind to her, I wonder?'

And it was curious with how sharp a pang he thought of the possibility that his marriage might mean complete severance from Catrin.

When it began to dawn, seeing that granny still slept, he gave way also to the drowsiness that was weighing down his eyelids, and when he awoke at last, the sun was shining brightly on the silent figure on the bed – so silent, so still!

'Sleeping still,' thought Goronwy, as he bent over her anxiously.

Yes, sleeping still, the sleep that knows no awakening, the hands clasped in their favourite attitude; a smile on the sweet sunken mouth, and the gentle eyes closed forever!

CHAPTER XV

SEEING THE WORLD

One day during the hay harvest when everybody, young and old, had gathered in the fields at Sarnissa, an unusual event occurred at Treswnd. On the brow of the hill, where the high road appeared to launch into space, a vehicle made its appearance, in which two men sat.

The haymakers were soon aware of it, and great curiosity prevailed, which increased to excitement when it passed the turning of the road to the vicar's house, and kept its way down the steep descent to the village.

'Who can they be?' was the question in every mind and on every tongue.

''Tis a man in black, so I thought he might be a clergyman,' said Morgan Hughes, 'going to see Morris ffeirad.'

'P'r'aps 'tis the agent – no; 'tis light clothes he wears! Who can it be then?'

'I better go home,' said "Esther, The Ship," 'because the door is shut, and something is wrong with the latch this last month,' and flinging her rake aside, she hurried home, arriving in front of the inn just as the gig drove up to the door. Recognising the driver as a servant from one of the inns at Caermadoc, her whole attention was centred upon the other occupant of the vehicle, a portly man dressed in shining black broadcloth, and wearing a tall hat of the glossiest and blackest. A chain of very yellow gold stretched across his waistcoat; one hand, ungloved, was white and fat, a massive ring of the same yellow gold adorning the little finger. His well-polished boots creaked as he stepped out of the gig, and a smile of pleased amusement spread over his clean-shaven red face, and his eyes lengthened into mere slits, as he observed Esther's series of curtseys, for one, she felt was not enough for such an evidently important visitor.

'Dy'da, ser,' she said, raising her hands to show the astonishment which she had no words to express.

His smile broadened into a laugh.

'We're having more than our share of those curtseys, little woman,' he said. 'Are you the housewife?'

'Yes, ser,' said Esther, with another bob, inserting her finger into the hole where the latch ought to have been, but it had slipped out of its place, and required much manipulation to reach before the door was opened.

The passage, paved with round cobblestones, was well sanded, as was also the floor of the parlour, the door of which she opened wide.

'In here, ser; thankee, ser. You'll be wanting something to eat, no doubt?'

'Yes – what have you got?'

'Oh, plenty of ham and eggs, ser, and ale and bread and cheese.'

'Ham and eggs will do,' and Esther, more at her ease, for her guest spoke good Welsh, soon placed before him a clean, though frugal, repast.

'Now, ser, I hope you'll he able to make a good meal, and don't eat too fast; you'll eat a great deal more if you eat slow. You must be hungry coming all the way from Caermadoc. Coming to see the country, I suppose, ser? But, dir anw'l, there's nothing here for gentlemen from London to see.'

'No, l suppose not; but I am not from London.'

'Oh, indeed, ser; where you come from then?'

'Not so far as that whatever,' said the stranger, much amused at her curiosity; 'from Glamorganshire. And look here, little woman, don't you trouble to ask me any more questions; I'll tell you all at once now. I come from Glamorganshire, my name is Jones, and I want to find a man from the village called Ben Bowen – a fisherman, I think. My niece is living with him since she was a baby. I am come to take her away. And now you can leave me to my dinner, and when I've done, I'll call you to show me the way to Ben Bowen's cottage.'

Esther positively gasped at the extent of the information that had been accorded her so freely, though it would certainly have given her greater pleasure to have extracted it from him gradually.

'Can I go and see how is my cow? She is sick today.'

The stranger nodded his assent, and before he had eaten many mouthfuls, Esther was running up the dusty road to Sarnissa fields, the haymakers all intently watching her. She carried her wooden shoes in her hand, and was enveloped in a cloud of dust raised by her energetic running. It was but fair that they should lessen her fatigue, so they ran in a body through the gap into the lower field to meet her. She arrived so breathless and panting that she could only deliver herself of her news in scraps.

'Oh! Ben Bowen, make haste – 'tis from the "Works" he is – splendid clothes! – ham and eggs he's having – gold chain and gold ring – and his hat and his boots shining like the sun. Yshbel Lloyd, 'tis thy uncle come to fetch thee – make haste, lodes! I can't stop,' and turning abruptly away, she ran out into the lane, leaving her hearers gaping with astonishment.

Ben Bowen flung his rake aside; Betto followed his example.

'Come on, Yshbel!' they said.

'Yes; go – go!' cried every one, except Goronwy, who had coloured to the roots of his hair, an angry red flush on his cheeks, and a dogged resistance in his eyes.

Yshbel, on the contrary, had paled a little, and had clung to her rake. 'I'm not going,' she said; 'tell him he's too late – tell him we are busy with the hay, when 'tis gathered I will come home;' and she led the way to the upper field, the rest of the haymakers following excitedly. Goronwy said nothing, but went on with his work in silence.

'Not going?' said one of the women under her breath. 'What wilt do then, Yshbel? Wilt not go with him at all?'

'Of course not,' she answered; 'my home is here for the rest of my life.'

'Oh, of course,' said the woman, 'and 'twill be a fine thing for thee to be mistress of Sarnissa, but, tan i marw, lo's, 'twould be grander to be a ladi, and come down here sometimes to see us in thy silks and satins, grander than Mrs Gwyn, Tredu. Oh, Yshbel think what thou art doing!'

The girl made no answer, but continued to toss the hay, her face gradually regaining its colour and her mind its composure. Later on, she found herself near Goronwy, and seeing a frown on his face, tried to find something to say which should dispel the cloud, but his expression was not encouraging, so she was silent.

'This is strange news,' he said at last, as they stood in the gap together, and watched the last load joggle into the lane. Morgan Hughes joined them, looking flurried and heated, and wiping his face with his red cotton handkerchief.

'Look here, Yshbel,' he said, with a curious sparkle in his eyes, which had not gleamed there so often since his jealousy of Simon Rees had subsided, 'my son Goronwy is not the man to be tossed about like a ball at the bidding of a stranger, remember you.'

'And I'm not the woman to behave in that way, am I?' said Yshbel, with a little toss of her head.

'No, she's not, father,' said Goronwy; 'but I am not the man, too, to force any girl to marry me against her will. So let her be – she shall do as she likes. I won't come down tonight, Yshbel, go you down and see this strange man.'

'You are all talking a lot of nonsense,' said the girl, with a little flash of temper. 'Most like Esther knows nothing about it, but guessed it all out herself?'

Goronwy had walked away with his rake over his shoulder, so she too turned down the lane to the village, accompanied by a group of girls, all eagerly discussing the object of the stranger's visit.

Leaving them, one by one, in the village, Yshbel crossed the sands towards her home in a strangely disturbed frame of mind which was by no means soothed by the sight of Betto, who came running to meet her.

'Come on, 'merch i; here's good lwk come to thee at last.'

She was too breathless to say more before they reached the cottage door, where the stranger stood waiting.

'Well, 'merch-i, and how are you?' he said, pleasantly. 'Quite well? That's right. You've been haymaking, they tell me. Well, upon my word, if there are many pretty girls like you in the fields, I'll go haymaking tomorrow too. Come, off with your hood, and let's see you plainly;' and Yshbel untied the strings of her sun-bonnet and threw it aside.

Mr Jones took a long look at her, noting the slender waist, and the graceful carriage. The lovely face he had already taken into consideration.

'Yes; she'll do,' he thought 'when she's trimmed up a bit.'

'Well, 'merch i,' he said sitting down in an affable, friendly way on the bench which ran along one side of the big chimney, 'come here now. Lemme tell you, you are my half-brother's child. Your mother died here when you were a baby, and your father – a sad roving fellow he was, as ever you saw – went abroad, and for twenty years I never heard anything of him. Lately I received a letter from him telling me about you, and begging me to go and fetch you, and take care of you, as he is married again, and never means to come home to Wales. That's a fine way to get rid of your family responsibilities – isn't it?' he said, looking at Betto and laughing. 'Well, as Merry Ann and I have no children of our own, we settled at once that we'd fetch you, my dear, and polish you up a bit, and see after you for the rest of your life. You're a lucky girl, I can tell you, for I've been a fortunate man, and our colliery has turned out well; and there isn't a gentleman in the neighbourhood that drives a better turn-out than I do. You shall drive about everywhere in your carriage and pair, and your aunt will dress you up like a lady.' Then, suddenly stopping, he raised his fat, white finger admonishingly, adding, 'All this is if you are a good girl, mind, and do everything to please your aunt Merry Ann. Come, 'merch i, what do you say to it?'

Yshbel was fairly bewildered by the prospect of good fortune thus suddenly offered her; a prospect which, however, she realised must be abandoned at once.

''Tis too late, sir,' she said. 'I waited many years in the hope that my father would keep his promise, and come to fetch me away; but now I've lived here so long that I'm feeling my home is here, and my heart would break if I couldn't see the sea, and the shore, and Penmwntan and hear the waves dashing against the rocks.'

'Oh, as for that,' said Mr Jones, with a smile of amusement, 'we are not ten miles from the sea ourselves, and you can see as much sand as you like. But stop a bit – lemme tell you again, my girl, your aunt Merry Ann and I can show you better things than these – grand houses, gay ladies in silks and satins! You shall go to London; you shall learn to dance; and—'

'But another thing, sir,' said Yshbel, 'I cannot come, because I have promised to marry Goronwy Hughes.'

Betto, who had carefully hidden this fact from her visitor, now looked much embarrassed, and suddenly found she was wanted by Ben, who was spreading his nets on the rushes.

Mr Jones' smile changed to a look of serious annoyance, and he expressed his feelings in a long whistle.

'Phew!' he said. 'Botheration! That's nonsense, my dear. There's lots of young fellows in our neighbourhood, with grand houses and carriages and horses, will be glad enough to have you, I can tell you, when they hear you are our adopted daughter. And we'll give the young man down here a nice suit of clothes, and a ten-pound note in his waistcoat pocket.'

'Goronwy Hughes is not the man to give me up for ten pounds,' said the girl, with a toss of her head.

'Well, well, well, we'll see about that – but I know the world better than you, my girl. And if ten pounds won't do, I'll make it twenty pounds; and, if he still holds out, why, I can make it fifty pounds, and not ruin myself;' and he jingled the money in his pockets.

His face once more beamed with smiles – in fact, Mr Jones of the 'Daisy' Colliery ("Jones, the Daisy," as he was generally called), went through life with a smile on his face, so much so, that even on the most solemn occasions, he found it difficult to control the corners of his mouth. Fortune had favoured him since first, as a youth, he took a place as shop assistant in London, afterwards setting up in a small business of his own; which, under his careful management, soon became an 'establishment', where the prosperous owner employed many hands and accumulated a large fortune.

Selling his business, he invested his savings in a colliery near his old home in Glamorganshire. Here riches had rolled in upon him. In his wife's own words, 'Everything Jones touched turned to money,' so it was no wonder that when he visited the simple, unsophisticated inhabitants of Treswnd, his face should wear a constant smile of amusement for he had forgotten the old thatched cottage where his childhood was spent, and the poor old mother who had scraped and saved to set up her favourite boy for his first journey to London, who had wept over his departure, and prayed for his return, and had died at last, her heart still hungering for the lad she loved. True, he sometimes paid her a hurried visit and left her well provided with money, but, alas! no money would satisfy the cravings of a mother's heart.

Mrs Jones, too, had been a cottager's daughter from the same neighbourhood and the only bitter drop in her cup of success was the fact that many of her relatives still lived in the village that lay at the foot of the hill upon which her handsome residence was built.

'We'll make it fifty pounds,' said Mr Jones, seeing that Yshbel still looked uncongenial and unimpressed, 'and if he won't be satisfied with that – well, he's a fool! And I don't know my countrymen. Come you now, open that box,' he said, pointing to a large trunk in the corner; 'here's the key. Your aunt has sent you some clothes to wear. You shall have plenty more when you come to Glaish-y-dail.'

Yshbel could not well decline the key which her uncle held out to her. She only placed it on the table, however, saying 'I won't open the box, sir—'

'Call me uncle, my dear.'

'Well, uncle; I won't open the box till you have seen Goronwy, and heard what he has got to say. As for offering him fifty pounds 'twould be an insult! Not five hundred pounds nor five thousand pounds, would tempt him to give me up. But I'm not saying that I wouldn't like just to see the world a bit before I marry, and settle down here. I wonder would Goronwy agree to that?'

'There's a sensible girl now!' said Mr Jones, patting her on the shoulder. 'Of course he will, and if you find you can't forget him, my dear, you can come back here and marry him when you like; but I'll bet my last shilling you'll think nothing more of him, when you've been with us a month. Come now, let's see the young fellow and settle the matter at once.'

'Oh, what will he say?' said Yshbel. 'Will I dare to fetch him?'

'I'll go,' said Betto, running out.

During her absence Mr Jones once more pushed the key towards Yshbel's hand, but she resolutely forbore to touch it.

'No,' she said, 'not till Goronwy has come; if he's not willing, you must take the box back without opening it.'

'Twt, twt,' said her uncle, 'he'll be willing enough. You like pretty things – my girl, eh? Silk frocks, pretty hats, a gold watch, and rings on your fingers?'

'Oh no,' said Yshbel, drawing herself up; 'such things would never suit me. I would like only just to see what the World is like beyond Treswnd, but – gold chains and rings! Ach-y-fi! They would not suit Yshbel Lloyd, and, indeed, I wouldn't wear them.'

'Well, well, we'll see about that.'

Presently footsteps were heard approaching, and Yshbel nervously awaited Goronwy's entrance.

'Hello,' he called, in his rather boisterous voice, as he crossed the threshold. 'Who wants me here?'

'"Tis I, young man,' said Mr Jones, without rising from his seat. 'I want to have a little talk with you.'

'And what about, sir?' asked Goronwy. 'Yshbel, lodes, what art looking so serious about? Betto has told me thine uncle wants thee to go with him, and I would not have come down at the call of a stranger, only I wanted to tell thee at once thee'st but to say thou wishest to give me up, and thee'st as free as the sea wind to go where thou pleasest. I am not the man to force a girl to keep a promise against her will. So, I think, sir,' he added, turning to Mr Jones, 'you have got your answer before you ask your question.'

'Yes, indeed,' said Mr Jones, rising and slapping Goronwy on the back. 'You are a sensible fellow, and see how wrong it would be to bind a girl down to a promise made before she knew her own mind.'

'That's between me and Yshbel, and nobody else,' said Goronwy. 'Tell me, lass, dost repent of thy promise to marry me in October?'

'Oh no, no! Goronwy, I will never break my word to thee; I have no wish to do such a thing. I have made my choice, and I will never change – unless, indeed, thou art tired of me, lad,' she added, with a smile that Mr Jones felt was fatal to his arguments.

'That's enough then, sir,' said Goronwy; 'there's no need for more talk between us. Yshbel is my promised wife, and in October we'll be married, and there's an end of the matter.'

'You're an obstinate fellow after all, l see,' said Mr Jones. 'I was hoping you'd see the sense of setting her free. You would not lose by it, my man. A brand new suit of clothes, with a ten-pound note in the waistcoat pocket – twenty pounds then – eh? Or I'll make it fifty pounds if you'll agree quietly with my wishes.'

Goronwy had grown white to the lips while Mr Jones was speaking.

'I don't want to insult Yshbel's uncle,' he said at last, 'or I would tell you what I thought of you.'

'Well, well, we won't quarrel about it,' said the visitor. 'Ask Yshbel if she wouldn't like to see the world a bit before she's married, and if she's a truthful girl I think she'll say "Yes".'

'See the world?' said Goronwy. 'What can she want to see the world for? The world has got nothing to do with us here at Treswnd; and if there are many people like you in it, sir, I think the less she sees of it, the better.'

The smile on Mr Jones' mouth broadened, and his eyes narrowed to mere slits.

'But surely,' he said, 'you are not such a selfish brute as to be unwilling for her to come and see her aunt for a few weeks before she gets married.'

'That's a different thing to seeing the world,' said Goronwy, 'and she's free, of course, to do as she likes. Speak out, lass – dost want to go and see thine aunt?'

Yshbel had been standing during this conversation, her fingers nervously tying and untying her apron strings. At Goronwy's last question, she raised her eyes to his, and said: 'Thou knowest me, Goronwy. I will never break my word. I am thy promised wife, and I will marry thee in October. But I would like to go and see my aunt. There would be no harm in that – would there? Oh, Goronwy, I have thought of it so often, when I felt my coral necklace on my neck. I should like to see the beautiful things my uncle tells about. I have seen them in my dreams, and heard such beautiful music!'

"That's enough then – go,' said Goronwy, 'though, tan i
marw! I don't see what help it will be to thee in managing
Sarnissa,' and he laughed, scornfully. 'But there – I'm not going
to be like Twm "Tredelyn", who would not let his wife see her
own mother! So – go thou, Yshbel, if thee likes. But you, sir,'
he added, turning to Mr Jones, who seemed more amused than
ever, 'remember she's my promised wife, and I don't give up
my claim to her.'

'All right, all right, my good fellow!' But Goronwy had
turned away and gone out into the twilight, whither Yshbel
followed him.

'That's a dogged fellow,' said Mr Jones. 'She'll be well rid of
him, I think.'

'True enough, sir,' said Betto, anxious to propitiate the man
who could jingle sovereigns in his pocket as if they were
halfpence. 'He's as obstinate as a mule!'

In a little while Yshbel returned, her eyes red and swollen.

'Here she is,' said Betto. 'She'll be a sensible girl and give
you no trouble – will you, 'merch i?'

'I am coming with you, uncle, to see my aunt,' said the girl,
ignoring Betto's question.

'That's right. Well, today's Saturday, I must be back on
Monday, so tomorrow you can go to church in your fine
clothes. But look here, Yshbel you must drop the Welsh
tonight. Betto tells me you can speak English.'

'Only very slow,' said Yshbel in that language. 'I can read it
very easy, but I am not used to speak. I will soon learn though,
if my aunt will have patience with me.'

'There!' said Betto. 'Didn't I tell you, ser? Oh, she was always
in her English books.'

'Well, I'll go now,' said her uncle. 'The Ship's wife has a lot
more curtseys ready by this time,' and he laughed till his eyes
were almost closed, and his ample waistcoat shook.

'There's a jolly man he is!' said Betto. She had seen him out
through the doorway with a series of curtseys, which she hoped

would put the Ship's wife's in the shade. 'Come on now, and let us see the grand things in the box. There's a ladi you'll be tomorrow in church!'

'No, indeed,' said the girl; 'I would never wear grand things here. They would not suit Yshbel Lloyd, and Goronwy won't be willing.'

'Goronwy!' said Betto, scornfully. 'What are you talking about Goronwy, when you'll have the pick of all the grand gentlemen in Glamorganshire?'

'Nanti,' said Yshbel, pausing before she raised the lid of the box. 'Look you here, Nanti, and make no mistake – I mean what I say. I will go with my uncle, because I've longed so much to know what the world is like – but 'tis Treswnd is my home, and I will come back before long. I have promised Goronwy Hughes, and I will never break my promise to him.'

Betto's only reply was an upward glance, and a pitying ''ts, 'ts, 'ts!'

The lid raised, Yshbel who had an innate love of pretty things, paused in delight.

'Oh, Nanti! Oh, Nanti!' and she drew out a hat of black lace, followed by a fichu of the same material.

'Oh!!' said Yshbel – 'Oh!!' said Betto, and for some time their conversation consisted only of exclamations, while garment after garment was taken out and examined. A dress of some thin, black material, all gauzy and frilly, was shaken out carefully. Then came the petticoats of white, embroidered and frilled, the dainty shoes, gloves, parasol – and Yshbel stood up fairly overcome with delight.

'Oh, Nanti Betto! How will I look in all these grand things?'

'Not so grand as they might be,' said Betto. 'If the gown had been green now, and the parasol pink!'

'No, no,' said Yshbel; 'they are more beautiful as they are. My aunt must be a wise woman and kind. She knew l wouldn't like to be dressed in gaudy colours. Oh, I wish Goronwy was quite willing, then I would be quite happy!'

'*That* for Goronwy!' said Betto, flipping her fingers. 'Now fit them on, 'merch i,' and Yshbel fairly trembled with excitement as she slipped on the skirts and the gauzy black dress.

'Now, this over my shoulders.'

'Anw'l! anw'l!' said Betto. 'Was there ever such a thing?'

'Now the stockings, Nanti – oh, think! Beautiful black silk stockings – and the shoes!'

'Now the hat,' said Betto, fixing it on the girl's head; and under its broad lacy brim, Yshbel's fair face looked very charming. Truly her aunt had chosen her dress with discrimination and good taste. Under the brim of the hat a pink rose peeped out, and at the top of her black parasol a bow of the same colour fluttered. A pair of soft grey gloves completed the costume. The only drawback to her content was that Goronwy, although not refusing his consent, had parted from her with a look of offended pride.

When everything had been examined and admired, Yshbel laid them reverently back in the box again. She nearly broke Betto's heart the following day, when she went to church in her homespun of blue, and her old felt hat, with the white wing. But Goronwy, looking across from the men's side of the church, was pleased and relieved.

She was the same Yshbel. She would return to Sarnissa, in spite of that black-clothed tempter, sitting in front of him, and reading his prayer-book through gold-rimmed spectacles, things unknown before at Treswnd.

It would not have been etiquette to walk home in broad daylight with his affianced wife, so Goronwy stalked homewards in dignified solitude.

CHAPTER XVI

GLAISH-Y-DAIL

On the side of a rocky hill, overlooking one of the most romantic valleys in Glamorganshire, stood the residence (for we dare not call it the house) of Mr and Mrs Jones. A snug, old-fashioned farmhouse when it came into the rich coal-owner's possession, Glaish-y-dail had been added to and improved out of all recognition. The front door had been enlarged, and a massive portico, with pillars of stucco, adorned it. The lawns were trim and soft, the gravel on the drives immaculate, foreign shrubs and trees stood stiffly where they had been planted. No trailing branches, no moss-grown stumps, were permissible in the grounds of Glaish-y-dail. But it mattered not much, for no eye could rest long on the formal and artificial foreground while beyond it stretched a scene of so much natural beauty.

The river Gele wound its silver length through the valley which, twenty years before, had been one of complete rural seclusion. Now, alas! its waters were polluted and utilised by the 'works' of copper and iron which stood on its banks, their noxious vapours rising in a brown cloud and hanging like a pall over that portion of the valley. The air was full of throbbing and hammering; the regular thud of the enormous bellows seeming to beat time to the chorus of infernal sounds which had come to invade the once peaceful dale.

Glaish-y-dail, however, was high above the turmoil of the 'works'; the throbbing and whirring, softened by distance, seemed like the pulse and breathing of some monstrous creature who toiled and moiled in the valley below to coin the gold for the rich owners of the handsome houses built on the sides of the hills above. Before it reached the village of Pontargele, the river still retained much of its sylvan beauty, the brown hills between which it meandered rising one behind another and growing bluer and greyer as they stretched further away from the haunts of men.

Looking out through the large bay window in the drawing room, "Mrs Jones, the Daisy," watched the turn in the valley where the cloud of brown smoke hung low. Here stood the railway station connecting the 'works' with the world beyond, and transmitting to a neighbouring port the rich products of the hills extracted by the toiling miners.

The sun was setting behind the smoky haze, gorgeous clouds of crimson and gold overspread the west, but Mrs Jones was too intent upon the little puff of white steam which she saw in the distance to notice such commonplace things as clouds.

She walked nervously up and down the room, which was furnished with every luxury that money and bad taste could collect. Her black eyes and her mouth had lost their natural kindly expression in their continual endeavour to look dignified and indifferent to her grand surroundings. She stood in awe of her servants, being conscious that village gossip had made them acquainted with her humble origin. She was a woman of rather stately appearance, of much natural shrewdness and adaptability, kind-hearted and generous when she allowed her character its free expression, but so much curbed and restrained by her constant endeavours after grandeur and fashion, that her life had become little more than a weariness to her; and she looked forward with pleasure to the arrival of her niece, who, she hoped, would give her the companionship and affection which her idea of the importance of her position prevented her seeking elsewhere.

She approached the bell, but withdrew her hand several times before finally ringing it. The door opened noiselessly.

'Is Morgans gone, John? The train will be in in five minutes. Is he gone, do you think?'

'I don't know, 'm, I gave the order.'

'Dear, dear! I hope he has!'

And the man, provokingly calm, closed the door, leaving his mistress in a fume which she might easily have quieted by stepping out herself through the French window and opening a door in the wall, which separated the grounds from the outbuildings. But this would have been undignified in a lady, in Mrs Jones' opinion; so she would have died sooner than satisfy her anxiety in that way. She walked restlessly up and down, at last ringing the bell again.

'John,' she said, 'if Morgans doesn't go at once, he'll be too late, and Mr Jones and Miss Isbel Lloyd will have to walk. Oh, here they are!'

And John, who had been aware all the while that the coachman had left in good time, turned away with a smile to open the front door.

"Mrs Jones, the Daisy," had a warm heart under all her vulgar gentility and dread of breaking the laws of etiquette, and when, following her husband from the well-appointed brougham, a fair, graceful girl stepped out, she for once threw dignity to the winds, and, hurrying to the portico, clasped Yshbel in her arms.

'Come in, my dear! I *am* glad to see you; indeed, there!'

And Yshbel, excited and happy, returned her aunt's greeting with a warm embrace, but with few words, for her English, though correct, was far from fluent.

After her, Mr Jones came bustling in.

'Well, Merry Ann,' he said, 'here we are, and pretty tired too. Yshbel—'

'Isbel!' corrected Mrs Jones, with a nudge and a look at John.

'Isbel then. Le'me tell you, she's not tasted a morsel since the morning. Looking at everything and asking, what's this and what's that as if she was just born into the world,' and his waistcoat shook and his eyes disappeared entirely with laughter.

'Jones! Jones!' admonished his wife. 'Come, my dear, and take off your things,' and in the privacy of the bedroom she embraced her niece once more.

'Oh, here's a beautiful house!' said the girl looking round in admiration as she took off the hat which her aunt had chosen with such good taste. 'And thank you for all these pretty clothes! Dir anw'l! I can scarcely believe I look like that – I, Yshbel Lloyd!' and she stood, surprised and pleased, before a tall cheval glass.

'Yes. You look very nice, my dear, and you shall have plenty more clothes, only try not to say Yshbel before the servants, but Isbel. Here's hot water, my dear, and that dress will do tonight.'

'Will do? Oh, aunt!'

'Well, I'm glad you like it, my dear. But now, before you go down to dinner, let me teach you a little how to behave,' and then followed a lecture, of which all that Yshbel remembered, as she followed her aunt down the stairs, was that she was not to put her knife in her mouth or drink out of the little glass basins 'that will be before you with the fruit, my dear'.

'Oh dear, dear! What will I do?' Yshbel said at last. 'I will watch you, aunt, and do the same exactly,' and her merry laugh rang out in the soft carpeted corridor, a sound so unusual there, that Mrs Jones looked round, reproving though smiling.

At dinner her exclamations of wonder and delight were sometimes uncontrollable, but, perceiving her aunt's finger raised reprovingly, she at last took refuge in silence, contenting herself with looking at everything with unbounded admiration.

'There's a long journey it is!' said Mr Jones. 'I was never so tired in my life. Nothing but green fields and rivers. Not a single 'works' nor flames anywhere, nor a tall chimney, if 'twas to save your life! You could never live there, Merry Ann. Not a collier or a truck did I see till I came back to Stranport. From there home we had the company of Jones, "the Belfield".'

'Indeed' said Mrs Jones, with much interest. 'What did he say?'

'Oh, he got one of his doleful tales as usual! James Lewis down the valley killed in the copper works. He was getting up a subscription for the family, and I had to give him something, of course. Many's the time I've told James Lewis to try and save a bit. 'Because,' says I, 'the best friend that ever you'll have is a shillin' in your pocket,' says I. I introduced him to Yshbel, seeing he was looking so hard at her.'

The servants had left the room, and Yshbel was sitting in much perplexity, with the little glass 'basins' before her, out of which she was not to drink, and Mrs Jones was able to give expression to her anxiety.

'Oh, Jones,' she said, 'how did you do it? Le'me hear exactly now how did you say?'

'Well, I said, "This is my niece," says I, "Miss Yshbel Lloyd," and he took off his hat very polite. "She's been brought up 'mongst the Cardis," says I, "so she's not seen much of the world." "That's not been much loss to her,"' says he. "Well, I dunno," says I, "but, however, we are going to keep her with us for a bit, and see if we can polish her up a little."'

'And what did he say to that?'

'Well, he didn't say a word, but he got as red as fire in his face, and Yshbel did the same, I dunno what about. "I hope," he says too, "we shall see her up at Llys-y-fran some day," and then we came to the station.'

'Well, indeed! There's for you! I daresay "Mrs Jones, the Belfield," will call here one of these days. Come, my dear, we'll retire to the drawing room," and Yshbel followed her in a dream of happiness.

She was beginning to realise the visions of beauty which had haunted her mind on the lonely sea shore. They were within her grasp, were things of truth and reality, and the world which she had longed so much to see was present around her in colours as vividly beautiful as those of her most romantic dreams. Soft carpets, glittering lights, the luxurious appointments of the dinner table, her aunt's kindness, her uncle's genial bonhomie – all were delightful to the simple peasant girl, and when, on entering the drawing room, the strain of the village band floated in through the open window, it put the finishing touch to her dream of happiness. This was the music whose mysterious echoes she had heard in the roar of the sea.

'Oh, aunt,' she said, 'it is all wonderful to me.'

Ever since she had left Treswnd in the morning, sitting by her uncle in a kind of awed silence, a crowd of admiring neighbours standing round to wave their farewells – ever since, on the brow of the hill, she had lost sight of the sea and the village – her mind had been gradually opening to fresh scenes, charming from their novelty, if not beautiful in themselves. Gradually, the memory of Goronwy's unwilling leave-taking had faded away. He had given his permission, though reluctantly, and with the natural buoyancy of youth, she soon cast from her any lingering compunctions which had somewhat spoilt the commencement of her journey; and as she stood beside her aunt, looking out into the night the handsome drawing room behind her, the valley, with its glow of crimson haze, spread before her, she felt as though she had been wafted at once to fairyland.

The brown cloud had changed to a luminous red mist from which came the ponderous and regular beats of the huge bellows and the hum of the works. Flames leapt into the air, lighting up the valley with a lurid glow, and bringing into relief the rocky points on the hillsides. No wonder was it that Yshbel stood silent and spellbound, only asking in a whisper, 'What is it then? Are these the works?'

'Yes, my dear. And that large house – you can see it by the light of the furnaces – is Mr Jones, of Belfield's. Llys-y-fran it is called. The gentleman, I mean, who came home with you in the train. A very rich man he is. His colliery (that's the Belfield) is about two miles from here; his nephew is looking after that.'

''Tis a large house,' said Yshbel.

'Not so large as this, nor half so well furnished; shabby and mean, I call it for such rich people.'

'Oh, look, aunt! The light on the windows is like the sunset on the sea; and that beautiful music! I have never heard such sweet sounds!'

Let us leave Yshbel a moment to her romantic dreams, and peep into the house on the opposite side of the valley, whose windows had attracted her attention. A quaint, old-fashioned house it was, and perhaps "Mrs Jones, the Daisy," had not been wrong in describing it as shabby, for evidently its occupants were reluctant to change the old, faded furniture of their ancestors for the newer and grander style so easily procurable at Stranport. An air of refinement and good taste, however, reigned over everything, which amply made up for the lack of grandeur. The appointments of the dinner table, though not so elaborate as those of Glaish-y-dail, had a simple refinement about them that was entirely wanting at that place.

The family, consisting of Mr Walter Jones, his wife, and son, were gathered around it.

'I travelled home from Stranport with "Jones the Daisy", today,' said Mr Jones, a tall, dark man, his hair sprinkled with grey, but looking as vigorous in his middle age as did his son of five-and-twenty. 'He was as smiling as usual, and as generous.'

'I don't know what that man does find so amusing in life,' said his son. 'I wish he'd tell me the secret.'

'He hasn't the heavy business anxieties that you have to weigh him down, probably,' said his father, with a little sarcasm in his voice.

'No, by Jove! said Jenkin; 'they say the old fellow's coining money.'

'He had a very pretty girl with him. In fact, I don't think I have ever seen a more beautiful girl.'

'One of Mrs Jones' vulgar relations?'

'Not at all. Very quiet and inexperienced, I should say, but not vulgar by any means. Very well dressed, too – all in black. with something pink about it.'

'I have noticed men always admire a black dress,' said Mrs Jones. "Mrs Jones, the Daisy", has very good taste in dress herself – she always looks quiet and ladylike.'

'Yes,' said Jenkin; 'it is when she puts on the *grande duchesse* airs that I feel compelled to set her down. The old man is not a bad sort.'

'He is a very good sort,' said Mr Jones. 'I had no sooner told him of poor James Lewis' accident, and of the subscription we're getting up, than he gave five pounds at once to head the list. He is very generous, certainly. He even managed to look serious, though the corners of his mouth seem made for smiling. Have you called there lately, dear?'

'No,' said Mrs Jones. 'I will go some day this week and see this pretty girl you talk of.'

'Shall I drive you, mother?' said Jenkin 'I should like to see her too. There isn't a pretty girl in the valley since Lily Owen left.'

'I shall be glad when George returns,' said Mr Jones. 'I am uneasy about the colliery. I must go up there tomorrow;' and the conversation turned upon other topics.

In less than a fortnight Yshbel had adapted herself wonderfully to the ways and manners of those around her. She was naturally of an observant nature, and, moreover, unusually receptive to all impressions of refinement and beauty, and she entered into the life of a more extended entourage with thorough enjoyment. Her uncle and aunt were proud of their beautiful niece, delighting in showering upon her all kinds of adornments, and were much surprised at Yshbel's indifference to them.

It was not until some weeks later that she discovered that her aunt had a 'skeleton' in her cupboard. She had spent the day at Stranport with her uncle, and at dinner that evening was amusing her aunt with her naïve description of their adventures.

'And what do you think, aunt? When we came to Rhoswen station there had been an accident in the – tunnel, you call it, where the train goes underground? Well, we couldn't come through there, so we had to go round some other way, and when we came to some station we had to change; and in the waiting room I had to stay a little while, and a woman came in, with a red shawl and a cockle hat. She had a basket on her arm, and strong leather boots. But oh, aunt, she was the very image of you! She asked me where I was going, and I told her I was stopping here with you; and she said, 'You tell Mrs Jones, my dear, that you've been speaking to Martha Williams, she'll tell you who I am.' Her voice and all was like yours. Uncle knew her, too, because he said, 'How are you, Martha?' Who was she, uncle?'

'Well, well, she was Martha Williams, I suppose – there's lots of Williamses about here. Try this champagne, Merry Ann. John, fill your mistress' glass.'

When Yshbel looked at her aunt she saw she had visibly paled, and that the glass of champagne was much needed. Very quick to discern where she had made a false step, she instantly changed the subject of conversation, and chattered as volubly as her imperfect English permitted. What had she done? What had so wounded or frightened her aunt, she wondered? She had scarcely reached the drawing room, however, before Mrs Jones began to enlighten her on that point.

'Isbel,' she said, 'le'me tell you, you must alter very much in one thing, my dear, or else you'll get me into trouble. Yes, indeed, there. You're a great deal too fond of talking about common people. It will never do in genteel sessciety. Talk about flower shows, or concerts, or about church, if you like –

say you like a high richial, mind! – or about the good singers
– you must learn their names, child – but, for goodness' sake,
leave the common people alone!'

'Aunt Mary Anne, what have I done? I am a common girl
myself, I know, and not fit to be in this grand house and
wearing these fine clothes; but what did I say?'

'What need was there for you to talk about Martha Williams
before John? I thought I would drop! And Jones smiling like
an image! – but he never knows how to keep up his pussition.'

'Who is Martha Williams, then?' asked the girl. 'She seemed
a very nice woman whatever, and said if I ever came to
Pontargele she would be very glad to see me.'

'Well then, she's my sister, Isbel; but there's no need to bring
her name before my servants.'

'Your sister? Well, indeed! But she looked poor, aunt, and
you are rich. How can that be?'

'It can be very well. She married a fool of a man who spent
all his money on drink. I married a man who knew how to
turn every penny into two. I can't help that, can I? It would
never do for me, after Jones has been so successful, and got
such a good pussition here, to disgrace him with my poor
relations. I wish to goodness we had not bought the Daisy
Colliery, then we could settle down somewhere else, but it's no
use wishing that now. Don't you talk about the common
people you meet, Isbel. I am very kind to Martha, poor thing!
I sent her a cheese and a ham last week, but there's no need to
talk about her, or else we would soon lose our friends, and it's
little of Llys-y-fran we'd see, I can tell you, or any other
respectable house in this neighbourhood.'

'I'd give up every Llys in the world for a sister,' said Isbel.
'Continually I am wishing I had one.'

'Oh, be joyful,' said Mrs Jones. 'When you've got nobody
but yourself to think about, you can sail through life pretty
smooth; but when you've got a poor relation 'kiwking' at you
from every shop in the village, they'll soon drag you down; and

you've got nothing to do but to hold your head high and take no notice.'

'Oh, aunt!' was all Yshbel's answer.

This was terrible! It was not only Nanti Betto, then, who could be mean and dishonourable; not only 'N'wncwl Ben who could swear the fish was fresh, when he knew it was stale, for had she not heard her uncle tell a fellow-passenger in the train, that he had a horse to sell which would suit him exactly, when he knew he was a 'bolter,' and that that was the reason for his being sold! It was all shameful! And into her mind there came the memory of the starlit sea at Treswnd, the lap-lapping of the wavelets, the soft murmur of the breeze, and for the first time she longed to return to the old shore and to feel the north-west wind on her face once more.

'I will try to behave better,' she said, when she bade her aunt goodnight; and as she went up the soft carpeted stairs she began to suspect that 'all is not gold that glitters'.

CHAPTER XVII

AWAY TO THE 'WORKS'!

Leaving Yshbel to her new experiences, we must return to Treswnd, where life wore on tranquilly, untroubled by the struggles and aims of the outside world.

It was evening, and the crimson sunlight streamed across the Pengraig hayfields, from which the last waggon had been led away, leaving the fields fresh and green. The haymakers, too, had departed, and were sitting at supper in the farmyard, where Bensha and Madlen were busily engaged in dispensing the viands.

At the further end of the field, where a gap in the hedge opened out to the cliffs Goronwy and Catrin were standing. He had worked all day at the harvest, his father, too, assisting energetically, for the old feud between him and Simon seemed to have died away with the fall of Parcglas, and Catrin had lingered a moment to thank him for his help. He had constituted himself director of the labourers for the day, and everything had gone well, as it always did under Goronwy's supervision.

'Thee art a good master, Goronwy,' said Catrin; 'and indeed I must thank thee and thy father for coming to help us.'

'There's no need for thanks; we couldn't do less, being neighbours,' said Goronwy.

She was picking idly at the sea pinks, her face lit up by the red sunset.

''Tis long since thou and I have been in the fields together, Catrin.'

'Yes, indeed, 'tis long since we have left our young days behind us. Canst think I'm twenty-one?'

Goronwy made no reply. He was looking out over the broad crimson pathway leading away to the west, his heart full of discontent and unrest.

Yshbel's departure had thoroughly disturbed him; a journey taken so suddenly, and with so little cause, was a thing unheard of at Treswnd. The object of it, too, appeared to him unreasonable and frivolous in a girl whose life was to be spent amongst the simple surroundings of a farm.

'To see the world!' he said, scornfully, to himself many times since she had left; ''tis all very well to see the world if you have a good safe ship to sail in, but to go like this, nobody knows where; to stop with an aunt, nobody knows who; to be amongst grand folks and grand houses, and music and dancing, and silks and satins! How will she feel, I'd like to know, when she comes back (if she ever does come back), and settles down here with the churn and the tubs and the milking pails – and only me for company? Tan-i-marw! I don't think she cares a cockle shell for me!' And he had worked at the hay with less peace and content than he had ever done before.

On this, the last evening of the Pengraig hay harvest, the old scenes around him, the glint of the sunset sea, the flutter of white wings in the air, the rosy tint on every bush and quivering blade of grass, Catrin's small fingers plucking at the sea pinks as of yore, her soft voice in his ears – an intense longing seized him for the old time past, when life was fully satisfying and complete. Why had he put away from him the happiness which was his in the old days? Why, with Yshbel's fair head on his shoulder, and her hand in his, did he never feel the ecstatic pleasure which he experienced in Catrin's presence?

He had been dimly conscious of this question for many long months – unvoiced, unrealised, perhaps – but tonight not only the question arose in his mind, but the answer came too with a full tide of consciousness – because he loved Catrin. The very ground she trod upon was sacred to him, the simple flowers she picked, and threw away, were precious in his sight, her voice was music in his ears, and her face was to him the embodiment of all that was charming, beautiful and pure.

He knew it all, as he stood there in the sunset, and he knew, too, that his life was hopelessly marred; that Catrin and he were separated by a gulf as deep as that which yawned between heaven and hell.

'Yes, those times are gone,' he said at last, and his voice was not quite steady; 'and we are growing older, and as for me, Catrin, I care not how soon the end will come – I am sick and tired of life.'

'Oh, Goronwy,' she said, gently drawing her fingers over the sleeve of his rough jacket, ''tis not like thee to give way like that. I have heard, indeed, how Yshbel went away, but listen, lad – she will come back as fresh and beautiful as ever, and she will love thee more than before, because she will see, that in the whole great world she can find no one like thee. Take heart, lad. Indeed, she will come back, and in the autumn you two will be married.'

A hoarse, scornful laugh was all his answer.

'Thou'rt talking about what thou dost not understand,' he said at last. 'Come, lodes, let us drop this subject and let us stray down to Traethyberil, and fancy we are children once more.'

'Yes – come,' said Catrin. 'But 'tis too late to fancy we are children, Goronwy. I, whatever, have had so many troubles, and learnt so many lessons, harder than those thou used to teach me, that 'tis impossible to feel like a child.'

'Come as man and woman then. See that red sun sinking down in the west – he will keep his promise and rise again tomorrow. See these flowers in the grass – they will keep theirs and come again next spring. Everything is true and plain, except my life, Catrin, and that is false and full of lies.'

The girl hid her face in her hands.

'Never say such hard, cruel words about thyself, Goronwy. *They* are false indeed, and thou art true as the light. Didst not teach me to tell the truth when I was a child, and thought it no harm to tell a lie to shield my father? Oh, Goronwy, thou art not false, though all the world should be!'

'I am a false liar.'

'Though thou wert to swear that to me, lad, I would not believe thee; I would know it was the first lie thou hadst ever told. But, dir anw'l! Why do we talk of lies, and age, and sorrows? Look at the sea, soft and grey; the edge of the sun is still sparkling on the ripples; see the white surf on the sands, and look up at the sky – look hard, and you will see a star over there in the east – 'tis all too beautiful for sorrow!'

'Let us stop here,' he said, 'in our old corner. Come, sit thee down, Catrin, thy hand in mine, like long ago.'

Her small soft hand stole into his, the sea wind blew a straying tress of hair over his shoulder, his very soul was flooded with the charm of her presence; but with the strong temptation to declare his love to her, the stern determination of his character came to his rescue. He would die, before he would be false to Yshbel, or tempt this pure and guileless girl to confess a love which he knew she must for ever after consider a stain upon her soul. And so he put away from him the bitter, sweet temptation, and, loosening his grasp of the brown hand, appeared to change his mood entirely.

'Come,' he said, gathering a handful of the brown and pink shells that clustered on the rocks around them, 'let us have a game of dandiss.'

'Let us, indeed,' said Catrin, acquiescing at once in his mood; and soon the little lonely cove resounded with their exclamations of amusement.

He could scarcely take his eyes from the lovely face that dimpled with merry laughter.

'I believe, lodes, if we lit a fire on Penmwntan, and broiled our mushrooms there, we could forget how old we are, and be children once more. Wilt try some night?'

'Yes, indeed; they will grow now after the hay. But the moon is rising; my father will be wanting his supper. I must go.'

'Yes,' said Goronwy, 'I suppose we must go. Jâri! I've a mind sometimes to run away to the cliffs, and live the rest of my life there.'

Catrin shook her head, smiling pensively. 'What would become of Yshbel then?'

Goronwy made no answer, as they retraced their steps through the fields now growing grey and dewy.

'Goodnight,' he said, rather abruptly, turning down a stony lane; 'this is the shortest way to Sarnissa.'

'Wilt not come and have supper?'

'No, no,' he called back, waving his hand.

'Another mood is upon him,' thought Catrin; 'he was never used to change like that.'

With love, doubt, despair, busily working within him, Goronwy reached Sarnissa, where he found his father sitting in the chimney corner, his legs stretched out to their full length before him, a cloud of smoke curling from the short pipe which he was smoking with lazy enjoyment. He had drunk of the Pengraig brewing, 'not wisely, but too well', and, under its influence, was more loquacious than usual.

'Where hast been so late, 'machgen i?' he asked, as Goronwy entered. 'I've been sitting here this hour alone, with only granny's empty chair for company, and Marged as deaf as a post. I had a mind to go down to the village to find some one to say "bo" to me.'

Goronwy drew a bench nearer the hearth, carefully avoiding the empty rush chair, which he rigidly insisted should be considered sacred.

'Well, here I am now,' he said, 'and my advice to you is, "Go to bed, instead of the village."'

'Go to bed thyself,' said his father. 'Where'st been so late? If

Yshbel was at home now, I would know – but there, she's gone! And look here, Goronwy,' he said, his expression suddenly changing to one of ludicrous solemnity, 'dost not think she'd better stop away? Mind thee, I won't have a ladi here, and I'm afraid that's what she'll be when she comes back, if she ever does come back. She'll be bringing English notions with her, I'm afraid, and wanting pewter spoons and basins, instead of wooden bowls. And perhaps she'll say she can't bear the smell of smoke. Dei anw'l! What will we do with her then? Finish with her, lad – that's my advice!'

'Twt, twt,' said Goronwy, and leaning back against the chimney wall, he too stretched out his legs, and his head dropped on his breast in an attitude of deep thought, while his father mumbled on.

'There's tidy and clean everything is at Pengraig now, and Simon so comfortable in his bed. The little girl is so clever and so kind to him, and speaking as soft as a pigeon. Simon might be worse off, I can tell him, if he is dying – as they say he is, though I don't believe it. Thee'st a great fool not to have tried for Catrin Rees, instead of Yshbel Lloyd; she'd never want to see the world! If I was a few years younger, I'd try for her myself.'

Goronwy changed his attitude uneasily. His father's tippling habits seldom went further than the maudlin stage, and generally ended with the hay harvest, so they were excused or ignored as much as possible, in consideration of their infrequency. But tonight the subject of his conversation irritated his son.

'Hisht! hisht!' he said, 'and go to bed. You are not fit to talk tonight. Who but you, I'd like to know, used to abuse Catrin Rees, and call her a witch?'

'Yes, but I was a fool then, my lad, and tonight I've got all my senses about me, and I'm quite sober, see you! So take my advice and get Yshbel home at once from those Saeson, or else finish with her.'

'They are not Saeson in Glamorgan,' said Goronwy; 'but, in my very deed, I think you are right, father, in spite of your tipsy talk. They say a drunken man and a child will speak the truth, and I'll go to the 'works' myself, and bring her home, or leave her for good. There now! I've said it, and I'll do it, as soon as Tredu hay is safe in.'

'That's right, my boy! Always take thy father's advice,' said Morgan Hughes, with a solemn look and a hiccough.

Under the influence of the Pengraig ale, and the pleasant glow of the fire, he fell asleep, and Goronwy was left to his dreams, which lasted long into the night. At the word of a drunken man, how fair a vision had stolen in upon him! Catrin always with him – in the fields, on the hearth, sitting in the old rush chair! Yes, even occupying granny's seat! What a fool he had been to ruin his own life! Then he thought of Yshbel's guileless face, her pretty ways, her bravery in the storm; and he cursed himself for an inhuman brute. Then, passing into another mood, he sank into a slough of despond and self-pity.

'God help me!' he said. 'Help Yshbel, for I see nothing but misery before us both!'

He tried with all his might to banish the thought of Catrin, and, rising, he strode up and down excitedly.

The night wore on, the sea wind sighed in the chimney, the moon shone in upon him, but the tumult of his feelings was not assuaged.

It was two hours after midnight – that hour when the line that divides the seen from the unseen world seems thinnest, and all we have ever heard of the weird and uncanny returns to the mind.

He heard the moaning of the wind, and the hooting of the owls on Penmwntan, and always there was the hsh-sh-sh of the sea, sometimes like the crooning of a mother who hushes her infant to sleep, sometimes like the rush of a torrent, and sometimes like a gentle whisper, through which every separate wave is heard breaking on the shore. But all fell unheeded on

Goronwy's ear, until, on the clear night air, there fell another sound – that of a light footstep surely, hurrying up the stony path to the farmyard. Now it is lost on the straw and stubble, now it enters the 'cwrt' and even before there comes the timid knock, some mysterious instinct has told him it is Catrin's step.

The knock, though gentle, aroused Morgan Hughes from his nap. Goronwy hurried to the door, and, raising the latch, saw Catrin, flurried and breathless.

What is it, lass? Come in.'

'Oh, Goronwy, why art up so late? I thought I would have to knock long before any one would hear me. 'Tis my father is so white and so weak – a faint, I suppose it is – and when I went to fetch some brandy there was none. Madlen has broken the bottle and spilt it all, she says, and I beg of thee, if there is any in the house, to give me a little.'

'Why, of course,' said Goronwy, 'only I keep it locked up. Wait till I fetch it from the coffer,' and he hurried up to the loft while Morgan Hughes stirred the embers on the hearth.

'Come nearer the fire, 'merch-i,' he said; ''tis cold at this hour, even in summer. Thee'st a good daughter, and I was just telling Goronwy 'twould be wiser for him to have chosen thee for a wife than Yshbel Lloyd; but he says, "How could he marry a witch?"' and he laughed the foolish laugh of a man whose brain is still clouded by his late potations. 'He is going to follow her to the "works" now, and bring her home. Art not, Goronwy?' he added, as the latter appeared.

It was the last straw which made Goronwy's burden too heavy to bear, and, with a deep oath, he pushed his father aside.

'Mind him not, Catrin,' he said; 'he has drunk too much of Madlen's strong beer. Give thy father a spoonful of this, and he will revive. I will come with thee.'

'No, no!' said Catrin, repulsing him, as she had done once before; 'I wish thee not to come. Can diolch! Go thou to bed.'

Goronwy watched the flying figure as it crossed the moonlit

clos, and turned at last, with a sigh, to the cold hearth, where even the grey embers were expiring.

Morgan Hughes, frightened at hearing so unusual a thing as an imprecation from his son's lips, was sobered a little, and retired to his bed in moody silence.

Goronwy, too, sought his, but found no rest until the dawn, when he slept heavily, and arrived late at the Tredu haymaking. Everything was propitious for the harvest, however, and when he arrived, strong and full of energy, every one felt a fresh zest in his work. In three days the hay was ready to be gathered, and Mrs Gwyn, coming into the hayfield for a last glance at the haymakers, sat down, well pleased, on the hedge at the entrance into the field.

She had aged a good deal, had a careworn, faded look on her face, and bent a little over her gold-headed cane.

As she sat on the hedge-side, her scarlet cloak and her broad-brimmed straw hat made a bit of bright colouring against the lush green of the hedge.

'Well, 'tis a good crop, and gathered without a drop of rain,' she said, as the last load passed her, leaving its trails on the wild roses that grew by the gate.

'Ah! Goronwy Hughes, good-day to thee! I have seen thee in the fields these three days. Many thanks to thee and thy father. Is all well at Sarnissa?'

'Yes – well thank you, mestress,' said Goronwy, cap in hand, 'only 'tis very lonely without granny. Jari! we didn't know how she filled the house till she left us!'

'No, no; 'tis always the way, and I can well understand how empty the hearth is without her!'

She could not help noticing the handsome erect figure of the man who stood before her. His sunburnt face, his brown wavy hair, his blue eyes, his brown neck exposed by his loose blue shirt, his broad shoulders, and the red handkerchief tied round his waist, made a picture that an artist would have been glad to seize. He was the man to whom Yshbel Lloyd had plighted her troth, and through her alone could she hope for her son's return to Tredu! She had long recognised this truth, and now that Yshbel had in a manner stepped out of the peasant rank and become a 'lady,' perhaps a rich one, she had woven many dreams in which Walto found Yshbel, and brought her triumphantly home as his bride! She was, therefore, somewhat taken aback when Goronwy said: ''Tis Walto's direction that I'm wanting, if you please.'

'Art wanting to write to him? Well, then,'tis 'George Cadwalader Gwyn, Esquire, Belfield Colliery, Pontargele, Glamorgan.'

'Jari! I'll never remember it,' said Goronwy, and producing a dog-eared memorandum book, he laboriously transcribed the address. '"George Cadwalader Gwyn, Esquire." We quite forgot the "George" down here.'

'Yes,' said Mrs Gwyn, ''tis "Walto" he was down here,' and her voice took a tender, longing tone. 'I wish he'd come back, Goronwy, and be "Walto" once more.'

'Yes, indeed, we are all feeling for you, mestress. 'Tis long since he went away, and 'tis strange he never came back. Perhaps I'll persuade him.'

'Thou!' said Mrs Gwyn, with a start.

'Yes; I'm going to the 'works' to fetch Yshbel home. 'Tis a long journey for her to come alone.'

'Fetch – Yshbel – home!' said Mrs Gwyn, sarcastically. 'Fetch her home, indeed! Don't be a fool, Goronwy; she has had a taste of the world, and she will never come back to thee! How wilt thou dare to show thyself there amongst her grand friends? She, a lady in her carriage, and thou, a farmer from the middle of the hay harvest!'

'Yes, and worse than that,' said Goronwy, 'a collier with a black face most like, for I'm going to work in the Belfield Colliery, if Walto will find me a place.'

'Not "Walto" over there, remember,' said the mestress, drawing herself up, 'but "Mr Gwyn," Goronwy.'

'Yes, yes – of course, mestress; I won't forget. He will be the master, and I will be only a collier, but Yshbel Lloyd is my promised wife, and she'll come home with me, or we separate for ever.'

'Thou art a 'penstif' man, I know,' said Mrs Gwyn, rising and preceding him through the gap.

'Will I take a message to him?' asked Goronwy, following her towards the farmyard, where the supper awaited the haymakers.

'Thee canst tell him, if thee likest, that if he doesn't come home soon, he will not find his mother here;' and she passed into the 'cwrt', and in the shadow of the tall box hedge, dried the tears which had gathered in her eyes.

The country people assigned no reason for Mrs Gwyn's failing health, except the real one, namely, that she was breaking her heart for her son.

We are told there are no such things as broken hearts, but this is a falsity, which those who have lived through middle age can refute. It is not only the sudden, sharp agony that breaks, but the long wearing sorrow, the hope deferred, the continued craving. The bow of wood that yields long to the bending is broken at last, as surely and completely as that of steel, which snaps at the first strain, and the torn fragments distinctly mark the severity of the wrench.

Goronwy shook his head, as he caught the last glimpse of her scarlet cloak behind the two peacocks clipped out on the box hedge.

'Pwr thing! pwr thing! I'll bring Walto home, if there's any heart in him!'

A few days after this conversation, he left Sarnissa in the early dawn, having delivered himself of sundry injunctions to his father on the necessity of looking carefully after the farm and avoiding the haymaking drinks during his absence.

'Thee canst trust me, lad,' said Morgan Hughes, in the strength of purpose born of the pure, fresh influence of the early dawn. 'I'll only go haymaking to the Wern and Llanrhyd.

They are teetotallers there, and only send buttermilk into the field. But, Goronwy, lad, 'twill cost a lot, that journey.'

'Twt, twt,' said Goronwy. 'I'll take employment in the colliery, and soon make enough money to pay for it, and a little over for my wedding.'

He began his journey through the Pengraig fields and round the side of Penmwntan, as, by so doing, he would cut off two miles of the distance. On his left, Pengraig's grey walls stood gilded by the morning sun; on his right, the broad sea shimmered and whispered, the seagulls and crows swept over him, and all around him spoke of peace and the fullness of summer.

He followed the very path over which he and Catrin had so often strayed together, and because that stalwart figure strode on steadily, and showed no signs of the restless discontent which possessed him, it would not be true to say the peasant nature within him was stolid and callous. On reaching the Tygwyn fields, where he lost the last glimpse of the old neighbourhood, a pang of regret swept over him, and though he made no sign, there was a wistful sorrow in his last look towards Penmwntan and Pengraig.

He was wearing his best clothes, and this in itself caused him to be fretful and uneasy. Could he but doff them, and don the fustian suit which he carried in his bundle, he would have felt more at his ease.

He reached Caermadoc as the shopkeepers were taking down their shutters, and, being still twenty miles from the railway station, took his seat in the mail coach, to meet which he had, years ago, driven Walto. 'Dei anw'l!' he thought, 'I won't be as long from home as he has been, and I'll bring Yshbel back with me.'

He was too absorbed in his thoughts to take much notice of the scenes of sylvan beauty through which he was whirled, and it was not until he had reached the station, and really entered the train, for the first time in his life, that he began to realise how far he had left the seclusion of Treswnd behind him.

The grey stone houses, each in its square patch of garden, the slated roofs, the stiff roads, and formal trim hedges all struck him as new and strange.

'Tidy people here whatever,' he thought, recalling to mind the picturesque untidiness of the Treswnd hedgerows. It was a little-frequented line, and he was the sole occupant of the carriage, until, at the first stopping place, a fellow-traveller entered.

A broad-shouldered, stalwart man like himself, but with all the signs of cultivation and refinement which mixing with the world may give, but often fails to do. A clean-shaven, dark face, a broad forehead, with deep-set black eyes, the mouth delicate and sensitive – there was something prepossessing in the appearance of the man, which made Goronwy glad of his company. His clerical garb by no means hid the fine proportions of his figure, and the soft felt hat shaded a brow on which deep thought and perhaps some sorrow had left their traces. There was no sign of them, however, in the genial voice with which he addressed Goronwy.

'Not many passengers on this line – there never are.'

'Perhaps not, sir. I have never been on it before.'

'Indeed! 'Tis one that often brings the country people to the haunts of men.'

'Well, 'tisn't often we Treswnd people want to visit the towns. I have never been a journey before, and I suppose I will never take another, once I get back to Treswnd.'

The stranger was silent, and Goronwy again fell into a reverie, from which at last his fellow-traveller aroused him.

'This is Trecoed station – do you change here?'

At this question Goronwy was much perplexed, though he was too proud to show it.

'I don't know; I'm going to Stranport, and there I have to take a ticket to Pontargele.'

'Then we shall be fellow-travellers all the way. Perhaps I can be of use to you at Stranport, which is a busy station, and you are not an experienced traveller.'

'Thank you, sir. There couldn't be any one less used to it.'

In the silence that followed, the newcomer looked keenly at his companion. There was something in the man that interested him, and made him wish to enter into conversation with him, for the Reverend Ivor Owen, curate of Pontargele church, was one who found his work, his happiness, and the chief interest of his life, in the study and society of his fellow-beings. To him, human character was a book whose pages he was never tired of reading, and his flock often benefited by his interest in them, for to see a difficulty or a trouble in the pathway of others meant, for Ivor Owen, an earnest endeavour to remove it; and as he watched Goronwy's face, which had once more settled into a brown study, he took note of the firm set lips, the line of perplexity between the eyebrows, which he felt sure was unnatural to that open countenance. He longed to know what troubled the man, who, for a few short hours, was to he his companion. He was, however, too thoroughly refined for intrusive curiosity, so he, too, at last settled himself down to his newspaper, and it was Goronwy who first broke the silence.

'What time will we be in Stranport?'

'About three o'clock, and Pontargele at four. You are going to see the world a little, I suppose.'

'See the world!' said Goronwy, with a little scorn in his voice. 'I have no wish to see the world. I am going to the Belfield colliery; I have a friend there.'

'Ah! That is halfway between Pontargele and Tregele, where the 'Daisy' colliery is situated.'

'Are they so near, then?'

'Yes; little more than a mile apart.'

Silence followed, until, at Stranport, Goronwy, bewildered and confused, realised how fortunate he had been in meeting with Ivor Owen.

'I don't know how I would fare in this station without you, sir.'

'Well, badly perhaps, the first time, but you will soon get used to it.'

On reaching Pontargele, Goronwy turned to wish his new friend 'Goodbye,' but the latter, following him from the carriage, said: 'Have you lodgings?'

'No,' said Goronwy. 'Will it be hard to find them?'

'No; there are plenty of a sort, but I will take you to a comfortable place. 'Tis here close by.' And, opening the gate of a small front garden, where cabbages and leeks filled the place usually given up to flowers, he entered at the open door without knocking. A pleasant-faced woman came to meet him.

'Dear, dear! Mr Owen, sir, how are you? There's glad I am to see you, and there's glad Mary will be!'

'I have no time to see Mary today, but I have brought you a lodger. Didn't you say you wanted one?'

'Yes, sir, indeed – and you never forget. Is he a countryman?'

'Yes,' said Goronwy, laughing, 'if ever there was a countryman. I am from Cardiganshire.'

'Oh, a Cardi!' said the woman. 'We have plenty of them here. But come in, 'machgen i, you shall have a clean bed and a warm hearth.'

'Well, I will leave you,' said Ivor Owen, 'for you are in good hands, and I shall see you again no doubt. My friends are all colliers, or nearly so. Goodbye.'

'Jari! he's a nice man,' exclaimed Goronwy. 'There's kind he was to me at Stranport.'

'Kind!' said Mrs Johns. 'He's the kindest man, and the best man that ever I saw. If there were more men like him in the world, we wouldn't want a better world! He's called the "collier's friend". But come, you'll want something to eat after your long journey.'

And with the clatter of the tea-things, and the frying of the inevitable chop filling his ears, Goronwy forgot for a moment the thoughts that had burdened him on his journey.

CHAPTER XVIII

AN UNINVITED GUEST

A tawny shore, a sky of light, a sea of blue all flecked with white, a cliff above, on which a boy and girl are roaming. Such was the picture that passed before the mental vision of a man who sat idle for a moment and mused. Again applying himself to his work, he tried, but in vain, to banish the vision. How different was the scene of reality around him!

It was Goronwy Hughes, who, for the first time, had begun to work at his 'piece' in the Belfield colliery. One hundred feet below the surface, and half a mile from the shaft, he toiled at his unfamiliar occupation, sometimes pausing to think over the train of circumstances which had brought him to this pass.

'I, Goronwy Hughes, who was never happy if he was not in the air and the sunshine. Tan i marw! I think I must have lost my senses,' and he looked round him at the walls of black with disgust. 'But I would be a fool not to make a little money when 'tis so easily earned.'

Above him, he knew, towered a high hill, on whose crest the sun was shining, on whose sides the grass bent in the wind, but here the air was heavy with sulphurous fumes. The clink-clink of the picks were all the sounds that fell upon his ear, except, indeed, the muffled rumble of trams, which rolled through the dark underground tunnels. Clink, clink, clink – and Goronwy actually laughed at the irony of the situation. 'And all for Yshbel,' he soliloquised. Deep down somewhere in his nature he rebelled against his fate, and giving way to temptation, dreamed of how gladly he would have borne the darkness and gloom if only it were for Catrin! Gradually, as his pickaxe loosened the blocks of ebony, a new hope rose up within him – a hope that Yshbel, having once tasted the joys of grandeur, would be so enamoured of her life, that her old love would be distasteful to her, and that thus she would refuse to keep her promise to marry him – and he would be free. Free! What a world of hope and happiness that word contained!

Until this vision shone before him, he had not realised how galling were his chains, how distasteful the prospect of his marriage had become. But now, as he threw his tools aside at the dinnertime, he stretched himself to his full length, and rising from his stooping posture, a longing desire to unravel the knot which had so suddenly tangled the thread of his life, throbbed through his veins. The darkness, the sense of suffocation, the confinement – he would escape them all, and, breaking his bonds, would fly to Catrin, the sunlight and the sea wind. Then came the thought of Yshbel's promise, and his to her, the memory of how she had imperilled her life for him, the bitter certainty that his fetters were too firmly riveted, even by this last act of leaving home in search of her. And sitting down, with his back to the rock of coal, he sighed heavily, and applied himself to his meal of bread and bacon, washed down with a draught of cold tea.

A few yards away from him another collier worked at his 'piece,' and drawing near Goronwy, sat down beside him, and spreading out the four corners of his blue cotton bundle, proceeded to regale himself upon its contents.

'You're from Cardiganshire?' he asked, unceremoniously.

'Yes,' answered Goronwy; 'and I wish I was back there, with all my heart. I don't see the sense of a man's being buried before he's dead – but there, 'tis my own doing, and I've got no one to blame.'

'Well,' said his neighbour, plodding away at his bread and cheese, clasped knife in hand, 'every man feels like that at first, and if 'twasn't for the good wages, I don't suppose anyone would be content to work here.'

'No amount of wages would tempt me to stay here long,' said Goronwy. 'You can get the best things in life without paying for them, and only those things will satisfy me, you see.'

'You're a gentleman, I suppose, then? But what things can you get without paying for, I'd like to know?'

'Why, light and air, the fresh sea wind, the open fields, the sky at night, and the moonlight – plenty of work in the open air, sound sleep, and a good appetite.'

'But what will you have to satisfy that appetite, 'machgen i? I know it all, I'm a Cardi myself, though it's many years since I saw the dear old country. 'Tis true you get a good appetite there, but twelve shillings a week will not give you much to satisfy it. Here we get fresh meat for our dinner, bacon for our breakfast, tishens and pies in plenty, and that's what I call the best things in life – in this life, mind you – for I'm not one who neglects his soul. No, no. There is not a service at my chapel that I don't attend. What chapel do you go to?'

'I'm a churchman,' answered Goronwy.

'Oh! Well, you've got a good man for your curate here, and no mistake!' and he tilted his tin bottle of tea, and washed down the last of his dinner.

'Time's up,' he said, and picking up his pickaxe, he set to work again, leaving Goronwy to his meditations.

He was not sorry when the day's work was over, and he was once more standing in the 'cage' which carried the toilers up and down to their work. He drew a long breath on reaching the open air.

'Dei anw'l!' he said, 'here's a life, and here's a figure I am!' Hands, face, hair – in fact, the whole body – was covered with the dust of the coal, at which he had worked all day. Fortunately for the colliers it is not unwholesome, or their lives would be seriously endangered by the clogging of their skin. Scores of other men in like condition wended their ways homewards with him. When he reached his lodgings, he hesitated at the doorway of the kitchen, fearing to pollute its speckless cleanliness.

'Come in, come in,' said Mrs Johns. 'Here's your clean clothes, my man, and here's your tub of water. You'll soon get used to our ways. Put your black clothes in this corner, and put on your clean ones, and tea will then be ready for you,' and, closing the door, she left him to his ablutions.

A huge tub full of water stood before the glowing fire, which had excited Goronwy's wonder and admiration ever since his arrival. Not only the walls of the broad, open chimney were whitewashed, but the hobs, the very bars of the grate, and even the culm balls of which the fire was built up. The only black object was the shining kettle which simmered beside the fire. All so white and pure, the red glow lighting up the white hearth with a rosy light.

It is a curious taste this, of the Glamorganshire collier for a white hearth – perhaps in the contrast with the dark surroundings of his work lies the charm. Every day the cleanly housewife renews the whitewash on any stain the previous day may have brought her spotless hearth or fire; and later on, when Goronwy, washed and dressed, was seated at his tea at the little round table with his landlady, he was obliged to confess that the red glow of the fire, and its pure white surroundings, had a peculiar charm of their own.

'I must buy new clothes at once,' he said.

'Well, you'll get them close by, and you get good wages to pay for them. If you're a sober, steady man you'll soon make money here.'

'I won't stop here long enough to make much money. I want to get back to Cardiganshire as soon as I can.'

'That's strange. For what did you come, then?'

'I came here because I was a fool, and had lost my senses.'

'To see the world a bit, I suppose?'

'I've seen enough, and you may depend upon it, as soon as

my business is finished, I'll go back to Treswnd, especially as the manager is from home. He is from the same place as me.'

'Well, indeed! Mr George Gwyn?'

'Yes; Mr Walto Gwyn, we were used to call him.'

'Everything is fresh and strange to you now, 'machgen i. Wait a month before you do anything;' and Goronwy, thinking it good advice, determined to abide by it.

He debated long within himself whether he should make a confidante of his hostess, but decided on the contrary, as he still felt entirely equal to bearing his own burden, though the confidence with which he was accustomed to quote his favourite maxim, 'A man can always do what he makes up his mind to do,' had considerably diminished.

'No, no,' he said to himself one evening, as he sat in the corner of the white hearth, and sent curls of blue smoke from his pipe up the chimney, 'Catrin is right, and no one can do exactly what he likes, somehow.'

He did not hasten to make known his arrival to Yshbel, preferring rather to wait until Walto should return to his post at the Belfield colliery, and accompany him to Glaish-y-dail, whose imposing front had been pointed out to him by a fellow-collier.

'Yshbel up there!' he thought. 'I wonder how they treat her?' But he kept his own counsel, never divulging his interest in the large white house, which was so conspicuous in the sunshine, on the opposite side of the valley. He had been a week at Pontargele, and had not yet made any sign of his presence to Yshbel. A spell was upon him, that he seemed unable to break. Every day seemed to increase the distance between them, and every day he felt more keenly the complete separation from Catrin and the longing for her presence.

'You are not eating, man,' said Mrs Johns. 'What's the good for you to think and think like that? Come, rouse yourself, and enjoy life like other young men. There's the Glaish-y-dail carriage,' and she rose from her seat to look at it.

Goronwy, too, looked after it with eager interest, as it passed slowly up the road in front of the cottage. It was a steep hill, and he had time to see the occupants plainly.

'There's for you!' said Mrs Johns, with a mock salaam. '"Mrs Jones, the Daisy," if you please! And see my grand horses stepping out and my grand coachman on the box, if you please, and me sitting like the Queen inside! My goodness! there's a pretty young lady she's got with her, and that young Mr Jones, of Belfield, talking to her. D'ye see her?'

'Yes,' said Goronwy, standing in the middle of the kitchen, glowering at the pretty girl, who was chatting merrily with the young man – he bending forward with every sign of admiring attention.

A wave of bitter feeling swept over Goronwy as he took in the scene. There was not a shred of jealousy in it, which fact in itself was a proof that there was no real love for Yshbel in his heart, but an utter distaste for the circumstances in which he found himself took possession of him, as the handsome equipage passed out of sight, and he turned his eyes upon his own rough hands, and remembered the heap of black soiled clothes of which he had lately divested himself.

Mrs Johns, who was rambling on about pride and grandeur – 'Ach-y-fi! and passing her own sister's door with her chin in the air,' etc, etc – was startled by an oath, and a sarcastic laugh from her lodger, who had hitherto commended himself to her by his abstinence from the bad language which is too prevalent amongst the lower class of colliers.

'Caton pawb! 'machgen i, what's the matter? But there! 'tis no wonder, when you are working hard yourself, and seeing people like that riding in their carriage! And if you knew them from the beginning as I do! "Jones, the Daisy's", mother was a poor woman in the village here till she died, though certainly he was always sending her enough to keep her respectable; and Mrs Jones' sister, Martha Williams, is living in that little house with the pink face and the box hedge in front, to this day, and—'

'Oh, I don't care about Mr Jones and his relations,' said Goronwy, impatiently. 'I suppose he worked hard for his money, or he would not have got it, and he's welcome to it, for all I care! All I want is to settle my business and get away from it all,' and he flung himself down full length on the settle, and fell once more into that bad habit which Mrs Johns so much deprecated, and thought and mused, until the twilight fell, and the whole kitchen was lighted up by the rosy glow of the snow-white hearth.

'What foolery it was altogether! How could he present himself, black and begrimed with coal dust, before that fine carriage, and ask that fair girl, who he felt was its brightest ornament, to step out of it, and come home with him to Sarnissa, and mind the cows and calves, and boil the uwd for dinner?' and again he laughed bitterly at the ridiculousness of the idea.

And yet there was a gleam of comfort in the very incongruity of the whole thing. Yshbel would feel it herself, and would refuse to keep the promise she had made. A flush of red suffused his face as he realised his own feelings.

'There's no doubt I'm a mean dog,' he thought. 'Tan i marw! I'll bear it no longer, but I'll have it all plain and settled at once. I won't even wait till Walto comes back. How unfortunate that he should be away. Let me see, 'tis Friday today. I'll go up to Glaish-y-dail tomorrow afternoon. I'll put on my best clothes, and won't frighten her with my black face, So help me, God! I'll put it all to the touch then, and if she is still true to me, I'll marry her at once, and, if I can help it, she shall never know that for her my heart is as cold as a stone – but for Catrin, it is warm – yes, burning like that glowing fire!'

Next day he was full of restless impatience, and could scarcely wait till the afternoon to carry his determination into practice.

Meanwhile, at Glaish-y-dail Yshbel's days were full of excitement, and she often turned with something like a longing

regret to the old time of peace and seclusion at Treswnd. Her
aunt, perceiving there was something unusual in the girl's
manner, did all she could to fill up her time with gaiety. She
took her to Stranport, and introduced her to all the young
people she could think of. Picture galleries, theatres, concerts
– all were crowded upon her, and all were enjoyed with a
wondering delight which should have satisfied her, but "Mrs
Jones, the Daisy," though not an educated woman, was shrewd
and observant, and the wistful look of sadness which followed
Yshbel's seasons of merriment, was noted and keenly felt by
her. 'Had she not loaded her with presents? dressed her in
fashionable attire? done all she could to amuse and entertain
her?' And yet this country girl seemed sad and discontented!
Such a thing was unheard of, and Mrs Jones began to feel a
little anger towards her beautiful niece.

'Taking her from a poor fisherman's cottage, too, where
there was nothing to eat but bacon and broth! Ach-y-fi! If you
put some people in a pot of honey they would not say it was
sweet!'

Yshbel, ignorant of the keen watch which her aunt kept
upon her, went on her way quietly, though evidently not at her
ease. Her aunt was mistaken in thinking her discontented with
her good fortune; she was not that, but she did feel a strange
disquietude growing up within her, which she found it
impossible to banish entirely from her face. This strange
feeling, she was conscious, was connected with Goronwy and
her promise to him. It was not that she was tired of the bond
which existed between them, but that she was irritated and
uneasy at her own conflicting feelings. She had had a glimpse
of the world, with all its gaudy grandeur, its hollowness, its
want of real refinement, and it had disappointed her, and made
her long for the simplicity of her former secluded life. She
would return to her romantic dreams, her solitary rambles on
the shore, and be happy again.

And yet, would her marriage with Goronwy Hughes satisfy

her – fill her life with content, as she had once thought it would? And here it was the discontent came in. She had seen other men – men who had struck her fancy, though none had touched her heart, and she had felt that Goronwy was not like them. He was true of heart, she thought, he was honourable, he was brave, but he lacked the outward refinement which she had seen in other men; and she felt her happiness had been spoilt by her one peep at the world.

Oh, to return to Treswnd – to marry Goronwy, and settle down amongst the pots and pans at Sarnissa! She had never called them, or thought of them, as 'pots and pans' before, but now somehow all was changed. She felt it was, and, regretting it, still felt unable to throw off the spell cast over her by her initiation into the ways of the world. It was glorious summer weather too. The craggy hills, grown golden in the sunshine which had ripened their scant herbage, reminded her of Penmwntan; the silent gliding river below, drew her thoughts away with it to the sea, to which it was flowing, and that soft sky brooding over her one afternoon as she sat in the verandah at Glaish-y-dail, reminded her of the sunny days at Treswnd, when she had lain in her boat in the shade of the rocks, and dreamt of the world in which she was now living.

Mrs Jones sat at her tea table at the open French window, handing her cups of afternoon tea to her guests, whom the heat of the day had drawn into the garden. Mrs Jones, of 'Belfield,' had called, and "Mrs Jones, the Daisy," was in the seventh heaven of happiness, for everything had gone well. Jones happened to be at home, and in his best suit. She herself was wearing her most becoming cap, and Yshbel, sitting there under the roses in her plain white muslin, looked 'quite the lady' in spite of her obstinate refusal to wear the jewellery with which her aunt loaded her.

'You will come early on Monday, Mrs Jones,' said her guest, 'will you not? For I would like to show your niece through the orchid house. She says she has never seen any.'

'Oh yes; certainly, Mrs Jones. We will come as early as we can.'

'A garden party?' said Yshbel, meditatively stirring her tea, 'I have never been to such a thing. All among the flowers, and out in the sunshine. How beautiful!'

'Yes,' said Jenkin, who was hovering near her, 'and as we shall have a good band, we are to have a little dance in the evening.'

'Oh! 'twill be lovely,' said Yshbel 'to hear the music and to see you all dancing.'

'But you dance?'

'Me dance? Oh no, indeed! Where would I learn to dance? – except I danced sometimes before the waterfall – 'The White Lady,' we called it, because the wind blew it just to that shape. 'Twas like a lady dancing and waving her skirts; and I was a foolish girl, and used to dance and sing on the sands before her, and hold up my old blue gown, and bow and toss my hair like she did.'

'You looked charming, I'm sure,' said Jenkin, with a little scorn in his voice.

'You have painted a lovely picture, Miss Lloyd,' said a clear, musical voice from the verandah, where the Reverend Ivor Owen was chatting with "Mr Jones, the Daisy". 'It makes me long for the seaside. My childhood was spent by the sea, and I never feel that any scenery, however lovely, is perfect without it.'

'Oh no,' said Yshbel – 'no, indeed! I could never be happy long away from the sea.'

Mrs Jones coughed meaningly, and tried to attract her niece's attention. The conversation was straying into a path that might lead to uncomfortable disclosures.

'Come here, Yshbel – fetch me my glasses, dear. Who is this man coming up the drive?' and all eyes turned to the grey figure of a man who approached the house.

'He has made a mistake,' said Mr Jones, going a few steps to meet the intruder.

'To the left, my man,' he called out, pointing towards a diverging road, which led to the stables and the back of the house; 'that way – that way!' but the grey figure came on steadily.

'A collier, I expect, in his best clothes,' said Jenkin.

'Go and speak to him, Jones,' said the hostess, who was always in dread lest some of her poor relations should turn up at an awkward moment.

'These colliers are so stupid,' she said, apologetically. 'But there! I must not say a word against them in Mr Owen's presence – must I?'

'He is very slow to believe any harm of them, certainly,' said "Mrs Jones, the Belfield".

'Well, I certainly have a warm corner in my heart for the colliers, and this one seems a very good specimen. What a fine physique! What a noble head he has!'

The stranger had now met Mr Jones, and was evidently holding an animated conversation with him.

'What do you want here?' said the latter. 'Didn't I tell you, my man, you made a mistake? That is the road to the back door.'

'I don't want the back door, or the front door either,' said Goronwy – for it was he – 'I only want to speak a few words with Yshbel Lloyd. I see her sitting there. Hands off, man! Tan i marw! I'll throw you into your own fish pond.'

But Mr Jones, alive to the importance of keeping up the dignity of Glaish-y-dail before company, laid hold of the young man's shoulders and endeavoured to turn his face by force in the opposite direction. Goronwy's hot temper flashed up in a moment. With Yshbel looking on, was he going to be turned about like a tramping beggar? No; and turning suddenly round, he seized hold of "Jones, the Daisy," and flung him bodily into the middle of a clump of rhododendrons.

In vain Mrs Jones tried to preserve the polite equanimity of her tea party.

"Mrs Jones, the Belfield," and Yshbel rose in a flutter, while Jenkin and Ivor Owen hurried down to Mr Jones' assistance. He was extricating himself with difficulty from his rough couch, his eyes half closed, and his black waistcoat shaking with laughter.

'Le'me tell you, he shook me off as if I was a fly,' he said, while the young man came to his assistance.

'Beg your pardon, sir,' he said, 'but I never allow another man's hands to be laid upon me. I only want to see Yshbel. She is my promised wife as you well know, and I've come up to claim her, and to take her home with me.'

'I say you shall not speak to her.'

'And I say I will,' said Goronwy, calmly walking towards the house.

'My fellow-traveller, surely!' said Ivor Owen. 'I thought your form seemed familiar to me. Here is Miss Lloyd, she has evidently recognised you.'

Goronwy was too intent upon the vision of beauty that flew down the lawn to meet him, to answer. It was indeed Yshbel, who, heedless of her aunt's reproving voice, and of "Mrs Jones, the Belfield's," astonishment, upon recognising Goronwy had started from her seat and rushed to meet him.

'Oh, Goronwy, lad!' she cried, breathless. 'I am glad to see thee,' and she clasped his outstretched hand. No warmer greeting would have been considered maidenly between a couple plighted to each other.

'How art, lass?' was his undemonstrative answer, though in his heart there surged a proud feeling of triumph over the rich man who had treated him with such contumely.

The latter now stood confounded. Yshbel's disgraceful behaviour had put the finishing touch to his discomfiture! And he turned towards the house much flurried and ruffled in appearance by the rough bed from which he had just risen. Ivor Owen and Jenkin accompanied him, the two Mrs Jones' awaiting them in the verandah.

'Did you ever see such impidence?' said his wife, brushing a dead leaf off his coat. 'What is Yshbel saying to him?'

'Leave her alone. She's got a pretty way with her, and I daresay she'll get rid of the fellow better than we can.'

'No doubt he's drunk, or mad, or something. Come in, Mrs Jones, and finish your tea in the drawing room.'

Every one looked flushed and uncomfortable, except Ivor Owen, who, with his clear brown eyes, was keenly alive to the situation.

'It strikes me we are all making a grand mistake,' he said, 'and owe an apology to the young man. He is evidently a friend of Miss Lloyd's, and she is glad to see him. Here she comes to explain.'

'Aunt,' said Yshbel, on reaching the verandah, 'this is Goronwy Hughes, the young man to whom I am going to be married, as I have often told you. I must have a little time to speak to him. We will walk up the hillside, as he is not welcome here. Goodbye, Mrs Jones. I told you I was only a fisher girl come amongst you for a little while. I will go back with Goronwy to my nets and my fishing, and you must forget all about me.'

Ivor Owen had turned away at once on hearing the words 'to whom I am going to be married,' and joined Goronwy, who stood a little way off, neither boldly assertive, nor unduly retiring, but simply waiting calmly for Yshbel's return.

'I have come to congratulate you,' said Ivor Owen in Welsh, holding out his hand, 'and to claim acquaintance with you. Don't you remember we travelled together from Cardiganshire a short time ago?'

'Of course I do,' said Goronwy, grasping his hand, 'and how you helped me, sir; but, in my deed, that 'Daisy' man angered me so much, that I never looked at you. What does he mean? No man ever laid his hands like that on me before, and I can tell him I'm not going to allow him to touch me.'

'But I'm sure he will apologise now. He did not know you were a friend of Miss Lloyd's.'

'Yes; he knew me well enough. He knows that Yshbel Lloyd and I were to be married in October, and he came to Treswnd and tempted her away from me, 'just to see the world,' he said. 'Well, she's seen it now, and she's got to choose between me and the world!'

'It's easy to see which she will choose,' said Ivor Owen, as Yshbel returned, her face glowing with excitement and shyness.

'Come, Goronwy,' she said, 'we will walk up the hillside. That path leads to the top,' and opening a little rustic gate, they passed together from the lawn.

'Goodbye, sir,' said Goronwy, looking back, 'I hope we shall meet again.'

It would be impossible to describe "Mrs Jones, the Daisy's," discomfiture, when Yshbel, after disclosing her 'disgraceful' connection with the 'common man', left her to gather together the rags of her gentility as best she could.

'I'm ashamed of her, Mrs Jones,' she said, hot tears of indignation gathering in her eyes. 'After Jones and me doing so much for her and all. Of course, after her behaviour today, I wouldn't think of bringing her to your garden party. She shall go from here at once, so don't you be afraid that we'll disgrace you with such company!'

'Well, look here now,' said Mr Jones, 'there's something to be said on her side. You know, Merry Ann, I told you she was going to marry this young farmer, and 'twas only on me promising that she should go back to him in a short time, that she would consent to come at all. Certainly, I never thought she would stick to him like this.'

'I cannot agree with you at all,' said Ivor Owen. 'On the contrary, I admire her immensely for her fidelity and her courage in acknowledging him before us all; and upon my word, he seems to me to be a man to be proud of! A fine manly fellow. A farmer, you say? Well, I know he is working at the 'Belfield' now.'

'A collier! The hussy!' exclaimed Mrs Jones, forgetting her gentility for the moment.

'I'm very sorry for your disappointment,' said "Mrs Jones, the Belfield." 'Miss Lloyd seemed to fit into her place so well, and we all thought what an acquisition she was to your household. Most certainly you must bring her to Llys-y-fran. She's a great favourite of mine.'

'Well indeed you're very kind,' murmured "Mrs Jones the Daisy," as her guest rose to leave. 'I don't know yet what Jones will settle about her, but 'tis very certain if she stops here, she'll have to drop that fellow.'

'Take my advice, Mrs Jones, and let the matter drop. Take her about as much as possible, and it will all blow over – but anyway bring her to Llys-y-fran on Monday.'

'I, for one,' said Ivor Owen, 'shall be charmed to see her there.'

As they drove away, "Mrs Jones, the Daisy," turned crestfallen to her husband.

'Well, Jones, here's the most dreadful thing that has ever happened to us. That's the worst of poor relations. Indeed, there!'

CHAPTER XIX

THE COLLIERS' FRIEND

Yshbel had returned from her stroll with Goronwy, much disturbed in mind: he had insisted upon her returning to Treswnd as his wife, and she could find no reasonable objection to the plan, but this sudden climax of her long betrothal had but brought out more distinctly her want of real love for him. It did not shake her determination to keep her promise, however, and when her aunt received her with sharp and bitter reproaches, she felt so unhinged by the interview with Goronwy, that she could only sink into a chair, and, burying her face in her hands, sob quietly.

'Oh, aunt, don't scold me! I know you think I'm ungrateful, but I am not, indeed. I told you I was going to be married to Goronwy, and now he has come to fetch me. That's all. Let me go quietly, and no one will remember I have ever been here.'

It was now Mrs Jones' turn to be frightened. She knew better than Yshbel did, how much her acceptance in the best society of the Gele valley depended on the presence of her beautiful niece, and to part with her, before she had passed safely through the ordeal of the garden party, was the last thing she desired, so she changed her tactics somewhat, and, with a little less anger in her voice, said: 'Well, I have tried my best to make you happy, but now I see you had better go back to Treswnd. You shall leave here next week, but not at a day's notice. I don't forget you are my husband's niece, so you can take time to pack up your clothes quietly. You must come to Mrs Jones' garden party now we have promised.'

'Garden party? What will I do there, aunt, with my heart so heavy, too?'

'Oh, don't bother me about your heart! You might have been the happiest girl in Glamorganshire, if you had behaved yourself. In my deed, there! But to bring a collier here, and then tell all my genteel friends that you are engaged to him – ach-y-fi! Go out of my sight.'

And Yshbel went away sobbing. 'What should she do? Where should she go until her marriage? Oh, that she had never left Treswnd!' And she sat a long time lost in thought, at last deciding to accede to her aunt's wishes and accompany her to the garden party, hoping that thus she might find a chance of a quiet talk with "Mrs Jones, the Belfield," who, the innate refinement of her own nature told her, would appreciate her constancy to Goronwy, and the dishonour her failure to keep her promise would entail.

She was somewhat comforted by this decision, so that when "Mr and Mrs Jones, the Daisy," and Miss Yshbel Lloyd arrived on the lawn at Llys-y-fran no one could have guessed the stormy hours that had preceded the visit. Mrs Jones received them with all the graciousness that her kindly heart dictated, and to Yshbel she was specially kind, keeping her near her, and introducing her to all her friends.

But the girl's thoughts were far away, for on the brow of the hill above the village, a rough spot on the green and a mass of scaffolding marked the mouth of the Belfield colliery, and here, she had learnt from Goronwy, he worked deep down under the surface of the very hill upon which the gay party around her were enjoying themselves. Ladies in brilliant costumes, flowers and fruit everywhere, and through all, the strains of music, which stole through the trees and filled the summer air with harmony. How lovely it all was! How like the dreams which had haunted her long ago! For already Yshbel was beginning to feel that a climax in her life had arrived, and that henceforth youth and happiness must be left behind, and dullness and duty alone must be faced! She looked at the fair girls around her, so full of laughter and gaiety. Why should she feel sad? Goronwy had waited long for her. Why should she now feel reluctant to put the final seal on her fate?

She sat under the shady elms, her hands clasped on her lap, so pensive that she was startled when a voice broke in upon her reverie, and Ivor Owen stood before her.

'Oh, Mr Owen!'

'I hope I haven't startled you; shall I leave you to your reverie?'

'Oh no,' she said, looking straight into the clear brown eyes, and feeling as every one did, that here was a man whom she could trust. 'I am very glad if you will sit with me a little while – they are all strangers to me.'

'They would all like to be better acquainted with you, I am sure.'

'That cannot be, as I am going away soon.'

'I am very sorry indeed, but if you are going to that golden shore and waving waterfall, which you spoke of the other day, I must not regret it. The picture you drew has returned to my mind many times.'

Yshbel smiled, but Ivor Owen thought he detected a tear in her eyes and a tremble on her lips.

'Yes, I am going back there. My aunt is very angry with me, and it is very natural, but how can I break my promise to the man who has waited so long for me? I would never do it indeed.'

'Certainly not, Miss Lloyd, and I honour you for your firmness, if that man is worthy of such fidelity.'

'Oh, he is good, and straight, and honest. He is a country lad, as I am a country girl – only for a time I have been here amongst ladies and gentlemen.'

'They have only been honoured by your presence amongst them,' said Ivor Owen. 'There are ladies and gentlemen in homespun clothing as often as in broadcloth and satin – perhaps oftener.'

'Yes, indeed I am beginning to see that since I have been here, but "Mrs Jones, the Belfield," is a lady – a real lady and kind and good,' she said, looking wistfully and inquiringly at her companion.

'Oh, certainly. Yes; a lady of the right sort, one who would help you in any difficulty I am sure – with wise and good advice, I mean.'

'Yes, I believe; and I'm going to venture to ask her advice.'

'You could not do better, and if I can be of any help to you, I should only feel it an honour and a pleasure. I already know your affianced husband, and I'm sure he is a splendid fellow.'

'Yes, he is; but will I venture to tell you my trouble, Mr Owen?'

'You may venture, indeed,' said Ivor, with a kindly smile, 'if you think I can help you. I know everybody about here, both rich and poor, high and low.'

'Yes, indeed; Goronwy has told me how the colliers all love you.'

'I hope they do – I know I love them, and never feel more at home than amongst them. The colliers have their faults, as every class of man has, but for genuine kindness of heart, for warmth of hospitality, for generosity and bravery, give me a collier! But what is troubling you? I see there is something, as there is in most people's lives.'

'Yes 'tis this,' said Yshbel, raising her eyes once more to his. 'My aunt wants me to go away some day this week, but Goronwy says we must be married before we go back to Treswnd together, and he is a very determined man. Well, then, where will I go till I am married?'

'Oh dear,' said the curate; 'there is no difficulty in that. Mrs Jones, our kind hostess, will be delighted if you will stay with her. I know her well enough to say so without hesitation.'

'Well, indeed, perhaps she will. She is so kind and gentle, but how am I to ask her such a thing?'

'You need not; I will manage that for you. I have only to

broach the subject to her, and I know she will be delighted to seize the opportunity of having you near her.'

'But Goronwy is a collier now?'

'That will make no difference to "Mrs Jones, the Belfield." I told you she was a lady, and that means a Christian woman.'

'Yes, of course,' said Yshbel 'I can see that, though I am an ignorant girl.'

'Ignorant! Well, there is ignorance and ignorance, and I would infinitely prefer such ignorance as yours to the superficial education of many people I know. Is that all the trouble?'

'Yes,' said Yshbel, looking down at the rose leaves which had fallen on her lap – 'at least I don't know. You are a clergyman, and perhaps many people must have told you their troubles. Can you tell me why there is so much unrest here?' and she pressed her hand on her bosom.

'I am a clergyman, it is true, and many people have confided their difficulties to me, but that does not give me the key to the secret of all hearts. There is only One who knows them, and, if you can lay them before Him and follow the dictates of your conscience, guided by His Spirit, you will have found the only comfort possible to a human being on his way through life.'

'I am trying to do that,' said the girl; 'but oh! I am not sure, I am not sure!'

'I feel I have no right to inquire more closely into your difficulty, but believe me, I could give you no better advice than I have just done. Don't be afraid to ask me any question; I shall be very glad if you will let me be your friend.'

'You are kind, but I couldn't tell you more. It is here,' and again she pressed her hand on her heart, 'very deep down, but 'tis here all the same. Here is Mrs Jones; will I ask her now?'

'No,' said Ivor Owen 'leave it to me, and before the day is over, I will arrange it all for you;' and looking at his watch – 'The train is nearly due,' he said. 'We cannot see the station from here, but we see the steam.'

'The train is in,' said Mrs Jones, as she passed them, intent upon making somebody else happy, and well pleased to see that Yshbel and her companion were engaged in conversation.

'Are you expecting anybody?' asked Yshbel.

'Yes, a great friend of mine – in fact, my best friend, George Gwyn, Mr Jones' manager. He has been away a fortnight, and this morning l heard from him that he might possibly return today.'

'Yshbel,' called a familiar voice, and "Mrs Jones, the Daisy" approached, 'come here, my dear. Here's the Miss Fothergills want to be introduced to you.'

Yshbel rose and Ivor Owen rose also, and bowing a farewell, walked down the drive towards the village.

'Poor girl,' he thought. 'She is very charming, very beautiful, and very unhappy. I wonder if she really loves the man she is marrying? I wish l could help her.'

His brows were knit in deep thought when round the corner of the road a man approached and almost reached him unobserved.

'Hallo, old fellow! Deep in thought? I'll bet you anything you like, I can guess the subject.'

'Gwyn, old chap, I am glad to see you. How are you? All the better for the change, I hope. Shaken off the blues? Come along, your aunt will be glad to see you too, to take a little of the entertaining off her shoulders. That's the only duty Mr Jones shirks; he's sitting now in the study with the vicar, both of them smoking till all is blue.'

'Garden parties are not much in uncle's line certainly, but I should have thought the vicar would enjoy it. It sounds very festive from the village.'

'Yes; the yearly dance in the evening makes it very popular with the young people too.'

'Any new people here?'

'No, I think not, except a Captain Ellis with the Fothergills, a jolly old fellow enough, and "Mr and Mrs Jones, the Daisy," have a very pretty niece with them.'

And while the two men walk up the road together, let us look at them, and we shall recognise in Mr Jones' manager our old friend Walto Gwyn. Not much altered, considering that five years have passed since we saw him last. His face a little less sunburnt perhaps, and wearing a heavy moustache, instead of the shadow of black which used to adorn his mouth. Tall and broad as his companion, but less thickly built, his handsome form was supple and graceful, and "Mrs Jones, the Daisy," was accustomed to say he was 'every bit the gentleman!' Looking carefully at his face, one saw there was missing in its expression the open air of content, which made Ivor Owen's countenance so pleasant to look upon. On the contrary, Walto's face, although it was frequently lightened by a merry laugh, seemed to return to a sober, thoughtful look as to its natural expression.

'You look very well, Owen,' he said at last; 'but what were you pondering when I came upon you?'

'Well, the young lady I mentioned, Mrs Jones' niece, seemed in a little difficulty, and I—'

'Didn't I guess it? You were thinking how you could set it right!'

''Pon my word, George, you are making me out to be a regular meddler, and there's nothing I hate more.'

'If you think that, you are putting quite a wrong construction on my words – but you don't think it.'

'No, no; I know, on the contrary, you have all sorts of golden opinions of me to which I have not the least claim. Here we are at the gate. Does it feel like coming home with all those people about?'

'Coming home! Oh Lord, no!' said Walto. 'My dear fellow, I should like you to see what those words really mean to me. An old yellow-washed rambling farmhouse, half covered with ivy, a trim high box hedge before the door with peacocks cut out of it. The sea shimmering down there to the right, the cows standing about, and the dearest old woman in the world, with a scarlet cloak on, standing at the gate. That's home to me, and I cannot live much longer without seeing it.'

'Well, remember you have promised I am to see it, too, some day.'

'Yes, I hope you will. I will go in this way and brush up a bit; I am not in trim for visitors,' and he turned away into a shady path in the shrubbery.

Meanwhile "Mrs Jones, the Daisy", was in her element in the thick of the company, looking complacently at Jones, who was safely embarked on a conversation with another rich coal owner 'up the valley'; but she cast more anxious looks at Yshbel, whose behaviour she was not at all so sure of, although she had found an opportunity of whispering to her, 'Not a word about the collier – mind!' and being a clever woman, she had thought it diplomatic to make an admission to the girls to whom she had just introduced her niece, 'Now, Miss Fothergill, I'll leave Isbel here while I go and speak to Dr Powell, and you must not be surprised at her ignorance, for she has only just been brought from her foster-mother in Cardiganshire, so she knows nothing of sessciety; indeed, there!'

In spite of her 'ignorance', the two Miss Fothergills found Yshbel very fresh and charming, and 'so original!' and they entertained each other satisfactorily until, when the shades of evening grew greyer, and the dew began to fall, the dancing began in the long old-fashioned dining room, whose windows opened out to the verandah.

Here Yshbel sat, her hands clasped on her lap, her thoughts flying back on the strains of the music to the happy days of long ago, and she wished with all her heart that she had never left her secluded home, for here new ideas had dawned upon her, and a restlessness and dissatisfaction with her fate had taken possession of her. Suddenly she was roused by a pleasant voice, and Ivor Owen approached in the twilight bringing with him a friend.

'I have brought my friend Gwyn to make your acquaintance. Miss Yshbel Lloyd, Gwyn,' and in a moment Yshbel had started to her feet, a crimson blush like the rosy glow of dawn overspreading her face. She stretched out both hands, crying 'Walto!' for it was a cry more than a greeting. To describe Walto's astonishment would be impossible. He grasped Yshbel's hands and stood silent, while she, sinking back into the seat from which she had risen, lost all the happy glow and excitement.

To Ivor Owen, the moment was embarrassing. 'I see you have met before,' he said, 'so I will just go and speak to a friend for a few moments.'

Thus left alone, Yshbel and Walto looked at each other earnestly.

'I thought,' he said, 'that you were married, Yshbel.'

'Not yet,' she answered, 'but soon I suppose 'twill be. Goronwy has come to fetch me.'

'Indeed!' and that simple word which is used in Wales to express such various shades of sentiment, seemed in this case all sufficient.

'Indeed!' said Walto again, and there was a long silence.

'Oh, Walto! speak to me,' said the girl. 'After so long years, say something to me.'

'There is only one thing I can say to you as long as the world shall last, and that – I must not say now.'

'No, no; you must not say it now.'

'Then there is nothing but 'God be with you,' Yshbel, and goodbye.'

When he was gone, she followed him a few steps down the darkening path, through the rhododendrons, away from the lights, the dancing feet and the glancing eyes, away from the happy and the gay, to sob alone in the shade of the tall shrubs. 'Oh, 'tis hard!' she said, throwing herself down on the mossy ground, and letting her tears flow unrestrainedly.

She was startled to hear a footstep approaching. There were

no means of escape, so she had to sit still and wait until, in the gloaming, Walto appeared once more.

'Yshbel,' he said, recognising her and seeing her distress. 'I was going back to ask you a question. Will I ask it? Will you answer me?'

'Yes; yes, what is it, lad?' she said, returning unconsciously to the old familiar term.

'Listen then,' he said.

And rising, she stood before him, self confessed – an unhappy woman.

'What was it turned you so suddenly against me long ago at Treswnd? I am going far away – to the West Indies, where a good appointment is offered me. We shall never meet again in this world, so tell me, once for all, what made you change towards me? You owe it me to tell me that.'

'I have never changed – 'twas your mother, Walto! The mestress came and told me I was spreading a net to catch you, and I was hot and proud and angry, and I promised her that I would never draw you away from her nor seek your company on sea or shore, and she was well pleased. I have kept my promise, and I thought sometimes I had forgotten you – but oh! 'tis hard to forget; try we ever so much, 'tis hard to forget.'

'Yshbel,' said Walto, 'one question more – do you regret that things are as they are between you and me, and – between you and Goronwy?'

'Oh! that question I will not answer – you have no right to ask it, Walto. I am to marry Goronwy at once, and go home to Treswnd as his wife; nothing can change that.'

'Goodbye then. 'Tis some comfort at least to know it was not hate that made you so cold and altered to me. Goodbye, Yshbel, once more. God bless you,' and turning from her she heard his footsteps dying away in the distance.

The twilight had darkened a good deal as, drying her eyes, she returned to the verandah, where the dancers were chatting and fanning themselves and flirting.

Ivor Owen amongst them was just leading his partner to a seat; looking round, he espied Yshbel, and was soon at her side.

'I was just this moment going to speak to Mrs Jones about your staying here. You will see how delighted she will be.'

'Oh, no, no!' said the girl.' I would rather not, l see 'twould be – I mean, I have changed my mind – I could not stay here. Don't think me very changeable, Mr Owen, but can you think of any woman in the village, kind and clean, who would take me in? I would rather go at once amongst those of my own class.'

'I see,' he said, and he *did* see. His keen, observant eyes had disclosed to him almost at a glance the significance of Walto's change of countenance and Yshbel's tears. He was abnormally sympathetic and sensitive to the feelings of others, thus it was his fate to bear the burden of many sorrows.

'I see what you mean, and perhaps you are right; at any rate, I can easily find lodgings for you. There is Martha Williams, "Mrs Jones, the Daisy's" own sister, the kindest, most unselfish creature imaginable, beautifully clean too! I know she will make you very comfortable.'

'Oh, how kind you are! I will never forget it. When will I come?'

'As soon as you like. I will see that all is ready for you – go straight to her house. I lodge close by. It is the little pink cottage near the colliery. She will be ready for you, and you can go there as freely as if you were going to your own home.'

'I have no home – but thank you, thank you! There is my aunt; l had better go to her.'

Mr and Mrs Jones were preparing to take their leave, and were no sooner seated in their brougham than they began to question Yshbel.

'Well, Yshbel, and did you enjoy yourself? Indeed, there! you were introduced to the best people in the Gele Valley sessciety. I saw Mr Ivor Owen taking young Mr Gwyn to speak to you too; I hope you were nice to him. All the young ladies hereabouts are setting their caps at him, but he will have nothing to do with them. What did he say to you, Yshbel?' and so on, and so on, until, finding the girl's answers growing shorter and lower, and Jones snoring audibly in the corner, she too sat silent until they reached Glaish-y-dail.

'A letter for you, Isbel,' said Mr Jones, looking into the letter-box on the hall table. 'A love letter perhaps!' he added, laughing.

'A letter for me?' Yes, it was so addressed in large black writing with many dashes. Yshbel was puzzled. Who could be writing to her? And, taking it up to her own room, read it with increasing astonishment, for at the end it was subscribed, 'Your sincere friend, Eleanor Gwyn.'

She tossed off her hat hurriedly, and with fluttering heart began to read the epistle, which had cost Mrs Gwyn, of Tredu, much thought, many sheets of paper, and quite an array of blotting paper, ruler, sealing wax, etc. It began:

'MY DEAR YSHBEL LLOYD –
'You will be puzzling very much when you see this letter from me, and wondering what I can have to say to you; and, indeed, I am wondering myself why I am writing to you, because l hear that Goronwy Hughes is gone to the 'works' to fetch you home. But, Yshbel Lloyd, before you marry him, I want to tell you all the truth. I have been a proud woman all my life, but now my health is giving way – my heart is broken with longing for my dear son, and I am stooping to ask your help to get back my health and my happiness. My boy Walto will never come back home again, if you won't draw him here, and all these years I have hidden a secret in my heart that has eaten the life out of me. He has written you, Yshbel Lloyd, two letters, and I have stopped them both; but 'twas soon after he went away, and then I was foolish enough to hope that he would forget you in time, although I mistrusted it sometimes sorely. But after

stopping the first letter, I was obliged to stop the second.
Never mind how I got them. Now, Yshbel, you are going
to marry Goronwy Hughes, they say, but I know 'tis Walto
you love, and I am writing to beg of you to consider well
before you do such a wicked thing. It is my fault, all of it, I
know, and a poor old woman is begging of you to give her
back her son and her peace of mind. Write to me if you still
love Walto, and I will write to him. I don't know are the
'Belfield' and the 'Daisy' colliery far from each other, but
they are both in Glamorgan whatever.

    'And now I will conclude, hoping this will find you well
and happy, and still inclined towards my son Walto.
Your sincere friend,
ELEANOR GWYN.'

Yshbel let the letter drop from her hand in sheer astonishment
– that the mestress should have written to her – Yshbel Lloyd,
in such a humble strain too! And oh! What good was it now?
What a maze of difficulties seemed to entangle her! The only
thing that seemed fixed and certain was her marriage with
Goronwy. 'Let it be soon then,' she soliloquised; ''twill end this
misery.'

    'Twas late in the evening when Walto Gwyn, having seen
the last of Mrs Jones' guests off, walked down to the village in
search of Ivor Owen, for they were bosom friends, and one was
seldom seen without the other. He was not in his lodgings.

    'At Martha Williams',' Walto was informed, and there he
found him sitting well back in the glow of the snow-white
chimney, a neighbour's child sitting on his knee and examining
his watch with busy fingers. 'What! open it again? There then;
no more till tomorrow. Home now, little man,' and off the
child trotted, meeting Walto at the doorway.

    'I thought, indeed, I should see you soon, sir. Here's Mr
Owen sitting with me. How are you? Are you better from your
jurrney, sir?'

'Oh, all right again, Mrs Williams, thank you; but I am going to take Mr Owen away. You won't bless me, I know.'

'No, indeed – but there, he is going to bring me a young lady tomorrow, and then I expect I shall have a good many visits from you both.'

'Very likely. Come on, Owen. 'Tis a glorious evening; the moon is rising. I want to talk to you.'

But when they had gained the road, Walto did not seem inclined to be communicative.

'Something's wrong, Gwyn, I know. Can I help you?'

'No,' said Walto, moodily; 'no man can help me, and I don't know that there's anything very wrong after all. I ought not to have called you out perhaps for such a trifle, but I thought you would like a walk on such a night.'

'So I do – nothing I like better.'

'I missed you at Llys-y-fran – what became of you?' said Walto.

'I left early, having some arrangements to make with Martha Williams about lodgings for that very young lady to whom I introduced you.'

'For her? Why is she leaving her aunt? Didn't you say "Mrs Jones, the Daisy", was her aunt?'

'Yes. Well, she has offended her, and has been politely ordered out of the house. She asked me to find lodgings for her, with some kind, clean woman in the village, and I thought Martha Williams just answered that description.'

'Exactly, I should think – but how has she offended her aunt?'

'Well, she is going to be married to a young man from her own home. He has followed her here, and insists upon being married at once, and small blame to him, I think. "Mrs Jones, the Daisy," is scarcely the woman to prepare a girl for farm life. The young fellow – Goronwy Hughes is his name – is working at the 'Belfield' at present. You will find him there tomorrow. Mrs Jones is indignant that a niece of hers should disgrace her by marrying a collier, hence the order to leave the house.'

'I see the situation. But if Yshbel has promised, it would take more than Mrs Jones' anger to make her break that promise.'

'You know her then? I thought as much when l introduced you to her. I never saw such a hue of rosy dawn as lightened up her face. But you, Gwyn – I cannot say as much for you.'

'Probably not'

And Ivor, seeing his friend showed no desire to explain, changed the subject, and endeavoured, as none knew better how to do, to wean him away from the gloomy thoughts that seemed to oppress him.

'Owen,' said Walto at last, 'we have not many secrets from each other, but there has been one event in my life which I have carefully hidden from you. I am not given to wearying my friends with my own affairs, especially when they are of so private a nature as this of which I am speaking. But tonight I feel some strange presentiment of evil – I cannot shake it off, I have struggled with it for days, and I should think that my experience at Llys-y-fran today ought to satisfy my evil genius, and the presentiment should be dispelled, but it is on me as strong as ever tonight. Perhaps if I tell you everything – as my mother used to say – I shall be quit of it.'

'Tell me what you think fit, old fellow, and no more.'

'Oh no; it shall be neck or nothing. Well, you are right; Yshbel Lloyd and I have met before. As babies we trotted together on the sands, as boy and girl we paddled together between the rocks hunting for crabs, as we grew older we loved each other, and, speaking for myself, it was a love that will last as long as I have any being. Suddenly, without any warning, that girl became cold to me. She did not say or do anything that I could reasonably find fault with, but love like mine is sensitive, and I felt the difference in her more keenly than if she had spoken bitter words to me. I charged her with the change in her manner, but she only laughed, and denied that there was any alteration in it. Perhaps there was not, but love is keen-sighted, and saw behind the manner.

'I made many attempts to tear aside the veil of coldness, which seemed to grow daily more dense between us, but in vain; and at last, in despair, I left home and came here. I wrote to her twice, but received no answer. Today, after you left us together, I persuaded her to tell me the cause of her sudden change. It was my mother's pride which came between us, and I wonder now that I never suspected it. I have heard from her today. Dear mother! She makes a clean confession, but it comes too late. Had I even read her letter this morning, instead of this evening, it might have prepared me for the discovery, which I make too late, that Yshbel loves me still. There, Owen, that's my story in a few words.'

'As far as it has gone,' said his friend.

'It has gone far enough to spoil my life. I will go home to old Tredu for a time before I go abroad. I don't ask for your advice, Owen, for there is nothing to be done – I simply craved for your sympathy, and that I know I have.'

There was no answer from Ivor except a warm grasp of the hand as they reached Walto's lodgings.

'Goodnight,' said the curate, 'you have given me much to think of. I won't come in; I shall see you tomorrow.'

CHAPTER XX

TANGLED THREADS

It was Sunday, and at Pontargele the clear summer air was full of the clangour of bells. The 'works' were silent, the colliers, washed and dressed in their best, sauntered towards their several places of worship, or hung about their open doors chatting and smoking. The elite of the neighbourhood had filled the church in the morning. It was now afternoon and the bells rang out once more, but Ivor Owen, having snatched a hasty lunch, was off a good hour ago on his tramp to the breezy hillside, where on Sunday afternoons he conducted the Welsh service in the old parish church, in which the sparse population from the hills beyond congregated. Amongst others, Goronwy Hughes strolled up from the village, attracted thither by its similarity in outward appearance to Penmwntan church, and by his landlady's information that Ivor Owen officiated there.

'Well, indeed, I'll go then! because I didn't like the performances in the big church you got here, at all. Dei anw'l! Is that the way you worship God in this part of the world?'

'Oh, it's grand, they say,' said Mrs Jones, sarcastically, she being a rigid Methodist. 'That's what they call "High Church", man!'

'Oh, I don't know anything about that,' said Goronwy; and he had made his way up the mountain side to the neglected, weather-beaten edifice, which lingered on from the old time past, and looked soberly down at its gay, new sister church in the village, where the silks and satins congregated, while Llanberi was content to welcome the country people in their homespuns and corduroys. Goronwy, accustomed only to Morris ffeirad's rather slipshod ministrations, was struck for the first time by the beauty of the liturgy, read in his own language in Ivor Owen's clear and refined tones; read reverently and impressively too, and not galloped through, as it had been in the morning at St Agnes', where the vicar and his congregation were wont to race through the service – the vicar, as it were, given so many yards at the start, and keeping well ahead of his congregation, who followed helter-skelter, *sauve-qui-peut*, all arriving at the end in an indistinct jumble. Goronwy had looked round at first in astonishment and had ended by hiding his face to laugh.

At Llanberi all was different. A sense of reverent worship reigned over the time-worn building, and when the sermon commenced every ear was strained to listen, every eye was fixed with interest upon the preacher. When the service was over, the congregation filed slowly out to the sunny churchyard, Goronwy turning aside to examine the tumbledown tombstones, and finding one convenient, to sit down and fall into a reverie, a thing he had done more often during the last fortnight than in the whole of his previous life.

One by one the people passed through the lych gate, and thinking himself alone, he was startled by the voice of the preacher, who approached through the long grass.

'I saw you in the church,' he said, 'and am glad to meet you again,' and sitting beside Goronwy, he pointed to where, along the mountain side, the fields grew hazy in the evening sunlight.

'We shall have another lovely sunset; did you see it last night?'

'Yes, sir, and it made me think of my own home, where the sun sinks down behind the sea. 'Tis splendid there sometimes. There's glad I'll be to go back again. I don't like anything here – not the people, nor the place, nor the work, nor anything.'

Ivor Owen smiled. 'Not even that?' he said again pointing to the distant view.

'Well, indeed, that's all right,' said Goronwy, laughing, 'and I must confess, sir, I liked your reading and preaching. I wish you would come to Penmwntan, instead of our clergyman.'

'That would be hard upon me; it would be a great trial to leave this place.'

'You're so fond of that black village and all those smoky chimneys? Well, I know the old saying, 'The chicken that is hatched in hell, likes no other place as well!'

The curate laughed.

'That's putting it rather strongly, but there's truth in it, as there is in all these old adages. I came here when a great trouble was upon me, and working amongst these colliers I found peace. They have endeared themselves to me, and I hope to end my days among them, as the living is in my father's gift.'

'Well they will be lucky men, sir.'

'Oh, I don't know. We all help each other, or the reverse, in our passage through life.'

'This churchyard is very full,' said Goronwy, after a pause.

'Yes. These old tombstones cover many a sorrow, many a tragedy. I have made myself acquainted with the history of most of those who lie beneath them.'

'That has opened the hearts of the living to you for sure, sir.'

'Yes; the Welshman loves to talk of his long-lost relatives. This little unmarked grave covers a sad story – a little child who died from swallowing a pin, while playing with her doll; that grand tombstone marks the place where lies the richest man in the parish; he died a year ago without a friend to mourn for him, or a relative to inherit his riches. There, in that shady corner, lies a woman who, having the reputation of being a witch, was shunned and hated by all her neighbours, and died at last, I believe, from sheer despair and loneliness. I can find no trace of anything bad or uncanny in her life, to account for the abhorrence in which she was held. Nothing but that she was exceptionally sensitive and reserved, living alone, and spending much of her time out of doors, roaming about the hillsides, in sunshine and starlight alike. It was many years ago, and I have only gathered the story from the old inhabitants of the parish. I have lately cleared away the weeds which hid her grave, and have placed that little cross with her name, to mark the spot.'

'Thank you, thank you, sir,' said Goronwy, excitedly. 'You are a good man, and a rough farmer from Cardiganshire says 'God bless you!' What can you call those people but devils, who shun and hate a poor girl because she is better and purer and higher than they? I, for one, will never desert her, but will declare as long as I live, that she is the most beautiful and good woman that God ever created!'

'You are alluding to a living woman, I see,' said Ivor Owen, surprised at the burst of eloquence from the quiet and rather reserved collier.

Goronwy, already ashamed of his outburst of feeling, said, with some signs of embarrassment: 'Well, yes, indeed; she and I have been together in the sunshine and the rain, ever since we were children; and so 'tis natural we should be friends – and – and I'll stick to her as long as I live, whatever they call her.'

'You are going to be married soon; what will your wife say to that friendship? Will she like it, do you think?'

'She'll have to like it. Yes, Yshbel is a wise girl, and I hope shell be kind to Catrin.'

'Remember, your wife must be your first consideration when you are married, and, if you take my advice, you will break away entirely from your friend, before you take a wife.'

'*Never!*' said Goronwy, firmly. 'I feel as if I could do anything for you, sir, but *not that*; and, if you knew Catrin, you would never ask me to do that. Dir anw'l! When she dies she will want but little change to make her a fit companion for the angels. That's my opinion of her whatever.'

The curate looked thoughtfully down at the nettles at his feet for some time.

'Well,' he said at last, 'I must not stay here longer, I hold a service – in the schoolroom this evening, and must hurry down. Are you coming? We must talk further on this subject.'

'No; I am going out over those hills yonder, to see can I fancy myself at home at Treswnd. And, begging your pardon, sir, there's no need to talk any more about Catrin. I was a fool to mention it.'

'Goodbye, then,' said the curate, 'but think of my advice when you are out on those hills.'

Goronwy did not answer, but turned rather sulkily away.

'He'll marry the wrong girl,' thought Ivor Owen, as he hurried down the hill, 'and there will be misery for three people. I wish I could persuade him.'

But, unfortunately, he was summoned to a sister's sick-bed next day, and although, in the interims of attendance upon the invalid, he often thought of the entanglement which had revealed itself to him at Pontargele, the impressions thereof were weakened by his more immediate anxieties, and it was not until the end of the week, when he was able to return to his parish, that Goronwy's and Walto's difficulties returned to his mind with full force.

On the morning following his interview with the curate, Goronwy, on going to his work, was startled by a sharp slap on the back, and still more astonished when, on looking round, he saw Walto Gwyn, for, in spite of the alterations which time and residence in 'the world' had made in him, there was no mistaking the deep black eyes and clear-cut features.

'Walto!'

'Goronwy!'

And their greeting was at least hearty enough to hide any want of warmth there might be in Walto's manner.

'Well, tan i marw! I am glad to see you!' said Goronwy. 'In this strange place, and with all these flames around me, I feel as if I was dead, man, and had awoke in another world!'

'Oh, thou'llt soon get used to it,' said Walto. 'I hated it at first, but now—'

'Now, it has put your home out of your mind, I should think, such a long time you have been away. And your mother, Walto—'

'How is she?'

'How is she? Fading away she is every day. Her message to you was, 'Tell him if he doesn't come home soon, he won't find his mother here,' – and, in my deed, I think she's right. What's the matter with you? I never thought you were the man to forget your old home for the sake of a parcel of strangers, half English, half Welsh.'

'Well, stop thy scolding now; I must go into the office. I am a busy man, Goronwy, and work fills up many a longing, and covers up many a wound. I am going home to see my mother at once – next week, most likely, before I go further away from her. But I will come and see thee tonight and thou canst finish thy scolding then.'

Frequently during the following week they met, and talked together of their past lives, their future plans, but always with a little reticence, for Walto could not bring himself to speak calmly of Yshbel's approaching marriage, and to Goronwy the subject was not so enthralling as to make him weary his friend with it. In spite of many an hour of intercourse and many a chat in the white ingle nook at Mrs John's cottage, there was no real and congenial exchange of confidences between the two friends, whom circumstances had so strangely brought together again. The week passed quietly away, but one evening, towards the end of it, Goronwy might be seen walking down the road that led from the vicarage with a determined step and firm-set lips. He had been, for him, strangely dilatory in carrying out his plans, but tonight he felt he had put the seal upon his future life; his banns were to be 'called' on Sunday, and there would be no more looking back. He must see Yshbel, if possible, and yet he hesitated, as he saw the Glaish-y-dail carriage roll by, Yshbel within it, sitting beside her aunt, looking no whit out of place in the smart equipage.

'Dei anw'l! she suits it well,' he thought; 'and what sense is there in taking her home to the churn and the cows at Sarnissa? God help me! If ever a man has made a muddle of his life, I have! And there's fond I used to be of saying, 'A man can always do what he makes up his mind to do!' In my deed, 'tis always the contrary, I think. No doubt Catrin is right, and there's Some One above who shapes our lives for us, whatever our own plans may be. She sees further than we do with those brown eyes of hers.'

And so the days passed by, unmarked by any further event. Even the weather seemed to be drowsy and still, a grey mist softening the sunlight, a brooding expectancy in the air hanging over everything.

At Glaish-y-dail Mrs Jones had said no more about Yshbel's 'disgraceful conduct' but had allowed the matter to drop, in accordance with her friend's advice. Yshbel had found it very difficult to answer Mrs Gwyn's letter, but had done so at last, to the effect that she was to be married before her return to Treswnd, and therefore it was better to let the past die out of their memories, assuring her, at the same time, that her earnest desires and prayers were always for the mestress' restoration to health and peace of mind. She wrote in Welsh, as Mrs Gwyn had done, and although her letter was expressed in simple language, it was grammatical and correctly spelt, for Yshbel had always been attentive to Jeremy Schoolin's instructions, and had rightly earned the reputation of being a 'good scholar'.

On Sunday morning, when the bells of St Agnes were ringing for morning service, Mrs Jones looked at her niece with disapproval in her eyes, although the girl's costume was perfect in its quiet simplicity.

'Why did you put that rough straw hat on, Yshbel, when I gave you a lovely pink silk one?'

'This suits me better, aunt! Will I change it?'

'No, no, it is too late; come on. Jones, have you got your gloves on?' and satisfied on this point, Mrs Jones stepped into her brougham.

When they entered the church Ivor Owen was in the reading desk. He had had a busy time since his absence during the previous week, and he too had felt the oppressiveness of the atmosphere.

He had thought much of Walto and Yshbel's unhappy prospects; Goronwy's state of mind too was very keenly impressed upon him, and he had resolved that in the coming week he would make some strenuous efforts to set matters straight amongst them.

In the background of the church he saw Goronwy, and wondered why he had again visited the church whose services were so distasteful to him.

It was his turn to preach today, and as the service proceeded his thoughts turned to his sermon, and for a time he forgot his immediate surroundings. He was startled beyond measure, therefore, when, after the second lesson, the words fell upon his ear: 'I publish the banns of marriage between Goronwy Hughes and Yshbel Lloyd, both of this parish.' Astonished and shocked, he started to his feet, a rush of deep regret and self-reproach swept over him. These people would be miserable if he could not prevent it; and following one of those impulses which are sometimes stronger than reason, he said, in clear firm tones, which reached the furthest corner of the church: 'I forbid the banns.' A wave of surprise rippled over the congregation, and the words fell distinctly on Goronwy's ear. He too rose to his feet and stared at the curate, while the vicar made the usual request for the objector's presence in the vestry after the service.

There were two others in the church, upon whom the publishing of the banns had come with a shock of surprise. Yshbel, who sat in the Glaish-y-dail curtained pew, was terrified, as she realised the anger which the announcement would arouse in her aunt, and she shrank deeper into the corner, wondering why Goronwy had acted so precipitately, and forgetting in her fright that she had consented to his proposal to hasten their marriage with the words 'as soon as thee likest, lad;' but she had expected a further intimation from him, and had intended to take refuge in Martha Williams' cottage before the inevitable disclosure came about. Trembling, she looked at her uncle and aunt, the former answering her look with a flash of anger in his eyes, but to describe "Mrs Jones, the Daisy's", horrified astonishment would be impossible! The ostrich tips on her bonnet quivered with her excitement, and the flood of crimson that had dyed her face at the announcement of the banns, had, at the prohibition, which would add so much scandal to the already disgraceful affair, fled from the rest of her face and taken refuge in her nose, a state of things which Yshbel knew from experience always added bitterness to her anger. It was not to be wondered at, therefore, if Ivor Owen's sermon fell upon deaf ears, as far as the Glaish-y-dail pew was concerned.

'Dreadful, dreadful!' were Mrs Jones' thoughts. 'The ungrateful hussy shall tramp. Oh, that I had driven her out before she had brought this public shame on us.'

When the service was over she rose, and beckoning to her husband, walked out of her pew, stooping towards Yshbel as she passed and whispering, 'Don't come with me; I won't walk with you,' and the girl had shrunk, like some guilty creature, thankful to be hidden from sight by the crimson curtains. The congregation filed slowly out of the church; she had sunk to the ground, and, with her arms folded on the crimson cushions, was sobbing in bitterness of spirit.

Goronwy looked angry and defiant as the curate bent towards him.

'What's the meaning of this?' he blurted out. 'I thought you were my friend, sir.'

'Don't judge me till you have been into the vestry; will you come there with me?'

'Yes, I'll come, to hear what you mean.'

'Then wait a moment, while I fetch Miss Lloyd,' and returning, he entered the Glaish-y-dail pew, discovering Yshbel in tears.

'For heaven's sake, do not cry,' he said. 'I am your true friend! I have acted for the best; and may God direct us further. Will you come with me to the vestry?'

'Oh, I can't, I can't!' sobbed Yshbel. 'What is the matter? What have I done?'

'Only come with me, and I will explain all; trust me,' and after some further persuasion, she accompanied the curate to the vestry, Goronwy joining them with every sign of flurry and anger in his countenance.

Yshbel turned from red to white and white to red, and, looking piteously at the vicar, asked once more: 'What is it? What have I done?'

'I don't know,' said the vicar, looking somewhat severely at his curate. 'Explain yourself, Mr Owen.'

'Yes; what do you mean?' asked Goronwy, indignantly.

'What just cause or impediment is there why these two should not be married?' asked the vicar. 'Have you any charge to bring against them?'

'Yes,' said Ivor Owen. 'I charge them both with nourishing in their hearts feelings which, as soon as they have entered into the bonds of marriage, will be a guilty passion, that will render their union a sin in the eyes of Almighty God. Goronwy Hughes, I charge you with marrying one woman while your heart is wholly given to another. And I charge you, Yshbel Lloyd—'

'Halt, man!' said Goronwy, hotly. 'Say what you like about me, but not a word against her! She is as true as the sky above her and as—'

'She is here to answer for herself!' said the curate, calmly. 'Yshbel Lloyd, I charge you with the same sin. Can you before the face of Almighty God deny the truth of this charge?'

'Are you not interfering too much with their private affairs?' said the vicar. 'Have you no graver accusation to bring against them?'

'None. It is enough,' said Ivor Owen. 'I have made my charge.'

'I think you have exceeded your duty in this matter,' said the vicar, 'and brought a public disgrace upon them without just cause.'

'I will abide by the consequences,' said the curate. 'What do you say, Goronwy Hughes?'

'You have behaved like a spy!' said the latter, still smarting under the publicity of the prohibition. 'You have found out my secret somehow, but you have no business with my private affairs.'

'Goronwy!' said Yshbel, her eyes flashing, her cheeks burning, 'hast been deceiving me all this time then? Would'st make me thy wife while thy love was given to some one else? Oh, shame! I will never marry thee.'

The vicar looked impatient and flustered, but Ivor Owen, ignoring her indignant protest, looked straight into Yshbel's face with those brown eyes of his which so few could withstand.

'And you, Yshbel Lloyd,' he said, 'what have you to say? Once more I make my charge; deny it if you can. You were about to marry this man while your heart was entirely given to another.'

'Yshbel!' said Goronwy, indignantly. The girl I thought was as true and open as the sky, and as free from guile as a dove! Hast thou been deceiving me all this time then?'

Yshbel flushed under that clear gaze, her eyes fell, her head drooped, and frightened and unnerved, she burst into tears. All the long strain of the years that had passed since she and Walto had parted at Treswnd, all her late discontent and misgivings presented themselves to her mind in their true colours. Goronwy's falseness, her aunt's cruelty – everything crowded in upon her, and she realised how miserable she had been. Her tears flowed unrestrainedly for a few minutes, while the three men looked on awkwardly and uncomfortably. The vicar began to disrobe, impatient at the delay.

'It is a ridiculous affair altogether,' he said, 'and another time I advise you to be sure of your own minds before you have your banns published, and I think, Mr Owen, you would have been wiser not to have interfered in the matter. What do you wish, young people?'

'Oh! I will never, never marry him,' said Yshbel, drying her eyes. 'Goronwy, thou canst not expect it!'

'Of course not! And I have to thank you for this disgrace,' said Goronwy, hotly, turning to the curate, who stood quietly waiting.

'You have to thank me for it.'

'Well, there's no more to be said, I suppose?'

'Will you come with me, Miss Lloyd?' said the curate, doffing his surplice and looking for his hat.

'Where will I go?' said Yshbel. 'My aunt will not be willing to see me at Glaish-y-dail; she told me not to come with her.'

'I saw her. Martha Williams is ready to receive you, so you had better come there at once.'

'Dei anw'l!' burst out Goronwy. 'Are we two going to be parted like this by a stranger? Not if my name is Goronwy Hughes. Come, Yshbel though we're not to be married we'll be friends still, lass. Remember the hours thou and I and Walto Gwyn spent on the shore and in the boats together at Treswnd.'

'Oh! I do, I do; and my only wish is to get back there once more.'

'Come on then,' said Goronwy; I know Martha Williams' house, and I will take thee safely there.'

'There could not be a better arrangement,' said Ivor Owen – the vicar had already departed in dudgeon.

'There's a fine muddle we've made, Yshbel,' said Goronwy, as they reached the lych gate together. 'If any one had told me when I was in the hayfields the other day, that such a thing would happen to me, I would have called him a liar. Yshbel, lass, don't thee look so downhearted. Before God, I did not mean to do wrong; I meant to be so good and kind to thee that thou should'st never know that – that—'

'That while I churned and spun and boiled the uwd, thou wert for ever dreaming of some one else. And of whom, I should like to know?' and she tossed her head, with the old action that Goronwy remembered so well.

'Yshbel, thou hast a right to ask me. Well, 'tis Catrin Rees then; but, believe me, lodes, I didn't know it when I asked thee first to marry me.'

'Catrin Rees,' said Yshbel, thoughtfully. 'Didst not say, "How could I marry a witch?" one day when I asked thee?'

'Shame upon me! I did,' said Goronwy, 'but I was not myself when I said that. Don't think too bad of me, lass.'

'No, no; I can understand that,' said Yshbel, upon whom the light was beginning to dawn, a light that inclined her to be more lenient to Goronwy's fault than she had been in the first shock of surprise. 'I have been wrong too,' she said; 'but indeed, indeed, lad, I did not know how – how – wrong I was, till lately. Canst forgive me, Goronwy, as I forgive thee, and let us be friends once more? I too meant to be a good wife to thee, and thought I would die before thou should'st know I cared for some one else.'

'Well, keep the secret still then, lass; until thou choosest to tell it me – I will never ask his name. Yes, yes; we must both forgive. Here's Mrs Williams's;' and he opened the little gate for her to pass through.

'Forwel, lass!' he said 'We have been very near making each other miserable for life today. In my deed, I am beginning to thank that Ivor Owen for his interference.'

'And I, indeed,' said Yshbel with another toss of her head. Then relenting, she held out her hand. 'Forwel, Goronwy; he has saved us both from our own mistakes.'

'Yes, tan i marw! I believe there's one good man in the world whatever,' said Goronwy.

CHAPTER XXI

THE EXPLOSION

Once more the clink, clink, of the picks was around Goronwy, as he worked in the dark coal pit, and as he loosened the shining black blocks, his thoughts were busy with the curious tangle of circumstances which had brought him to this pass in his life. The past years of his intercourse with Yshbel the realisation that he had been an unhappy man, and that even while he courted her, he had been hungering for Catrin's love, became clearly impressed upon his mind; then came the thought of yesterday's scene in the church, and a hot flush rose to his face as he remembered it.

''Twas like the bitter physic my mother gave me sometimes, but, in my deed, I think 'twas a good thing, now that I have swallowed it. Yshbel deceiving me all that time, and what for, I wonder? Well – she's free to marry him now whoever he is. I don't care. But he'll be a lucky man, and no mistake,' he said, picking away at the coal, 'and I'm free – free once more, free to go home to Treswnd, when this week is over! Where will I find Catrin, I wonder? God bless her brown eyes! What will she say to me?' And a happy smile hovered round his mouth as he worked and mused, for some instinct bade him hope, and even rejoice. 'What will Walto say to this muddle? Was he at church? I wonder.'

And thinking thus the morning hours passed rapidly. When dinner-time came he was not left in ignorance of Walto's opinion, for to his astonishment as he sat on the ground at his dinner, his neighbour as usual sitting beside him, forging his way systematically through the blocks of bread and cheese, and hunks of cold meat which lay spread out on his lap, Walto suddenly emerged from the gloom of a tunnel.

'Goronwy, man,' he said, 'what's this I hear – thy banns published and forbidden! What does it mean?'

'It means,' said Goronwy, 'that I thought I was a fool to come here at all, but I find 'twas down at Treswnd I was a fool, and now I'm a wise man – thanks to thy friend Mr Owen. There's a man worth calling a man, Walto! In my deed, he looks through your body and into your very soul with those eyes of his. There's something very nice about brown eyes! Well, 'tis all off between me and Yshbel. There's two fools we have been, Walto. Courting these years, banns published and all – and now it seems we never cared a cockle shell for each other after all!'

'You've been a long time finding it out,' said Walto, curtly, 'and Yshbel – is she glad to be free, I wonder?'

'Well – yes, I think,' said Gorowny. 'But what brings you here, Walto, in the pit? I thought you never came down yourself—'

'Only sometimes on special occasions. Today I came with a party of engineers to examine the North Shaft. There's some disaffection amongst the colliers – hast heard of it?'

'Why, yes; I'm glad I don't work there. They think they are getting too near the old workings, shut up ten years ago. 'Tis dangerous, I should think.'

'I fancy the engineers were somewhat doubtful,' said Walto. 'They are going to consult with my uncle about it tonight; and depend upon it, the North Shaft will be closed at once. For my own part, I would like to be out of it. Come home, Goronwy, man; we're not in our right places here – 'tis death in life for thee, and for me, 'tis bondage that I hate, though it brings in good money. But the sea, the sands, the boats for me, the sea gulls and the farm and the dear old mother in her red cloak! Goronwy, sleeping or waking, the picture is continually before my eyes.'

'You've made up your mind very suddenly too,' said Goronwy. 'Dei anw'l, man! I thought with your gentleman ways, and your coat fitting like a mould, you were booked for this black country for ever. But for me, too, 'tis Treswnd and the cliffs, and the seagulls are calling. I tell you, man, I can't breathe freely till I'm back there. This man here owes me a bit of money, and he can't pay till Saturday, or else I wouldn't be here this week. Look here, Walto, will we go home together? – and take Yshbel Lloyd with us, for 'twill be goodbye to the Glaish-y-dail carriage now, depend on it. She's lodging at Martha Williams'.'

'Yes – so I hear. Ivor Owen came in last night to tell me about it all. Will she come back, I wonder?'

'She'll come, b't shwr she will, and see that chap she's fond of, whoever he is. Is it Ben Roberts, I wonder? Dei anw'l! He's not good enough for her. Now if you had been at home, Walto, l should think p'raps 'twas you, and, in my deed, I wouldn't mind that – but Ben Roberts! Ach-y-fi!'

Walto did not answer; he was lost in a maze of hopes and fears – of delightful possibilities – when, with the suddenness of the 'Last Trump', there came a blast, a shock – a roar as of thunder, followed by a sound of crashing debris. They spoke not a word to each other, but ran for dear life away through the dark passages – whither they knew not – but anywhere, anywhere; for if darkness was before them, certain death was behind, and they flew from that deadly blast, which strikes terror into the bravest heart.

The man, with the clasp-knife was first in the race, Goronwy and Walto following close upon him, while a boy of twelve brought up the rear. There was no time for speech; every muscle, every nerve, was wanted in the endeavour to get as far as possible away from the explosion. Suddenly another dreadful shock seemed to shake the foundations of the earth.

There was a sound of falling rocks behind them; so close, indeed, was it, that a flying block struck Walto on the knee. He wavered and fell, expecting instant destruction; the boy

294 A Welsh Witch

had leapt over him in the darkness, but Goronwy, missing him, turned back hurriedly.

'Run, Goronwy, run!' said Walto; 'run for thy life. The deadly damp will be upon us – even now I think I feel it – go on, man, and leave me,' he said, almost fiercely. 'Why make it two lives? Thou mightest escape.'

But Goronwy, wasting no time in words, lifted his more slender friend from the ground, and, getting him on his shoulders, carried him bodily along the dark passage.

'Stop, stop!' said David Humphrey, the man with the clasp-knife; ''tis no use. We're shut in here; there is no outlet. We're in some old workings, and that last fall has cut us off from life for ever.'

They were standing up to their knees in a pool of inky water, whose surface glittered in the light of their lamps.

'We must cross this pond whatever,' said Goronwy, and splashing through it, they reached a raised bank of black mud. Around them, the walls closed, with no further outlet; behind them, divided only by the black pool, the mass of debris which had fallen with the last shock, cut them off entirely from the passage through which they had run.

''Twill keep the blast away,' said David Humphrey, 'but 'twill bury us alive.'

Walto, who had fainted from pain, moaned a little and opened his eyes as Goronwy laid him gently on the bank of black mud.

'If I had a drop of water just to moisten his lips!'

'Here,' said the boy, who was trembling with fright, 'here is water dropping, but very slow,' and taking a tin box from his pocket, he filled it under the falling drops, and Goronwy held it to Walto's lips.

'We shan't die of thirst whatever,' said David Humphrey. 'What's the matter with him?'

''Twas a block flew out at him in the last shock,' said Goronwy. 'What will I do for him?'

'Nothing to do, but let him die at once. 'Twill be worse for us to starve to death.'

'Starve!' said Goronwy. 'Don't talk nonsense, man. They'll miss us, and find us out.'

'Will they?' was Humphrey's laconic reply.

Slowly Walto regained full consciousness, the pain in his knee grew less acute, as he rested on his bed of mud.

'Goronwy,' he said at last, 'art hurt thyself?'

'Not a bit,' said Goronwy, stoutly; 'and, thanks to that last fall, we are safe from the fire damp. I think 'tis thick enough to keep it out.'

'I shall be able to stand soon,' Walto said, endeavouring to rise.

'Not for the world, man, until your knee is better. Well, try then, if you must,' but Walto fell back with a groan.

'Impossible!' he cried, 'so leave me here, and run yourself, Goronwy.'

'Run! There is no outlet from this hole and if there was, is it likely I'm going to desert a Treswnd man? Why, we've faced death together before, and here 'twill only be for a time. They'll hunt for us, and rescue us.'

Humphrey sighed heavily.

'Who is that?' asked Walto, looking at the small group crouched round the inky pool.

'David Humphrey, a Cardi like ourselves, and a lad who followed us up. What's thy name, 'machgen i?'

'I am Will Thomas,' said the lad, his voice trembling, and his lips twitching nervously.

'Oh, well, be a brave boy, and don't cry, we'll get out of this before long.'

'Mother, will be waiting for me tonight. She'll cry shocking,' said the lad.

Another heavy sigh from David Humphrey.

'Don't sigh like that, man,' said Goronwy, 'sprack up a bit; sighing will never help us.'

'Nothing can help us,' said the melancholy man. 'If that fall is thick enough to keep away the fire damp, it is thick enough to bury us. I know where we are, we're in the old workings that were closed ten years ago; they stopped them then, because they were not safe. Oh, 'twas not for nothing that we heard those knockings a month ago.'

'Knockings?' said Goronwy, curiously. 'I heard Dan Ellis talk about them. What were they?'

'Well – nobody knows, but certain it is, that whenever they are heard, there comes misfortune in the pits. Hark! I hear them now.'

And they all listened intently, but not a sound fell upon their ears, except the drip, drip, of water from some crack in the roof.

'Not a knock!' said Goronwy. 'I wish I could hear it. 'Twould cheer us up.'

'H'm!' said the man, with a groan and a shake of his head. 'Twould be no human knock in this depth under Cribddu.'

''Tis on the side of Cribddu my mother lives,' said the boy, now beginning to cry in earnest.

'Hisht! hisht!' said Goronwy. 'Thee'llt be home with thy mother soon.' And the boy dried his tears.

They had all eaten their midday meal before the explosion occurred, except Walto.

'Thee art hungry, man,' said Goronwy, searching in his pocket for the remainder of his own dinner. 'Here's bread and some cold meat.'

Walto ate sparingly, however, remembering that hunger might be their first visitor.

'Now, to see if thy leg is broken.' And Goronwy, bending it gently, discovered to his satisfaction that at all events that was not the case. 'I must rub it for thee, Walto. 'Twill be our only physic here, and 'twill give me something to do.'

And thus he cheered his companions with words of hope, though, truth to tell, a deadly fear weighed him down. He knew how far his 'piece' was from the mouth of the shaft; he knew, too, how much further he had run in his endeavours to escape, and realised, with a thrill of horror, that he and his companions were entombed deep underground, and they sat silently waiting in the first agony of suspense.

At last Goronwy took out his watch. ''Tis eight o'clock,' he said, and little Will Thomas began to cry again. This time they let him cry until, tired out, he went to sleep. 'Twas supper-time, but they were not hungry, or at all events stayed off their hunger with no great difficulty. The long hours dragged on wearily, marked off only by Goronwy's watch, which he took out periodically, as if to show they had not yet done with time.

David Humphrey, who, from the first, had resigned himself to his fate with profound hopelessness, did not even exert himself to look at his. Hour by hour passed slowly by. At midnight Goronwy said: 'I wish I had my pick. I'd make a try for it where that water oozes through.'

'Yes, but we haven't one,' said David Humphrey, 'and a good thing, too, for you'd drag the roof upon us.'

'But we must knock, somewhere,' said Goronwy.

'Here's a hammer,' said the boy, bringing one out of his trousers pocket, and with that and some large stones lying around them they commenced to knock at their grimy walls, wondering that they had not sooner thought of this device for making known their whereabouts. Clink! clink! clink! They knocked and listened, but no answering clink was heard. Together they shouted, but in vain – no response came through the black air around them. David Humphrey sighed again.

'Come on, we'll all take it in turns,' said Goronwy, 'and keep up the knocking. 'Tis certain they are looking for us.'

'There may be scores besides us in different parts of the pit, and by the time they are all taken out, we'll be starved.'

'Hisht, man!' said Goronwy, 'if thee canst not talk sense. Why mayn't we be the first to be saved and not the last?'

And so they whiled the weary hours away, each man taking his turn with the hammer to knock at the rocky walls. Walto, exhausted by pain, was the first to sleep. Goronwy, taking off his jacket, had rolled it into a cushion for his knee, thus affording him some relief.

Towards morning, of which, of course, there was no sign in their dark dungeon, Goronwy, sitting silent beside his friend, and watching the surface of the inky pool round which they were all crouched, saw first a ripple on the water, then another and another, each bearing with it two bright black eyes that sparkled even in that dim light.

'Rats,' thought Goronwy, 'and all swimming this way.'

He flung a stone into the water; it made a broad splash in the black pond, and when the motion had subsided not a rat was to be seen. From time to time he resorted to the same device, never telling his comrades, however, of the fresh horror which threatened them in the darkness.

Walto wandered a little as he woke from sleep.

'Oh, mother,' he said, 'I am tired.'

Again the little tin of water was held to his lips, and before long he was thoroughly awake, and alive to his dismal surroundings.

''Tis morning, I suppose,' he said. 'Canst fancy the sun rising over Penmwntan, Goronwy?'

'Hisht, lad!' said his friend. ''Tis better not to think about it.'

'Is it morning?' said the boy, beginning to yawn. Then, remembering where he was, he started to his feet. 'Aren't we out yet? Oh, what will I do?'

'Here, 'machgen i, try this shelf cut in the coal – 'tis long enough for thee. Yes, in my deed, as if it were made for thee. Well, there's a bed for thee, high and dry from this damp ground.'

The boy looked at it with little favour.

'Will we be here another night?' he said. 'D'ye think the sun is rising, David Humphrey? I wish I could see it.'

'l wish we could,' he replied, with a deep sigh; 'but never again! Never again!'

Come,' said Goronwy, 'give me the hammer. We have not searched all round the walls yet;' and tapping carefully on the rocks of coal, he made a journey of discovery, and found that the passage or cave, although it had no outlet, yet penetrated a few yards further into the mountain than they had at first imagined. 'This will give us a little more room whatever,' he said, 'and we can stretch our legs a little. I had hard work to keep mine from the water last night.'

'Yes; I was watching thee,' said Walto, wearily. 'In my deed, I believe thou fancied thyself sitting on the sea shore, for all night thou wert throwing stones into the water.'

''Tis a trick I have,' said Goronwy, 'when I am sitting by the water. Well, to breakfast, now, to strengthen us for the day, and before many hours they must reach us; 'twill be a poor meal, but never mind, we'll make up for it when we get out. Now, let's see – a hunch of bread and cheese, a lump of rice pudding, and some biscuits. Not so bad!' and he divided them into four equal portions.

'Will doesn't require so much as we,' said David Humphrey, glowering at the boy. 'I am famished with hunger.'

'Share and share alike,' said Goronwy, and the boy attacked his portion hungrily.

Each one felt, as the frugal meal was consumed, that another prop to their frail chance of rescue was disappearing. Walto alone was fully satisfied with his meal. His knee pained him much, and it required all his stoicism to bear in silence.

'Well, I couldn't eat a morsel more,' he said, as cheerfully as he could.

'But that's not good news, lad,' said Goronwy, whose heart sank as he noticed the weakness of his voice, and the difficulty with which he moved. 'Knock again, and listen, Humphrey;' but no sound reached them save the monotonous dropping from the roof.

The hours dragged on without a break in their deadly silence, varied only by the splash of the stones which Goronwy continued to fling into the pool.

'Thou'lt fill it up,' said Walto. 'I think 'tis beginning to rise.'

"Tis rising fast,' said Humphrey, gloomily. 'Some stream is loose; 'tis not the stones. But leave off thy foolery, man; this is not the time for childish games.'

'True,' said Goronwy, with a stretch and a yawn, both feigned to hide his uneasiness; but when Walto fell into his next doze, with a nudge he drew Humphrey's attention to an approaching ripple in the water, from which rose a little head with two fierce black eyes.

'Oh! Duw anw'l!' said the man. 'I understand your game now. They'll eat us alive, man,' and henceforth he too flung stones into the pool, for 'amusement'.

'Two of you at it now,' said Walto, as he woke, and he smiled languidly.

''Tis something to pass the time,' said Goronwy.

'It does drag, indeed,' said Walto, smothering a groan.

The lamps had gone out, they were now in total darkness, and there was no supper to divide amongst them. Little Will Thomas did not wait to be told it was bedtime, but quietly stretching himself on the shelf, or seat, hewn out in the coal, he made room for the others, who, from the rising of the water, were obliged to retire a little closer to the back of the cave.

'We'll be drowned, if we are not starved,' said Humphrey, gloomily.

'Oh, for God's sake, man,' said Goronwy, who was beginning to feel the strain of the long watching, 'hold thy tongue, if thee hast not something cheerful to say!'

'Cheerful! I tell thee, Goronwy Hughes, I am dying of hunger. I have always had a big appetite – they say I have 'the wolf' inside me – and I tell thee, I must eat before long, or die.'

'Well, try and sleep,' said Goronwy.

'Who'll keep those water devils off?'

'I will. I watched last night. Tonight I must stone them without seeing them. Thou shalt watch tomorrow night.'

'Tomorrow night!' said the man fiercely. 'D—n thee! Twelve hours more!' And again he knocked wildly against the wall which closed them in. But in vain – nothing but deathly silence, the drops in the pool, and the splash of the stones in the water.

At last they all slept, except Goronwy, on whom the long tension was beginning to tell seriously. Splash, splash – and the foe increased in numbers and in daring. A sharp movement and a moan from Walto.

'Something has bitten my hand,' he said.

'The devils!' muttered Goronwy; and moving closer to Walto, he continued incessantly to pelt at the invisible foe.

Again he thought of the sunrise, and of the blue sky over Penmwntan, of the soft grey shore in the early dawn, of the sea growing silver in the morning light, the corn growing yellow for the harvest; a grey farmhouse, and within it – oh, the thought was unbearable! Death in that fearful tomb! Was there a God? Did He know of their distress? Yes. Was it fancy, or had he heard granny reading aloud, 'The darkness and the light are both alike to Thee.' 'Yes, God lives,' he thought, 'Catrin is too sure for that to be a mistake, and she would say, 'Hope on, and trust Him.' Well, for thy sake, lass, I will try to hope.'

Ere long his three companions were awake, and hunger was beginning to add its bitterness to their misery.

It was the fourth day of their entombment, and. hope was dying fast in their hearts, and black despair was taking possession of them. The rats, now bolder and more numerous, approached closer and closer, but still scurried at the flutter of a coat or the raising of an arm.

Little Will cried softly on his shelf, for his weakness made him disinclined to rise.

'Get up, 'machgen i. 'Twill be at least a change for thee.'

The child obeyed, and holding his little tin box under the drops, tried to satisfy the cravings of his empty stomach with water.

'Poor lad!' said Goronwy; and he drew his hand tenderly over the rough, yellow head.

The touch of kindness was more than the childish heart could bear, and sinking down to the ground beside Goronwy, he leant his head against his arm, and burst into a fit of wild sobbing. Goronwy tried to soothe and comfort him, but in vain. He was 'a mother's boy', delicate and sensitive, and accustomed to all the endearments of a tender home, and the long strain, the darkness, and the hunger had quickly undermined the constitution, which had never been strong.

Goronwy drew him closer, and passed his arm around the little thin body; the boy nestled into his lap, and his sobs grew fewer and fewer.

A strange change had come over Humphrey, he talked incessantly, sometimes abusively, sometimes in wandering self-pity, and sometimes incoherently.

He sat as far from the others as the small compass of their tomb allowed, his knees crouched up to avoid the encroaching water, and some instinctive feeling of repulsion told Goronwy that the man with the clasp-knife now looked on his former companions as enemies. He muttered curses, he clamoured for the food with which no one could provide him, and henceforth Goronwy felt there was a new terror in the darkness.

As hour followed hour, Walto grew weaker, and sometimes wandered in his mind. It was not only once, nor twice, but many times, in those dark hours, Goronwy had caught the word 'Yshbel' on his lips, sometimes in tones of sorrowful reproach, and in others of loving greeting; and sitting there on the banks of the Styx, as it were, his bodily strength fast waning, his hours numbered, as he thought, his life finished –

his mind grew clearer, and with a keen perception which had not belonged to him in the heyday of youth and health, he saw before him, clearly written in characters of fire, the story of his life – his mistakes, his sins, his follies.

'Yshbel,' he thought, 'always Yshbel! Yes, yes; 'tis plain.' And even as he spoke he tightened the leather belt round his waist to try and stay the gnawing of starvation. 'I see it all. 'Tis Walto Yshbel loved, and 'tis Yshbel is in his heart this moment, and I, with my headstrong folly, have come between them somehow. I was a fool – so proud, so wilful. "A man can always do what he makes up his mind to do," says I, and here's the end of it! To die in a deadly hole, to be eaten by rats – and, Catrin, oh, Catrin!' And starting to his feet he flung himself wildly against the black rocks. 'Oh! my God – for Thou art, and Thou hearest me – save us from this dreadful death!'

In rising so suddenly, he had let little Will slip off his lap, but he took him tenderly again on his knee, and supporting him with his arm, spoke words of kindness and comfort, such words as came first to his tongue, though he knew they were false.

''Twill be all right soon, lad.'

David Humphrey continued to jabber and jibe, and Goronwy distinctly heard the opening click of his clasp-knife.

'Let that boy alone,' he said, in a hoarse whisper – their voices had all grown strangely hoarse and hollow – 'let him die, that we may live. I must eat.'

'Humphrey,' said Goronwy, trying to speak calmly, 'I thought thou wert a good man, a man who prayed to God, and taught the young to pray. I never made pretences to be religious, but, man, I would be ashamed to act like thee. Give me that knife, or I will fling thee into that pool, for the rats to eat thee. Give me that knife, I say.'

Humphrey, springing to his feet, flung the knife at Goronwy's face with a deadly aim, an aim which, however, missed its object, for the weapon, passing close by him, fell clattering to the ground.

In a moment Goronwy had seized it, and, thrusting it into his pocket, had grappled with the madman, who was now in a paroxysm of fury, but, weakened by hunger, was no match for Goronwy, who, though in the same starving condition, retained enough of his muscular strength to force the raving man into a crouching position, where he held him at bay by sheer force of will.

'Sit there,' he cried, 'and if thou dar'st to move, I swear I will keep my word, and throw thee to the rats.'

The rats were evidently a terror to Humphrey, for his mood changed, and he began to whimper like a child.

'Not to the rats, Goronwy Hughes – I'll be quiet. I'll pay thee the money I owe thee. Here; 'twas in my pocket all the time – thou'lt not throw me to the rats?'

'Not as long as thou art quiet.'

Then followed the hours of terror and darkness and agonised waiting, which were never entirely to be effaced from Goronwy's memory. Walto's voice had grown weaker, his incoherent ramblings were ever of the boats, the shore, the sands – and woven through all his fantasies was 'Yshbel,' ever 'Yshbel'.

How many hours passed in this climax of misery, Goronwy could not count, but to him they seemed a lifetime. Little Will had nestled again into his arms, his head upon the young man's breast. He moaned sometimes, 'Mother, mother!'

'Goronwy,' he said at last, 'wilt sing for me?'

'Sing, lad? My heart is too heavy for a song.'

'Not a song,' said the boy, 'the hymn they sing in Sunday School – I can't remember it all.'

And the clear treble, weak and trembling with suffering, set up a strain which surely had never echoed from those walls before:

'Hide me, O my Saviour, hide,
  Till the storm of life be past;
Safe into the haven guide,
  O receive my soul at last.'

'That's it, Goronwy; sing with me. Hark to the children; I hear them.'

'While the nearer waters roll,
  And the tempest still is high.'

'Sing, Goronwy;' and to please the child, he sang verse after verse, hymn after hymn – words of faith, of hope, and trust. Ah! how hollow, how unmeaning they seemed at first, but as his trembling voice grew stronger, and the little boy's treble grew weaker, some inward calm awoke within him, some strong faith, some hope revived, and with clear and sonorous voice, he sang:

'Other refuge have I none,
  Hangs my helpless soul on Thee;
Leave, ah! leave me not alone,
  Still support and comfort me;
All my trust on Thee is stayed,
  All my help from Thee I bring;
Cover my defenceless head
  With the shadow of Thy wing.'

The boy had ceased to sing, but in the dark foul atmosphere of their tomb rose another voice, clear, melodious, and true. It was Humphrey, whose mood had changed again. With hands clasped, his eyes closed, he sang the old familiar hymn.

'Yn y dyfroedd mawr a'r tonau,' and Goronwy joined. Walto, too, seemed to hear the familiar strain, and though his voice was too weak to sing, he repeated the words in a whisper. Little Will alone was silent.

'Art not singing, Will?' Goronwy asked bending over the drooping head; but there was no answer. The yellow head drooped lower and lower, and, frightened, Goronwy felt the hands; they were cold and damp. He listened for the breathing; but the heart had ceased to beat. Little Will was dead! And Goronwy, strong man as he was, broke down entirely. He stretched the little body on the shelf, upon which he had lain almost continuously, and as he straightened the limbs and closed the eyes, deep sobs shook his frame. Alone! With the dead, the dying, and the frenzied around him, Goronwy was brought face to face with the deep mysteries of life.

'Yes, God is here – I am not alone. If He chooses He will save me; if not, I will die at His bidding.'

But he felt his work in life was not ended, for Walto still lived, and at any moment David Humphrey might change his mood. He took no notice of Goronwy's movements as he lifted little Will's body to its couch, but continued to fill the dark vault with strains of melody. Every hymn he had ever sung at his mother's knee, in his chapel, at his fireside – all, all came crowding to his memory, and he poured them forth in an ecstasy of frenzy.

They had ceased to knock, had given it up in despair; they had ceased to struggle against the encroachments of the rats, Goronwy alone endeavouring to stave them off from Walto. But as he sat, no longer able to stand, and languidly moved his arm occasionally, to show there was still life in the tomb, he was horribly conscious of a scuttering and crawling on the shelf upon which little Will lay, too still to frighten them away.

Sometimes Humphrey stopped for breath, and then Goronwy gathered his strength together, and prepared for a final struggle with the madman, but a line of some old hymn suggested by him, would set him off again, in another flight of uplifted song; and in this continual music Goronwy felt was his only hope of safety.

Silently he sat beside his friend, feeling that but a few hours more would end the struggle, when Walto surprised him by calling his name softly.

'Goronwy – art there?'

'Yes, lad,' and he took Walto's hand in his.

'Wilt take a message to Yshbel for me?'

'If ever I see her again,' said Goronwy.

'Tell her I loved her, and her only, from my childhood; and, Goronwy, we may never roam the sands at Treswnd together again, but death cannot sever our friendship.'

'No, no,' said Goronwy.

'Thou hast been good to me. I have only thanks to give thee, lad.'

But Goronwy did not answer; he had heard something which sent a throb to his heart.

Hark again! – a clink! And seizing the hammer with renewed strength, he knocked in return. Yes – there was no mistaking – that was the clink of a pick.

'They have found us, Walto! They're coming. Humphrey, man, we are saved!'

But Humphrey still sang on, distraught.

'Dost hear them, Walto?'

'Yes,' he said, 'I hear them. Oh God, 'tis too late!'

But in Goronwy's veins the blood coursed once again. Hope sprang up within him, and awoke every pulse of his strong frame; the heart that had almost failed beat with fresh vigour; and falling on his knees on the black mud he cried: 'Catrin, thou art right – there is a God and He does hear us!'

Again the clink of the picks was renewed – one, two, three, and Goronwy, using all his strength, answered with one, two, three strokes of the hammer. Yes! he was heard, and among the miners on the other side of that bank of debris there arose a shout of gladness, for hope had almost died within them, so long had been their search, and so fruitless!

It was hours before they worked their way through the fallen mass, but with every moment strength returned to Goronwy's heart. When at last, however, a rush of air came over that black pool of horror, and the glimmer of a lamp shone in upon its surface, he himself gave way, and swooned in sheer excess of joy.

CHAPTER XXII

UNDER THE HAWTHORN TREE

'And so that's how it was, you see, that Mary Ann and I got separated when we were married, because she had a man who went up and up, till he came to his carriage and pair, and I married poor Jim Williams who went down and down till he got to his grave. Yes, indeed;' and Martha Williams paused to turn the slices of ham which she was frying for dinner.

''Tis a pity, indeed,' said Yshbel.

'Yes, yes. There's fond we were of each other! Running down the hayfields together, my arm round her neck, her arm round my waist – we would scarcely loose our hold to pick the flowers;' and she sighed as she broke the eggs in the pan. 'That is life, 'merch i; 'tis full of bitterness – but, caton pawb! There's plenty of sweet in it too, more sweet than bitter, and the bitter God will turn to sweet in another world. So there!' placing the appetising dish upon the table, 'we have no cause to grumble, after all. Poor Mary Ann! Her heart is very full sometimes, I know, because I see the tears in her eyes when I am sitting with her in her bedroom talking Welsh – soft so the servants won't hear – and then, when she opens the back door for me, I know her heart is aching, by the pain in my own, my dear. And there's kind she is to me! This ham, that cheese she gave me. Oh, she will never let me want. But 'tis pity for her, poor thing!'

Yshbel, who was sceptical as to her aunt's deep feeling in the matter, made no reply, but, silently eating her dinner, cast frequent glances towards the heterogeneous mass of boarding and machinery that marked the mouth of the 'Belfield' colliery, in which she knew both Walto and Goronwy were engaged.

'Yes, we can see the pit very plain from here,' said Martha Williams, following the direction of her eyes. 'Ten years ago I could tell one man from another who was about there, but now my eyes are not so good.'

'What is that red shed with the whitewashed roof?' asked Yshbel.

''Tis the manager's office. Mr George Gwyn is his name. There's a handsome young man he is – dark skin, black eyes flashing like a Spaniard's, like my poor Jim's used to do. He's great friends with Mr Owen, the curate. Oh God!' and she started to her feet, Yshbel too, for against the clear blue of the sky, a column of smoke rose from the mouth of the pit, while the air was rent by a loud report as of a cannon. The ground shook beneath their feet, and the sky was darkened by clouds of smoke.

'What is it?' cried Yshbel, 'are they blasting, or what is it?'

''Tis an explosion in the "Belfield", child. Come, come!' and she rushed out, followed by Yshbel, who hastily snatched a cloak and hat as she went.

The shock was followed by a few moments' ominous silence. Then, from the village below, came signs of frightened hurry; from every cottage men and women pouring forth, all making their way up the hill towards the colliery. Young men and old, who had toiled all night underground, now started from their sleep; mothers and sisters distracted with fears, pale wives, and little children wailing in affright – all trooped up the hillside together, for there could be no doubt of it, there was death and disaster in that awful shock. Their dear ones were deep underground, exposed to a fate too horrible to contemplate. But hope, the ever faithful friend of the sorrowful, upheld them – suggesting that though some unfortunates might be killed, many might be saved, and that their dear ones might be amongst the rescued. Oh yes! It must be so; they must, they must return to their homes. And in tears and dread they drew near the pit, where already preparations were made for help and rescue. Amongst the rest, Martha Williams and Yshbel had hurried up, the latter faint with terror. Goronwy in that dreadful pit, from which the smoke belched forth in a column of blackness! And Walto – where was he? She was thankful to remember that his employment did not necessitate his going underground, and she anxiously scanned the hurrying figures around her in search of him. She dared now to open her heart to the long repressed love, and in the agony of those first moments of terror, she spoke aloud the feelings she had so long hidden in her heart. 'Walto, where are you? Oh, come to me! It is Yshbel calling you, f'anwylyd!' The door of the red shed was open, hurrying figures passing in and out. She approached, and anxiously looked in; it was filled with men who spoke in serious whispers, but no Walto was to be seen. 'He is directing those at the pit's mouth,' she thought, and gliding in between them, she sought with anxious eyes for the form so familiar and so dear to her.

'Walto, Walto!' she cried again.

'Hush! 'merch i,' said a woman, whose pale face was drawn with fear. 'Is it your husband or brother – or perhaps your lover – you're seeking?'

'No, no – neither,' said Yshbel, ''Tis the manager I want to see.'

'The manager is no good now,' said the woman, 'no better than the plainest collier. 'Tis the dear ones *I* want to see who went out hale and hearty this morning.' And breaking down, she threw herself on the ground and moaned, rocking herself backwards and forwards in her misery. 'My sons, my sons, my brave boys!' was her continual cry.

'Oh! I hope they will return to you,' said Yshbel, 'I don't understand. I am a stranger here. Will you tell me what has happened?'

'What has happened? 'Tis an explosion, child! Death and

destruction to the men, sorrow and poverty to the women ever after. Oh, my sons, my sons, my handsome lads!' Yshbel, having no solace to offer, moved further into the crowd and asked again for the manager.

'Can any one tell me where he is?'

'The manager? Yes,' said a man, who turned his pale face for a moment to answer her. 'He's in the pit; went down this morning with the inspector. He has come up, but Mr Gwyn is down below.'

A shiver ran through her frame as she turned away with a despairing cry: 'Walto, Walto! and Goronwy! Both gone! Both buried in that frightful hole!' The calamity seemed too great to realise, and joining a group of women who seemed to wait for something, she knew not what, she asked: 'Must all be killed? Can none escape?'

'All?' answered a woman, whose face of misery Yshbel never forgot. 'All? No, no. Some must escape. Some always do. My boy with his yellow hair and his blue eyes! It can't be. God will not be so cruel! I am a widow, and there's only little Will to comfort me. Yes, 'merch i, many will be saved. Who have you down there?'

'Two friends,' said Yshbel, 'very dear friends.'

'Oh, friends,' said the woman, scornfully. 'Wait till you have father or husband or brother there, or your own bonny boy, bone of your bone, flesh of your flesh, down there in the darkness. Oh, God, save him, save him! But He will,' she added, with sudden calmness. 'You'll see, my girl, we'll be happy women tonight. You wait with me, will you?' for she felt drawn to the girl's tender, sorrowful face. 'We'll wait together, my dear, and we'll rejoice together. Come, sit under this thornbush.'

'Yes, indeed, and thank you,' said Yshbel, 'for I am very lonely.'

'Is it your lover down there?'

'No – yes – at least, I was going to be married to one of them, and the other is—'

'Pwr thing! I'm sorry for you; but still, 'tis not so bad as to have your only child there – no, no!' and she moaned and rocked herself again.

'Here's Mr Jones,' said somebody, and the owner of the 'Belfield' colliery approached hurriedly, and with signs of great agitation on his kind face. The crowd pressed close upon him, questioning, suggesting, clamouring.

'Hush, hush, my dear friends!' he said. 'We will talk tomorrow; today we must work. Let me pass.'

His troubled face made more impression than his words, and directing, questioning, and sympathising, he passed in and out amongst the crowd. But little could be done until the first burst of smoke was over; then, there was no lack of brave hearts and willing hands ready to enter the cage which might carry them to the jaws of death, but which, at all events, they hoped would bear them to the help of their suffering fellow-creatures.

It is in such times of tension that the true character of the collier shows itself. His bravery shines out resplendent, and his self-sacrifice kindles a glow of pride in every Welsh heart.

Sitting under the shade of the thornbush, Yshbel and her new friend waited patiently, until, as the sun went down, the cage came up bearing its first load of the rescued. Then there were eager faces gathered round. Three men but little injured were enthusiastically seized upon by their friends, and walked away quietly with them, astonishing Yshbel by their appearance of stolid calmness. It was all in their day's work! They had been saved, and went to their homes prepared to take up their work again as soon as the pit should be pronounced safe. Three others seemed dazed and trembling, and had to be supported to the shed that had been hastily prepared for them.

Yshbel and Mary Thomas had rushed forward at the first appearance of the cage, but had returned sorrowfully to their thornbush when the six men had been taken possession of by their friends.

'Not mine!' said Yshbel, 'and not your little boy!'

'No, no, 'merch i,' answered Mary, with set lips, and clutching at her throat, as if to press down the sobs that would rise in it. 'Never mind,' she said, 'there's plenty more to come. See those first three how brave they walked away, and the others will soon be all right. Oh yes, there are many saved, and that's how our dear ones will come up, my dear. God is faithful, and He has promised to help those who put their trust in Him. My little Will will come up safe and sound, and your two friends too.'

'I hope so, indeed,' said Yshbel, who was reproaching herself for want of faith.

The sun went down in a bed of fleecy golden clouds, the fields around slept cool and peaceful in the evening light, the crows cawed as they sought their nests, the wood pigeons cooed in a wood near by – all spoke of peace and rest, except around the coal-pit, where, although a solemn silence had taken the place of the first wild outcry, all seemed trouble and disquiet.

When the moon rose round and yellow, the work of rescue was still going on. Many men had been brought to the surface in different stages of collapse, but Yshbel and Mary Thomas, who had been joined by Martha Williams, still sat under the shelter of the thornbush, pale and silent, pressing forward when the cage appeared, and returning with ever-increasing anxiety as the night wore on, and still their dear ones were not restored to them.

Even Mary began to lose her confidence as the stretchers continued to pass, bearing the straight, silent forms of the injured, the dying, and the dead. She turned to Yshbel in the moonlight, her face white and drawn, 'Go you this time, my dear, and look at them; they are all too tall for my little Will!' and Yshbel, supported by the tender Martha, entered the long, low shed again, where lay side by side the stiff, stark forms of those who had gone out in the morning, full of life and vigour.

Over some the doctors bent with interest, over others the concealing sheet was mercifully drawn.

Steeling her nerves to a pitch of endurance which she had never thought herself capable of, Yshbel forced herself to brave the whole grim tragedy, and looked at every face in that silent row. She spoke not a word, but, leaning heavily on Martha's arm, shook her head sorrowfully as one by one she passed them by. Still one remained.

'Is it your father? asked a doctor, touched by her look of shrinking horror. If not, you need not look at him,' and he pointed to the last straightened form; 'he is an old man, with long, grey hair.'

'Oh no, then, thank you!' said Yshbel, turning away sick and faint.

All night they sat under the thornbush, waiting, waiting, while the hours went by. At last there was a longer interval than usual before the cage returned from its errand of mercy. There was a murmur at the edge of the pit.

'What is it?'cried Yshbel and her companions, hastening forward.

'That's all!' said a man, with haggard face and drawn voice. 'The rest are buried under the 'falls,' or beyond them, and my boy is there!'

'Yes, indeed; true,' said one of the rescuers in answer to Yshbel's tearful inquiries.'We have brought up all we can find, but there are heavy 'falls' and the rest must be under them or behind them.'

There were still twelve men missing, and down below the search was not relaxed. Strong arms and brave souls toiled at the dangerous work, delving through the falls of debris, and daring the insidious fumes of the deadly after-damp.

Outside, the weary watchers must be content to wait for hours.

'Come home with me,' said Martha Williams. 'Breakfast will strengthen you; you cannot go on without food.'

'No, no,' said Mary; 'not a step will I go from here till I see little Will. Go you to breakfast both of you, and, leave me here.'

'We'll take her some,' said Yshbel, as she sat to her dismal meal, her eyes swollen with tears, her heart aching with an intolerable weight of hope deferred.

With difficulty they persuaded Mary to swallow a cup of tea, but she refused to eat, saying: 'I can't, I can't; not till little Will comes. I will keep the bread and butter for him, he must be hungry by now,' and folding it in her apron, she sat still and rigid watching the pit with unflinching gaze. All through the long, sunny day the work went on, and before night six more bodies were brought to the surface – but, alas! crushed by the heavy falls, they were only bodies! And again Yshbel went through the terrible ordeal of seeking amongst them for those whom she had now very little hope of seeing alive. Oh, how the old sweet past returned to her thoughts! How plainly came upon the evening breeze the sound of the seagulls calling! How clearly she pictured the yellow sands where strayed three children full of life and gaiety! How she would chase the receding wave while Walto and Goronwy stood laughing at her! How, later on, when childhood had merged into girlhood, she had teased and frightened those same companions by hiding behind the rocks! And now! Was it possible that she alone might stand under the bright sunshine, while they lay buried deep beneath that frowning mountain, never again to hear the music, of the waves or the singing of the birds?

The third day had dawned, and before its close, she felt her strength was giving way under the continual strain of anxiety. The realisation of her worst fears would have been scarcely worse than this prolonged tension.

Feverish and ill, she threw herself occasionally for an hour's rest on the settle in the chimney corner, but she was quickly out again under the old thornbush watching and waiting, hope growing ever fainter in her heart, and giving place to a dread that grew hourly stronger.

On the fourth day all had been found with the exception of three men and a boy, of whom no trace had hitherto been discovered. There could be no doubt who these three were. Their names were passed about from one to another of the crowd, now grown smaller, around the pithead. There was little hope of reaching them alive, but still there was no thought of desisting in the search.

'Alive or dead, we'll have them, boys,' said the brave, warm-hearted colliers, and a cheer arose in answer. But the hours still wore on without success.

Mary Thomas had been carried home in a state of unconsciousness, having sat day after day, without food or sleep, until at last one of the doctors had ordered her forcible removal to her home, and to her bed, where she lay in silent, stony despair.

Five days had passed, and yet the missing colliers had not been reached. Under the thornbush Yshbel still sat waiting, and the crowd had grown accustomed to that slender, grey figure who watched so intently and so patiently. Ivor Owen was almost continually beside her. Every moment which he could snatch from the pressing work which the disaster had brought upon him, he spent with Yshbel for to him too the long suspense was a trying ordeal. Walto and he had been firm and fast friends, so that it was not only pity for Yshbel that kept him there through the chilly night, and the burning sun by day, but a deep anxiety on his own account.

Every moment was now lessening the chance of finding the men still alive, and as the sun went down he looked at Yshbel with tender pity.

'You have been very brave and hopeful,' he said, 'and I have tried to follow your example, but now I think it is time for us both to prepare for the worst'

'Yes,' said the girl, her head drooping, and the tears falling heavily down her cheeks.

'Ah! I am glad to see those tears,' he said. 'There you women have the advantage over us. They are Nature's safeguard, and I have grieved to see how dry-eyed has been your sorrow.'

But if the tears had been few before, it was not so now gradually the slow, falling drops increased to a shower of tears. She stretched herself on the grass, and a fit of uncontrolled sobbing took the place of her hitherto silent grief.

'Oh dear, oh dear!' she cried. 'How can I go home without Walto and Goronwy? Oh! if l could go into the pit and die with them!'

'No, no,' said Ivor Owen, gently. 'You must keep up your strength so that you may be able to help them should they be brought up alive. Will you take my advice, now?'

'Yes,' she moaned, 'if I can,' and allowing herself to be persuaded, she accompanied him to the cottage, and in sheer exhaustion, threw herself on her bed, where Martha had scarcely arranged her pillows before she had fallen into a deep, calm sleep, which lasted many hours.

When, at last, she awoke, it was to see Ivor Owen entering, with a smile on his lips that raised a wild hope within her.

'Are you smiling? What is it? Are they safe?' she asked, starting up.

'They are found and are alive. Now be calm and brave, as you have hitherto been. Thank God! Thank God!'

In a moment she had passed him, and was running with all speed towards the pit, Ivor Owen following with little less eagerness. Slowly the cage once more made its appearance, and was at once surrounded by eager inquiries.

'Alive?' they asked.

'All but one.'

First little Will was laid upon the grass, a sheet thrown over him which told its own tale; then Humphrey was carried out, still attempting to sing, though his voice was now a whisper only. He was borne at once to the shed, and then Yshbel felt her heart stand still. Ivor Owen, too, was very white, as Goronwy was lifted out of the cage, Walto next, straight and motionless.

'Oh, dear God!' said Yshbel, 'Is he dead?' And she would have rushed towards them, had not Ivor Owen withheld her forcibly.

'No, no, not dead; alive, and you must be satisfied with that. They will do all that can be done for them in the shed. The doctors are there. You must be guided by me in this matter.'

But this injunction was needless, for, from the moment when she had realised that both Goronwy and Walto were in truth alive, the powers of nature had given way, her body seemed unstrung, her mind a blank, and Martha Williams' strong arms carried her to the cottage, scarcely feeling her burden, and lay her on her own bed, where she lay as motionless and silent as Walto. The long tension was relaxed, and nature was bringing her own remedy, for Yshbel slept all the next day, being roused only momentarily for the refreshment which Martha prepared for her. In fact, the second day was well on its way before she awoke to a real consciousness of the events which had preceded her long sleep.

In the shed, meanwhile, Goronwy had recovered sufficiently to give some account of their terrible experiences and of Humphrey's sudden frenzy. There had been no one to wait for the latter at the pit's mouth, for he had been a lonely, morose man all his life, and as soon as he was sufficiently recovered, he was taken to the nearest lunatic asylum.

Little Will was carried home to his mother. Alas! for the yellow head which she had thought to press once more to her heart. It was smirched with coal-dust, and on the cheek was a wound which not all Goronwy's stones had prevented.

The latter's strong frame had stood him in good stead, for though he was but the shadow of his former self, gaunt and hollow-eyed, his spirits were not daunted.

Walto, too, though more prostrated by his prolonged incarceration, soon began to show satisfactory signs of recovery, and it was Ivor Owen, bending over him, who answered his first conscious look of anxious inquiry with the words: 'She is here, close by; only waiting to be allowed to come to you.'

And during the following week the same faithful friend made continual journeys between Goronwy's and Yshbel's lodgings, carrying news of them frequently to Walto's bedside, feeling amply repaid for his trouble by the light which shone in the latter's eyes at the mention of Yshbel's first despair and present joyful expectancy. He had been taken possession of by his uncle and aunt, and at Llys-y-fran was making rapid strides towards recovery. His knee had received but little injury, the delay in attending to it alone causing the inflammation, which was rapidly subsiding, with proper dressing and nourishing food.

'It will be a blow to your vanity, though,' said Dr Powell, 'to hear that you will walk with a limp for some weeks; but you must be thankful to have escaped as you did.'

'You are not as cheerful as you ought to be, under these providentially happy circumstances, George,' said Mrs Jones one day. 'What can be grieving you?'

'Two things, aunt; the first, that I am unable to be with my uncle at this time of trial to him. I know so well how entirely free from blame he is in the matter. How satisfactory was the Inspector's last report of the workings! Who could have divined that danger would have developed so rapidly?'

''Tis terrible, indeed! but he will bear his share of the trouble bravely. My dear boy, you must not let that weigh too heavily upon your mind. And Jenkin has already taken your place very well, and has been most energetic in carrying out all the plans for help in the village. I think this experience will do him good. But what is the second thing?'

'Well, it is that I ought not to be receiving all this kind care from you, knowing that as soon as I can travel I am going to leave you.'

'To leave us? Going to Bermuda, I suppose?'

'No, no, aunt; going home, back to Tredu, to look after the old mother and the old farm.'

And then came the whole story of his love for Yshbel, a story received by Mrs Jones with every sign of satisfaction to Walto's great relief, for he had feared some opposition from his relatives.

'My dear boy, what a ray of light upon this dark tragedy! That sweet girl! I pitied her so much! So gentle, so refined in feeling. What a happy ending to it all! It is quite idyllic. Jenkin will be jealous of you.'

Walto threw himself back on his couch, with a look of great relief.

'But, aunt,' he said, 'do you know, I have not yet spoken to her? She has never heard from me what I have told you.'

'Ah! but she knows it all,' said Mrs Jones. 'I understand it, my dear. I am not so old that all romance has faded out of my heart. You must get well quickly and go to her, and bring her up here if you can. I begged Ivor Owen to persuade her to come here and stay with me, but he says nothing will induce her to leave Martha Williams, and she could not be with a kinder or more respectable woman certainly.'

Not for many days was Goronwy sufficiently recovered to make the short journey from his own to Yshbel's lodgings, although the doctor had declared he 'had never seen such a fellow to recuperate!'

'Here, Martha Williams!' called a familiar voice one afternoon, however, as Yshbel sat knitting, with a happy smile upon her lips. 'D'ye want a scarecrow for your leek bed?' and Goronwy made his appearance round the kitchen doorway. 'Yshbel! In my deed, I ought to say, 'Beg pardon,' for coming into the presence of a pretty girl in this shape.'

'Oh, Goronwy!' cried Yshbel, rushing towards him. 'Welcome, lad; a hundred welcomes! Indeed, I am glad to see thee! Come, Martha, come. What will we do to welcome this brave man? Sit down, Goronwy, bach, and here's a stool for thy feet. Mr Owen has told us all about it, and how thou kept up their spirits in that dreadful tomb. Oh, 'tis too terrible to think of!'

'In my deed, yes, lass!'

'And now to have you safe with us again – there's happiness!'

And Martha aiding and abetting her, she did her very best to spoil him; shading the light from his eyes, and placing a cushion for him on the hard oak settle, which luxury, by the bye, he ungratefully flung across the kitchen before he sat down. The little round table was drawn up to the rosy ingle, the cakes were buttered, the pink ham was sliced, and such a meal was partaken of, as a week ago Goronwy had never thought to taste again; and as he cut slice after slice of the flat griddle loaf, Martha Williams looked more and more pleased.

'Well din, well din!' she said. 'Here's the man to get well; he'll be fit to go to work again before the pit is ready for him!'

'Work?' said Goronwy. 'Yes, in the cornfields, at the herring-fishing, or anywhere in the fresh air and in the sunlight, or in the moonlight on the bay, Yshbel – eh? But you'll never catch me underground again, not while there's life in my body whatever. Ach-y-fi! 'tis not fit for a human being. 'Tis home we'll go, Yshbel; home to Treswnd, lass. Wilt come with me and Walto Gwyn? Dei anw'l! Look at her, Martha! 'Tis easy to know where her sun is when you see his red light on her face like that. She never blushed like that at my name.'

Martha's shoulders shook with laughter, and Yshbel hid her face in her hands.

''Tis thy foolish nonsense, Goronwy,' she said at last.

'Well, wilt come home then?'

'Yes, indeed,' she answered, clasping her hands; ''tis all I desire, lad. Home to Treswnd – there's music in those words!'

'Hast seen enough of the world then?'

'Oh, too much, too much! It is not for such as us, lad. Our world is where the sea wind blows, and where the birds are singing. I have learnt my lesson well. 'Tis all here, Goronwy,' and she pressed her hand on her heart; ''tis here I feel that if I had stopped at home none of these dreadful things would have happened.'

'None of these happy things, too, so there's no need for thee to grieve about that. Only pack up quick; for Walto is getting better every day. I have been to see him today, and he is limping about his room. Mr Owen was driving past Llys-y-fran, and took me there and brought me back again. There's a tea I've made; and, in my deed, I believe I'll be ready for supper again!'

He did not seem inclined to enlarge much upon the subject of his entombment in the pit, and Yshbel, quickly discerning this, restrained Martha's eager curiosity.

'Let him alone,' she said, 'gradually he will tell us all. I can't bear to hear it now.'

Goronwy looked thoughtfully into the fire.

''Tis a thing I want to forget,' he said, 'though I know I never will.' And talking of other things, chiefly of the delightful prospect of going home together, a subject which Goronwy seemed never tired of, they let the time go by unheeded, until at last he started to his feet, and taking Yshbel's hand, said, 'Well, goodnight, lass; we understand each other now! Thou'rt looking more like a lily than a rose, like myself,' he said, jocularly, as he went out. 'Never mind, Treswnd air will soon colour our faces.'

Oh, the happy waiting of the next few days, the fluttering breath at the click of the little garden gate which Ivor Owen came through so often, until at last, one afternoon, when the sun was blazing down upon the pathway strewn with cockle shells, Yshbel heard a new step, accompanied by a tapping sound. She rose to her feet, and stood waiting while a shadow darkened the passage, and Walto stood before her!

For a moment neither spoke, but looked earnestly at each other, he realising that time, which had been so heavy footed with him, had left her as beautiful – nay, more beautiful – than ever; while she took note of the deep shadows under the eyes, the halting gait and the emaciation which even Mrs Jones' care and nursing had not yet banished. She had stretched out both hands involuntarily, and he had seized them as unconsciously, but although he wrung them almost to pain neither could find words easily to speak their feelings.

He drew her with him to the settle. 'Oh, how I have longed for this hour!' he said at last. 'To meet you again, Yshbel, to feel your hands in mine, and now, I have not a word to say! 'Tis too much joy, lass. I cannot believe it is true.'

'But it is, indeed, Walto,' said Yshbel, endeavouring by her smiles to chase away his grave looks.

'Yshbel dost see me, what a wreck I am? Goronwy has escaped uninjured through his fiery trial – but I – can I dare to ask you what I am longing to know?'

'Well how can I answer then if you won't ask?' she said, bending her head to hide her blushes.

''Tis not Goronwy whom you love. Tell me then, Yshbel.'

'No, no; you know it, Walto.'

'Is it me, beloved?'

'Yes, indeed you; always, always – since the old time at Treswnd when we were little children. You, and only you. Forgive me, Walto, for all that has passed! Ask Ivor Owen; he will tell you all the truth.'

'He has, Yshbel, he has. Dost give me leave to believe him then?' and a smile of so much happiness came back to his lips, such a light of love to his eyes, that she, too, was satisfied; and for them, the time dragged wearily no more.

'Five? Impossible!' he said, as the clock in the corner struck the hour. 'Must I go then, f'anwylyd? Art certain now thou'rt willing to marry an old lame man?'

'Well, yes, a lame man, but not old,' said Yshbel, laughing.

'See then,' and raising a clump of his thick black hair, he showed her where on the temples it was touched with grey.

'Oh!' she cried, with a short, sharp gasp, realising from the sight the fiery ordeal through which he had passed, more thoroughly than she had hitherto done.

'What have you gone through, Walto!'

'Through the darkness of the grave, beloved. And now to stand in the sunshine, your voice in my ears, and your hand in mine, is too much for me. Ah, Yshbel, are you not making a mistake again and choosing the wrong man? If you could have looked into that dark tomb and seen Goronwy as I saw him, I fear you would never have chosen me. Sitting there hour after hour, Yshbel, allowing no sleep to his eyelids, but flinging the stones into the water – pelt, pelt all through the long night, to keep the hungry rats away. ''Tis something to pass the time,' he would say, and he thought, poor fellow, that I believed him, but I understood it all! Nursing the little boy as tenderly as his mother would have done, cheering us, comforting us! Singing out bravely with the child when his voice was weak with hunger! Staunch and true to the very last! Yes, Goronwy is a man! Art sure I am thy choice, Yshbel?'

'Sure, sure and certain for ever.'

'Well then, let us waste no more time. In a week I will be well enough to travel home. Come, Yshbel, let us be married before we go. I have waited long enough.'

There were footsteps on the cockle shells.

'Come, answer quick!' he said.

There was a hurried 'Yes' and a flurried kiss before Ivor Owen and Goronwy arrived on the scene.

'Just in time, Owen,' said Walto, 'we've settled it all, and we want to be married at once. Will you marry us at old Llanberi?'

'But we must wait three weeks,' said Yshbel, 'because of the banns.'

'Banns!' said Walto, 'not a bit of it. I'll have nothing to do with banns, for fear this fellow will stand up and forbid them.'

'Yes, beware!' said the curate. 'See that you know your own minds this time.'

'No, I'll have nothing to do with banns. We'll be married by licence on Monday morning, next week, and we'll go home to Treswnd that day.'

'Jari,' said Goronwy, pushing his fingers through his hair,

'there's a good thing now that I could not afford to buy a licence! Why, we'd have been married slap off at once, and Mr Owen would have had no chance to set us right,' and he looked so serious at the possibility of such a fate, that all burst out laughing.

'Well, wilt be ready to come home on Monday?' said Walto.

'Ready and willing and thankful,' said Goronwy, with a thump of his fist on the table, 'but, in my deed, there's in the way I'll be all day!'

CHAPTER XXIII

JOHN LOVELL

Now we must return to the day on which Goronwy Hughes left Treswnd, to begin that journey which led to such important changes in his life.

It was a glorious summer day, the air brooding in quivering heat over the freshly cleared hay fields.

At Pengraig, Catrin sat silently sewing beside her father's sick-bed, sometimes looking out at the sunny landscape with sad eyes that often filled with tears.

She knew that Goronwy was gone, had even seen him as he took the short cut over the cliffs, when, standing on the hedge, he had cast a last longing look at Penmwntan and Pengraig; but at that distance she could not know what thoughts were busy within him, making his journey one of cheerless discontent.

Madlen was never slow to impart her budget of gossip.

'Think,' she said, 'Goronwy Hughes is gone all the way to the 'works' after Yshbel Lloyd. There's fond of her he must be! They'll be married now at once, no doubt.'

She waited for an answer, so Catrin said, 'No doubt.'

This did not satisfy Madlen, so she began again.

'Thee'lt lose thy friend now – no more loitering about the cliffs! Yshbel will soon put a stop to that.'

This time there was no answer, so Madlen had to content herself with muttering her own reply, 'No, no; no more sitting under the bushes and picking flowers and such nonsense!'

Still no answer, so she set herself to polishing the brass pans.

The day wore on wearily for Catrin. She was in a curious
frame of mind, a kind of lethargy had fallen upon her, a dreary
inability to realise the trouble that had overtaken her, a state
of mind which often mercifully softens the first pangs of grief
to the bereaved and blunts their sharpness.

Goronwy was gone! He would never return except as the
husband of Yshbel! Her father was daily growing weaker and
requiring more constant care and attention. At the present
moment he wanted his midday meal; she must see to it. In the
afternoon she must work at her bodice; it must be done before
evening; it would occupy every moment until the daylight
faded. And thus thrusting from her the giant despair, who
stood lurking in the corners ready to pounce upon her if she
gave him a moment's opportunity, she kept her foe at bay and
fought bravely with her sorrow until the evening shadows fell;
then, when she had smoothed the tumbled pillow and given
the sick man his supper, she escaped to the cliffs, seeking solace
under the calm majesty of the starlit sky.

One day was over! 'But how many in the year!' she cried,
'and how can I spend them without Goronwy?' The tears
welled up into her eyes, but she would not let them fall. 'No,
no,' she said; 'not that, I must not cry, or my tears will never
stop. There is another way, I know, if only I can learn it, "to be
happy, because he is happy!"'

And standing in her favourite attitude looking up at the
stars, her hands outstretched as if imploring help, she waited a
moment in silence, and then as calm and placid as the pale
moon which was rising behind the hills, she turned
homewards. But that moon is seamed and scarred by many a
fierce battle with the elements, volcanic fires have rent her
bosom, and her calm serenity, like Catrin's, is but an outward
show.

Bensha was sitting at supper when she entered. Merlin too,
as usual, with eager eyes fixed upon the bowls and platters.

'Where'st been?' he said, reproachfully. 'Thee might'st stop in now; he won't trouble thee long,' and he jerked his thumb towards the box bed.

'Trouble her long!' the words pierced Catrin's heart. The only being who still loved her and required her help; the father who, so long estranged from his child, had turned to her with double fervour of love in his sickness! 'Trouble her long! No!' she realised the truth as she stooped to kiss the pale forehead and smooth the grey locks.

'Father anwyl! Are you worse tonight?' she asked.

'Worse? No, no, 'merch i, 'tis better I am,' and somewhat comforted she stretched herself on the little truckle bed beside his, in which she slept or, oftener, watched.

The first wakeful hours of the night were followed by a long refreshing sleep, and when the next morning's sunlight reddened the kitchen wall, it fell on the sleeping forms of the old man and the girl. Later on she woke with a start.

'Dir anw'l! That I should sleep so long, and father too.'

'Oh, yes,' cried Madlen from the penisha, 'if people stay out at night, they're apt to be late next morning. As for me, I have made a cheese this morning, and given Bensha his breakfast. Oh yes, I don't let the grass grow under my feet.'

Catrin, having no excuse to make, dressed silently, and prepared her father's breakfast.

Then came the long, sunshiny morning, followed by the hot noontide, and her father slept.

Madlen and Bensha had both set off to a funeral which meant an absence of four or five hours.

Catrin prepared to spend the afternoon alone with her father. The house door stood wide open, letting in the soft sea breeze, and all the pleasant sounds of a country neighbourhood. A cow lowed in the distance, the sheep bleated, and an erratic cock crowed, as loudly as if he were not making a mistake in the time, and above all rose the song of the lark, distinctly audible in the farm kitchen, where the old man lay peacefully ending his days, and the young girl began hers in the strife of sorrow.

'Oh, the lark!' she cried, dropping her work, and pushing back her thick hair from her ears to listen. 'There's hope and joy and gladness, in that song. Why can't I feel it as I used to long ago?'

Suddenly, with the sharp hearing of a country-bred girl, she detected on the distant high road, the sounds of voices and footsteps.

'Madlen and Bensha were returning early,' she feared, but the voices retired, while one man's footsteps drew nearer, entered the clos, and reached the kitchen door.

Looking up, she saw a square-built man, whose swarthy skin and liquid black eyes proclaimed him one of the gipsy tribe, who had been accustomed for years to pay periodical visits to Penmwntan.

'Good-day,' he said, standing at the doorway, 'I am John Lovell – do you remember me?'

'Oh yes,' said Catrin, 'I remember you now: you were with Nancy Wood long ago, when we had supper with you on Penmwntan.'

The man smiled, showing a row of very white teeth.

'Well, 'tis Nancy Wood has sent me today. She wants to know how's all with you, and how's the old man? She doesn't forget you're a relation, you see, though, maybe, you don't care to remember it.'

'Oh yes, indeed,' said Catrin; 'I am so lonely, and I often wonder whether my mother's people would care for me?'

'Of course they would, lass. The gipsy blood is warm, I tell you. We haven't been here for many years, but Nancy Wood never forgot to ask William Bray about you and your father. 'Tis his company has been round here lately, bringing ponies to sell, but this time I had business in Pembrokeshire. I should like to speak to the old man.'

'Yes; he'll awake soon. Nancy Wood must be very old.'

'Oh, ask the white owl in the rock up there how old she is, and I expect Nancy was in the world long before him.'

'Who is that?' said Simon, in a weak voice.

''Tis some one come to see you, father bach. John Lovell is his name.'

'John Lovell,' said Simon, turning his head round, and extending his hand. 'How art, man? 'Tis many years since I saw thee. How's all with thee? And Nancy Wood, is she alive still?'

'Alive, and well and hearty,' said the visitor, taking the outstretched hand. ''Twas she bade me come to thee, to see thee and thy daughter. She doesn't forget she's Dolly Wood's great-grand-child.'

'Sit thee down, and let us talk a bit,' said Simon.

And while the two men conversed, Catrin took note of her visitor. His dress was that of the ordinary gipsy who haunts the fairs; his velvet waistcoat, red neckerchief, and numerous pearl buttons, making quite a brilliant show in the shady old kitchen.

'Oh yes; Nancy is alive and well,' he said. 'She can't walk now, so we wheel her about with us; but her mind – bless you, she's as sharp as a needle! Your lass here came to see us once, and ever since, Nancy's had a hankering after Dolly's great-grand-daughter. She's just like her mother, Simon.'

'Not so purty,' said the old man; 'no, no – not so purty. Poor Jinny! I broke her heart John.'

'Well,' said Lovell, shuffling his feet uneasily, 'that's long ago anyway.'

'Yes. I'm not long for this world myself, John, and I'm uneasy about the croten.'

'Have you made your will?' said the visitor. 'That's what Nancy Wood said, "Tell him to see to it, that the girl is provided for, or my curse will be upon him." That's her way of speaking, you know,' he added, as he saw the old man cower a little.

'No, no; tell her not to curse me! I have made my will, but 'tis several years ago, and I was not so clear in the head then as

I am now. Jones, the lawyer, said 'twas the best I could do, but, in my deed, I am not easy in my mind about it – keeps me awake o' nights, man. I'd like to alter it,' he whispered. 'But where's Bensha and Madlen?'

'Oh, they're safe enough,' said Lovell; 'I took care of that. I met them going to a funeral miles from here. I knew them by the eye and the tooth.'

'If I could see a lawyer.'

'There's no need for those devils. I'll draw you a will out – will stand an army of them.'

'Canst?' said Simon, his eyes glittering and his cheeks glowing with excitement.' Make haste then, Catrin, pen and ink and some paper.'

'No need for paper,' said John Lovell. 'Here 'tis, all in print. Aye, Nancy Wood's as 'cute as ever. "Take it in thy pocket, man, all ready," says she, "or they'll be a week finding pen and ink in those inconvenient houses." So here it is, Simon Rees.' And he read in a loud monotonous voice the usual formula at the commencement of a will. 'Now then, here's the place, "I devise and bequeath all my real and personal property to my daughter, Catrin Rees, and I appoint her sole executrix of this my will." There you are, man. Now stop!' And going to the doorway, he whistled shrilly through his fingers – once, twice, three times – until he saw on the hillside the flutter of garments, and two girls came running down, in a very short time arriving at the farmhouse.

'I don't want you both – only you, Matta. Melia's no good.'

Matta approached the bed.

'Can she write?' asked Simon, looking dubiously at the brown-skinned gipsy.

'Bless you, yes! Been to school in Birmingham last winter. Can sign her name to anything – a will, a document, or a receipt – don't care what it is. Now, Matta, watch this man sign his name.' And Simon, with great difficulty, appended his name to the will, John Lovell and Matta adding their signatures.

'There!' said the former, 'the Queen herself couldn't stand against it.'

'Art sure of that?' said Simon. 'Then I shall die easy.' Meanwhile, Melia had been amusing herself with closely examining Catrin's dress, the neatness of which contrasted much with her own gaudy costume.

'I 'spec he's booked for "Kingdom Come",' she said, indicating the sick man with a very brown finger adorned with a ring.

'No can spik much Ingleesh,' said Catrin.

'My golly! then I can't splosh much Welsh. Matta can.'

'Now, you two hussies,' said John Lovell, conducting the two girls unceremoniously to the doorway, 'you go home, and mind go straight and look after the old woman.'

He was dimly conscious that Catrin lost nothing by her ignorance of the language most familiar to the girls.

'Now come here, lass,' he said, drawing her towards the bed. 'See this paper? This is your father's will. Keep it safe till – till 'tis wanted.'

Catrin stooped and kissed her father's forehead.

'Don't let the old walrus get hold of it – you understand?'

'Yes' said Catrin, thrusting it inside her bodice, 'I will take care of it.'

'Well, we've done our job neatly,' said Lovell, pushing his hands into the pockets of his corduroy breeches. 'I don't think old Nancy herself would have done it better.'

Simon seemed much exhausted by his exertions.

'Tell Nancy Wood—to be—kind—to my—little girl,' he said, panting.

'So I will. Now you must rest easy,' said Lovell, kindly though roughly. 'Where's the chap who came with you when you were up with us?' he asked, turning to Catrin. 'Goronwy Hughes, of Sarnissa, he was.'

'Yes. He went away yesterday to the "works" to be married.'

'Ah!' said Lovell, drawing his hand thoughtfully over his

dark beard. His glittering black eyes roamed incessantly from one object to another, and before he left there wasn't a single article of furniture in the room of which he had not appraised the value, and that was small indeed. Every item of Catrin's dress, and appearance too, was carefully noted for Nancy Wood's benefit; it was not likely, therefore, that by such observant eyes, the blush that crimsoned her face at the mention of Goronwy's name, and the subsequent pallor, had escaped unnoticed. The gipsy mind is quick to draw conclusions.

'She's in love with that Georgio chap, d—n him!' was his thought, but there was no sign of this suspicion in the tone of his next remark.

'Ye'll maybe come up and see us some day. We'll be here about a fortnight.'

'Yes; I'll come, indeed, if father can spare me. I am running out every night for a little air before I'm going to bed.'

'And no wonder,' said the visitor. 'Pagh! I could not breathe long between these walls. You lie easy now, old man. We've done the walrus between us. Take care of the paper, lass. I must go. We've got to pitch the tent and cook the supper before night.'

'Stop and have tea with us,' said Catrin; ''twill be ready at once.'

'Tea! Not I! But thankee the same. I'll maybe come and see thee again, Simon Rees. Goodbye, lass; I'll tell Nancy Wood ye're coming to see her some day.'

He was gone without more ado, and looking through the window, Catrin saw him striding up the hill at a pace that would soon take him to the encampment.

'Who is John Lovell, father?' she asked, as she brought him his tea and tempted him to eat.

'He's one of Nancy Wood's tribe, lass. There's lots of Lovells, and they're close related to the Woods. Thy mother's grandmother was old Dolly Wood, and she was cousin to

Nancy Wood. Ah! The farmers round scoffed at me because I married a woman with gipsy blood in her, but she was a good girl, Catrin – a good girl like thee – too good for me. She died, poor thing, and after that I never tried to fight the drink, but let it get the mastery over me. Oh, 'twas a good thing she went, for she was fond of me – and I – Caton pawb! I would not let the wind blow roughly on her! When I was sober – but I was often drunk, so 'twas a good thing she went so soon. Och i, Och i! it won't be long before we meet again. Dost think she'll forgive me, Catrin?'

'Yes, father anwyl! I know what I would do myself, and so I think what she would do. I am *sure!*'

'Yes, I think thou knowest, lass.'

'You look so well tonight, father; such a nice colour in your cheeks.'

'Yes, 'merch i, I am better; the pain is all gone. Now lay me down quiet.' And doing as she was bid, Catrin sat beside him, occasionally drawing her fingers through his grey locks.

'You always like that, father,' but Simon was asleep, and he continued to sleep till Madlen's sharp voice awoke him.

'Well,' she said, bustling in, 'there's old Shenkin Shôn laid by again. I wonder who'll be the next? There's a large funeral it was!'

Simon looked at her with dreamy eyes. 'Is Shenkin Shôn dead?' he asked.

'And buried,' said Madlen.

'We used to play quoits together on the sands when the *Albatross* came in. Shenkin Shôn!' he called, and looking round the room in a dazed manner, he smiled. 'He's gone,' he said; 'gone home to his supper. The sun has set – 'tis getting dark.'

The eyelids dropped, the smile died away, and Simon sank back on his pillow.

'He's gone,' said Madlen, in a hard, matter-of-fact tone, and Catrin recognising the truth, sank down beside the bed, sobbing unrestrainedly.

The first moments of her grief were acutely bitter, for she had loved her father with a tender protecting love, ever since his accident had thrown him so completely upon her hands. Even before then, when he had neglected and beaten her she had loved him.

She realised now that her last friend was gone, and that her work was done, and when Madlen at last drew her away from the bed, she slipped from her grasp to the floor, where she lay still and white until Bensha, called in from the barn, helped to lift her up.

'Take her straight to the llofft,' said Madlen; 'she'll be no good here,' and Bensha, carrying her as easily as if she had been a swathe of hay, laid her down on a straw bed, clean and dry, but very close to the rafters.

'She's fainted, I think,' he said returning to his wife's assistance. She was too busy to answer, moreover fainting was considered the most appropriate mode of showing the depth of one's feelings upon the occasion of a death, and Madlen was rather pleasantly surprised to find that Catrin in this instance, at all events, acted like a reasonable being.

They removed the poor worn-out body which had lain so long in the box bed to the penisha, and laid it upon the old black bedstead which had once been Catrin's. Two lighted candles were placed at his head and two at his feet a large pewter plate full of salt was placed on his chest, the door was closed so softly upon him, and then they sat down to discuss the situation.

'I'll watch tonight,' said Bensha, 'and thou canst sleep in the barn.'

And so interested were they in their arrangements for the successive nights' watchings, the funeral, etc, that neither remembered Catrin who was still lying quietly on the bed in the llofft.

She had revived soon after Bensha had left her, but it was with a strange feeling of lassitude and bewilderment that she gazed around her. Her head ached, her hands were burning, her lips parched – in fact, for the first time in her life Catrin was ill. Heart, mind, and body were all overstrained, and had suddenly succumbed when the call for active work was over.

Gradually the sun sank behind the hill, the little room darkened, and still she lay on alone and almost unconscious.

A strange feeling of lethargy had overwhelmed her, indicating plainly how great had been the tension of the last few weeks, and how pressing was the call for rest, but there was no one to notice this. It was quite dark when Madlen at last appeared carrying a lighted dip.

'Come, get up,' she said; 'he's laid out in the penisha and he's looking splendid. Bensha's going to watch tonight;' but here something unusual in the girl's appearance struck her, and bending over her, she called her, 'Catrin! Catrin!'

'What is it?' said the girl 'I want to sleep,' and seeing that she breathed and answered when spoken to, Madlen said, 'Sleep on then, thou hard-hearted croten,' and leaving the candle disappeared down the stairs.

All night Catrin lay restless and feverish, and next day refused all food except milk, with which Madlen sulkily supplied her. For many days she lay in a kind of lethargy, but little conscious of what was going on around her. While she was in this state of semi-consciousness her father's funeral left the house. She heard the shuffling footsteps, and the rising and falling of the mournful funeral hymn as if in a dream, but still felt no inclination to move. A low fever consumed her, the days went on unheeded, and a fortnight had gone before she had begun to rally; but the healthy constitution which she had gained during the years she had lived in the open air, now came to her aid, and almost every hour found her with recuperated energy. Madlen had at last thought fit to send for the doctor, fearing lest she was going to be burdened with a helpless invalid for life.

'Lying here like a stone,' she said, ushering him into the low-roofed llofft, 'and her father's corpse, druan bach, carried out of the house!'

'What's the matter, 'merch i?' said the doctor, kindly.

'Nothing, only I've been ill,' said Catrin.'I am better now, and I will get up tomorrow.'

'Why didn't you send for me sooner?' he asked, looking sternly at Madlen. 'She has been very ill, and might have died. It is only her strong constitution has pulled her through.'

'How am I to understand the freaks of her?' said Madlen. '*I* didn't know she was ill,' and she flounced indignantly out of the llofft.

'Well, you don't want medicine, 'merch i,' said Dr Jones. 'You've had what you wanted most, a long rest, and you've regained your strength wonderfully. Madlen and Bensha have been left master and mistress here, I understand! Ach-y-fi! 'tis a scandalous shame! but you be a good girl, and I've no doubt they'll look after you as your father meant them to do.'

'Oh yes,' said Catrin, 'It is all right. My father loved me dearly, and did the best he could for me.'

'Well, get up when you feel inclined, and eat well. Goodbye!'

Two days afterwards Catrin was quite prepared to leave her rough bed. She dressed herself, and to Madlen's satisfaction entered the kitchen as she and Bensha were sitting down to their tea.

'That's something like behaving,' she said, pouring out a cup of tea for her. 'And now, there's nothing like plain speaking, so I'd have you to know at once that Pengraig has been left to Bensha and me, and we to look after you. So try your best to please us, and we'll take care you don't want for food and clothing.'

'Yes, I understand,' said Catrin quietly, and when tea was over, she washed up the tea things, and put them away in the same impassive manner.

Madlen nodded her head with a shrewd wink at Bensha.

'She knows which side her bread is buttered,' she whispered, as the girl, taking down the old blue cloak, went silently out of the house.

It was night, and the stars were out in bright array as she took her way to the cliffs.

Let it not be thought that Catrin's brave spirit had utterly succumbed to the trials which had befallen her. No; her simple faith bore her triumphantly through the ordeal of her father's death and Goronwy's departure, and in the long hour of her listless inactivity, her mind had been busily occupied in arranging her plans for the future, for as day followed day she had become more and more fully aware that although she might learn to endure the bitterness of Goronwy's absence, his return home with Yshbel would be more than she could bear. Out in the starlight once more her mind was clear as to her future course, and under the solemn silence of the night sky her heart regained its strength and courage. The fact that her father had passed through the portals of death was deprived of much of its bitterness to her by her vivid faith in the Unseen, and her long communings with Nature in the lonely hours of her solitary life, and the lethargy that overcame her had mercifully softened to her the depressing accessories of a funeral. She knew it was necessary and inevitable, but she shrank from the details with horror. They were entirely dissociated in her mind from the fact that a spirit had taken its flight from 'this bourne of time and space,' and it was more with a feeling of solemn joy than sorrow, that she stood once more on the bare Pengraig fields, looking out over the sea and up to the starry sky.

During those long days of inactivity she had silently thought out and matured her plans, while Madlen thought she slept. She would leave Treswnd and go far from the scenes where she had once been so happy. It would be a relief to Goronwy, and would enable her to bear her sorrow better.

'Perhaps you will come and see us!' John Lovell had said,

and she had made up her mind to take him at his word, and to test the friendliness of the strangers with whom, at least, a distant kinship linked her.

Suddenly she saw on the side of the hill the glow of the gipsy fire, and a feeling of hope awoke within her. As she drew nearer the light, she saw that the two girls Matta and Melia were dancing vigorously in front of the tent, while, lying in the full glow of the fire, a youth of dark visage was playing a wild Zingara tune with no mean skill upon a concertina, whose harsh tones were softened by the open air. John Lovell sat on an upturned box looking critically at the dancers and applauding sometimes. Here and there sat other groups of the dark-skinned company, some lying prone on the ground, others hugging their knees and watching with interest the savoury stew which bubbled in a large pot over the fire just within the door of the tent. Catrin recognised the face and figure of old Nancy Wood, reclining in the hand-barrow in which she was wheeled about by her devoted tribe. She was but little altered since the night when she and Goronwy had first made her acquaintance. Time had deprived her of the use of her limbs, but had left her otherwise apparently untouched.

So intent were the company upon the dancing and the bubbling pot, that Catrin had advanced close to the circle before she was observed, and it was Nancy Wood's keen eyes that first detected her presence.

'Who's that?' she called, and instantly every one was on the alert, the dancing stopped, the concertina was silent, and Lovell, starting to his feet, repeated the old woman's question.

Catrin drew still nearer, and in the full light of the fire he recognised her.

''Tis the girl from Pengraig,' he explained. 'Come on, my lass, you're welcome.'

'I have been ill,' said Catrin, 'or else I would have come before.'

'Come here, child,' cried Nancy Wood, in her curious

croaking voice; 'come here, let's see, are you like Dolly Wood?' and Catrin approached rather nervously, for the old woman's eyes gleamed in the gloom like sparks of fire She stretched out her claw-like hands and drew the girl towards her. 'Make a blaze, John,' she cried, and he kicked the burning logs till they flamed afresh.

Every black eye was turned upon Catrin.

'Yes, very like Dolly,' was Nancy's verdict. 'Sit down, child, on that basket – anywhere near. Aye! And I'm sorry to hear your father's gone! 'Tis a sore trouble for you, but wasn't it a good thing I sent John down when I did?'

'And what did the walrus say when she heard?' asked Lovell.

'I have not told her about it yet,' said the girl, timidly.

'What?' screamed Nancy.

'What d'ye mean, lass?' said Lovell.

'Oh, indeed,' answered Catrin, ''tis that I'm wanting to tell you.'

'Tell Nancy,' muttered Lovell, with an admonishing nudge, and so low that only Catrin caught the words.

''Tis now that I'm alone, I feel so friendless,' continued Catrin, turning to Nancy Wood. 'So I've come up here to see will you help me.'

'Aye, you did right, child; you knew where to come. Yes, I'll help you all I can for Dolly's sake; so take heart, 'merch i, and tell me all your troubles.'

'Not before supper, mother,' said Ando, the youth who had played on the concertina. 'I'm that hungry I could jump into the pot.'

'Supper first, then,' said the old woman.

And bowls and platters were soon filled with the savoury stew; Catrin receiving her portion with the rest, and enjoying it too, for the fresh night air had restored to her the appetite that had been sorely missing in the llofft under the slates. Between the spoonfuls of her stew Nancy drew from the girl an account of her father's death, and her subsequent breakdown, as far as she was able to remember it; and far more than the simple girl beside her imagined, the shrewd old woman, with her long experience of love affairs, gathered.

'You're grown a tall girl since we saw you last, my dear. How's things been going with you?'

John Lovell had told her every word of his conversation with Catrin on the occasion of his visit to Pengraig, and had described every article of her dress; neither had he omitted to mention the blush that had overspread her face at the mention of Goronwy's name, nor his own suspicions with regard to it.

'Where's the young man that came with you here last time?' asked Nancy, with a keen look at her.

Again the wearisome question, and the answer that cost her so much, and had to be given so calmly.

'He's gone away to the "works" to be married, and to bring his wife home with him.'

'H'm! I thought he was going to be thy husband, child.'

'Oh no, no; only my friend he was.' And the memory of the words, 'marry a witch,' came back to her mind with such scorching force that her face burnt in the gloom. She endeavoured to turn the conversation to other subjects, but Nancy Wood was not to be baulked.

'Who is his wife?' she asked.

'Yshbel Lloyd – down in the village.'

'What – old Ben and Nanti Betto's foster child? Well, well! Let the blackguard come up here again, and he'll feel the weight of my crutches about his ears!'

'Oh, Nancy Wood!' cried Catrin, in tones of real distress, 'not that name for Goronwy Hughes. You don't know him. He wouldn't tell a lie to save his life. You don't know him, indeed, indeed.'

'He has told you a good many lies, I guess?'

'No; never, never! But 'tis getting late, and I want to ask you something.'

The crock of stew had been emptied, and the satisfied company were once more settling themselves down to gossip and smoke, Matta and Melia drawing nearer the tent, with John Lovell, and seemingly much interested in their visitor.

'What about the will?' he asked; 'that's what I want to know. When are you going to turn that grumpy old couple out?'

''Tis about that I want to speak,' said Catrin.

She seemed much embarrassed, and, but for the gloom in which they sat, her keen-eyed entertainers would have detected the deepening colour and fluttering breath.

''Tis this. I have been here many years, and I want to go away for a bit now. I've got nothing to do, and – and I was thinking if I was to show this will, everybody would be wondering why didn't I stop at home, and look after the farm. But if I leave Bensha and Madlen as the first will settles, no one will wonder why I'm going away – and if I come back some day, 'twill be time enough to show the will and claim the farm. But, indeed, I don't think I will ever come back to disturb them.'

'My sakes! you are an odd one,' said Lovell. 'What d'ye want to go away for?'

''Tis only I feel I must go,' said Catrin. 'Oh! I would like to go and see the world a bit – there's tired I am here! I must go, and I was thinking perhaps Nancy Wood could help me and show me the way. I'll come back again some day perhaps, and if I do there's Pengraig ready for me.'

'Have you got money?'

'Not much. Madlen took it all out of the bag where father kept his money, to pay for the funeral and things, but I've got £3 that he gave me, and about fifteen shillings.'

'You won't go far upon that, unless you travel with us; and if you do, you must give me your money to keep.'

'Yes. I will, indeed.'

Nancy Wood had been listening intently to this conversation, and now broke in with her croaking voice: 'Let the girl have her own way. She is quite right to go away a bit. She has been ill, and our free life will do her good. You shall come with us, my girl'

'Oh, there's kind you are to me! 'Tis to the wool mountains I want to go, and earn my living as a shepherdess – those blue hills across the bay. Peggy Bryn used to go there every year, and bring home enough wool to keep her in petticoats all the winter. She is dead now, or else perhaps she would take me with her.'

'The wool mountains? The blue mountains across the bay? D'ye know how far off they are, child? 'Tis eighty miles at least, or a hundred, perhaps.'

''Tis there I want to go whatever, ever since we used to sing:

'Fair land beyond the sea,
When shall I come to thee?'

I have been wishing to go there, and now the time is come.'

Nancy Wood turned to John Lovell.

''Tis there she shall go,' she said 'The Cribor mountains, my child, are just beyond the Snowdon range, and there William Bray has a farm, eight hundred sheep he keeps, and shepherds many. I will give you a message to him, and Nancy Wood's name will help you on there as well as here.'

'Thank you, indeed, can diolch!' said Catrin. 'But how will I go?'

'Well, come with us as far as Pontwenardi, that will be fifty miles on your way, and there we must separate. We turn off to Bala, but you keep on towards Snowdon. You are young and strong.'

'Yes – only put me on my way, and I will find it out.'

'Well, you'll have to be sharp then,' said Lovell, 'for day after tomorrow we tramp from here.'

'So soon as that? But I will be ready.'

Yes – she would be ready. A feverish longing possessed her to reach those blue hills, where the shining bay would stretch between her and the shore where Yshbel and Goronwy lived.

CHAPTER XXIV

ON TRAMP WITH THE GIPSIES

The sun had scarcely peeped over the crest of the hills, when Catrin rose from her rough bed in the llofft on the morning when she was to join her gipsy companions. For the last time she ran down the little ravine to Traethyberil for her daily plunge into the sea.

'Oh, how will I do without it?' was her thought, as she returned to the dim old kitchen to snatch a hurried breakfast. She had arranged her dress the day before, and had been much puzzled as to what to wear, deciding at last upon her brown and green homespun gown. Her rush hat would do well, and her shoes were strong and good. But what for her shoulders? And she stood for some time before the old coffer undecided. Here was her mother's scarlet 'mantell'; here her mulberry cloak; but neither seemed suitable, so they were laid reverently back in their places. Here was a long cloak of brown cloth which had evidently seen better days, and throwing it over her shoulders, she decided to wear it. A few necessaries and a pair of dry shoes were easily contained in the small bundle which she strapped over her shoulders, and thus equipped, she was ready for her journey. She smiled as she looked at herself in the looking-glass on the kitchen window. 'Well, indeed,' she said, 'I look like a gipsy already; 'tis the bundle, I think, but I must have that!'

She had shut Merlin in the stable with a goodly supply of food the night before, to prevent his following her, so she had nothing to do now but to slip out silently and leave the old place for ever. This was not done without a pang of regret; but it was down on the edge of the cliffs that she felt the keenest sorrow. The long white line of the surf on the shore, not yet touched by the light of the sun, the silver bay, waiting cool and placid for the rosy light which should tinge its sparkling ripples, the white wings wheeling round her, the cawing crows, the rising lark, how dear were all to her! How well she knew every dent and crag of that rugged coast! ''Twas there the tide shut us in one moonlight night, and we had to wait till it went out again; and 'twas down there we played at dandiss together! There's foolish I am to look at it!' and she turned away, with a firm resolve not to turn back.

As she reached the gipsy encampment, she saw that John Lovell was already bustling about.

'Good morning to you, lass,' he called out as she approached. 'You've brought a fine morning with you!'

'Yes, braf indeed,' said Catrin, and her voice seemed to wake the community, for in a few moments all were astir, emerging, one by one, from the most unexpected quarters. Nancy Wood and one or two of the elder women slept in the tent, but in fine weather, the rest found their beds anywhere. A party of children climbed down from a covered cart; some rose from under a bush or a square of tarpaulin; Ando came, buoyant and bright, from a crate full of straw; Matta and Melia stepped out of the children's cart. All gathered round Catrin with eager interest.

'Well done!' they said. 'Ye're a girl to yer word! And you're really coming with us? Well, lend a hand with the breakfast then!'

'Yes, indeed; let me help you.'

A loud croaking from the tent showed Nancy Wood was awake.

'Here, child!' she cried, and Catrin entered the tent. With clawing fingers stretched out towards her, the old woman asked in a whisper, 'Where's your money, child? I'll take care of it for you!'

'Here it is,' said Catrin, carefully untying the corner of her pocket-handkerchief. But the knot was stubborn, fortunately for Catrin, for John Lovell, entering opportunely, arrested her hand, saying : 'Halt! I take care of the coin. Here's half-a-crown for your pocket, lass. Will that do?'

'Oh yes! I will never spend so much.'

'Well, then, the rest is safe with me till you leave us. That's right, mother, isn't it?' he said, looking, with concealed amusement, at the old woman, whose face was a picture of cunning and disappointed greed.

'Yes, yes; quite right,' she said, in an off-hand manner. 'I was only going to keep it safe for her, but you're so devilish suspicious. Go, then, 'merch i, and help Sylvia with the breakfast,' and a kindly smile softened the wrinkled face; but that moment had revealed to the girl the shady side of her kinswoman's character.

'Will I help you?' she asked a slender, gentle-faced girl, who was kindling a fire. 'Will I fetch the water?' and fleet of foot, she sped to the well, and returned, bearing a can of water in time for Sylvia's crackling fire.

'You need not have gone so far,' said Matta, 'this stream would do. You won't be so particular when you've lived out of doors with us a bit.'

'Perhaps, indeed,' was Catrin's reply, though her thought was, 'I have lived many years out of doors, but I like clean water for tea.'

When the tea had brewed, and Melia and Matta had cut plateful of bread and butter, they gathered round the alfresco meal with keen enjoyment and healthy appetites.

'That's a good cup of tea, anyway,' said Nancy Wood, turning her cup upside down in the saucer, having first swung it round once or twice, and gazed intently at the sediment of tea leaves.

'Yes,' said Lovell. ''Tis no worse for the spring water. And now, to work!'

And in a few minutes every hand was busy. Tents were pulled down, poles were taken up and slung on the backs of the patient donkeys, the carts were packed, and Nancy Wood in her barrow was hoisted bodily into the covered cart, which Ando drove, enlivening his journey by frequent tunes on the concertina, the reins hanging loosely over his arm, for Alexander, the old horse, was in no danger of running away. The fowls were caught and bundled into rough crates and baskets slung under the carts. The babies were used to fill up the corners, their little sunburnt faces peeping out in every direction.

John Lovell, with a string of rough ponies, which he was driving to Brynferri fair, led the van, and Jim Boswell, the knife-grinder, brought up the rear.

When they were once on their way, there was time for chatter and talk, Matta and Melia especially entertaining the company with their gossip and merry laughter.

Sylvia generally lagged a little behind, except when Catrin walked abreast of her, when she stepped out bravely and seemed to enjoy the tramp over the breezy hillsides. The sun was now risen, and between his golden light, and the bloom on the gorse, the world was all ablaze, and Catrin, to whom the beauty of nature was as the elixir of life, drank in all the loveliness of the scene. True, a dark shadow lurked in her heart, but, with her temperament, and with such scenes around her, to say nothing of the merry company, it was impossible to be wholly miserable.

'Well, 'tis time for me to ask where are we going, I think,' she said, laughingly, to Sylvia, who had caught her up again.

'Don't you know? 'Tis to Brynferri fair; 'tis a big town, and a grand fair. Have you ever been there?'

'Me? No, indeed; I have never been anywhere from Treswnd. I would never venture to move from there, I think, only Nancy Wood is so kind to let me come with you all. And John Lovell – there's kind he is too!'

'Yes,' said Sylvia, 'you can trust him. He thinks the world of you; and he told me to keep with you as much as I could, only I don't like to push myself when Matta and Melia are with you.'

'Why not?' said Catrin. 'There's pretty they are, and merry and light-hearted! They make the road bright for you.'

'Yes, sure they do. I am not so lively nor pretty.'

'Aren't you pretty?' said Catrin, looking at the pensive face of her companion. 'I think you are.'

'Do you like me then?'

'Yes, better than any of them.'

A bright red flush swept over the girl's face, and a smile of pleasure illumined the dark eyes.

'Well indeed; I must try to be merry for you, but it doesn't come easy for me, because I have seen so much trouble. My father is dead this long time, and my mother was burnt in the tent, and my little brother with her, that I loved so dearly.'

'No wonder you are not merry then,' said Catrin. 'But why did John Lovell tell you to keep with me?'

'I don't know, but I think because Matta and Melia are using bad words sometimes, and are smoking, both of them, and they so young! Matta's father got plenty money in the bank, and Melia's father – William Bray is his name – is very rich, they say.'

And thus chatting together, they made rapid progress towards their destination and left the old neighbourhood behind them. It was all new and strange to Catrin, and the companionship of those of her own sex was a new and pleasant experience to her.

For miles their route lay along the hillsides, and over breezy moors, where the crisp, short grass was like velvet under their feet. The air, redolent of the scent of the gorse, which covered everything with its mantle of gold, the little pools in the peat bogs reflecting the blue of the sky, and the modest brown flowers of the tufted rushes – all was new and beautiful to the girl whose life had hitherto been so unvaried. The butterflies fluttered from bush to bush, and the bees filled the air with their musical humming.

Catrin had determined not to look back, but when Sylvia exclaimed, 'Look, there's the last sight of the sea!' she turned eagerly, forgetting her resolution. Yes, there it was! The dear old bay, now glimmering like a sheet of silver in the distance, the haze of noontide brooding over it and veiling the blue hills on the other side. A sigh escaped her lips, and Sylvia cast a furtive glance at her. Was she, too, unhappy? The girl who seemed to her to have stepped out of the grand world of regularity and propriety, where people had their meals upon tables, and slept upon feather beds, to cast in her lot with the children of roughness and hard living! But Catrin was reticent by nature, and breathed not a word of her own sorrow. At a turn of the road the rest of the company waited for them, Matta and Melia evidently thinking that Sylvia had been sufficiently favoured.

'You come along with us now,' they called, and Catrin, anxious to propitiate them all, fell in with their wishes, but with a backward smile at Sylvia.

They were still treading the mountain ways, the soft-footed donkeys winding in and out between the low bushes, the scent of the wild thyme rising like incense from their steps. John Lovell and his ponies had already disappeared, having reached the spot where they had, perforce, to travel on the high road.

'How can you care to walk with that Sylvia?' said Matta.

'Horrid thing!' ejaculated Melia.

'Oh, don't!' said Catrin. 'Don't you like her?'

'Ach-y-fi, no! There's no 'go' in her. She hates Matta and me. She thinks to please the 'boss' by her sneaking ways, but I can tell her he don't like her, and if you don't please him, 'tisn't long you'll be in this company!'

'Is he the master here, then?' asked Catrin.

'Yes, of course; and he's a hard man to please, though you

wouldn't think it by his jolly ways. You'll see him at Brynferri tonight, how sharp he watches us. What between him and old Nancy's cuteness, there's no getting a bit of fun anyway; and 'tis no use trying to hide anything from her, you see. She's that knowing, she reads the stars!'

'Tchut!' said Melia. 'I know all about that; and I mean to take up the same trade myself some day, when I'm old and ugly, you know. 'Tis only cuteness, nothing more, and I've got my share of that!'

'And no mistake,' interpolated Matta.

'Yes. Look you here now. I'll play Nancy Wood, and you, Catrin Rees, sit here between Matta and me.'

Sitting in the shade of a broom brush, she drew Catrin down beside her, and holding her hand palm upwards, gazed fixedly for a few moments into the clear brown eyes that looked into hers.

'Well, you're a pretty girl, so 'tisn't likely you've gone so far without a sweetheart – eh? Well then, if all is right between sweethearts they don't want to part with each other. Well, you wanted to come away with us, so 'tisn't all right between you and your sweetheart, and you're coming with us to get away from him. See? That's how she does it. Stop a minute; I haven't finished yet. I'm beginning to read now myself!' and her eyes took a strange dreamy look. 'Yes, I think he's going to be married to somebody else.'

Catrin's face had become gradually suffused with blushes. She tried hard to withdraw her hand from Melia's, but it was held in a firm grasp.

'No, no; let me see,' she said, 'what I can read in it for the future!'

Matta, who was beginning to be interested, stooped also over the open palm, saying:

'Melia, what do you see?'

'Well, here's a sharp cross, and here's a long journey; and at the end of it is sorrow and loneliness. No, no; wait! Here is all of a sudden brightness and happiness – yes, and love. Catrin Rees, you shall meet your lover at the end of your journey, and you will have a long and happy life together. There now!' she continued 'Nancy Wood could not have told you a truer fortune!'

'Oh, stop, stop!' said Catrin, freeing her hand with a struggle. 'You are talking nonsense. Indeed, indeed, I never had a lover!'

'Tell that to the horse marines!' said Melia, with a laugh.

'To the what?' asked Catrin. 'What is that?'

'Oh! 'tis a regiment of soldiers, I think. That's nonsense, my dear, but that's the only bit of nonsense I've talked since under this bush I've been.'

'Melia!' said Matta, under her breath, 'I do believe you see! Will you tell my fortune?'

'Yes, some day perhaps, but not now. Come on,' she added, springing to her feet. 'We mustn't be late tonight; we've got to dance, you know.'

'Oh, I am glad,' said Catrin. 'I will like to see you, and to hear the music.'

'Ando plays first-rate, and no mistake; but don't you talk about music till you've heard Lovell sing!'

'Can he sing too? He is a clever man!'

'He is that!'

'Is he married?'

'Not he. He was married when he was quite young, they say, and his wife died, and a good thing, for she led him a life! 'Twas one winter when they were stopping in Liverpool. Perhaps, if they'd been on the road, it wouldn't have happened.'

'Perhaps, indeed,' said Catrin. ''Tis very hard to get well in the close house, even in the country.'

Noontide found them on the high road, a merry company, for the weather was perfect, and there were no sick loiterers. They made no halt for a midday meal, but every one seemed prepared with some kind of food, which they drew from their pockets, and ate with zest as they walked, Matta and Melia giving Catrin a generous share of their portion.

''Tis a beautiful pie,' said Melia; 'we had it from the yellow house beyond Sarnissa.'

'Oh, I know,' said Catrin, smothering a sigh; ''twas the mestress.'

'She's a good sort whatever,' said Matta, munching.

All day the motley cavalcade tramped on till the afternoon was nearly spent and the sun drew down to the west. Catrin, unaccustomed to so much walking, grew rather weary, and lagged behind a little, where Sylvia soon joined her, she too looking tired and dusty, but with a pleasant smile on her sweet face. She was not so dark in hue as the rest of the company, and perhaps it was this difference which caused the slight estrangement between them. Certainly, Matta and Melia never lost an opportunity for a sarcastic remark, if she ventured to join in the conversation.

'We won't be long now,' she said as she rejoined Catrin. 'There's our camping ground, just over the shoulder of the hill; and there's Brynferri beyond those trees. 'Tis a big fair there today!'

'I have never seen a town,' said Catrin, looking at the grey haze that hung over it. 'I will keep close to you, Sylvia. Will we be in the fair?'

'Well, of course; 'tis for that we have travelled so far today. John Lovell wants to sell some of his ponies, and Cordelia and I will sell some tins. Nancy Wood will take a lot of money telling fortunes, but 'tis Matta and Melia will make the most by their dancing.'

'Well, indeed! you can all do something except me!'

As they reached the camping ground, John Lovell came towards them. 'Well, my lasses,' he said, 'are ye very tired? That's right! Sylvia and you keeping together all day—'

'No,' said Sylvia, and the pale face blushed a rosy red as she encountered the reproachful eyes of the gipsy. 'I did my best, but Matta and Melia—'

'Matta and Melia! Tchut! You *promised*, but there, you're a bad 'un like the rest!' and he turned on his heel, with what Catrin thought was a smile on his handsome mouth.

Sylvia, however, seemed to have missed the smile, for her eyes filled with tears.

'Was he angry,' asked Catrin. 'I thought he was smiling.'

'Smiling? Oh no. He thinks the world of a promise, and I would not break mine for the world! Not to him, whatever.'

But there was no more time for talk; all were busy preparing the camp for the night.

The tent was set up, and Nancy Wood wheeled into it before any other arrangements were made.

Then came the sustaining 'cup of tea', Catrin's services being again called into requisition. It was a very informal meal, some partaking of it seated on the ground, some standing, but no time was wasted over it, as the stew had to be prepared for supper.

There were dire shrieks and scuffles, when four of the fowls which had been their travelling companions were summarily despatched, cleaned, and thrown into the pot. All the crusts that could be gathered were thrown in with them, as well as a large basket of vegetables, which Ando had bought or 'gathered' on the way. A dash of pepper and salt, and a tin of water were added. The crock, full to the brim, and hanging from the trivet over the fire, was soon sending forth an appetising odour. Nancy Wood was left in charge, while the rest of the company trudged to the fair, Sylvia and Catrin amongst them, while John Lovell followed, accompanied by Jim Boswell carrying a mandoline. As they drew near the town, the hum of voices reached them on the evening breeze, mingled with all the other sounds which proclaim the delights of a country fair: the clash of cymbals, and the braying of a brass band, whoops and calls, the laughter of men and the barking of dogs! Catrin's heart beat high with excitement. If only she could have stifled the sorrow that lurked behind everything, how she would have enjoyed the scene that met her eyes upon entering the town! Such a concourse of people she had never seen before. As Matta and Melia, accompanied by Ando, appeared, the crowd made way for them, for they were evidently known and welcomed. 'The dancers! the dancers!' they exclaimed, and closing in at their rear they followed the gipsies to an open square around which were ranged vans, booths, and 'shows' of every description, a gorgeous sunset lighting up the scene, aided by cressets of flaming coal tar and naphtha, which flickered and wavered in the evening breeze.

Ando spread a square of carpet on the ground, while Matta and Melia disappeared into one of the vans. 'They are gone to dress,' whispered Sylvia, and in a few moments they emerged, and tripped lightly on to the square of carpet, greeted by the shouts and cheers of the crowd. Ando struck up a lively tune on his concertina, and the two girls bowed. They wore dresses of brilliant chintz, with stockings of crimson, and shoes of black velvet, and to Catrin's eyes appeared more beautiful than anything she had ever dreamt of. With waving arms and glancing feet, they danced lightly to Ando's inspiriting music, their tambourines tinkling merrily, and their bright skirts fluttering round their agile limbs. It was a graceful and pretty dance, and the whole picture was full of charm; the soft sunset light, brooding over it all in a golden haze. What a scene for Catrin, so alive to every impression of beauty!

As she stood with Sylvia in the crowd, and watched her quondam companions of the road, she almost doubted whether it was no dream, which would fade away ere long, and for a while she forgot her sorrow in the gaiety around her.

When the dance was over, the girls made their way through the gaping crowd, holding out their tambourines, into which the pennies and halfpennies, and even coins of silver, fell with a pleasant jingle. While they rested, sitting on the shafts of a cart near by, their white teeth gleaming, their black eyes sparkling, as they chatted and flirted with the admiring yokels, John Lovell stepped on to the carpet, and, taking his mandoline from Boswell, struck a few chords, which instantly riveted the attention of the crowd, who filled the air with shouts of welcome. Thrum, thrumpy thrum thrum, thrum thrum; every ear was intently listening, and there was an audible hush in the hum of the fair, as their favourite commenced his song. And what a voice he had! – full, soft, and rich in melody, a tremble in the tones, which nature and not art had endowed it with. It was a wild gipsy song, with a Spanish refrain, which his quick ear had caught, in the days of his youth, as he travelled through Spain with a company of strolling players.

'Oh,' exclaimed Catrin, 'to think he carries so much of Heaven about with him!'

Sylvia made no reply, for she too was wrapt in such delight as music alone has the power of awakening.

'Hush!' she whispered; 'he is going to sing again,' and both girls listened breathlessly, while again the musical voice filled the air with melody; and while he sang the common-place gipsy figure was transformed: there was a smile on the lips, a flush rose in his dark face, and surely Love never found more perfect expression, than in the voice of this simple gipsy. The last words of the song died away amidst the loud cheers of the crowd. It was a Welsh crowd, and the music had reached their hearts; nothing else could have moved them to so recklessly throw their pennies into the tambourine which Ando carried amongst them.

'Sylvia,' said Catrin, 'I am sure 'tis true! John Lovell loves somebody like that.'

'No, no; not any one! There is no woman as happy as that in the world.'

'Well, indeed, I could not understand the words much, because I am so dull with the English, but the music was plain to me. Tell me in Welsh what was that last song.'

'Oh well, 'twas a lover telling his sweetheart (she was going to marry some one else, mind you), that when she would hear another man speaking words of love to her, then she would remember him.'

''Tis beautiful indeed!' said Catrin, to whose heart the simple sentimentality of a love-song was a fresh sensation, and seemed a wonderful expression of her own feelings. But Matta and Melia joining them soon banished sentiment.

'Two pounds,' said Matta, handing the money to Lovell, 'one in our tambourines, and the other Ben Jingo pays you for the bridle and collar.'

'Right,' said Lovell, laconically.

It was brilliant moonlight as they all tramped back to the encampment together. The glamour of the music, the lights, and the sunset had disappeared, but the words of Lovell's song still remained with Catrin, as Sylvia had translated them.

'Come, come,' said Nancy Wood, on their arrival, 'you've been long enough. The supper's ready, and I'm hungry. What takings, Lovell?'

'Oh, very good,' he answered. 'I sold four ponies, too, and sent the others on to Llanwarren for the fair there next week. After supper I've got something to tell you all, so come on. Here, Catrin, here's the bellows for you to sit upon. Sylvia, there's my jacket for you. Matta and Melia, you can sit upon your tambourines if you like. Come, Ando, bowl it out, man; I'm as hungry as a hunter.'

'Now for the news,' said Ando, when every one was satisfied, and the empty crock, with the bones only, was thrust aside for the dogs.

'Well, then, listen. Jim Boswell, I saw you examining a new van in the fair square.'

'Yes,' said Jim. 'Never saw such a van in my life! And no one about to tell me who it belonged to. Curtains in the windows, a seat with a velvet cushion all round, pots and pans, all bran new in the boot, plates and cups and glasses fit for a king! The two horses were there too, splendid strong animals. The lad as held them said they all belonged to a gipsy, and that's all l could find out.'

'That gipsy's me,' said John Lovell; 'that van is mine.' And now I want to know which of you women is coming with me to keep it clean and tidy?'

'Me! Me! I will!' rose from every direction.

'Well, there's one here that hasn't answered,' said Lovell. 'Sylvia, lass, will you come and be my servant?'

'Yes, will I, boss, if you're not joking,' answered Sylvia.

'Come away, then, while I settle the terms with you.'

And, rising, he passed out of the light of the circle, Sylvia following, with her hand pressed to her side, as if to still some unruly throbbing there. 'Come round the broom bushes, lass, they're tall enough to hide us. Sylvia,' he said, taking her hand, 'I've watched you since first you joined this company, and I never heard you tell a lie, nor use a bad word, and never saw you behave but as a good, honest woman ought to, and if you'll have me, lass, to be your wedded husband, why, I'm your man; and you're the girl for me!'

Sylvia's head drooped, her hand pressed harder on the throbbing heart, which was too full for speech.

'Come, answer, sweetheart!' he said. 'There's no need for many words; a kiss will do, for I know you love me. If it were not for that I would not have bought the van, and I would not have ventured to get the licence, lass. 'Tis all ready. The van is yours, and I am yours, only to say the word. Will you marry me, Sylvia, though I am much older than you? You know me well. Will you be my wife?'

Is it needful to tell Sylvia's answer? At all events, when John Lovell brought her back to the wondering circle round the fire, he seemed well satisfied, and there was a look of radiant happiness in her eyes, which told its own tale.

'Do tell, boss!' said Jim Boswell. 'What's the meaning of all this?'

'It means, my lads,' said Lovell, raising his voice a little, and drawing Sylvia to his side, 'that I have bought that van for me and my wife to travel about in. Here she is. I've had my eye upon her for a long time, and I challenge you all to say a word against my choice!'

There was a moment's silence of astonishment, broken by a cheer from Ando, and a somersault, which brought him perilously near the fire.

'Hooray for Sylvia and the boss,' he shouted, and everyone joined, the women half-heartedly, the men with stentorian tones.

Nancy Wood's excitement was so great, that, not feeling her croaking 'Hurrah' sufficiently emphatic, she flung both her crutches towards the affianced pair. Amid shouts of laughter, Ando returned them to her with a sweeping bow, while Lovell, mounting on a barrow, called for order.

'Listen, mates, once more. That's my van, as I told you before; this is my wife – or will be tomorrow, for I've got the licence in my pocket, and she's willing. So tomorrow we'll be married – in church too, mind you! None of your 'registers' for me, but a real stand-up again before a clergyman. So come on, my lads and lasses all, let's show them what a gipsy wedding can be, straight and smart and sober. Jim Boswell, there's a 'sov' for you, that the company may drink our healths; but, remember, no fighting, no lying about the road drunk for Nancy Wood's company! Now for business. I'm going to bid you goodbye tonight.'

At this there was a loud murmur of disapproval.

'Oh, not for good; bless you, no! I've travelled with this company since I came from Spain many years ago, and I hope to end my days with you. But there's the van. I've got to look after it as if 'twas my own child. It's been a fortnight at Brynferri, and I've been in it, off and on, as often as I could. You know I've been away from you a good deal lately. The vicar, he says to me, "You must reside a fortnight in this parish, you know, before you can be married." "Bless you, sir," says I, "there's my van in the market-place – been there this fortnight, and that's my pair of horses in the Lamb stables close by. Where else could I reside? And "if you want a pair of carriage horses, sir," says I, "there they are for you; fifty guineas a-piece. I ask no more, and I'll take no less." "All right," says he, laughing, "when I can afford it I'll buy your horses."

'Well, it's all right for our wedding tomorrow, you see, and I hope you'll all be there at ten o'clock. Then we turn down to Pembrokeshire – that's my wife and me – in the van, mind you; the ponies are gone on. And then we'll take a round through Carmarthenshire and Glamorganshire, and so work round to meet you at Pontwynedi this day three weeks.'

Here the cheering was loud and long.

'There's one thing more I would like to say; first, about my gal here. Once she's Sylvia Lovell, remember she's the wife of your boss, and I expect you all to treat her as such. The next thing is with regard to this young woman who has joined us for a time. You know she's related to Nancy Wood, and when I've said that I'm sure I need not say any more to make it plain to you all, that she's to be well treated and taken care of while she's under our charge. I've got her money in my keeping. And now I've finished.'

'I've got a word to say,' screamed Nancy Wood, waving her crutch. 'We wishes you all health and happiness, John Lovell and Sylvia Jones, and we'll be at the wedding by ten o'clock tomorrow. And another word. If any harm comes to my blood relation Catrin Rees, I'll have Jim Boswell's ears,' and again her crutch came flying into the fire, from which Boswell himself rescued it amidst the laughter of the company.

'Aye, aye! she knows her man,' they cried. 'He's a rogue among the lasses!' And Jim, by no means denying the soft impeachment, only shrugged his shoulders and laughed.

'By George,' he said, 'yer a slandering lot! But the boss he knows me better. Depend upon me, John Lovell, I won't neglect my jooty.'

'Well, goodbye, then,' said the latter, when the laughter at

Jim Boswell's expense had subsided. 'We'll meet at Pontwynedi this day three weeks.' And snatching up a brilliant new cart-whip, with a loud flick of the lash he made an unceremonious departure, only waving his hand to Sylvia, but with a look of love in his black eyes, which she alone saw.

CHAPTER XXV

SYLVIA'S WEDDING

Next morning, a little before ten o'clock, the church of St Peter's at Brynferri was pretty well filled with curious spectators, as it had been bruited abroad that a gipsy wedding would be solemnised there, and the road leading to the moor had for the last hour been narrowly watched from the town for signs of the bridal party.

Five minutes before the appointed time, John Lovell entered the church alone, no idea of groomsman or friend having entered his mind. He wore a new coat of brown velveteen and a scarlet necktie, and as he sauntered up the aisle a gleam of light shining through the painted window brought out the glitter of his numerous pearl buttons.

'What a handsome man!' was whispered in the pews, and in truth, as he took his place in the chancel, he looked every inch a gallant bridegroom.

It was not long before the rest of the party arrived, as was evident by the sound of footsteps in the porch.

Nancy Wood, who had charge of all the finery belonging to the company, had done her best to carry out Lovell's wishes, and show the town what a 'proper' gipsy wedding was like, and as the bride and her party entered, they were eagerly scanned by the spectators.

There was no order or arrangement in the procession, as, to tell the truth, few, if any, of their number had ever been in a sacred building before, and their idea of a marriage ceremony went no further than a business transaction at a Registry

Office. Matta and Melia were dressed in their dancing costumes, and only in the porch had Jim Boswell suddenly observed that they carried their tambourines. There was a decided tussle before they agreed to discard their usual musical appendages, Matta revenging herself upon him by a smart jingling blow on his head.

'Hush-sh-sh!' said Boswell. 'Blam'd if you know how to behave yourselves in church!'

Having bustled the tambourines under a back seat he turned to look for the bride, who, in an access of shyness, was lagging behind the less subdued members of her party.

With a very audible 'Come on!' Boswell endeavoured to pilot her towards the bridegroom, whose white teeth showed the smile with which he watched Sylvia's nervous mistakes. Here were no orange blossoms, no bridal veil, no bows of white satin! But Sylvia looked beautiful in the gorgeous colouring of her gipsy dress: a skirt of red silk with a bodice of black velvet, having sleeves and habit-shirt of white muslin. Her jet black hair was arranged high on her head, upon it a little cap of scarlet; from her ears depended a pair of massive gold earrings, the 'present of the bridegroom', and from her shoulders trailed a long cloak of yellow satin.

She was all blushes and confusion, and had it not been for Jim Boswell, would never have found her way to the altar.

Cordelia Spriggs was resplendent in a green velvet gown, much bedizened with spangles. All the men of the company wore crimson silk sashes, but there was no one who excited such general interest, or who was watched more intently, than old Nancy Wood, the queen of the gipsies, for she had insisted upon being present. The handbarrow upon which she reclined was decked with green leaves and flowers, and she herself attired in a crimson cloak, from the hood of which her shrewd wrinkled face of over a century looked out with keen, observant eyes.

It was Jim Boswell's forethought which had abstracted from

her barrow, without her knowledge, the crutches with which she was so apt to emphasise her remarks.

Behind the brilliant procession Catrin followed, like a silent brown moth. Nancy Wood had been anxious to adorn her in crimson and gold, but she had earnestly entreated to be allowed to keep her everyday apparel; and as she entered a pew, and looked at the throng of brilliant colouring before her, she was awed in spirit, for thus had Goronwy and Yshbel doubtless stood at some altar, and perhaps under some vaulted roof like this under which she found herself.

Very little of the service was intelligible to her, but she saw that Lovell drew a ring from his pocket, and placed it on Sylvia's finger; she heard the solemn question, and Sylvia's low reply, and felt with every word how completely such a service had bound Goronwy to Yshbel, and severed him from her for ever!

It was not with a light heart, therefore, that she saw John Lovell and Sylvia walk arm-in-arm down the church, although she rejoiced much in the happiness of the gentle girl, who had been her companion.

Outside the porch, the brilliant-coloured group attracted much attention, the gipsies themselves appearing quite unconcerned at the interest they aroused. Lovell, though much elated at having got safely through the marriage ceremony, was divided between his pride of his wife and anxiety for the arrival of the van. Suddenly it appeared round the corner, driven by another dark-skinned gipsy; the harness glittered in the sunshine, the glossy strong horses trotted jauntily towards them, with much jingling and rattling of chains.

He helped the shy Sylvia up the steps, and now, for the first time, she saw the glory of the van's interior.

Standing at the open door, she bade 'Goodbye' to her companions. Matta and Melia, though sick with envy, were loud in their congratulations.

'Goodbye, boss – Sylvia, so long!' And amidst much waving of hands, and shouts of 'Hurrah!' the van rattled up the road, and turned the corner. As they disappeared, Nancy croaked a farewell, and hunted about for her crutches.

We must now leave Sylvia to doff her grandeur, and see to the arrangement of her own pots and pans and crockery, while the company turned their faces once more towards the moor, on which their encampment stood.

Sylvia's wedding was long remembered by them, for its wonderful effects upon the public funds, as day after day – more especially, night after night – during the remainder of their stay, Nancy Wood was besieged by lads and lasses from the town, who came in batches to have their fortunes told.

Once more, in the early dawn, the motley cavalcade set off on its march, by winding road or mountain paths, towards the appointed place.

Catrin, having lost Sylvia's companionship, was glad to be on the road again, her thoughts and hopes centring upon 'the blue hills across the bay', of which she and Goronwy had so often sung in the summer evenings.

'Perhaps,' she thought, 'he would still look across those shining waters sometimes, and wonder where she was! Perhaps he might even guess that she had flown to those blue hills – perhaps even, she might send a message across to him on the wings of the wind!'

John Lovell's quick eye, his clear head, and ready hand, were much missed by the whole company.

'Blam'd if I don't feel like a 'oss as 'as slipt 'is 'alter,' said Jim Boswell, 'and glad enough I'll be when Lovell comes back, especially,' he added in an undertone, 'with this cussed old woman always a-clawing after the fun's! Being "boss" ain't all pleasure!'

Catrin, too, was glad when, three weeks afterwards, on the brow of a hill, Matta and Melia, pointing to a grey haze in the valley, said: 'There's Pontwynedi! Tomorrow we'll see Sylvia. I wonder has she and Lovell had their first clawing yet?'

'Oh, Matta!' said Catrin.' I don't think Sylvia would ever quarrel with him; she is too fond of him.'

'H'm, h'm,' said Matta, 'we shall see! However I shall bear to walk afoot, and see m'lady a-driving in her van, I can't think!'

'I'm sure she'll give you a lift sometimes.'

'Me a lift!' was all Matta's reply, but the spite and scorn expressed in those simple words are indescribable.

Once more the camp was fixed, the tents set up, the donkeys unloaded, and preparations made for a week's stay, during which Catrin was to bid them 'Goodbye,' and set out on the rest of her journey alone.

It was not without deep regret that she prepared to part with those who had befriended her so cordially, when life had seemed too strained to bear.

'Will it be a large fair tomorrow?' she asked, as they sat round the evening stew as usual.

The nights were getting colder, and many of the women were glad to share the shelter of the tent.

'Will it be like Brynferri? Oh! I will never forget that,' said Catrin. 'Matta and Melia dancing, the sun shining so red on them, and those flaming lights hanging over the shows, and John Lovell singing – oh no, I will never forget it!'

''Twill be a much bigger fair tomorrow, so you'll see it all over again,' said Matta. ''Twill be a fine day too, I think.' And true enough the next day was one of autumn's golden gem days, with all the beauty of summer and the mellowness of autumn mingled – a day of blue haze, and soft breezes, one that remained in the memory as a thing of joy.

This time the gipsies were early in the marketplace, Cordelia's tins glittering bright in the sunshine, Jim Boswell's wheel whirred merrily, while Matta and Melia passed in and out through the crowd, eagerly scanning every vehicle in search of John Lovell's van.

At last it arrived in the Market Square, the owner himself on the box, flicking up the horses with his new whip. There were rosettes of red satin on the horses' foreheads, in honour of the occasion, for John Lovell was intensely proud of his 'turn out,' and still more so of the pretty wife, who stood at the open door behind him, chatting and laughing, with a blithesome ring in her voice, which had been absent before her marriage.

Here they were at last all the company, except Nancy Wood and a girl of no account, who stayed in the camp with her, and, amidst much chatter and laughter, the newly married pair were greeted by their friends with loud huzzahs, to the amusement and perplexity of the rustic crowd.

'Here she is,' said Lovell, helping Sylvia out of the van; 'quite a different girl since I took her in hand. Why, the tears were as near as the smiles before we were married, but now, I can tell you, she's always as merry as a grig. And, bless you, she knows how to order Caleb about. "Now," she says, "gently with those 'osses up the 'ill!" She don't forget she's the wife of the "boss", you see!'

Sylvia shook hands delightedly with all her old friends, her happiness not a little augmented by the feeling that whereas she had formerly been the shabbiest of the company, she now wore a becoming dress of crimson merino, while her ears were adorned with earrings of solid gold, matched by the brooch which fastened her neat linen collar.

Matta and Melia were speechless with envy, more especially when Sylvia addressed most of her conversation to Catrin, kissing her on both cheeks, and 'Remember, all of you,' she said, 'John and me wants you all to come to tea to us tonight. There'll be plenty of room between the box and the shaft boards.'

And oh! What a tea that was! Sylvia at the top of the table, her back and shoulders quite out through the doorway, John Lovell beside her, for he could not banish himself to the end of the shaft boards. The tea – how strong it was! The cake – how rich! The muffins soaking in butter! And the jam as pink as 'Pink' could make it!

All the while, outside, the clashing of cymbals, the beating of drums, and the roar of the fair; but they were not disturbed, for their ears were accustomed to the sounds.

Every feast must come to an end; and when the table had been pretty well cleared, the men alighted and mingled with the crowd, while the women helped Sylvia to wash up the tea things, and lay them on the shelf running along the top of the van.

'Oh, there's chinee!' said Cordelia. 'Fit for the Queen! Lucky girl you are, Sylvia!'

'Yes,' said the latter modestly, 'I am a lucky girl indeed!' and, sitting on the shaft of the van, she watched the gipsy entertainment, which Lovell and the dancers always contrived to make the most fetching item in the programme of the fair.

Catrin, too, watched and listened with deep interest. She would never see such a thing again; never would she hear such singing as Lovell's, for on the 'wool' mountains she would be alone with the sheep and the rushes. Ah! but there would be the fresh mountain air, the sunlight, the moonlight, and the splendid stars! But somehow the thought of them did not bring such rapture to her heart as they did of old.

When at last the fair was over, when the streets were emptying, when the swinging, flaring lamps had been extinguished, the gipsy company once more returned to their camping place.

'Goodnight Sylvia,' said Catrin. ''Tis goodbye, too, because perhaps I will never see you again. I must begin my journey tomorrow, because the autumn is passing, and I want to find a place before the winter.'

Sylvia kissed her warmly, both girls shedding some tears at parting.

'But I will see you again, because John and me are coming up to the camp tomorrow.'

'Well,' said Catrin, 'I must wait for him, because he has got my money.'

She reached the encampment before the rest of the company, and after making Nancy Wood acquainted with her wish to start on her journey next day, she sought her bed in the corner of the tent. It was hard and rough, only removed from the bare ground by the heather, which she cut for herself, a shawl thrown over it, her bundle for a pillow, her cloak for a covering, but the hardy girl had been accustomed to sleep the sleep of youth and health. A bath in some neighbouring mountain pool or stream and the rough meals of her entertainers satisfied all the requirements of her simple life; but tonight it was otherwise – she could not sleep. Nancy Wood snored, and Cordelia talked in her sleep. There were no clocks to mark the time, but peeping through a slit in the canvas, Catrin knew by the moon that it was midnight.

Rising softly, she crept between the sleeping figures to the doorway. Out on the moor she was at home, and once more she stood beneath the stars, and with outstretched hands sent up a wordless prayer – wordless because the aching void within her was unexplainable to herself; she had no words in which to express it, but knew that she was miserable.

At last, stretching herself under the shelter of a furze bush, she set herself to endure, and to submit. The task was hard, but when the day dawned and the pink flush of morning spread up behind the hills, a fresh lesson had been added to Catrin's store of experiences, a fresh adornment to her spirit, and when she brought to the camp her tin of water for the tea, no one would suspect that the placid, quiet girl had spent half the night in tears of self-surrender.

''Tis a bad fire to light today,' she said, as she knelt before the newly kindled fire. 'Sylvia – 'tis she can light the fire.'

'Whistle to it' said Ando; ''twill light in a minute.'

'P'r'aps, indeed,' said Catrin; and she whistled a merry tune as she hung the kettle on the hook; but before she had reached the last stave of 'The Men of Harlech', there was a movement of lively excitement in the camp, for round the shoulder of the hill, on the smooth white road, the Lovells' van was seen approaching.

The whole company were proud of their 'boss's' equipage, it shed a lustre on the tribe, and would be an imposing addition to the cavalcade on the march.

That breakfast was a lively meal; Sylvia came amongst them again with a sweet humility which never suggested her possession of a husband who was the 'boss', the best van on the road, and a pair of gold earrings, which would put even Nancy Wood's in the shade.

''Tis sorry and glad I am, to give you your money, lass,' said John Lovell after breakfast. 'Glad that I have kept it safe for you, and sorry that you are going to leave us. But there's nothing to be done about that; the best of friends must part. But take my advice, Catrin Rees,' he added in an undertone, 'and come back to your home before very long. 'Tis good to follow the road in the summer, but in the winter, lass, you will be glad of a house to shelter you. 'Tisn't as if you had a van, like Sylvia and me. And remember to keep that will safe, and when you turn out the walrus from Pengraig, may I be there to see! We'll be back in the old place next spring; p'r'aps well see you at home then, lass. Sylvia would be glad enough, I know, and so would I.'

Catrin shook her head sorrowfully.

'Goodbye, boss,' she said, 'and thank you a hundred times for all your kindness to me. I will only take two of those sovereigns. Will the other pay for my keep since I have been with you?'

'Twt, twt; no,' said Lovell. 'You're a blood relation, child. Put your money safe. Goodbye and God bless ye! And where ye going?'

'I don't know; I can't say goodbye to the others. Will I slip away when I'm fetching water?'

'As you like, lass.'

'My love to Sylvia,' said Catrin, and Lovell was gone.

Now to bid Nancy Wood farewell, for she dare not leave her in so unceremonious a manner.

She was reclining as usual in her barrow, her wrinkled face almost hidden under the folds of her shawl, her keen eyes watching with interest the movements of the camp.

'Eh, child,' she said, 'ye're come to say "goodbye"? Well, 'tis time ye should be starting, but I'm sorry to part with 'e, lass. Let me look at yer palm before ye go. Yes, there's trouble,' she said with a shake of her head. 'Here's tears too, and sickness in store for ye.'

'Sickness for me!' exclaimed the girl. 'Oh, indeed, I hoped I should never be ill again!'

'Well, ye will! but there's joy beyond. Yes,' she said, peering closely at the outstretched palm, 'there's light beyond for thee, child, and right glad I am.'

'Pr'aps,' said Catrin, ''tis beyond this world – 'tis in the life to come.'

'Bosh!' said Nancy Wood. 'I can see a long way, child, but I've not seen a glimpse of any life to come; and I think if there was any, Nancy Wood would have found it out.'

'Oh, Nancy Wood! there is – there is, indeed. I am as sure of it as that I am standing here now.'

'Go 'long!' was the old woman's irreverent rejoinder. 'I ain't got nothing to do with that now. Look here, child, have yer paid John Lovell for yer keep while ye've been with us?'

'I offered him a sovereign, but he wouldn't take it.'

'A sov, did ye? Well!' she said, 'a blood relation – and he's a generous man! However he got so rich I don't know. But half a sov now – eh?'

'Yes, indeed,' said Catrin, holding out the required sum, 'but will that pay for my keep all this time?'

'No, no; but never mind, child; there's no need to talk about that amongst blood relations.' And her clawing fingers clutched the half sovereign, and hid it at once in the pocket of her gown. 'Well, goodbye, child, and I hope we'll see ye again

at Pengraig some time. Now, here ye are,' and she drew out
carefully from the folds of her shawl a curious object, which
she laid on the girl's palm. 'I prepared this yesterday for yer,
when ye were enjoying yerself at the fair; so don't say old Nancy
Wood forgot Dolly's great-granddaughter. 'Twill be worth
more than the half sov. to ye, child,' she added. 'Show it to
William Bray, and let no one else meddle with it. Tell him who
ye are, and he'll do all he can for 'e. Goodbye, child.'

'Goodbye, Nancy Wood; a hundred thanks, and God bless
you!'

The old woman did not answer, but her keen eyes followed
the girl whose voice had trembled a little, and whose eyes had
filled with tears as she turned away.

'Aye, aye; but she's a tender-hearted lass, anyway!' And was
it a tear which the old woman dried hastily from her keen black
eyes?

In another moment Catrin's face reappeared at the door of
the tent.

'Nancy – dear Nancy Wood,' she said, 'there is another life
indeed!' And in a moment she was gone.

Carrying a tin on her arm, and humming a merry tune, to
disguise her intentions, she reached the spring, and, having
filled her can, left it where she knew it would be sought for,
and, fastening her bundle more firmly to her shoulders, ran
down the side of the moor to the high road which led by
Pontwynedi in the direction of the blue Snowdon range, which
marked the line of the horizon. Now she had time to examine
the object which Nancy Wood had pressed into her palm. A
curious knot or plait of straw, interwoven with which was a
circle of pink twine; the whole had been pressed flat and was
of rather an intricate design. Catrin folded it up carefully in
paper, and resolved to sew it into her bodice, with the 'will',
which interested Lovell more than it did her.

Her first care was to provide herself with sufficient simple
food for the day, and for the early morning of the next day,

together with a tin mug, in which to boil the water for her tea. And thus equipped, she started on her lonely journey with a brave spirit.

For many miles after she left Pontwynedi her way lay through a deep wood, whose long dark glades were full of mystery to her, for though she had often looked towards the trees skirting the further side of Penmwntan parish, she had never ventured so far from home. It was a pine wood, interspersed here and there with birch and stunted oaks, and although she had yet thirty miles to walk e'er she reached the 'wool' mountains, she could not resist the temptation to stray from the beaten path to explore its recesses. The wind whispered and sighed in the tree tops, and she stopped to listen, for it reminded her of the sea: the birds that sang on the branches were, for the most part, new to her; neither sea gulls nor little sea crows were there, but brown birds that crept up the trees and flitted amongst the branches. 'How still it all was! like the church in which Sylvia had been married!' A soft, green light pervaded the place, through which Catrin walked carefully, almost reverently.

Here and there were open spaces where the sun shone on the brown bracken and undergrowth, and the blue sky looked down with fleecy clouds that hurried by on the breeze. In these open spaces the butterflies flitted from place to place, and Catrin was never tired of watching them, for on the bare brown cliffs they were rare visitors.

And thus the hours passed by unnoticed, until the level beams of the reddening sun stretched up the long glades, and she knew that evening had come, and that she was hungry. Laying her ear to the thick undergrowth, she detected the trickling of water, and soon found a clear stream, from which she filled her tin mug. It was never difficult for Catrin to kindle a fire, and in a few moments the water was boiling, and she dropped in her tea, and drank it without milk or sugar, satisfying her hunger with bread and butter which the baker at Pontwynedi had cut into slices for her. Plain fare indeed! but Catrin did not think so, for youth and health and hunger brought such an appetite to the feast that her simple meal was all she desired.

If only the sighing of the wind in the branches did not remind her so much of the sea; if only the fire she had kindled did not bring back so distinctly to her memory the fires which she and Goronwy had so often lighted on the cliffs at Penmwntan – and if only those happy days had not passed so completely out of her life!

But she did not allow herself time to brood over these regrets; she must leave these sylvan glades and hasten on her way for many a mile yet, before resting time. She had been careful not to stray too far from the beaten path, and now hurried back to it, after carefully extinguishing the fire, and thenceforward she walked, with steady pace, along its beaten track. Where it would lead to, she knew not, but as long as she kept that blue range before her, it mattered not, she was drawing nearer to her goal. At last the woodland path merged into a high road, which led her, as the sun was setting, into a small country town.

Tired labourers came home from the fields, jaunty shop girls strayed up the principal street, dirty children played on the pavements, and many an idle man looked curiously at Catrin as she passed.

Would she seek for lodgings in the town? No, she would be better and freer in the open country, and only entering a baker's shop, she once more supplied herself with bread, cheese, and butter for the next day.

'And two eggs, if you please,' she added, for she was beginning to feel a little weary with her journey.

'There 'merch i,' said the woman, 'in your tin cup, with the bread and butter on the top, they will be safe – but where are you going so late?'

'About two miles further,' said Catrin; 'the moon will be up directly.'

'Yes; yes, to Bryndu farm, I suppose?'

'No; to the "wool" mountains I am going.'

'Oh! 'merch fach i, that is many weary miles – thirty or forty more from here.'

'Yes, I suppose; but I will get there in time,' and the old dimpling smile lit up the girl's face.

'Take my advice, my little girl, and sleep at Bryndu, tonight; they will give you lodgings. 'Tisn't safe for a pretty girl like you to be roaming the road alone.'

'Oh, I will be quite safe, thank you,' said Catrin, nodding as she left the shop.

Out again on the hard high road, with the twilight darkening fast, and a pale glow behind the hills, showing where the moon was about to rise, she walked steadily on for two or three miles before she began to look about her for a resting place for the night.

Away from the high road, she found a sheltered corner where she could venture to light a small fire, on which to boil one of her eggs, and once more to make her tea. After this sumptuous repast, she rose well satisfied, and again debated within herself whether to seek for lodgings at Bryndu or not; but looking around her, and seeing no likely spot where she could spend the night, she decided to venture up to the quaint, old, thatched porch and ask for shelter.

As she neared the door, a sound of voices blending in rich harmony reached her ears.

It was Griffith Ellis' two sons and two daughters, who were regaling themselves with the usual evening glee, before retiring to rest, and Catrin waited for a pause in the music.

'Among the heather and the rushes,
Between the green and gold broom bushes,
Whose turn to fetch the cows tonight?'

'That's good!' said Griffith Ellis himself, 'but the bass rather too strong, Tom; and you, Mari, oughtn't you to rest longer on that "E"?'

'Yes, p'r'aps-but let's try it again,' but Catrin's low tap interrupted them, and the bass rose and opened the door.

'I beg your pardon for disturbing you, I am going to the "wool" mountains, and the woman that sells the bread in the village told me you were kind people, and p'r'aps would give me lodgings for the night.'

Perhaps it was the soft voice – perhaps it was the brown eyes – that paved the way for Catrin; at all events, Tom said graciously:

'Come in. Mother, 'tis a lass who seeks for lodgings. Can you take her in?'

'I have had my supper,' said Catrin, 'and can sleep in the hayloft or barn.'

'Can you?' said Griffith Ellis. 'Well, we can't refuse you that. You can sleep in the barn certainly; there's plenty of clean hay and straw there – but come in first and warm your feet.'

Mari Ellis held a candle high above her head, and took a long look at the girl.

'Come in,' she said, seconding her father's invitation, and Catrin entered.

'Sit there on the bench,' said the old man. 'Wouldn't like some supper, lass? 'tis rice and milk we have.'

'No, thank you,' said Catrin; 'I have had my supper.' And there followed an awkward silence, which, however, did not last long, for in Wales such opportunities are quickly seized upon for curious questioning.

'Have you come far?'

'From Treswnd.'

'Where is that?'

Catrin was rather puzzled how to fix the locality.

''Tis not far from Brynferri whatever, and not far from Caermadoc; 'tis on the edge of the shore looking over the bay.'

''Tis very far,' said Mari, 'and you are going to the blue mountains?'

'Yes.'

'Alone?'

'Yes, indeed,' said Catrin, and again that wonderful play of dimples which lighted up the pensive face, and made it beautiful, 'because I have no one to go with me.'

'Have you walked far today?'

'About ten miles, I think – from Pontwynedi. I am tired now, and would like to go to rest. Only one thing – will you sing once more that beautiful song you were singing when I came to the door?'

'Yes, indeed, with pleasure,' said Tom. 'And now, Mari, mind your 'E,' and I'll mind my bass.'

And again the rich, full voices blended in easy harmony, for the Ellis's were a musical family, that charming combination so common in Wales.

Catrin, in whom the national love of music was strong, gave a little gasp of pleasure as the last long-drawn notes died away.

'Oh! thank you,' she said, rising. I will never see you again, perhaps, because I will be on my way before the sun rises tomorrow; but, indeed, I will never forget your singing. There's easy it flows.'

'Yes,' said the old man, opening the door for her, and lighting his lantern to guide her to the barn, 'it comes as easy as breathing to my children, as it did to me and my brothers and sisters when we were young together.'

'I will pay you now, if you please,' said Catrin, because I am going so early.' And she held out a sixpence.

'Oh no!' said the old man, almost angrily. 'We are not lodging-house keepers, 'merch i. Go you to the barn, and sleep well. But I can't allow a candle. See the moonlight on the straw?'

'Oh yes; I want no candle,' said the girl.

'There's the red calf in the corner, but he's safe in his cratch. Goodnight, 'merch i.'

'Goodnight,' said Tom, who had followed.

'Here's the key inside the door; you can lock it,' said Griffith Ellis.

'Oh no,' said Catrin; 'I am not used to keys. Goodnight, and many thanks.'

When she opened the barn door in the morning, Tom was already at his ablutions under the pump in the yard.

'You are up early,' said Catrin, pointing to the sun, which was just appearing above the hills.

'Yes; you can't see too much of the sun when you've been a year underground as I have. I have only just come home from the "works".'

'Well, goodbye, and thank you all.'

'Oh, no need,' said Tom.

And the girl went her way, the old gnawing hunger at her heart, the same grim shadow hanging over her, and darkening the very sunshine itself.

'Why am I like this?' she asked herself, as she turned her face to the blue hills once more. 'Goronwy is happy, and I ought to be glad. But oh! indeed I'm not!'

CHAPTER XXVI

THE CRIBOR

It was late in the evening three days afterwards that a girl entered the yard of a farmhouse on the side of the Cribor range, so near the top of the hill that no other houses seemed inclined to keep it company. Very lonely and bare it looked in the twilight, the autumn wind sighing round it, a fine rain beginning to fall, which had threatened Catrin all day, as she toiled over the last ten miles of her journey. She was weary and footsore, and, withal, very nervous, as she approached the closed oak door, which did not look very hospitable. It was grey and scarred with age and storms, as she noticed when her first timid knock had brought no response.

While she stands waiting, we may look at her, and note the change in her appearance, which seemed out of proportion to the amount of fatigue she had undergone since she left Treswnd. She had grown very thin, and there were shadows under the eyes, no longer sparkling with smiles; the dimples, too, had fled, and there were lines of sadness about the mouth. Her brown cloak and rush hat were travel-stained too, and when William Bray himself opened the door to her second knock, he might well be excused if he took her for a beggar.

A hard, close man, his first impulse was to close the door violently, but a second look at the patient face made him hesitate.

'What d'ye want?' he asked, roughly.

'Does William Bray live here?' asked Catrin, her heart beating hard against that brown cloak, for what if that stern man should refuse to give her work?

His dark skin and jet-black eyes proclaimed his connection with the gipsies, but his Welsh was so thorough and so broad, that it was difficult to realise that he came of a different race to the other farmers of the neighbourhood.

'He lives here; what do you want with him?'

So flurried was she by the man's brusque tones that she could scarcely stammer out her simple answer.

'If you please, do you want a shepherdess?'

'A shepherdess!' scoffed William Bray, who, in truth, happened to be very much in want of one just at that time. 'And what if I did? Do you think I am going to take the first tramp that comes to my door? Where's your character from your last place?'

'I haven't been a shepherdess ever before, but—'

'Then be gone,' said Bray, and he closed the door.

Once more the grey, seamed, rugged door stood before Catrin with an appearance of stolid inhospitality. While the owner had been speaking to her, she had caught sight of a cosy interior, where a fire of logs and coal blazed on the stone floor, and the dark oak table was laid for supper, a huge crock, too, over the fire, which reminded her of the gipsy cauldron. It looked warm and tempting to a tired wayfarer, but that sturdy door stood between her and the warmth, while outside the soft rain continued to fall, and the wind to sigh mournfully through the solitary thorn bush which stood by the door. While she stood there hesitating, it was opened again.

'Well, what are you waiting for?' asked the man. 'I tell you I do not employ tramps and beggars.'

'Only just to say I am used to watch my father's sheep.'

'How many had he got?'

'About twenty – 'twas not a sheep farm.'

There was a burst of laughter from the kitchen, followed by the vision of a young man standing in the background.

'Twenty sheep!' he cried, scornfully. 'Why, we have from eight hundred to a thousand!'

'I couldn't mind them all, but some, p'r'aps. I would be very careful.'

'Well, you've had "your answer", said Bray; 'so don't stand about here any longer.'

At the same moment a girl's voice cried 'Supper, father!' and both men drew back, closing the door once more.

Catrin's heart sank, and the tears gathered in her eyes, as she turned away proudly. 'Beggar!' 'Tramp!' she was neither; but oh! that she had been more fortunate! And she left the farmyard feeling very lonely and puzzled. She had had no doubt of being able to find work, and this rebuff had utterly disconcerted her, but she took herself severely to task, as she turned into a lane where the high banks made a shelter from the rain.

'What is the matter with thee, Catrin?' she asked herself. 'Thou who used to be so brave and fearless, where is thy courage gone? There are more farms on the Cribor mountains, and a night under the sky will not hurt thee!' But, alas! it was a dark grey sky above, and a damp cold ground beneath. 'Where were the stars that used to light up that dark sea of blue? Where was the silver boat that glided over it?'

'There, behind that dark grey curtain,' thought the girl, 'though I cannot see them!'

The lane led away to the open fields, whose loose stone walls made no shelter from the wind or rain, but she lighted a small fire under the wall, and made her usual supper on a hot cup of tea and a hunch of bread and butter with cheese, after which, on reconnoitring, she espied a shed high up on the mountain side, and hurrying towards it, found it already occupied by a shock-headed steer, which had roamed from the herd and lain down for the night.

His large brown eyes looked at Catrin with astonishment, but no anger; she approached gently, and rubbed the rough curls on his forehead, and bending her face towards him with caressing words, she breathed into his nostrils a cooing passage of love, a method of taming the wildest animals which seldom fails. From that moment there was no fear of antagonism between them, but a complete friendship. A sheaf of rushes, which she found in the corner, she spread on the ground, and lying on it, with her bundle for a pillow, she slept safe and warm for the night; for the little steer's soft breathing and munching seemed all conducive to rest.

Not so the sounds which first met her ear in the morning; a loud barking approached, and as she rose in affright, a large dog rushed towards the doorway, and would have entered, had he not been forcibly held back by a man's strong arm.

The same arm did not hesitate to administer some harsh blows.

'Oh, please don't hurt her,' said Catrin, 'I beg of you; she would not hurt me.' And she passed her arm round the beautiful creature's neck, who wagged her tail, and looked inquiringly at her master.

'Down, Trodwen!' said Watcyn Bray, the young man whose contemptuous laugh had preceded his father's gruff dismissal the previous night. 'Leave Trodwen alone, you'd better,' he said, harshly; 'we don't like strangers making friends with our dogs.'

His tone was coarse, and his blue eyes looked angrily at the girl, 'Sleeping in our shed without leave!' But as he spoke the expression of his eyes altered; his anger died away, and it was in tones more gentle that he added, 'You done no harm, of course, only my father does not like – er—' He hesitated to bring out the word 'tramps', but Catrin saved him the trouble.

'Tramps nor beggars,' she said, with a smile which, in spite of her look of fatigue had not lost its charm; 'but indeed I'm not a tramp or a beggar. I know your sister, Melia Bray, and Nancy Wood is a relation to me.'

'Nancy Wood!' said the young man. 'Why didn't you tell my father? But he wouldn't believe, p'r'aps?'

'I was too frightened last night, and I forgot, too, until the door was closed. I have a message for him from Nancy Wood.

Here it is,' and she drew out the little packet or tablet of straw, and held it on her palm.

'Give it to me; I will take it to him.'

'No,' said the girl; 'Nancy told me not to let any one touch it, until William Bray took it from me.'

'Well, go back, then, lass, and have breakfast; I'm sure thee'st ready for it. I am going to fetch the cows, but I'll soon catch thee up.'

When he was gone, Catrin performed a hasty toilet by a pool under the nut trees, where she could see, not only her own image on the glassy surface, but the brown gold pebbles that lay at the bottom, and following the grassy sheep walks which the soft rain had freshened after a long drought, she reached the farmhouse door, where Watcyn rejoined her.

When they entered the kitchen, breakfast was standing ready on the long table.

'Father,' he said, 'this lass has a message for you from Nancy Wood.'

'What lass?' said the gruff tones of the farmer.

''Tis me,' said Catrin. 'I forgot last night to show you this.'

She held the little straw circlet towards him, and William Bray took it carefully in his fingers, carrying it to the doorway to examine it more closely.

'Yes, 'tis Nancy Wood, and no mistake,' he said 'Where got'st it, lass?'

'From her own hands,' said Catrin.

'And yet,' he said suspiciously, 'thou never gav'st it to me last night.'

'Indeed, I was too frightened, but now I can speak. I am Catrin Rees, my father lived at Pengraig farm, my mother was a great-granddaughter to old Dolly Wood, the gipsy, and Nancy Wood was very kind to me because of that. I wanted to come to the 'wool' mountains, if I could find work here as a shepherdess, and Nancy said, if I would show this to you, you would give me work.'

'Why, yes, of course,' he said. 'Here, Olwen,' and a dark-eyed girl came round the corner of the settle, 'this lass comes from Nancy Wood; and let me see, she's some sort of a blood relation, though 'tis very far off.'

'Come in,' said Olwen, and Watcyn placed a stool for her at the fireside.

'I have been living with Nancy Wood's company lately,' said Catrin. 'I travelled with them all the way to Pontwynedi.'

'What! With John Lovell's company?'

'Yes, indeed, and Matta Ling and Melia Bray – she is your sister I know, because you are so like her.'

'Oh, anw'l! Father, she has seen Melia! Yes, she is my sister, and Matta Ling is my cousin. But 'tis time for Melia to come home now, and let me travel a bit. Father has promised I should go to the south some day, and travel with Nancy Wood and John Lovell – say now, haven't you, father?'

'Yes, yes, when I see a good opportunity; don't bother me now, but give the lass a good breakfast.'

'Come, lass,' said Watcyn, 'Trodwen and I were near giving thee a rough greeting this morning, thee must forgive me.'

'Yes, indeed; but I'm not afraid of dogs or any animals.'

'Wert afraid of me, then, for thee looked pretty scared?'

'Well, I am afraid of men and women sometimes.'

'Of me, last night, I suppose,' said William Bray. 'Well, if thee'lt do thy work well, thee'lt find me a good master.'

'Indeed, I will do my best,' said the girl, and so she slipped easily into her place.

''Tis over the hills and far away' is everything here,' said Olwen. 'Thy flock is up yonder among those rocks. It will be lonely for thee.'

'Oh, no; never lonely out on the hills!'

'Well, we'll see,' said William Bray. 'Here, take care of this, Olwen. 'Twill be the last time we'll see the old woman's name sign, I expect. Why, she's over a hundred! How does she travel now?'

'She's wheeled about on a hand-barrow,' said Catrin. ''Tis put in the cart to travel. She seldom moves off it now, but she's lively and well, and throws her crutches at us sometimes.'

William Bray laughed. 'Aye, aye; the old woman's not changed, I see, and never will be, I expect. Well, thou'lt tell her I treated thee well, as soon as we saw her sign. I wouldn't like Nancy's curse upon me, I can tell thee! Before I settled down on this farm I was travelling in her company, and I saw a man not far from here, rich and thriving he was too. Well! We camped on a bit of wasteland belonging to him, and he drove us off like dogs, and shot his gun after us, just to frighten us, I suppose. But aye! Nancy Wood she turned upon him, and cursed him, and if ever I saw the evil eye, 'twas that look that Nancy cast upon him. Well! as true as I'm here, that man never throve after. His sheep died, his barn caught fire, his horse fell over yonder crag, and he died a poor man at last! No, no; 'tis wise to make friends with a surly dog!'

'You'll rest today,' said Olwen, kindly. 'There's glad I am to have a companion;' and Catrin was glad enough to avail herself of the offer, to sit on the old farm settle, to make friends with the dogs that lolled about the fire, to watch Olwen at her work, and to help her preparations for the evening meal, to which the farmer and his son returned, and the shepherds gathered from the pastures where their flocks lay safely folded.

'This lass will take thy place,' said Bray to an old man, whose coat of many capes and slouching hat tied under his chin, told of storms of wind and rain. 'Thee canst go tonight if thee lik'st; I'll pay thee what I owe thee,' and he flung a few shillings on the table, which the old man gathered one by one, and put into his pocket; then, with a long look at Catrin, he sat down at the end of the bench, on which the other shepherds and servants were ranged.

'Well, I've done my best for thee, William Bray, for many years, but I'm old now, and the sheep stray far, and the wind is cold o' winter nights, the lassie's young and hardy p'r'aps, and she'll do better!'

'Well, she can't do worse.'

The old man did not answer; his dim eyes were raised again to Catrin's face, and as she saw the long grey locks and the stooping shoulders, her heart was full of compassion.

'Am I taking his place?' she said, her eyes filling with tears, which the old man saw.

'No, no, 'merch i; 'tis time I gave up. I'm too old to climb the rocks, and seek the sheep amongst the rushes. Thee'lt find it cold up there, lass, and lonesome, very. But there! the young have merry hearts to bear them up,' and he sighed as he supped his porridge.

When supper was over, he gathered his old coat about him, and, leaning on his staff, said: 'Well, goodbye, master; I hope the lassie will serve thee well. Be kind to Trodwen, lass, she's the best dog on the Cribor mountains.'

'Goodbye,' said William Bray, curtly. 'Thee canst bring thy baskets and brooms to show me; if they're good I'll buy them;' and the old man went out into the darkness. Catrin slipped out after him.

'Which is Trodwen?' she said, laying her hand on the arm, whose frayed cuff he was drawing over his eyes 'I'll be kind to her, I promise; she'll be my only friend up there. P'r'aps you'll come up sometimes.'

'Aye, aye, p'r'aps I will. Here's Trodwen, 'merch i,' and an iron-grey sheep dog sprang towards them, and fawned upon the old man. 'Aye, aye, here's thy new mistress,' he said, and he held Catrin's hand in his, letting Trodwen lick the two together. After that, they were friends, and the old man disappeared in the gloom.

Before the sun rose next morning, William Bray took Catrin up the mountain side to where, on the brow of a hill, a rocky escarpment caught the sun's first rays.

''Tis on that green slope just under the rocks thy sheep are folded; thee'll know them by the red marks on their backs. See, here is one that old fool missed last night. 'Twas full time to send him packing.'

'Will I drive him on?'

'Aye, Trodwen will see to that,' and with indignant barks Trodwen drove the wanderer towards the fold.

'Now, I'll leave thee, lass; thee'll let the sheep out, and count them night and morning. There's a hundred under thy care. There's the hut for thee to shelter from the sun and wind behind yon crag. Come home to supper.'

His hard face relaxed a little as he turned to leave the girl alone. 'Now – mind thy work!' and he disappeared down the hillside.

Left alone, Catrin began to look about her. First she would unfold the sheep and count them as they passed through the gap.

'I will soon know their faces,' she thought, 'though now they are all alike.'

And she turned her steps towards the hut, which stood a little higher up the mountain, but sheltered by a towering crag.

The floor, of course, was of hard, bare earth. Old Gower's crook lay beside the door; a few charred embers on the ground showed where his fire had been; an upturned box for a seat, and another, which no doubt had served him as a table, were all the household furniture. Catrin looked round the bare tenement with a smile of congratulation. 'Here I will be safe and alone whatever.' And hanging the little wallet, which Olwen had filled with dinner for her, on the wattled wall, she proceeded to arrange her household. Searching amongst the old man's tools, she found a billhook, with which she had soon cut sufficient sweet green heather for a couch. The soft rain of the previous day had gathered into white, billowy clouds, which passed across the sky, sometimes obscuring the sunshine, but not staying long, leaving occasional glimpses of blue sky, from which the sun poured down its rays upon a scene of exquisite beauty. Far below her, down the sides of the mountains, stretched miles of moorland, brown with bracken, here and there streaked with the purple and gold of the furze and heather.

Beyond, lay more fertile fields and meadows, through which a river trailed its silvery length. Further away, old Snowdon and his companions reared their rugged heads; while beyond them, southwards, stretched the blue hills, range behind range, fading soft into the grey distance, where at the horizon gleamed a streak of burnished silver.

'Oh, the sea!' said Catrin. 'No doubt it is the sea! 'Tis the dear old bay across which I looked so often at these hills, when Goronwy and I were singing:

> 'Blue land beyond the sea,
> When will I come to thee?'

Oh, I wonder are he and Yshbel sitting there now.'

And into her mind, though she had fallen into a silent reverie, the words of John Lovell's song floated; but she thought they were treason to Yshbel, and endeavoured to thrust them from her, with the constant effort of will which was wearing her strength away.

All through that long sunny day she roamed the hill, and watched her sheep, or sat and feasted her eyes upon the lovely scene stretched out before her. Continually her eyes sought that line of silver on the horizon. The first thing in the morning, the last thing at night, looking towards it, her thoughts strayed to the old home, and the old times; and as day followed day, and she fell into the routine of her monotonous life, she was secretly disappointed to find that peace did not return to her spirit, nor was there any cessation to the unrest that pervaded her thoughts.

Watcyn and Olwen were kind and considerate to her; even William Bray's harsh voice lost some of its brusqueness as he gave his orders or greeted her night and morning. But day after day found Catrin losing strength.

''Tis tired I am,' she thought. 'I will be well when I have quite rested.'

But her step grew slower, the dark shadows under her eyes more marked, and the brave spirit was bowed down under the stress of the storm through which she was passing.

'What's the matter with that lass?' said William Bray to his daughter, as Catrin rose from the early breakfast one morning and left the house. ''Tis always, "Tired I am after my journey," or "I'll be better tomorrow, master." But the same pale face I see every day.'

'Yes, I'm asking her often, was she always like this,' said Olwen,'and there's red she is getting then. 'No,' she says, ''tis walk too far I did. Have you patience with me, and I will soon get well' But, in my deed,' continued Olwen, with a shrewd shake of her head, ''tis my opinion there's something on her mind. Why did she want to come so far from her home at once?'

'Oh, that's plain enough,' said Watcyn, upon whom the pathetic brown eyes had made some impression. 'Her father is dead, and there is no home for her; besides, Nancy Wood wouldn't send her to us if there was anything wrong about her.'

'Well, she won't trouble any one long, poor thing, unless she alters very soon; every day she is fading away, and I will be sorry, because I'm very fond of her whatever.'

'She minds the sheep all right,' said Bray, 'but I don't want any sick maids hanging about my place, and if she don't get better soon, she'll have to tramp. Dang my buttons! I don't want no funeral to pay for here,' and he banged the door as he went out.

CHAPTER XXVII

THE TWO AUNTS

The Llys-y-fran pony carriage had been standing some time before the portico of Glaish-y-dail.

In the drawing room the two Mrs Joneses were engaged in an animated conversation. "Mrs Jones, the Belfield," had discovered that Yshbel was much distressed at her abrupt parting with her relations, and she had determined to make an effort to restore peace between the irate aunt and her offending niece.

'No, indeed, then. You cannot think what trouble it has brought upon us. Jones and me to be disgraced in this way before all our friends! The ungrateful thing! I can never forgive her.'

'But,' said "Mrs Jones, the Belfield," 'I assure you no one remembers that little episode any longer, so deep has been the interest felt in the entombed men. That has buried it all out of sight, and now that your niece is going to be married to my nephew—'

'What?' exclaimed "Mrs Jones, the Daisy," the pink bows in her cap quivering with her excitement. 'Married to your nephew, Mrs Jones?'

'Yes. On Monday next. Ivor Owen is going to marry them at Llanberi Church. I do think it is most delightfully romantic, don't you? And so I thought the two aunts of the young people, you know, would be very suitable company. I know from Mr Owen that your niece is truly grieved at having offended you, so I thought if you could forgive the past and come to the wedding, you know, it would be all right. It would be so strange if no one accompanied her!'

'Well, of course!' said "Mrs Jones, the Daisy". 'Of course, I will be there. Poor little thing! I don't forget she's my husband's niece, and I wouldn't leave her alone at such a time for the world, indeed, there!'

'I knew you wouldn't!' said her visitor; and she drove home feeling satisfied that she had secured the presence of the bride's aunt at the ceremony. She was in her element. Not for years had she been in touch with so real a love affair, and she thoroughly enjoyed her connection with it.

"Mrs Jones, the Daisy," too, was exceedingly pleased with this turn of affairs. If she had been disgraced in the eyes of her friends, here was now the sure prospect of being reinstated in their good opinion. Her niece to be married to "Mrs Jones, the Belfield's," nephew! The most genteel family in the valley. Here was a substantial and enduring glory that would throw a continual lustre on the annals of the Joneses of Glaish-y-dail! When her husband returned in the evening, she could scarcely wait till he had entered the room before she burst upon him with the news.

'Here's good news for you! What d'you think? Little Isbel is going to be married to "Jones, the Belfield's" nephew, Mr George Gwyn!'

'What?' said Jones, smiling, 'George Gwyn? What's become of the other chap then?'

'How do I know? What does that matter? I wonder you mention such a low fellow! "Mrs Jones, the Belfield," has been here asking me to go to the wedding with her; and now, Jones, you get that man, Price or Ellis or something, who writes so nice to the papers, you know, to put in an account of the wedding, and say the bride was attended by her aunt, Mrs Jones, of Glaish-y-dail, and the bridegroom by his aunt, Mrs Jones, of Llys-y-fran. That'll settle us for ever in sessiety here!'

Jones thought so too, but added, ''Tis a pity she's not married from here.'

'Well, 'tis; but we can't have everything. I must manage somehow to prevent Martha going to the wedding. Indeed, there! It would be a fine thing for her to be there, with her boots and her cockle hat! But I've only to give her a hint, and she'll keep away safe enough!'

The following Monday dawned with all the beauty of summer and the freshness of autumn. Yshbel arrayed herself in her simple grey dress with the trembling fingers appropriate to brides, mislaying everything, finding them and losing them again, in the regular orthodox fashion.

'Oh, Martha! Where's my hat?'

'Here, 'merch i!' and the patient Martha held it towards her for the third time. 'There's a pretty white feather is in it! And here's your white gloves, and now you look beautiful, and like a bride! Oh! I would like to see you married, my dear! But poor Mary Ann, she wouldn't like to see me there, and she with "Mrs Jones, the Belfield!" Never mind 'merch i, I will never forget you; and if I shan't see you again in this world, I will in the next.'

Yshbel flung her arms round her neck, hugging her closely to her heart.

'Martha, Martha; let me whisper to you. I'd rather fifty times have you at my wedding than Aunt Mary Ann. You have been like a mother to me; and 'tis with you I have passed through the most miserable and the happiest days of my life! Oh no, I can never forget you; and I love you so much!'

'Yes, dear heart. 'Tis time now. Goodbye, goodbye!'

'Yes, indeed; here's Goronwy. I must go!'

'Art ready, lass?' he called, coming up the path 'Priodas dda! There's nice she looks, Martha! Come on, then, or we'll be late.'

When they had reached halfway down the cockle-shell path, one of Martha's heavy boots came trundling after them, restoring them all to gaiety and good spirits.

Up through the brambly lane, away from the village, they made their way towards the little grey church that stood alone like a sentinel watching the coming and going in the busy valley below.

Reaching the lych gate, they saw the church door was open, and that in the porch stood the two Mrs Joneses.

'My dear child, where have you been?' said both at once. 'Poor George has been waiting such a time.'

'I am ready,' said Yshbel, and taking Goronwy's arm, she entered the porch, the two aunts following.

One glance at the chancel, and she saw Walto accompanied by Jenkin. He was looking round rather nervously, for he could not yet believe with certainty that all was right. Yshbel caught the smiling light in his eyes as she entered, and all her nervousness took flight.

'Who gives this woman to be married to this man?' and Goronwy stepped forward, looking as cheery and bright as the bridegroom himself.

When the service was over, that makes or mars so many lives, they turned to the vestry.

'We are a happier party today,' said Ivor Owen, 'than when we last met in the vestry.'

'Yes,' said Goronwy; 'but if it hadn't been for that, this wouldn't have come about. We've got to thank you, sir, and I don't know what the others feel, at least – yes, I do – but I know I feel that you untied a hard knot in our lives by speaking out so brave. I'll never see you again perhaps, so I'd like to thank you today, sir.'

Walto was busily engaged in directing Yshbel where to sign her name, but looked up to say: 'Right, Goronwy, every word! Why, thou'rt growing quite eloquent, man. There! "Isbel Lloyd" for the last time!'

Then came the witnesses' names, and the deed was done; an event which began for these two a long life of health and happiness. Goronwy had grown silent after his speech, thinking within himself how soon he and Catrin would take upon them the same vows.

Out in the sunny churchyard Ivor Owen bade them farewell, and God-speed, with a promise that some day he would find his way to Treswnd, and visit the old yellow farmhouse by the sea.

"Mrs Jones, the Belfield" kissed Yshbel warmly and "Mrs Jones, the Daisy" followed suit, with much appearance of warmth, more especially towards Walto; Goronwy she did not condescend to notice.

In the corner, by the lych gate, stood a square country car, which Goronwy had procured at Walto's request, and towards this humble vehicle the eyes of the three friends turned with pleasure.

It was the first step to freedom. A beginning of the old, simple, rough ways to which they were returning, and they climbed into it triumphantly.

'Oh, but I am going to drive you, my dears,' said "Mrs Jones, the Belfield".

'No, thank you, aunt,' answered Walto. 'We are going to drive to Brynmain station to meet the express. We shall reach home earlier, and escape the bothers of Stranport station. A hundred thanks to you all!'

The car jolted forward and turned up the rough lane to the high road, Yshbel and Walto in front, and Goronwy behind, with the farm lad who was to bring the car back.

The two Mrs Joneses looked at each other rather blankly, as people always do after a wedding.

'Well, really,' said the one, 'I feel quite sorry to lose them.'

'So do I, in my deed,' said the other. 'Isbel is a sweet girl, and I hope she and her husband will often come and stay at Glaish-y-dail.'

'Well, d'you know,' said her friend, confidentially, 'I don't think we shall ever see them again; they belong to a different state of existence to ours, and they have been longing for it ever since they left it. But, upon my word, I am glad to have had something to do with that interesting wedding.'

'Oh, here's your carriage!' and with smiling 'goodbyes', the two ladies separated.

"Mrs Jones, the Daisy" stepped complacently into her handsome brougham, and, as she passes out of our sight forever, we may bid her farewell with a tender pity, such as Martha Williams would feel for her, and send after her a hope that she may awake to the true realities of life, that are alone worth struggling for. But, alas! For the criminal and the outcast there is more hope than for the worldly-minded.

Exposed to all the numbing influences of luxury and riches, how seldom do they see the truth, until the last awakening comes upon them with its startling revelations, and they find themselves entering upon a spiritual existence, entirely unprepared and unequipped for their new experiences. What can we say but 'Poor Mary Ann; indeed, there!'

The country car containing our wedding party rolled briskly along the roads, where the hedges were growing gay with the rich tints of autumn. The briony trailed its scarlet berries from branch to branch, the hawthorn showed its crimson berries between the leaves, and the wild roses put on their last adornment of scarlet hips and mossy tufts. High overhead the lark sang her lightsome song, down in the stubble the partridge called, and in the copse the pheasant crowed. What wonder, that that rough car bore three merry hearts.

'Who'll be the first to see the sea?' said Goronwy.

'Why, thou wilt, of course,' said Walto, thou'rt facing it, lad, sitting there at the back.'

'Facing it? That I'm not! D'ye think I mean this wishy-washy stuff they call sea here? No, no; 'tis the sea on the west, man, I'm looking for. The bright blue sea, and the white waves of Cardigan Bay.'

'Well, we won't see that till we've left the train, and reached the top of Gledwyn hill this evening in the mail coach. How will we get home from Caermadoc? Is it the day for Bensha's waggon?'

'Monday! Yes, I think,' said Goronwy; 'but if not, we'll walk. Canst walk, Yshbel, after the Glaish-y-dail carriage?'

'Yes, indeed; let us walk! 'Twould be like old times.'

'It would be beginning them again,' said Walto; 'but, Yshbel, lass, you forget you've married a lame man!'

'Yes, I forgot, indeed. We'll go in the waggon!'

But when, after a long day's journey, they reached Caermadoc, they found it was not the day for Bensha's waggon, so they once more hired a country car, and in it made the rest of their journey to Treswnd. Over the old familiar road once more; where the pigs and fowls roamed at will, and at every cottage door somebody nodded to them or greeted them with a 'Nos da'. The car bumped perilously sometimes over the little heaps of road scrapings which had turned into grassy mounds, waiting so long to be cleared away.

'Have a care, man,' called Goronwy from the back, when the car made a fiercer lunge than usual. 'It takes two arms to drive; and that one round Yshbel won't hold her up if you upset us all into the ditch!'

There were laughing denials from Walto and Yshbel, and when at last they reached the crest of the hill, it was their turn to expostulate, for Goronwy, standing up, waved his arms about in such an excited manner that Walto looked round in alarm.

'Goronwy, man, art mad? What's the matter with thee?'

'What's the matter?' said Goronwy. 'Hooray, hooray why, there's old Penmwntan's brown head, and there's the sun going down in the sea the same as ever! My heart is warming to it all. Never, never again will I leave the old bay!'

They had reached that spot where the lane to Sarnissa diverged from the main road.

'Here – put me down,' said Goronwy, and jumping out hastily he hoisted his bundle on a stick over his shoulder. 'And now,' he said, 'nos da to you both; and remember me to the mestress, and 'Priodas dda' once more. Dei anw'l! I've half a mind to undo my bundle, and throw my old pit shoes after you; they'd beat Martha Williams'. Goodbye, goodbye,' and Walto and Yshbel drove on, leaving Goronwy standing and gazing, as if in amaze that sun, sea, and mountain were still unchanged. When he had seen the last glimpse of the car as it jogged down the hill, he soliloquised: 'There's two of us all right whatever. 'Tis Catrin's and my turn next,' and he deliberately placed his bundle on the ground, while he waved his cap towards the old hill where all his hopes were centred.

Down the rough lane, and through the clos he passed to the open door, where Caesar barked furiously, and then apologised profusely for his mistake.

'Hello!' he shouted, rousing Morgan Hughes from his nap, and even Marged from her ironing. 'Where are you all here? '

'Why, here, to be sure, lad. How art, 'machgen i? Welcome home indeed!'

'Well, there's well he looks!' said Marged. 'In my deed, I scarcely knew him.' This, being her invariable greeting to everybody who was not absolutely in his coffin, Goronwy took no notice of it, except by a smart slap on the shoulders.

'Where's Yshbel?' was Morgan Hughes' next question, and his son, flinging his bundle down, sat down on the settle, and endeavoured to explain as best he could; Morgan Hughes at first looking very indignant but gradually changing his expression, until at the end of the story, told in unvarnished words, he grasped the full meaning of the situation.

'Thou'st been buried alive, my boy, and art come home safe again? Well, let Yshbel go! I never cared for her. So come to tea, and thou'lt tell me the rest afterwards.'

'Tea? I should think so! And herrings from the dear old bay. I smelt them from Pendrain.'

And they drew their chairs round the table, Marged filling their cups, and retiring to a corner to partake of her herring, her tea cup beside her in the embers.

It was a prolonged and merry meal, and though the board was rough and primitive, and the food of the simplest and plainest, there was abundance, and Goronwy declared that Glamorganshire food lacked the relish of a Cardiganshire meal.

'And how have things been going on here?' he asked.

'Oh, same as usual; very good weather for the harvest, splendid crops of barley in Parcgwyn, and the oats looking first-rate on the hill.'

Over their pipes the subject of Yshbel's marriage was thoroughly discussed, and it did not take long to satisfy Morgan Hughes that things had turned out for the best. The important point was that his son had made a little money over his journey, had had a long visit to the 'works,' had seen the world, had been in a coal-pit explosion, and had come home untrammelled by a wife, and all this at very little expense.

Goronwy made little of his terrible experiences in the 'Belfield' colliery, partly from a shrinking dislike of recalling them to his own memory, his greatest desire being that that event should be clean wiped out of his thoughts.

'Well, to tell the truth, 'machgen i,' said his father, 'I'm glad that Walto's got Yshbel, and not thee! I never cared much for her since she took up with those grand people, away. Besides, there's Ellen Tyrhos, now 'tis all off between her and John Owen, and she's got a tidy bit of money.'

It was now Goronwy's turn to make inquiries, but the question nearest to his heart he put off to the last.

'And how's all going on at Pengraig?' he asked at length. 'How's Simon by now?'

'Simon!' said his father. 'Hast not heard? Simon is dead and buried.'

'Heard? How would I hear when you never wrote to tell me? Simon dead! Druan bach; well, his life was no pleasure to him. And Catrin, how is she?'

'Catrin?' echoed his father again. 'Dei anw'l! Hast heard nothing, then? I thought thee wast sure to hear from some one. Why, Simon died directly after thou went away, and left Pengraig to Bensha and Madlen.'

'Where's Catrin, then?' burst from Goronwy.

'Wait till I tell thee. Simon made his will at that time when the croten was a child, when every one thought she was a witch, and mad, and he put a proviso in his will that Bensha and Madlen were to look after her all her life. They say 'twas a wise will as far as he knew then, for who would guess that Catrin would alter as she has, and behave like another girl? Well, no one knows what has become of her. She didn't like Bensha and Madlen being master and mistress at Pengraig, I suppose – and no wonder – and so she went away.'

'And where?' said Goronwy, starting to his feet. 'Tell me where she is, man, and no more words about it!'

'How do I know?' said his father; 'nobody does know. Bensha and Madlen saw her at supper one evening; and that's the last they ever did see of her. They hunted high and low, every field, and all over the country, but never a sight of the girl have they seen. Madlen thinks she's gone over the cliff, like she used to go long ago.'

'If I had known,' said Goronwy, 'I'd have come back to help her, whatever happened,' and he paced up and down the kitchen excitedly.

'I didn't know thee'd care so much about it,' said his father.

'Care? I care so much that my feet shall never rest till I find her. If she's in the land of the living I'll find her, and if she's dead I'll follow her.'

He looked through the deep-set window up to where, on the side of Penmwntan, the grey walls of Pengraig showed clear against the evening sky. The blue smoke curled up from one of its chimneys, a light glimmered in the window, for the sunlight left that side of the valley early. Turning, he caught up his bundle from the corner into which he had flung it, and carried it upstairs to the llofft.

'He feels bad about it,' muttered his father, with a shake of the head. 'Where'st going, bachgen?' he added, as Goronwy, dressed in his ordinary farm clothes, passed through the kitchen.

'I'm going to look for Catrin,' he answered, with such a firm set look about his mouth, that his father knew it would be useless to oppose him.

Out into the cold, calm evening air, where he could breathe freely, could try to realise what had happened, and where he could curse his fate – but stop, he would not do that, for Catrin would have placed her little hand on his arm and bid him to be patient. Yes, he would be patient, for, of course, he would find her. And rising, he set off with steady tramp towards Pengraig.

When he entered, Madlen was stirring the crock which hung over the sprawling wood fire, Bensha, sitting by, was whittling at something which he held almost on his shoulder so as to bring his crooked eye to bear upon it.

'Goronwy Hughes!' exclaimed the former, dropping her ladle in surprise. 'Well, bendigedig, man! Where'st come from?'

'Where's Catrin?' was Goronwy's only reply.

'There 'tis now,' said Bensha, shuffling awkwardly in his wooden shoes. 'Where is she? That's what nobody knows.'

'How is it she's not here in her own home?'

'That's where she ought to be, no doubt but 'ts— 'ts,' and he clicked his tongue against the roof of his mouth. 'Thou knowest her of old, I should think, and there's no telling her comings and goings.'

'How is it you are here, and she, the owner of the place, is not?'

'The owner of the place, indeed!' said Madlen, unable longer to control her temper. 'Stop a bit, my man, till you see Mr Jones, the lawyer. Simon Rees left everything to us, only we are to take care of the girl, and 'tis her own fault that she's not here now to have this "uwd" and every comfort; but if she won't stop with us, we can't help it.'

'That's her father's "will",' said Bensha; 'and no doubt he knew what was best for his own child. That's what the lawyer said, and that's what everybody else is saying.'

'I'm not saying so,' said Goronwy, bringing his heavy fist down with a thump on the table till the bowls and platters clattered. 'That "will" was made many years ago, when the child, driven out by cruelty, had become like a wild cat. But 'tis different now, and has been for many years, and I'll never believe that that "will" can stand. I'll spend my last penny to fight it out. But first to find Catrin.'

'Ha, ha!' exclaimed Madlen, an evil look in her eyes, 'to find Catrin – that's it! Thee canst do that very well. Go down to the edge of the cliff, and jump over it, as she used to do.'

'Listen to me, you two devils. I'll search every corner, behind every bush, under every haystack, in every box and coffer that stands in this old place, and if I fail at last, I'll call the law to help me. You are responsible for the girl, and if she's not found 'twill look black for you.' And he turned on his heel and strode out of the kitchen.

The long journey of the day had tired him a little, as he had not yet recovered his usual strength, and the disappointment was intense. The possibility of such a termination to his long-deferred hopes had never entered his head. Catrin's absence was the last idea that he could entertain, and as he walked moodily homewards the very spirit of the man was in revolt.

'God Almighty is fighting against me,' he thought, 'but I have given in long ago, and I'm willing to confess 'A man never does what he makes up his mind to do.' Why, then, does He continue to persecute me?' And with his heart full of rebellious feelings, Goronwy, for the first time in his life, sought his bed in an evil frame of mind.

With the first rays of the sun next morning he was out again on the cliffs; the cool morning air, the sea breeze that fanned his forehead, brought more soothing feelings in their train. He began once more to hope, for surely the girl who had learnt so young to provide herself with food from the stores of nature – who had accustomed herself to sleep with only a bush for shelter, and the sky above her for canopy – surely she could exist in safety and in seclusion if she so desired. He looked down at the swelling sea below the point at which she had been accustomed to disappear. The wild birds flitted about the crags, the sea gulls hovered halfway down, the clumps of samphire and sea pinks still decked the cliffs, but there was no sign of Catrin! Down on Traethyberil, he sought behind every nook, and in every crevice, but in vain! No footmarks, no discarded flowers, marked the path she might have taken, only the lark filling the blue air with melody; only the crows balancing themselves on some wind-blown crag; only the seagulls sailing overhead!

He roamed the fields where they had spent the sunny days and the soft evenings together, but nowhere could he find any trace of the girl. Noontide had come, and over the valley he saw the fields of Tredu, now ripe for the sickle; a scarlet speck against the gold of the cornfields, two darker figures beside it, and Goronwy knew the 'mestress' was leading her son and her newly-made daughter through the rich promise of harvest. Yes! he could fancy it all – the love-light in Walto's eyes, the happy smile on Yshbel's lips, the light of restored happiness in the 'mestress's' face! Old Tredu, lying low in the shade of the ash trees – while he, his heart hungering for the love of a lifetime, sought her in vain, and was roaming alone through the scenes where he had once been so happy.

'Catrin!' he called aloud; 'I *will* find thee – but O God! I must not say that, or I will never find her, for 'tis plain I am thwarted in all my plans. God help me! God help me!' It was spoken reverently and brought some comfort to his heart, for rising from his seat on the hedge side, he turned his face steadily towards Pengraig once more. 'There is one more place to search. In my deed, I thought never to see its dismal darkness again, but anywhere to find her – in hell itself I could go – but 'tisn't there I would find Catrin,' and he smiled sorrowfully.

Reaching Pengraig, he did not enter the precincts of the house, but kept on his way to where the untidy garden, reaching up the bare hillside, was lost in a wilderness of crags and wind-blown thorn bushes. Here he sought for, and found, the cleft in the hillside through which Catrin and he had emerged on their return from the underground shore.

'I hoped I had finished with the underground, till I died anyway – but here goes!' And with a shudder he began his way down the rugged path across which the bats still flitted, and the white owl hooted.

At the turning the wind rushed upwards as before.

'Here she stopped,' he thought, 'and stretched her little hand towards me, and bid me beware. Oh, Catrin! Canst have come to such a dreadful place as this for refuge from the cruel world?'

Down the rough steps, until at last his feet were on the shore, where, in the dull green light, the waves still broke monotonously. A shudder passed over him as he recalled his incarceration in the coal pit, and he hastened to cross the dark strand to the further end, where the bleached skeleton still lay with outstretched arms on the dry sand. Then to bend over every dark heap left at the highest edge of the waves, to turn them over, and make sure that no human body lay under the sodden debris. No! that dreadful trial was spared him. She had not in her despair leapt over the cliffs, or fallen into the 'Deep Stream'!

He was turning hurriedly away towards the steps again when something white and moving caught his eye.

He re-crossed the strand to the further end where the skeleton lay, and where a sudden fall in the ground made a passage for the receding waves which rushed through it with a rumbling sound like thunder.

Again the white object moved, and he stooped to touch it, though it was close to the skeleton's hand.

A fluttering paper, which the wind, always blowing through the cave, moved up and down. He picked it up. Was it a message, that that gruesome figure held out to him? He raised it to the dim green light and with difficulty read 'My dear

Goronwy,' – Catrin's letter – a leaf torn out by the wind from the old copybook. Yes! here was the book lying near, a sodden mass. Goronwy, whose nerves were not at their strongest pitch, trembled as he read.

'Was this a message from the dead? Was it a bad omen?' he asked himself, as he climbed the steep path to the outer air. No sooner, however, had he emerged from that dark crevice, than all the healthy sensations of a country life returned to him. 'Bad omens? Nonsense! What had Catrin to do with omens, good or bad? Nothing!' he said. 'Her life, wherever it is, is spent under the open sky, and she has nothing to do with dark caves and bad omens. 'Tis plain how this sheet came there; the wind blew the copy-book out of the shepherd's hut and over the cliff, and the 'Deep Stream' caught it, and bore it in to that dark shore. Well, I'm glad I have it safe!' And spreading it on the grass, he lay down on his face to read it.

'My dear Goronwy – I am sorry that my first letter to thee must be to say 'Goodbye!''

Oh, how blind he had been! How plainly now he saw it was her unselfish love for him that had prompted every word of that letter. That, indeed, he had known at the time, but how callous he had been – how hard! 'Fool! thou art awake enough now, at all events,' he muttered.

He had forgotten his midday meal, and now, feeling hungry, turned his steps towards home, thinking that for him the light had died out of life. He thought of Walto and Yshbel. Should he go and tell them of his misery? No, he would not mar their happiness with the sight of his mournful face.

Another morning dawned, and Goronwy rose feverish and exhausted after a sleepless night. He scarcely waited to taste his breakfast but left his father and Marged at theirs.

'I must go,' he said. 'I cannot rest!' And once more he turned to Pengraig, where Madlen accorded him no hearty welcome.

'Hast come to look in the churn and the brewing tub?' she said, with an angry snort.

'Yes; and if l don't find her I'll fetch a policeman to hunt for her.'

The word 'policeman' was a power at Treswnd and Madlen cowered a little and answered more civilly.

'Well it isn't likely I'd hide her anywhere, Goronwy Hughes. I'd be glad enough to have her help with the cows and the housework.'

There seemed to be some reason in this, so he tried to speak calmly, and curb his angry feelings.

'Who saw her last?'

'Bensha and me, most like. 'Twas a Friday night; the old man was buried a fortnight before, and you might think 'twas the kindest father in the world was gone, by the way she was crying after him. Well, we were having our supper – porridge and milk it was – and she was sitting there on the stool in the chimney, because she wouldn't sit at the table with Bensha and me, so she was sitting there quite silent, with her bowl on her knees, and the tears dropping down one after another, so sulky she was. Then, when she finished, 'Dere Merlin,' she said, and out through the door with the biggest porridge bowl she could find, and full to the brim, me calling after her, 'That's enough for three meals for him.' 'Yes, I know that,' she said, and out she went, Merlin jumping after her. And that's the last we saw of her, but next morning I found Merlin shut in the stable with the big porridge bowl before him. And that's all I know, or I'm willing to die for it.'

Out again in the stable Goronwy sought high and low, until, late in the evening, he stayed his search in despair.

At every farmhouse he inquired, and at every cottage on the shore, where he stood the broad banter of the villagers as patiently as he could.

'Going all the way to the "works" to fetch thy sweetheart, and bringing her home the wife of another man! Haw! haw! haw!' laughed Dyc Pendrwm.

'Well, she's married to the right man!' said Goronwy, angrily.

'And if I find Catrin thou'lt see me married to the right woman!'

'What! Now that she's a beggar as well as a witch?' said Dyc.

But he had gone a step too far, for in another moment Goronwy had struck him a blow that sent him sprawling into the corner under his mother's brewing utensils. She helped him to rise, but Goronwy followed up his blow with so big a fist close to Dyc's pale face, that both mother and son drew back frightened.

'Listen, Dyc,' he said, 'once and for ever. Say what thee lik'st about me – I will not trouble to punish thee – but if ever again I hear a word disrespectful of Catrin Rees, as sure as thy name is Dyc Pendrwm, I'll give thee a thrashing with the cart-whip, and I can make a good mark with that!' and he turned away with such a look in his eyes as Dyc never forgot, and his mother only told her neighbours in a whisper.

The whole day was spent in a fruitless search. Walto had joined him at noon, and not a field or cliff or wood escaped their close scrutiny. When the sun set, Walto went home to Tredu with the sorrowful news, and Goronwy to his tea at Sarnissa, where his father was beginning to grumble.

'Canst not sit at home an hour, lad, and let's hear something of all the grand things thou hast seen away?'

But Goronwy ate silently; and as soon as his meal was over, turned his steps once again to the old familiar ways. He was growing very disheartened at the dead blank which seemed to check all his inquiries. Reaching the cliffs, he sought the shepherd's hut, where Catrin had so often passed the night; but as he approached it, his attention was attracted to a bright red flame that shot up from the mountain side. 'The gipsies,' he thought; 'John Lovell and his company, and they have lighted their fire in the old spot.'

He felt irresistibly drawn towards that glowing fire, so well he remembered the night when he and Catrin had shared the supper of the merry company. And he continued to sit leaning against the hut, his thoughts roaming backwards over the simple events which had filled his life on those cliffs and fields.

The twilight deepened, the moon came up, and still he sat on, ever feeling more and more drawn towards the red glow. Suddenly he started.

'What if Catrin should be there? What if, goaded and driven out by Madlen, she had taken refuge with these strangers?'

He remembered now that Nancy Wood – the 'Queen', as she was called – was related to the girl's mother; the connection was often brought up against her by the villagers, but it had slipped out of Goronwy's memory. Now, however, it came as a gleam of comfort to his mind; and he drew near the tent in front of which most of the gipsies were gathered, with an eager smile on his lips.

John Lovell himself was there, stretched at full length on an old sack in front of the fire, over which the regulation pot was hung, a savoury smell from its bubbling contents as usual filling the evening air.

Near by sat two girls, whose merry laughter first reached his ear, while others sat about hugging their knees, all evidently waiting with interest the cooking of the stew over the fire. In the gloom of the tent, just inside the door, Goronwy saw the little barrow, or hand-cart, in which the old 'Queen' reclined.

'Nos da,' said Goronwy, genially.

'Nos da,' said John Lovell, curtly.

'You have come round once more,' said Goronwy, by way of opening the conversation; but the gipsy did not seem inclined to continue, for he only answered:

'Yes, we have.'

Goronwy was rather taken aback. He scanned the faces of the girls eagerly in search of Catrin; but although their dark eyes reminded him of hers, she was not there.

'I have sat over your fire before,' he said again, 'and shared your supper years ago, when we brought you some fish – do you remember?'

'Maybe I do – maybe I don't,' said John Lovell. 'I have a convenient memory.'

'You're a lucky man, then!' said Goronwy. 'Well, at least you remember a young lass, Catrin Rees by name, who was with me then?'

'A young lass, Catrin Rees by name!' and a general laugh went round the fire. 'Is that the way you ask me if I remember my own relation? Yes, I do, then; better than you do, I'm thinking. What about that?'

The taunting tone was very trying to Goronwy's hot temper; but the one important question of finding Catrin thrust everything else into the background.

'Well, I've been away in the "works" lately' – another laugh went round the company, while in the gloom of the tent Goronwy saw old Nancy Wood raise herself to a sitting posture, and her shrill laugh joined the others.

'What's the laugh about?' asked Goronwy, looking round fiercely. 'Can't you give a civil answer when a man asks you a civil question?'

'What's the question?' said John Lovell.

'I was just telling you I went away to the "works" about two months ago, and left Catrin Rees here at Pengraig, alive and well, and now I come home, and can find no more sign of her than of last year's hoar frost. Do you know anything about her?'

'Maybe I do – maybe I don't,' said John Lovell. 'You went away to fetch a wife – what business have you so soon to be asking after another girl?'

'Aye, that's it, that's it,' screamed the old woman, and her fierce eyes seemed to sparkle like live coals through the darkness. 'Throw him out! We don't want him here, with his civil questions and his civil answers! Throw him out, I say,' and she flung her crutch at him across the flames, with such a vindictive aim, that it struck him on the shoulder.

Now it was one of two things with Goronwy, either he must have flung himself upon that taunting crew, and laid about him in right down earnest, or he must master his own temper, and bring the meeting to its senses.

He stooped calmly, and picked up the crutch, keeping it in his hand while he spoke.

'Listen to me,' he said. 'I'm not afraid of you; I'm stronger than any two of you, but as God is my witness I cannot bring myself to fight with Catrin's friends unless I'm forced to it. What is your quarrel with me?'

'What business have you to go on for years courting a girl who is related to Nancy Wood, and then to throw her aside and marry another girl?'

'What a pack of fools you are! I'm not married!'

An awkward silence fell upon the group, whose dark faces gathered round the fire.

'Not married?' said John Lovell. 'I'll find the truth about that.'

'Not married?' croaked the old woman's voice from the tent door. 'Where's the wife you went to fetch home from the "works" – Yshbel Lloyd, they called her?'

"Now listen to reason," said Goronwy, sitting down fearlessly amongst them. 'I brought home with me three days ago Yshbel and her husband, Walto Gwyn. Go to Tredu today, and you'll see them there as happy as two birds. Stop a bit,' he added, as he saw Nancy Wood's shrivelled finger pointed at him and her lips opened for another remark, 'I don't want to hide anything from you. I had found out before I left here, that it was Catrin I loved and not Yshbel; but I had promised to marry Yshbel, and I could not break my word. I was only hoping that after seeing the life of grand rich people she would want to change her mind and would set me free; and true enough, the clergyman there found out how it was with me, and with her too, for it was Walto she cared for all through, and he set it all straight for us three. Walto and Yshbel were married, I gave her away, and as soon as ever I could, I came home to marry Catrin, and now I find her gone!'

The two girls drew nearer; John Lovell kicked at the embers and looked thoughtful.

'Now, for God's sake,' said Goronwy, 'if you know anything about her – tell me.'

'You ask her,' said Lovell, pointing his thumb over his shoulder towards Nancy Wood.

'Yes, you, Nancy Wood,' said Goronwy, entering the tent, 'have some pity for me. You are old, and your blood runs slowly through your veins, but remember I am young, and my blood is hot and impatient, and I have had trials enough to daunt any one lately. Where is Catrin?'

'Tell him, tell him,' said one of the girls; 'I'm sure he is telling the truth.'

'Come here,' said the old woman, 'give me your hand.' And holding his palm to the firelight she scanned it narrowly, and her black eyes rose and fell alternately from his hand to his eyes. 'I think you are telling the truth,' she said at last. 'Wheel me outside,' and Goronwy did as he was bid.

The moon was hidden behind a cloud, but the sky was full of stars, and the old woman looked up at the brilliant galaxy for some time in silence and her lips moved. It was characteristic of the simplicity of Goronwy's nature, as well as evidence of the influence of Catrin's habits of mind upon him, that while the old woman gazed up at the stars, he doffed his cap. The action told in his favour, not only with Nancy herself, but with all the company.

'Now, listen, my lad,' she said at last. 'I know where Catrin Rees is – you shall know tomorrow. Come here exactly at twelve o'clock, and I will show you where she is.'

'Show me? You're not going to show me where she is buried? I can't bear that, in my deed, I can't.'

'No, no; she is alive.'

'Why not show me now, then, mother? 'Tis long hours till twelve tomorrow.'

'Tomorrow at midday. Wheel me in again. And now,' she

said, when she had been deposited safely inside the door, 'have some supper with us; the stew is ready.'

And Goronwy, fearing to offend her by a refusal, and partly because he was really hungry, and still more, because he was drawn towards the only people who seemed to feel any interest in Catrin, and moreover were related to her by ties of blood, sat down in the circle gathered round the huge crock. Wooden bowls and spoons were handed round, and a portion of the stew served out to each.

'Well, I never tasted such a stew, I think, since the last time I supped with you.'

'Well, come and sup with Sylvia and me in our van some night. 'Tis in Brynferri tonight, but will be here in a month's time again, and you'll taste a better stew.'

'That will I, if I find Catrin, and bring her with me.'

'Aye,' said John Lovell, with a shake of his head, 'Sylvia will be glad to see you both.'

The two girls, Matta and Melia, sidled closer to him. 'Give us an apple,' said Matta; 'or plums,' said Melia.

'Indeed, there's sorry I am! I have not got one in my pocket, but come to Sarnissa tomorrow, and I'll give you plenty of both.'

'We'll come, then, about ten. Are there any dogs about?'

'Only old Caesar; I'll shut him up,' said Goronwy, and he felt more cheerful than he had done since his return home.

'How did you like Glamorganshire?' said John Lovell.

'Ach-y-fi!' answered Goronwy, with a shrug and something like a shudder, ''tis a place I hope I may never see more; but, indeed, I have made up my mind nothing will ever make me leave home again. 'Tis here I was born, 'tis here I wish to die, and since you say you will show me where Catrin is. Is any one keeping her against her will? In my deed, 'twill be a bad day for them when I meet them if there is.'

Again Nancy Wood's shrill laugh came from the tent.

'You are only a fool after all, Goronwy Hughes,' she said; 'softly, man, softly. "I have made up my mind, indeed." Ha! ha! "Nothing will ever make me leave here again." Can you rule your fate, man? Can you fight with the stars? I tell you before we return to Penmwntan you will have travelled many miles from here.'

Goronwy was silent for some time, looking thoughtfully into the fire.

'Well, you are right,' he said at last, 'and I ought to have learnt my lesson by now. You call it "the stars"; Catrin always said "God". 'Tis all the same, I suppose, for well I know now that 'tis madness for a man to make up his mind to any plan without remembering the Almighty or the "stars", as you say. I am an ignorant man, and I make no pretence to be religious, but l am willing to submit my way to God, trusting only that I may find Catrin.'

'Well, go now,' said the old woman, ''tis late, and come tomorrow at twelve. I will help you, and if Nancy Wood will help you, you are pretty safe.'

'Well, goodnight,' said Goronwy; 'I'll go and try to sleep the hours away till tomorrow.'

And as he hurried down the mountain side the grass once more felt springy under his feet, the waves splashed musically on the shore. All nature around him was full of buoyant life, and within him, hope and joy reigned once more.

At noon the following day, the sky was clear, the sunny air tempered by the fleecy clouds, which crossed the sky as Goronwy, punctually at twelve o'clock, drew near the gipsies' tent. He saw no sign of Nancy Wood, but all around were tokens of a hasty flitting. Two donkeys stood waiting by, while Matta and Melia, armed with sticks, stood ready to guide them, munching the apples which Goronwy had supplied them with. John Lovell and the rest of the party were already many miles on their way. A covered cart alone remained, on the shaft of which a dark-eyed youth sat idly dangling his legs, underneath it were slung the hen-coops, through the bars of which the cocks crowed defiance at each other.

Drawing nearer this motley group, Goronwy discovered that the covered cart contained Nancy Wood, still reclining in her barrow.

'Come up here to me, my lad,' called out the old woman, when she saw him arrive, and he climbed up into the ramshackle vehicle, and stood as well as he could close beside the barrow.

'Now, Nancy Wood,' he said, eagerly, 'tell me now where is Catrin? I was shocking frightened, when I saw the tent was gone, but you promised you—'

'I promised, man, and the gipsy breaks no promise – 'tis the Georgio does that. John Lovell had to start early for Pembrokeshire to meet a man of our tribe who owes him money. We are going to follow, Now listen to me, you Goronwy Hughes, who art never going to move from home again!'

She pointed with her shrivelled finger to where the bay shimmered in the noontide light stretching away to the far horizon.

'I told you I would show you where Catrin was. Well, look!'

'I see only the bay – not a sail or a boat,' said Goronwy, with a fresh terror.

'But what beyond the bay?'

'Those blue hills,' he said, starting. 'She was often talking about them. Is she there?'

'There,' said the old woman. 'See the Snowdons, towering highest of all? Behind them lie the Cribor mountains; you see them fainter and farther off.'

'I see them.'

'Well, she is there! I could not show you in the darkness last night, but now I have kept my promise and we must start.'

'Oh, wait a moment. Tell me why she went so far? Tell me how am I to find her!'

'Why she went so far? Ask thyself that. How to find her? Find the Cribor mountains, and then ask for Brostetyn,

William Bray's sheep farm, there thou wilt find Catrin. Oh yes; if you get Nancy Wood's help, you are all right, my lad.'

'Well, indeed, I don't know what to say, nor how to thank you; but one thing I can say, if Catrin and I will ever be so happy as to settle down at Sarnissa, we will not forget that we are related to you.'

'Well, well! Perhaps old Nancy Wood will come and bring you a blessing some day. But remember you, 'twill not be a blessing that I will bring you, but a curse, if you are false to that girl!'

'Oh, Nancy! Let me find her only, and then come and see. I'll find a ship before three days are over, bound for Merionethshire, and I'll cross the bay in that, and then I'll tramp it over those hills. There's the *Swallow* goes regular to Bermwth.'

'That's the place,' said Nancy; 'no better starting point. Goodbye now, my lad – we must start. Go on, Ando.'

'Goodbye, then,' said Goronwy, alighting. 'A good journey to you, and my best thanks. Can diolch!'

Matta and Melia, who were now quarrelling over their apples, stopped to say 'Goodbye.'

'Goodbye; we'll be back in a month, some of us, perhaps not Matta and me – but if not, keep some apples for us.'

'I will, you may depend,' shouted Goronwy, as the cavalcade jolted over the moor.

When they were out of sight he sat down to consider. Was there ever such a strange fate? That he, Goronwy Hughes, who three days ago desired nothing better than to stay at home in peace and quietness to the end of his days, should once more be seeking about in his mind for something which should bear him away from Treswnd! But Catrin's brown eyes drew him, that pensive face rose up before him, and he longed for the moment when the white wings of the *Swallow* should bear him over those shining waters.

CHAPTER XXVIII

MOUNTAIN ECHOES

The wind whistled through the rigging, and the long blue pennon streamed on the wind as the *Swallow* sped on her way across the bay, leaving Treswnd rapidly behind, and drawing ever nearer the blue hills, which lay fully eighty miles away.

Goronwy was on board, his thoughts forestalling her arrival in port, his eyes continually drawn towards the hills on which his hopes were centred. The wind blew straight with his wishes, the foam flew back from the vessel's prow, as she cleaved through the green waters, but all too slow for him for if he could, he would have left the *Swallow* behind, and flown to the distant shore.

'Patience, man!' said the captain. 'We've never had such a fair passage before; what's drawing you across the bay like a magnet?'

Goronwy smiled. ''Tis a brave little ship, indeed,' he said, 'and makes good headway, but I've always been an impatient fellow. Tomorrow noon, you say, we'll be at Bermwth; well, indeed, I must try to sleep the time away,' and stretching himself on the deck, he was soon asleep, or at all events, Captain Owen thought so.

Perhaps the clear blue eyes under that peaked cap still gazed towards the north. Perhaps the thoughts that kept him silent company flew on before that bounding vessel, and on some sunny slope he pictured Catrin, and rehearsed in fancy their happy meeting. At night, lying in his bunk, and listening to the rushing waters at the prow, his mind roamed backwards to the day on which he parted with her. How had she fared since then? If she loved him, as he hoped she did, what sorrow must have shaded her life! What a heavy heart she must have borne with her through that toilsome journey, over moor and road and river, by which she reached the goal towards which the little *Swallow* was bearing him so swiftly and so smoothly! Merlin, curled up at his feet, was fast asleep, for, as Goronwy had passed down the Pengraig slopes, the old grey dog had followed him, fawning upon him, and with wistful eyes appearing to ask him for his lost mistress.

'Come on, then, old dog,' he said. 'We'll go in search of her, and surely thou and I together will find her.'

Next day, at noon, the *Swallow* was in port, and Goronwy, accompanied by Merlin, once more unwillingly found himself in the busy haunts of men.

Gladly he turned his steps from the town, and, with a cheerful step and a buoyant heart, set his face towards where, in the distance, old Snowdon reared his rugged head.

'I'll keep that old fellow in front of me,' he said, 'and, once there, surely I'll find the Cribor mountains.'

After all, it was a long tramp, though relieved by many a 'lift' in cart or waggon, and sometimes by a ride in some rough country car, which he hired at a wayside inn, always with the same directions— 'Towards Snowdon, and then to the Cribor mountains. D'ye know them?'

'The Cribor mountains? Oh yes; but 'tis full twenty miles, and my horse is old. I can only drive you ten miles on your way.'

And towards evening he alighted, and sought a night's shelter in a little inn.

At last Snowdon was behind him, and before him rose another range of rugged hills.

'What hills are these?' he asked his hostess.

'The Cribor.'

'All right,' said Goronwy. 'Only give me a little bread and

cheese and a bed to sleep on, and I'll make a closer acquaintance with them tomorrow.'

'They are very bare and wild,' said the woman. 'Only at the bottom are farms and villages. The sheep have scarcely footing at the top.'

''Tis there I want to go whatever. D'ye know one William Bray, who keeps a sheep farm thereabouts?'

'No,' said the, woman, with a shake of her head. 'I never heard the name. 'Tis English.'

'P'raps, indeed, but I must find him tomorrow.'

And when, next morning, the sun shone full upon his face and woke him, it was with a bound of happiness that he rose and joined his hostess at breakfast. When, before starting on his journey, he paid the modest sum which she asked for his night's lodging, he added a silver coin thereto.

'Yes, indeed, you must take it, because this day is going to be a wonderful day for me.'

'There's an odd man,' said the old woman, gazing at the money in her palm as the traveller disappeared down the lane. 'P'r'aps he isn't wise, druan bach!'

But if he was not wise, Goronwy was at least happy, as he trudged along the dusty roads, Merlin beside him, increasing the length of his journey by continual circuits round the fields and hedges, which were new to him.

'Come back, old boy!' called Goronwy. You'll be tired enough before night;' and in the exuberance of his own joy, he sang, till the hills around resounded with his mellow voice:

> 'Blue land beyond the sea,
> When will I come to thee?'

The longest day comes to an end at last. The sun was sinking in the west as he reached the foot of the craggy Cribor range.

On the verdant pastures in the valley stood a few scattered

houses, and at one or two of these he inquired for William Bray's farm, 'Brostetyn, it is called.'

'Brostetyn? Oh! 'tis far up yonder; some of the pastureland reaches down there to that hollow. See, there are some of the sheep; but the most of it is up there among the crags. You're a butcher, I suppose, and want to buy sheep?'

'A butcher? Not I!' said Goronwy. 'Anw'l! I never could make out how a man can live by such a trade, though I eat my meat as well as anybody when I get it.'

'That's it,' said the farmer. 'Are you wanting to buy a horse, p'r'aps?'

'Wrong again,' said Goronwy, laughing. 'P'r'aps I'll call on you on my way back, and show you what I was looking for.'

He was already round the corner of the road, and facing the rugged heights, which now rose close in front of him, and with a swinging step every moment mounting higher towards the summit, Merlin bounding before him, and barking with delight, as though he too anticipated a happy ending to his journey.

At Brostetyn, it had been a day of trial for Catrin, for William Bray had grown irritable and captious; and, although he could find no fault with the girl's care of his flocks, he took every occasion to hint to her that 'sick maids were not fit to be shepherdesses'. Every day Catrin's step grew slower, her form thinner, her eyes more hollow.

Olwen sometimes expostulated, for Catrin had won her way into her heart: 'Oh, father,' she said, 'don't be hard upon her; remember she's a relation, and so friendless. She'll get better in time, and she minds the sheep well.'

'Yes; but who's going to bury her, that's what I want to know?' and he went out, slamming the door.

Meanwhile, Catrin, alone on the hill top, although pale and languid, was certainly not thinking of being buried. She was sitting, at the very moment of Bray's conversation with his daughter, under the shadow of a rock, looking over the long velvet pastures, where Trodwen, having met another shepherd's dog, was enlivening the day with an impromptu race. Catrin called and whistled in vain; her face dimpled with the old smiles as she watched the gambols of the two happy creatures. Round the rocks and over the stone walls, they chased each other with joyous barks, the sheep looking on with solemn astonishment, until at last, tired with their game, they separated, and Trodwen returned apologetically to her mistress.

It was plain to Catrin that she must seek for work on another farm ere long, for William Bray's black looks had not escaped her notice. She would be sorry to go from here, feeling some tie of kindred between her and his daughter. Moreover, she had grown to love her simple flock, and 'Trodwen, fach!' she said, 'how will I part with thee? Thou art a faithful lassie, in spite of thy foolish pranks! But, indeed,' she thought within herself, 'it is no wonder he wants to get rid of me; what is the matter with me, I don't know, but I think it is because I don't want to live! 'Tis so many years till you're seventy – and all that long time without Goronwy! No, no, Trodwen; 'twould be impossible!' and as the day wore on her strength seemed rapidly to fail her.

The sun was sinking low in the west, behind bars of gold and purple; overhead, the blue was flecked with tiny feathers of gold. The far-reaching slopes faded away into a golden haze, and gold was upon the crags behind her, and adding brilliancy to the furze and heather stretched before her.

'And yet, 'tis a beautiful world,' thought Catrin. 'I am sorry to leave it, if only I could be happy in it! 'Tis because I have not eaten my dinner, p'r'aps, that I'm so weak today!' And rising, she turned towards the shepherd's hut, where her little wallet had hung untouched since early morning. She opened it, and spread the coarse food upon the grass beside her, fare which she would once have eaten with relish, but now she turned from it with loathing.

'No, no; I cannot!' she said. 'Here, Trodwen, lass, take it all!' and, leaning once more against the crag, she gazed at the gorgeous scene before her, until her spirit seemed to melt into its beauty.

Suddenly she roused herself and listened intently. She thought she must have been dreaming, for on the still sunset air, came a bark so like Merlin's, that before her eyes rose a vision of the Pengraig slopes, with Goronwy sauntering up towards the cliffs.

'Oh, if it could only be once more!' and she sank back into the same languid attitude. Again, the clear, short yaps fell on her ear, and again she listened eagerly. 'So like! So like!' she thought; and with the sound, came over her so strong a flood of happy memories, that the tears welled up in her eyes. But the bark came nearer, and she stood up to listen. 'Surely – surely it was Merlin!' And – hark! Upon the evening air came another sound – 'Catrin! Catrin!' – a voice was calling her. 'Was it Goronwy's?' Again she heard it, but more distant, and now it ceased altogether. 'Was I dreaming?' she thought. 'Am I dying? I have heard people see and hear strange things when they are dying – but no – surely!' From another direction now, there came the same short, sharp yap, like Merlin's when he chased a rabbit, then again came the long call reaching her with those slanting beams of gold which seemed to bring enchantment on their level rays. 'Catrin! Catrin!' and the echoes around took up the call, and answered 'Catrin!' from one blue hill to another.

She looked round bewildered, holding her hair back from her ears, and again came the long-drawn call, but fainter now, as if more distant, and further still, until it died away in echo amongst the hills.

She listened with intense eagerness, straining her ears to catch the sound, but though, in the momentary pause, the air seemed full of echoes, the phantom call had died away. How loud was the song of the lark as it hovered above her! How clearly the sound of the river in the valley fell on her ear! – the beetles' drone, the late bee hurrying homewards, the tinkle of the sheep bells in the fold – all the sweet sounds she knew so well, but not the strangely familiar voice, that seemed to come from some mysterious spirit world to mock her.

When, for some time she had listened, but heard only the eternal silence of the mountains, she fell into a deep depression of spirit.

''Twas some strange dream of the past,' she thought, 'that had slumbered in her brain, and suddenly woke to life again. There's a foolish girl she was, to hope that she should ever hear that life-stirring call again! And yet, what was that faint echo of a voice that now seemed to come from behind, and beyond the hill on which she stood?'

It was, it must be, though faint and distant! 'Catrin! Catrin!' and, like the will-o'-the-wisp, the strange sound flew from hill to hill – now near, now far – but ever eluding her.

'Tis a spirit, I think; will I answer it? 'Tis so like Goronwy's voice!' And trembling in bewilderment, she stood expectant.

Suddenly, round the shoulder of the hill a figure appeared, and Catrin's eyes were riveted upon it in utter astonishment, for surely that grey coat, those leather leggings, belonged to no spirit, that dog bounding towards her was real and material – was Merlin! for his paws were upon her, her arms were around his neck. Then, standing expectant once more, she saw the grey figure advance nearer and nearer, and had William Bray been able to see her now, he would not have called her 'a sick maid,' for as she recognised Goronwy, a rosy flush dyed her cheeks, the light in her eyes brightened, the red lips a little apart, showed the white teeth, and with a fluttering breath she clasped and unclasped her fingers in the old childish habit.

Yes, 'twas Goronwy! and for a moment Yshbel and all else were forgotten. He held both hands towards her, but she seemed chained to the spot, and could only hold out her hands towards his.

Truth to tell, the newly arrived seemed quite as excited as she was; he blushed like a girl as he drew nearer.

'Catrin, lass, hast not a word to say to me?'

She pressed her hand to her bosom to still its throbbing.

'Oh, Goronwy, what will I say? Indeed, indeed! Where hast come from, lad?'

'Why, from Treswnd, of course; dost think I could stop there without thee? A fine dance thou hast led Merlin and me! All across the bay in the *Swallow*, and then over roads and rivers!'

He had hold of her hands now, and was guiding her towards a seat on the wild thyme.

'Sit down, lass,' he said there's a spirit look about thee I do not like. Thy little hands are thinner; thy face too. What ails thee, Catrin?'

'I have been ill,' she said, with embarrassment. 'I think the air here is too strong for me.'

'Of course it is. Come back, then, lodes, to Treswnd. 'Tis on the Pengraig cliffs, and in Sarnissa fields we ought to be – thou and I.'

Catrin shook her head, smiling sadly.

'No, no, Goronwy. I have made my home here now, and will never go back to Treswnd.'

'Hast indeed made thy home here? And what have I to do? Must I, then, leave Sarnissa, and come up here to live amongst these barren rocks?'

'Leave Sarnissa? Thou? Oh no!' And for a moment a serious, puzzled look passed over her face, which Goronwy watched with a mischievous smile. 'How is Yshbel?' she asked at last.

'Oh, quite well. She is at Treswnd.'

'Yes, I suppose; and thou must go back, Goronwy. How will I ever thank thee for coming all this way to fetch me? But, indeed, it cannot be; I cannot go back. They think I am a witch, and do not love me there; though I've tried so hard to make friends with them. Go thou back, lad, and be happy with Yshbel at Sarnissa.'

'Catrin,' said Goronwy, 'let me tell thee a story, lass, like granny used to tell me long ago. "There was once a boy and girl called Goronwy and Catrin; they grew up together, and spent their lives together on the cliffs and sands by the seaside. He was an uncouth, rugged lout, but she was a beautiful girl as gentle as a lady, and as pure as an angel from Heaven. Well, this great clumsy lout loved her with every fibre of his heart, but he didn't know it, so dull was he! And just to be like the other lads around him, he took up with a sweetheart – Yshbel was her name – and it went on from courting, till at last they were going to be married; but the lout gradually came to his senses and found out, when it was too late, that he didn't care a cockle shell for his sweetheart, and loved Catrin as his own life. Well, this stupid fellow and Yshbel had their banns put out – "thy hand is trembling; cariad anw'l! Don't take it away; wait till I finish" – well, they had their banns published, and his heart was as heavy as lead. But a good man had found out how it was with him, and also that Yshbel loved another man, and he stopped the marriage, and let the two birds free. Yshbel flew to her mate, and Goronwy has now found out his beloved." Wilt refuse me now, lass? I have told thee all the truth. Canst love me after all? Let me see thy face. Turn thine eyes upon me, Catrin; I could always read them like a book.'

Catrin turned her face toward him, and the answer that he saw in those soft brown eyes satisfied him entirely.

'But a witch, Goronwy!' she said, mischievously.

'Yes, a witch indeed, Catrin, for thou hast bewitched me completely, if ever man was bewitched! Why, I tell thee, lass, not only now, since I have opened my eyes, and know that I love thee, but long ago, when we roamed about the cliffs together like children, and like brother and sister – why, even then, I worshipped the ground thy little foot had pressed; and the dimples in thy face, and thy merry laugh, were light and life to me. But no more partings for us, Catrin! We'll go home together in the *Swallow*, we'll be married in Penmwntan church, and thou shalt be the honoured and loved mistress of Sarnissa.'

'Oh, Goronwy!' was all Catrin could gasp, ''tis so sudden.'

'Sudden, indeed! 'tis so slow; all these years I have been waiting for it.'

'Wilt marry a witch, then, and go to church on a broomstick?!'

'Catrin,' he said, and for once Goronwy's voice took a solemn, serious tone, 'never say those dreadful words to me again; they have stung me, lass, a hundred times, since I spoke them once thoughtlessly to Yshbel Lloyd. Oh, Catrin! I knew then I was lying to her, but some evil fate seemed to urge me on. 'Tis strange thou shouldst use the words that have so often wounded my memory.'

'Forgive me, lad; I did not mean to wound thee. 'Twas a foolish word that came first on my tongue.' And she never told him that she had overheard those words, and that to her, too, they had often returned with a cruel sting.

'But where is Yshbel?' she asked, halting a little at the name.

'Why, at Treswnd, as I told thee; and as happy as a bird. Married to Walto Gwyn, and living at Tredu.'

'Oh, anw'l!' was all Catrin's answer; but what a load of doubt and fear was removed from her mind, what a cloud of sorrow lifted from her life!

It was a happy hour that they spent there in the sunset together, an hour to compensate them for all the bitterness that had gone before; an hour that restored to Goronwy the peace of mind, and the delight of living which had been dried up within him, longer than he liked to remember, and that worked a marvellous change in the 'sick maid'.

'Oh! 'tis getting late,' she said at last,'and William Bray is a hard man. I am afraid of him to stop out longer.'

'Wait till I have talked to him a bit,' said Goronwy. 'I'll let him know who thou art, and who thou'rt going to be. Down, Merlin! 'tis too free thou art, pushing thy nose under Catrin's chin.'

'Oh, Merlin, bach! Let him alone.'

'Nay, I am jealous of him;' and Catrin laughed the old, happy, dimpling laugh.

Arrived at Brostetyn, again the grey scarped door confronted her; but how different were her feelings tonight to those with which at other times she had crossed its threshold.

'Where's been so late?' was Bray's first greeting.

''Tis talking to a friend I've been; here he is,' said Catrin, blushing furiously, and Goronwy stood at the open doorway, holding Merlin by the collar.

''Tis true what she is saying,' he said, looking fearlessly into William Bray's angry black eyes. 'I am an old friend of hers. We grew up like brother and sister together, and Nancy Wood told me I would find her here with you, William Bray.'

'Nancy Wood! And what dost want with the lass, I want to know?'

'Well, I want a great many things,' said Goronwy, 'but first I want you to know, she is my promised wife, and I have come all the way from Cardiganshire to fetch her. I am Goronwy Hughes, of Sarnissa in the parish of Penmwntan, in the county of Cardigan; and now I will go to my lodgings, that white house down there in the valley – 'Tygwyn' they call it. They have promised to lodge me there tonight.'

William Bray scratched his head. 'Well, we've no bed for strangers – but if thee'rt a friend of Nancy Wood's –' And he looked round at his son and daughter, who were standing with Catrin in the background.

'No, no,' said Goronwy; 'I will trouble no one. Merlin will wait no longer, so goodnight, Catrin, lass; I will come up tomorrow;' and without waiting for an answer he was gone into the darkness, and William Bray turned to Catrin for an explanation.

''Tis all true what he says. He is Goronwy Hughes, of Sarnissa, and he has come all the way from Treswnd to fetch me; so the day after tomorrow I will go back with him in the

Swallow. I am sure old Gower will be glad to watch the sheep for you instead of me.'

'Oh, don't thee trouble about that,' said Bray. 'I have a lad ready to take thy place. But what will Nancy Wood say? – pretending to be such a steady girl here, and then going off with the first lad that asked thee!'

At this, the girl looked sorely troubled.

'Well, indeed, why not?' she said, ''Tis home I'm going, and Nancy Wood will be glad to see me when she comes round next, and Melia will be glad to hear about you all, too.'

William Bray sulked a good deal over his supper, and Olwen looked sad at the prospect of losing her new friend; but, in spite of all, before many days had gone by, the *Swallow* sailed from Bermwth with Goronwy and Catrin on board.

The moon shone straight down upon the heaving bay, the breeze blew fresh for land as they drew near Abersethin harbour.

In one of the cornfields at Tredu, Yshbel and Walto stood watching it, guessing that Goronwy would be on board, and wondering whether his search had been successful, and Catrin would accompany him home. No prudish doubts as to the propriety of such a proceeding had entered into the minds of either, any more than into that of Catrin and Goronwy. Their simple rural lives had been passed in a seclusion into which such ideas had not yet entered.

The corn stooks stood around them, the moonlit air was full of the scent of the ripened grain, and as they stood there, side by side, he in his dark and manly strength, and she in her fair and graceful beauty, they gave to the silent scene around them the added charm of living humanity, which was all the picture needed for perfection; their voices were low and tender, all the old look of dissatisfied care had disappeared from his dark face, giving place to an expression of perfect content and peace – and hers, as the moonlight fell upon it, showed nothing but radiant happiness.

'See, Yshbel, they're crossing that silver pathway, and by that light on board, I see we shall have fish for dinner tomorrow.'

'Oh, greedy man! 'tis not a fishing smack!'

'No; but the sailors are amusing themselves, and I know the bay is full of mackerel tonight.'

'Well, we must go in, Walto, or your mother will think we have fallen over the cliff.'

'Yes, indeed! 'Tis wonderful how she has taken to you, Yshbel. She cannot bear you out of her sight. I suppose we must go. I hope Goronwy and Catrin are safe on the *Swallow*. We shall see them tomorrow.'

'Oh, Walto, will they ever be as happy as we are?'

'Well yes, indeed, I think so. He loves her with all his heart, and Goronwy Hughes' love is worth having, Yshbel, although I'm thankful you did not prize it. What would have become of me if you had?'

Their conversation was interrupted by a call from the doorway of Tredu, where the 'mestress' stood waiting for them.

'Come in, children, come in; supper is ready.'

And they passed through the little gate behind the two peacocks cut in the box-hedge, into the old-fashioned passage, and the green door closed after them, its brass knocker shining bright in the moonlight.

And so Walto and Yshbel pass from our sight. What lies in store for them in the dim future we cannot tell; but, whatever events may happen, their path will be sweetened by the joy of a true and abiding love.

Half-an-hour later the *Swallow* entered the little harbour of Abersethin, Goronwy and Catrin standing side by side at the prow, and watching the old familiar cliffs with hearts that beat high with happiness and hope.

'Well, goodbye,' said the captain, 'and I hope you'll come another trip with me some day. Here's a word in your ear, my dear.' And stooping towards Catrin he whispered, 'You shall have your wedding-trip on the *Swallow* for nothing, if you like.'

'What art saying to her?' asked Goronwy. 'I see by the moonlight it has brought the red to her face.'

'Ha! ha! My lad – secrets! But I'm not too old to see how it is with thee and the lass. Well, goodbye, and good luck to you!'

The ship's boat was lowered, and on landing Catrin and Goronwy turned their faces towards the cliff that separated them from Treswnd.

'What did he say, lass?'

'Oh, nothing – nothing, indeed! 'Twas all nonsense. But here's a lovely night, and there's old Penmwntan. There's the shepherd's hut, and there's old Pengraig. Oh, Goronwy! Is it true? Have we come back indeed to the old fields and rocks? Will we light a fire some night, and fry our fish, and eat our supper in the moonlight again?'

'Yes,' he said 'that will we; and I'll challenge thee to a game of dandiss on Traethyberil. So there, lass!'

'Oh, 'tis too happy I am! Goodnight, lad.'

'I'll be up tomorrow early,' said Goronwy, 'and bring thy father's will with me, and read it aloud to Bensha and Madlen. Goodnight, lass.'

And he retained her hand a little while, but Catrin, with a strange perversity, slipped her hand out of his, and flew unceremoniously over the grass, as she only knew how to fly.

'Dei anw'l!' said Goronwy. 'I would never catch her. She flew away like a frightened bird. Well, never mind; I'll catch her safe enough one of these days.'

And he trudged down the path to Sarnissa with a heart as light as he had borne in his boyhood.

On reaching Pengraig, Catrin had found the door closed and the lights out, for Madlen and Bensha went to bed at sunset from motives of economy. She had some difficulty in restraining Merlin's exuberant delight at finding himself in his old quarters again, but opening the 'boidy' door, and shaking out his bed of straw, she shut him in and began to reconnoitre. No; there was no mode of entering the house, except by the old bedroom window, which would not close.

'I must try it whatever,' she thought. 'I don't think I'm fatter since I've gone away!'

And she found no difficulty in slipping in, in the old fashion. She felt the bed carefully. It was empty, and she knew by the snoring which she heard from the kitchen that Bensha and Madlen had taken possession of the box bed, and in an incredibly short time she was asleep, the old red and blue coverlet drawn over her as of yore. But if she slept heavily she woke early, and with the first faint flush of morning she was out on the cliffs, and running down the little gorge to Traethyberil, across its golden sands, and into the foaming breakers once more.

'Oh, 'tis a happy world!' she said, as she dressed in the sunshine, and climbed up the path, entering her bedroom through the window as before, for she would not disturb the snorers until she had finished her toilet, and searched in the old coffer for another gown to replace the brown and green, which had grown faded and travel-stained.

'What will I wear?' became suddenly a question of importance, for Goronwy would be up before long, and he should not see her any longer in shabby clothes; and opening the old coffer, she began her selection from amongst her mother's gowns; at last, fixing upon a black with yellow spots, its sleeves reeved tight at the wrist and shoulders. A yellow silk kerchief filled up the low neck, and when her brown-black hair was drawn into its massive knot at the back of her head, her neat best shoes on her feet, she looked at herself in the tiny looking-glass with a smile of satisfaction.

The clattering of pots and pans in the kitchen proclaimed Madlen's preparations for breakfast, and when at last she called Bensha at the doorway, Catrin opened the door of the penisha, and appeared also upon the scene.

Madlen's astonishment was indescribable, and not a little tinged with superstitious fear.

'Well, bendigedig!' she said. 'Where hast come from now – earth, sea, or sky? And where's thy broomstick?'

'Well – sea, this time,' said Catrin, laughing. 'I've left my broomstick in Abersethin harbour.'

At this moment Bensha entered, and his astonishment was not less than Madlen's. He squinted frightfully, and twisted his head to look at her.

'Jari! 'tis the croten!' he said 'Well, in my deed, I'm glad to see thee, Catrin. Where hast thou been? But mind thee, lass,' he added, suddenly changing to a solemn voice, 'these witch ways won't do – going away nobody knows where, and coming back nobody knows how! And looking fresh and fair as a new-laid egg. Dost know, lass, Morris ffeirad read out from the Bible, 'Thou shalt not suffer a witch to live' – and tan i marw! my thoughts went to thee at once – didn't they, Madlen? Didn't I tell thee coming home from church?'

'Oh, hold thy tongue, with thy texts and thy new-laid eggs, and come to breakfast. I suppose thee must have breakfast, Catrin, though thee'st done nothing to earn thy salt?'

'Well, I'm hungry whatever,' said the girl, sitting down to the table with a merry laugh, and a look of radiant happiness in her eyes that irritated Madlen beyond endurance.

''Tis all very well to smile like that, with nothing to do. Here have I been toiling and moiling in this old farm, while thee'st been, goodness knows where.'

'Well, I'll help you after breakfast,' said Catrin. 'I'll press the curds for you, and wash the dairy out.'

'Oh, no meddling with my work; thee'lt milk the cows, and feed the pigs, and clean out the stable. I'll manage the rest myself.'

'Well, we'll see,' said Catrin, as she cut the long slices of the flat barley loaf.

'Thee hasn't lost thine appetite whatever,' said Madlen.

'Let her eat druan fach!' said Bensha; 'thee'st too hard upon her.'

Madlen only answered with a snort, as she pushed away her platter, and went about her household duties, Catrin taking her pail and singing as she went down the fields to milk.

'What did it matter that Madlen was grumpy, and Bensha was dull? Goronwy was coming; everything would be right.'

She bore the frothing pail into the dairy, where the cool green light came in through the tree mallow at the lattice window, and, adhering to her first intention, washed it out, as it was not the spic-and-span place it had been when under her control; Madlen continually interrupting her and frustrating her plans in every possible way.

'Let that cream alone, lodes!'

'But 'tis mouldy,' said Catrin.

'Mouldy let it be, then! I won't have it touched. I am the mistress here;' and she brought down her fist with a bang on the stone slab.

But nothing annoyed Catrin today; her temper was angelic. There was no flashing of the brown eyes, but with a pleasant smile she answered, 'Well, wait till noon, Madlen, and we'll see about that.'

'See about that indeed! See about giving you a good thrashing; that's what somebody ought to do!' And she went out, slamming the dairy door so violently that the cream quivered on the surface of the pans.

'Bad for thy next churning, Madlen,' said Catrin, with a smile of amusement, and she went on quietly with her work, until, about noon, she heard the sound of footsteps approaching, and Goronwy entered, followed by Walto Gwyn.

She came in from the dairy, her face suffused with blushes, her eyes falling shyly before Goronwy's ardent gaze.

'Catrin Rees,' said Walto, 'I am glad to see thee, for my own sake, and more for Goronwy's. He has been breaking his heart for thee, lass, and we only wanted thee to make our happiness complete. Yshbel will be glad to see thee, too. We were out in the cornfields last night when the *Swallow* came in. Yshbel had been there a dozen times in the day, I think, to watch for thee!'

'Well, indeed, there's kind!'

Goronwy and she had greeted each other with a cool nod, and the dry 'Well, Goronwy!' and 'Well, Catrin!' considered the appropriate manner for lovers' meetings in public.

Madlen, who had a keen suspicion that Goronwy's visit boded her no good, was by no means cordial in her greeting.

'Wel wyr,' she said, 'it is enough to moider one – to be alone in the house, with no one but Bensha to tread the doorstep for weeks, and then suddenly to have three visitors pouring in! And what is your business here, Goronwy Hughes?'

Catrin busied herself at the dresser, to hide her embarrasment, for she felt a critical moment had arrived.

'Well, 'tis this,' said Goronwy. 'I have something to say to thee, Madlen, and a paper to read to thee, and Walto is with me, to hear me reading it. You and Bensha think you are master and mistress in this house.'

'So we are – what of that?' said Madlen, her face flaming defiance.

'There's no blame to you for thinking so, because Simon Rees left it to you in the will which was read at his funeral. I don't blame you for that – but I do blame you for your want of tenderness to his orphan daughter; but never mind that now. Here is a will which he made after the one you have – made, indeed, the very day he died. You read it, Walto,' and Walto Gwyn read it plainly and deliberately, first in English and then translated it into Welsh.

Madlen's flushed face grew pale, but, not easily subdued, she said: 'I don't understand that English gibberish, and you can translate it as you like. I am mistress here by Simon Rees' will, and you are talking nonsense, to try and frighten me and Bensha out of our rightful home, that you may place this

croten here, I suppose! But I'll have Jones, the lawyer, to you
– he'll look after my rights.'

'Yes,' said Goronwy, 'I am going to him tomorrow, and I
will bring him here in the afternoon, and he will tell you the
rights of the case. But remember – I tell you now – Catrin is
mistress here; every stick and stone, every creature and every
article of furniture, belongs to her.'

At this juncture Bensha entered.

'What's the matter?' he said.

'Matter enough,' said Madlen, beginning to cry. 'These
"fileined" have come here today to turn us out of house and
home – saying that old Simon made a will the day he died,
leaving everything to the croten – the blackguard! But I don't
believe it!'

'Did he?' said Bensha, turning to Goronwy. 'Is that the will?'

'Yes; I will read it to you,' said Walto, and once more he read
it from beginning to end.

''Tis plain enough,' said Bensha, 'and thank the Lord that it
is so. As true as I'm here, I have never had peace of mind since
Simon died, and I will be thankful to turn out to the road, and
beg my bread, rather than spend the sleepless nights I have had
lately – the croten roaming about somewhere without a home,
and Madlen and me enjoying the comforts she ought to have.
No, no! the Almighty is just, and I am glad to give it up to her.'

Catrin, who had been listening with deep interest as she
dusted the dresser, could no longer remain passive; she flung
her duster away, and sitting beside Madlen on the settle, gently
drew her fingers over the hands with which she held her check
apron over her face.

'Madlen, fach, don't cry,' she said. 'You could not be
expected to know there was another will. I ought to have
shown it to you sooner. But don't cry, Madlen, fach; you and
Bensha shall never be turned from Pengraig, but shall live here,
as you did in my father's time. Only, Madlen, I must be
mistress, and you must never call my dear father a bad name.'

But Madlen was not to be pacified, and before they left, Walto and Goronwy found it necessary once again, and more firmly, to impress upon the angry woman that her place was subordinate to the new mistress, who would now take her proper position for the first time.

Bensha seemed much relieved by the turn affairs had taken, and accompanied the two young men as far as the clos gate, assuring them, over and over again, of his satisfaction.

''Tis just right now,' he said, 'but what stress of weather I shall go through with Madlen, I don't know – in my deed I don't.'

The sun had not long set that evening when Goronwy once more went up the side of Penmwntan, to where the Pengraig fields grew grey in the evening light.

Catrin was not yet there, but he knew she would come, for he had looked with an inquiring glance from the cliffs to her face, and she had answered with a look of shy assent, as he silently pressed her hand at parting. Yes – here she came through the twilight, running down the fields as of yore, Merlin bounding after her.

Goronwy rose to meet her, and they turned together to the further cliffs beneath the shepherd's hut. Together now – no reproachful shadow beckoning him away, no haunting sadness weighing her heart, but the same happy lass and lad who had strayed therein the days gone by! She had been looking into his face with a wistful, inquiring expression in her eyes.

'What is it, lass?' asked Goronwy. 'Dost want to ask me something?'

'Well, yes, indeed, but I don't know what to ask. 'Tis that I see some change in thy face – I don't know what it is – but I marked it the first moment I saw thee on the Cribor mountains.'

'Not less love for thee, f'anwylyd.'

'No, no; nothing like that but a look in thine eyes, as if thou hadst been in a storm.'

'Catrin, thou art a witch! I have been through deadly peril lass. But wilt promise me not to ask me about it, until I choose to tell thee?'

''Tis hard, indeed, but I will never ask nor want to know till thou tellest me, Goronwy.'

'Canst trust me, then? A bargain! Then when we are sitting round the hearth at Sarnissa, when the wind is howling in the big chimney, my father smoking in the corner, I sitting on the bench, and thou in granny's chair opposite me, there's stories I will have to tell, thou clasping and unclasping thy little hands, as thou dost when thou'rt listening eagerly – yes, and sometimes turning pale, Catrin! Oh, I know thee! But there will be stories to make thee laugh, too; for, oh, I have seen strange things and places since we were here last! People running about like mad to make money, and getting no pleasure out of it that I could see, others trying their best to be grand, and thinking the best way to begin was to forget their own language! And even in church, Catrin, racing for their lives to get through the service! Oh, in my deed, we are simple down here, but we are not fools!'

'Oh, well, indeed! thou'lt not be wanting to go away again?'

'Never, indeed! With thee always by my side, Catrin – out in the fields, here on the cliffs, at home by the hearth – how could I wish to go away? In three weeks' time thou'lt come to Sarnissa, thou hast promised! We'll keep Pengraig, and farm it well, and Bensha and Madlen shall live there as our servants. Hast nothing to answer me, f'anwylyd?'

'Oh, Goronwy, 'tis too happy I am!'

The moon rose over Penmwntan, the waves whispered on the long beach, and Goronwy drew Catrin's cloak around her, for the autumn was waning, and as they sauntered homewards together, they settled all their plans; and before the winter winds had come to ruffle the bay, and when the corn stooks were all gathered into the barns, the little bell at Penmwntan church rang out as merrily as it could, to announce their wedding. And there was no prouder, happier man than Goronwy Hughes, when he took his bride home to begin their life at sunny Sarnissa!

GLOSSARY

Ach-y-fi!	Ugh!
Anwyl/anwl	Dear
Andras	Curse
Bach/fach	Little
Bastwn	Cudgel
Bendigedig!	I'm blest! (literally, Blessed!)
Beudy/boidy	Cowshed
Braf	Fine
Bryn	Hill
B't shwr	To be sure
Bwdran	Gruel
Bysse cwn [bysedd y cwn]	Foxgloves
Can' diolch	Many thanks (literally, a hundred thanks)
Cardi	Person from Cardiganshire
Caton Pawb!	Save us all!
Cawl	Broth
Cerrig	Stones
Clos	Yard
Crochen/crochon	Cauldron
Croten	Wench
Cwrt	Court
Cwtchi	Curtsy
Cythrael	Devil
Dandiss	Jacks (a game played with white pebbles)
Dir anwl!	Dear me!
Diwss/dewss	Deuce
Druan bach	Poor dear
Du/duon	Black
Dy'da	Good day

Ffeirad	Priest
F'anwylyd	My love
Feleined	Villains
Fforwel	Farewell
Ffrind	Friend
Gentriss	Gentry
Gwae fi!	Woe is me!
Gwrecs	Wrecks
Gwn bach	Bedgown
Jar-i!	Dear me!
Ladi	Lady
Lodes/ lo's	Young girl
'Machgen i	My boy
Mawredd anwl!	Dear God! (literally, Dear Greatness!)
'Merch i	My girl
Mestress	Mistress
Mishter	Mister
Nanti	Aunt
Nos/Nosweth dda	Good night
N'wncwl	Uncle
Penisha	Lower end
Penstiff	Stubborn
Priodas dda!	Happy marriage!
Saeson	English people
Sayloom	Asylum
Stryd/stryt	Street
Tan i marw!	I'll be damned! (literally, Were I dead!)
Tishen	Cake
Uwd	Porridge
Wel wir!/wyr!	Well really!
Wirion	Foolish

Welsh Women's Classics

Series Editor: *Jane Aaron*

Formerly known as the *Honno Classics* Series, now renamed and relaunched for Honno's 25th Anniversary in 2012.

This series, published by Honno Press, brings back into print neglected and virtually forgotten literary texts by Welsh women from the past.

Each of the titles published includes an introduction setting the text in its historical context and suggesting ways of approaching and understanding the work from the viewpoint of women's experience today. The editor's aim is to select works which are not only of literary merit but which remain readable and appealing to a contemporary audience. An additional aim for the series is to provide materials for students of Welsh writing in English, who have until recently remained largely ignorant of the contribution of women writers to the Welsh literary tradition simply because their works have been unavailable.

The many and various portrayals of Welsh female identity found in these authors' books bear witness to the complex processes that have gone into the shaping of the Welsh women of today. Perusing these portrayals from the past will help us to understand our own situations better, as well as providing, in a variety of different genres – novels, short stories, poetry, autobiography and prose pieces – a fresh and fascinating store of good reading matter.

*"[It is] difficult to imagine a Welsh literary landscape
without the Honno Classics series [...]
it remains an energising and vibrant feminist imprint."*
(Kirsti Bohata, *New Welsh Review*)

*"[The Honno Classics series is] possibly the Press'
most important achievement, helping to combat
the absence of women's literature in the Welsh canon."*
(*Mslexia*)

Titles published in this series:

Jane Aaron, ed.	*A View across the Valley: Short Stories by Women from Wales 1850-1950*
Jane Aaron and Ursula Masson, eds,	*The Very Salt of Life: Welsh Women's Political Writings from Chartism to Suffrage*
Elizabeth Andrews,	*A Woman's Work is Never Done* (1957), with an introduction by Ursula Masson
Amy Dillwyn,	*The Rebecca Rioter* (1880), with an introduction by Katie Gramich
	A Burglary (1883), with an introduction by Alison Favre
	Jill (1884), with an introduction by Kirsti Bohata
Dorothy Edwards,	*Winter Sonata* (1928), with an introduction by Claire Flay
Margiad Evans,	*The Wooden Doctor* (1933), with an introduction by Sue Asbee
Menna Gallie,	*Strike for a Kingdom* (1959), with an introduction by Angela John
	The Small Mine (1962), with an introduction by Jane Aaron
	Travels with a Duchess (1968), with an introduction by Angela John
	You're Welcome to Ulster (1970), with an introduction by Angela John and Claire Connolly
Katie Gramich and Catherine Brennan, eds,	*Welsh Women's Poetry 1460-2001*
Eiluned Lewis,	*Dew on the Grass* (1934), with an introduction by Katie Gramich
	The Captain's Wife (1943), with an introduction by Katie Gramich
Allen Raine,	*A Welsh Witch* (1902), with an introduction by Jane Aaron
	Queen of the Rushes (1906), with an introduction by Katie Gramich
Bertha Thomas,	*Stranger within the Gates* (1912), with an introduction by Kirsti Bohata
Lily Tobias,	*Eunice Fleet* (1933), with an introduction by Jasmine Donahaye
Hilda Vaughan,	*Here Are Lovers* (1926), with an introduction by Diana Wallace
	Iron and Gold (1948), with an introduction by Jane Aaron
Jane Williams,	*Betsy Cadwaladyr: A Balaclava Nurse* (1857), with an introduction by Deirdre Beddoe

Clasuron Honno

Honno also publish an equivalent series, *Clasuron Honno*, in Welsh, also recently re-launched with a new look:

Published with the support of the Welsh Books Council

ABOUT HONNO

Honno Welsh Women's Press was set up in 1986 by a group of women who felt strongly that women in Wales needed wider opportunities to see their writing in print and to become involved in the publishing process. Our aim is to develop the writing talents of women in Wales, give them new and exciting opportunities to see their work published and often to give them their first 'break' as a writer.

Honno is registered as a community co-operative. Any profit that Honno makes is invested in the publishing programme. Women from Wales and around the world have expressed their support for Honno. Each supporter has a vote at the Annual General Meeting.

For more information and to buy our publications, please write to Honno at the address below, or visit our website: www.honno.co.uk

Honno, 14 Creative Units, Aberystwyth Arts Centre
Aberystwyth, Ceredigion SY23 3GL

Honno Friends

We are very grateful for the support of the Honno Friends:
Gwyneth Tyson Roberts, Jenny Sabine, Beryl Thomas.

For more information on how you can become a
Honno Friend, see: http://www.honno.co.uk/friends.php